BOSTON
PUBLIC
LIBRARY

FIRST WORLD
FANTASY AWARDS

Edited by GAHAN WILSON

FIRST WORLD FANTASY AWARDS

1977
DOUBLEDAY & COMPANY, INC., GARDEN CITY, NEW YORK

All of the characters in the book are fictitious, and any resemblance to actual persons, living or dead, is purely coincidental.

Library of Congress Cataloging in Publication Data

Main entry under title:
First world fantasy awards.

1. Fantastic literature, American.
2. Fantastic literature, English. I. Wilson, Gahan.
PS509.F3F5   813'.0876
ISBN: 0-385-12199-7
Library of Congress Catalog Card Number 76-2830

Copyright © 1977 by Gahan Wilson
All Rights Reserved
Printed in the United States of America
First Edition

ACKNOWLEDGMENTS

"The Bat Is My Brother," copyright © 1944 by Weird Tales for *Weird Tales*, November 1944. Copyright © 1972 by Robert Bloch.
"Beetles," copyright © 1938 by Weird Tales for *Weird Tales*, December 1938. Copyright © 1966 by Robert Bloch.
Excerpt from "The Forgotten Beasts of Eld," copyright © 1974 by Patricia A. McKillip; reprinted by permission of Atheneum Publishers.
"Pages from a Young Girl's Journal," copyright © 1972 by Mercury Press, Inc.; reprinted by permission of the author's agent, Kirby McCauley.
"The Events at Poroth Farm," copyright © 1972 by Harry O. Morris, Jr.; reprinted by permission of the author's agent, Kirby McCauley.
"A Father's Tale," copyright © 1974 by Mercury Press, Inc.; first published in *The Magazine of Fantasy and Science Fiction*.
"Sticks," copyright © 1974 by Stuart David Schiff; reprinted by permission of the author's agent, Kirby McCauley.
"Come into My Parlor," copyright © 1949 by Avon Publishing Co., Inc.; reprinted by permission of the author's agent, Kirby McCauley.
"Fearful Rock," copyright © 1938 by Popular Fiction Publishing Co.; reprinted by permission of the author's agent, Kirby McCauley.
"An Appreciation of Lee Brown Coye," copyright © 1974 by Stuart David Schiff.
"The Bait," copyright © 1973 by Stuart David Schiff; reprinted by permission of the author.

"The Vampire in America," copyright © 1973 by Stuart David Schiff; reprinted by permission of the author.
"The Shortest Way," copyright © 1974 by Stuart David Schiff; reprinted by permission of the author's agent, Kirby McCauley.
From "Chips and Shavings," copyright © 1974 by Stuart David Schiff; reprinted by permission of the author.
"The Soft Wall," copyright © 1974 by Stuart David Schiff; reprinted by permission of the author.
"Toward a Greater Appreciation of H. P. Lovecraft," copyright © 1973 by Dirk W. Mosig.
"The Abandoned Boudoir," copyright © 1974 by Stuart David Schiff; reprinted by permission of the author's agent, Kirby McCauley.
"Cradle Song for a Baby Werewolf," copyright © 1973 by Stuart David Schiff; reprinted by permission of the author.
"Guillotine," copyright © 1970 by the Acrostic Press; appeared in *The Fantastic Acros*.
"The Farmhouse," copyright © 1974 by Stuart David Schiff; reprinted by permission of the author.

Dedicated to the Old Gentleman from Providence, of course

CONTENTS

Introduction ... 9
Map of Providence ... 11
The Convention ... 15
About the Fantasy Awards ... 17
The Awards ... 19

LIFE ACHIEVEMENT:
The Bat Is My Brother – *Robert Bloch* ... 21
Beetles – *Robert Bloch* ... 36
Acceptance speech ... 46
About Robert Bloch ... 53

NOVEL:
The Forgotten Beasts of Eld – *Patricia A. McKillip* ... 55

SHORT FICTION:
An Essay – *Robert Aickman* ... 63
Pages from a Young Girl's Journal – *Robert Aickman* ... 66
The Events at Poroth Farm – *T. E. D. Klein* ... 97
A Father's Tale – *Sterling E. Lanier* ... 137

BRITISH FANTASY AWARD:
Sticks – *Karl Edward Wagner* ... 168

SINGLE AUTHOR COLLECTION OR ANTHOLOGY:
Come into My Parlor – *Manly Wade Wellman* ... 187
Fearful Rock – *Manly Wade Wellman* ... 198
About Manly Wade Wellman ... 253

SPECIAL PROFESSIONAL:
The Ballantines ... 254

BEST ARTIST:
Lee Brown Coye // An Appreciation – *Grahan Wilson* ... 256

SPECIAL NON-PROFESSIONAL:

From *Whispers* — edited by *Stuart David Schiff*:	258
The Bait — *Fritz Leiber*	260
The Vampire in America — *Manly Wade Wellman*	263
The Shortest Way — *Dave Drake*	268
From "Chips and Shavings" — *Lee Brown Coye*	277
The Soft Wall — *Dennis Etchison*	279
Toward a Greater Appreciation of H. P. Lovecraft — *Dirk W. Mosig*	290
The Abandoned Boudoir — *Joseph Payne Brennan*	302
Cradle Song for a Baby Werewolf — *H. Warner Munn*	302
Guillotine — *Walter Shedlofsky*	303
The Farmhouse — *David Riley*	304

INTRODUCTION

There we were, the professional monster makers, seated in a row to form a panel, staring in our various ways at the small sea of friendly, intelligent faces before us, waiting for the next question and hoping we'd be able to answer it wittily, or profoundly, or at least in some way which would not cause us embarrassment. A hand rose from the audience, one of us nodded, and we heard:

"Why do you write *all that scary stuff?*"

There was not the usual polite rush to grab a microphone, as with previous questions; there was a pause on all our parts. A noticeable pause. I noticed it being noticed.

Joseph Payne Brennan, mild-mannered veteran of *Weird Tales*, author of *Slime*, was the first to answer. Brennan is a small, dark, quiet man who examines his words thoughtfully as he speaks them. One might not be surprised to learn he is a librarian, one might be to learn he makes part of his living by animating cadavers in readers' minds and causing horrors to creep about in fictitious back yards.

"I can't say," he said, and elaborated on the theme. He guessed. He guessed it might have something to do with his Irish genes, he guessed it might have something to do with his lonely childhood, he guessed it might have something to do with his early attraction to ghost stories, but he had no idea why he'd been early attracted to ghost stories. He couldn't say. It appeared to depress and confuse him.

Robert Bloch, justly famous for his *Psycho* and insufficiently appreciated for his many contributions to the truly horrible, is a far more worldly man than Brennan—you get pretty worldly writing motion pictures—and much, much cagier. Pretending smoothly the question hadn't made him pause (but I was sitting next to him and had seen him pause), he did what many intelligent people do in alarming situations. He made jokes. He explained that he had been unable to decide whether to work or starve and so had combined the two by becoming a writer of horror stories, a field which had attracted him all along because of its tolerance for sloppy writing.

Gratefully following Bloch's lead, and taking advantage of the general hilarity he'd created, I, too, delivered a few one-liners, gave a nod of familiarity to Brennan's lonely childhood, and then turned expectantly to Frank Belknap Long. Perhaps he would have the answer.

Mr. Long is a dear, gentle, kindly man who has written some of the most literally haunting stories which have been printed. His *The Space Eaters* is based on his long friendship with Howard Phillips Lovecraft, and is perhaps the best evocation of that particular horror of indifferent cosmic violation Lovecraft worked so well which was not written by H.P.L. himself. Mr. Long stroked his neat gray beard with a thin, small hand, gazed thoughtfully upward, and, speaking in a voice barely loud enough for the microphones to pick up, explained that what had spurred him into writing such things was a brooding fear of, he paused, "encroachment." From the quiet stir of the panel, we all knew he had found the right word.

The last to answer was Manly Wade Wellman. Mr. Wellman's prime speciality in rendering spooky stories is a wonderfully convincing folksy quality, though he is certainly not restricted to that. He is a man of few trimmings and much practicality, and he confessed to me as he settled himself at the table that he had had the intelligence to consume three fingers of bourbon as a sensible precaution against the rigors of participating on a panel. He smiled at the specific human who had posed the question and drawled his answer:

"Even when I was a kid I was making those things up, and telling them, and seeing my friends' eyes stick out of their heads."

Wellman paused, a man recalling happy moments in some dark, southern wood, with maybe a fire crackling before, maybe even some dog baying in the distance.

"I *liked* that! I *still* like it! I think that's why I write it—*to make your eyes pop out!!!*"

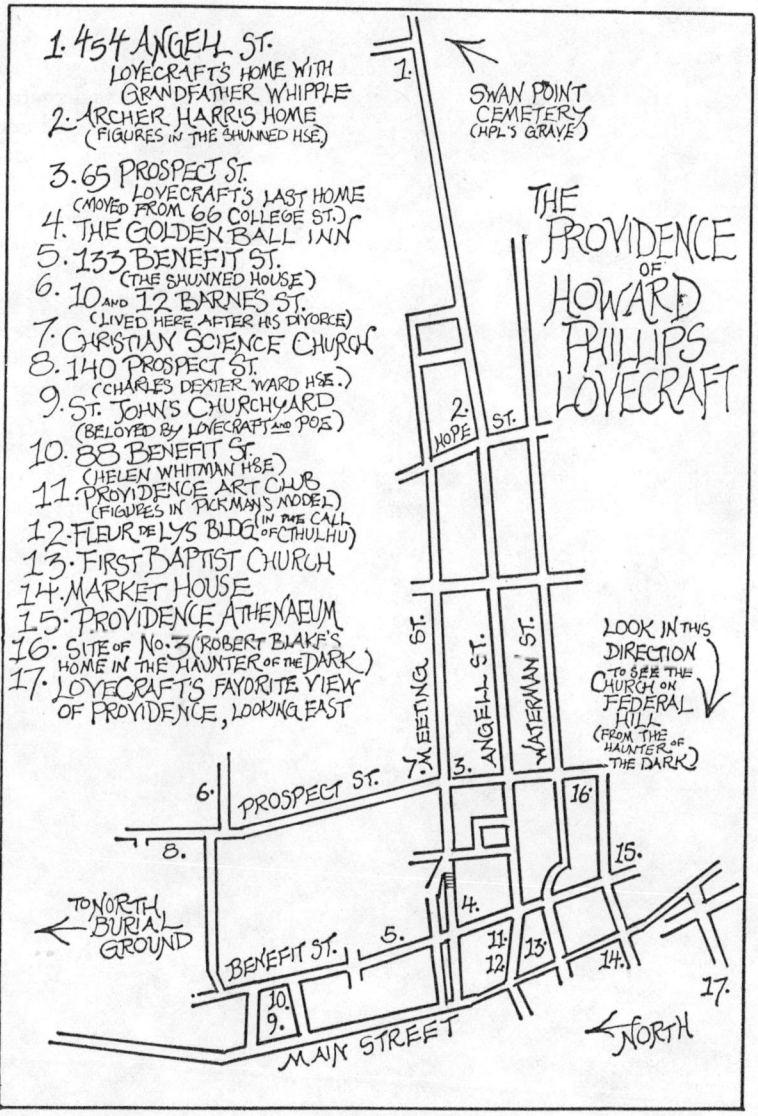

FIRST WORLD FANTASY AWARDS

THE CONVENTION

Howard Phillips Lovecraft, usually referred to as "Howard P. Lovecraft," now and then more familiarly as "H.P.L.," and, *very* rarely, only by those who knew him in life, or by those who have known one who knew him in life long enough to dare to take the plunge, as "Howard," dominated the First World Fantasy Convention, and was meant to dominate it. Lovecraft's influence over macabre fantasy and anybody interested in it has increased steadily and formidably over the last fifty years, and it's obvious it will continue to grow. He and his fellow workers in the old, extinct *Weird Tales* (indeed it was "The Unique Magazine"!) are viewed with increased respect and affection as time's gone by, and the convention was an unabashed tribute to how much H.P.L. and his circle meant to us all through the years, no matter what our individual counting.

If it could have been done we would have held it in Arkham, Massachusetts, but Arkham is only, unbelievably, a figment of Lovecraft's imagination. So we held it in Providence, Rhode Island, which was Lovecraft's birthplace, and the one spot in an otherwise alien cosmos which he considered home.

If you want to see Providence, especially Lovecraft's Providence, the best way to do it is in the company of one Harry L. P. Beckwith, Jr. Harry is a Yankee, through and through, and knows and loves his New England with a thoroughness which I found touching and inspiring to behold, and which made me wish I, too, had firm roots in some part or the other of this world. If you can't get ahold of Harry—he is obliging, but he is busy—do take along the map I copied from one he gave me, which is reproduced here for your convenience. It doesn't have the twang, nor the gentle jokes, but it will serve to guide you to the major points of interest. Keep your eye peeled for the cats in St. John's Graveyard.

I was fortunate enough to be driven around Providence in a small car by Harry, given the full tour with stops and rambles, but my good luck did not stop there, for sitting next to Harry, in what is known in racing circles as the death seat, was none other than Robert Bloch, on his very first visit to the home of his friend and mentor, H.P.L. I count it a rare privilege to have been present when Bloch was pointed out the church where Lovecraft had him find the shining trapezohedron as Robert Blake in *The Haunter of the Dark*, and the original site of the house where later he'd been blasted by the sight of the "three-lobed burning eye." Nor am I liable to forget the sight of him standing in the Phillips' family lot in Swan Point Cemetery, gazing at the inscription on the gray obelisk: "*Their Son, Howard P. Lovecraft,* 1890–1937."

The convention was full of memorable events. Imagine having breakfast at the Holiday Inn, which is where it was held, sitting across the table from Forrest J. Ackerman, he of *Famous Monsters* magazine, seeing him wear on one hand the scarab ring which Karloff bore on a withered finger in *The Mummy*, on the other the bat-crested wonder which Lugosi waved at us so hypnotically in his *Dracula*s, and on his chest a large plastic jewel which lit up in the presence of a pretty woman, as it did for my wife. Try and forget L. Sprague de Camp, angry as hell, as usual, with Lovecraft, primarily for not getting on with his career, and Willis Conover leading those fighting back, and Tom Collins and Frank Long somewhere in the middle, trying to pull it together. The whole battle very touching. Then there was Mayor Vincent Cianci, kind enough to burst into the banquet and give us a rouser of a speech, kind enough to promise to put Lovecraft in marble on his favorite perch looking east over the city if a committee would meet with him —I have no idea if any committee ever did—and let us by no means pass over the sentimental display of Lovecraftiana put on at the John Hay Library: enormous pulps with lurid covers, a letter from H.P.L. patiently explaining how to try and pronounce "Cthulhu" with a human mouth, and, most particularly wistful, a selection of the tiny newspapers Lovecraft painstakingly manufactured as a child. It was easy to imagine the wan, little Howard seriously, probably even solemnly selling his bulletins to indulgent elders.

The names of those who helped put the whole thing together must be here inscribed. First let be written Kirby McCauley, the chairman of the whole thing, who, together with Donald M. Grant and T. E. D. Klein, came up with the idea of holding the thing in Providence, but they couldn't possibly have brought it off without the help of Dave Hartwell and Don Grant, not to mention John Stanley, Bill Desmond, Bob Booth, Lupe and Charles Collins, and, life always being reliably unfair, too many others to mention here.

ABOUT THE FANTASY AWARDS

The point of the awards was, is, and hopefully shall be to give a visible, potentially usable, sign of appreciation to writers working in the area of fantastic literature, an area too often distinguished by low financial remuneration and indifference on the part of the critical establishment. It was noted that an Edgar or a Nebula or Hugo award not only gave their recipients a pleasing boost to the ego and a comforting feeling of being loved, the printing of a notice on their books saying as how they had won an Edgar or a Nebula or a Hugo tended, demonstrably, to increase the sales of the recipient's books and give him or her a reasonable income for his or her labor.

The 1975 awards were for material published in the English language during 1973-74. Instead of popular ballot, a specific awards committee was gathered and pressed into service as judges. David G. Hartwell, editor at Putnam/Berkley, was the awards administrator. The rest of the committee included: Ramsey Campbell, British horror writer; Edward L. Ferman, editor and publisher of the *Magazine of Fantasy and Science Fiction;* Fritz Leiber, renowned writer, critic, and poet; and yours truly, Gahan Wilson.

This done it soon dawned on us all we had nothing tangible to give whoever eventually won. It would not do to shake their hand, merely, or pass over a scrubby bit of paper with "Well done" or "Congratulations" or something of that sort scribbled on it. No, we would actually have to provide something they could clutch and be photographed clutching, something they could later take back home to place prominently on a shelf so that they could stare at it fondly over the years and tell little stories about it to friends and loved ones.

Needless to say, it had to be something on the spooky side; an adapted standard bowling trophy would not do, nor a small statuette of a character from *Peanuts*—it would have to suggest weird goings-on. A bat? Somehow it didn't seem right; perhaps too directly Halloweenish. Possibly a likeness of one of Lovecraft's ghastly gods, say Cthulhu, maybe (all those tentacles would be nice), or possibly Yog-Sothoth. But would that be the right thing to give to some author of a gentle little whimsey—eventually it was possible the author of a gentle little whimsey might win —and would an octopoid blob or a congeries of iridescent globes reproduce well, reduced and printed on the corner of a paperback?

I offered a suggestion: Why not follow the example of the Mystery Writers of America with their famous bust of Poe, known far and wide as the Edgar, and make our award take the form of a bust of Lovecraft, perhaps in time to be known as the Howard? When this suggestion was well received I offered another: Why not let me sculpt it?

Of course Lovecraft's face had been familiar to me since childhood's happiest hour, or at least pre-adolescent's. I first saw it gazing out at me, hollow-cheeked and solemn, from the pages of *Marginalia*, the starter of Arkham House's welcome spin-offs on H.P.L. I had read his fiction and often wondered how he looked. Now I knew—for H. P. Lovecraft, he looked just exactly right!

My second suggestion having been accepted, I went back to *Marginalia*, and to the other books which had accumulated since, to study once again that lean and kindly, yet sinister cranial appendage; this time with the slightly nervous air of one committed to producing a feasible likeness of it.

I surrounded myself, literally, with pictures of Lovecraft, placing the books opened to his photograph or portrait all around my drawing table and chair, and I studied them in sequence and at random, taking notes and making sketches, observing how Virgil Finlay and Lee Brown Coye had handled the problem, seeing Lovecraft posing, inevitably a little stiffly, before stoops and fences and barn doors, perched on a sofa between friends, looking oddly younger, and certainly more assured, as the long-gone years went by.

Unfortunately for me, no one thought to take a picture of the back of H.P.L.'s head, and so I had to extrapolate, working round behind the visible edges. Some who knew him have told me that my guess, while not awesomely accurate, is still a good approximation of how the Old Gentleman looked when facing in another direction from the observer.

The statue has an Easter Island look to it on purpose, both because Lovecraft's jaw and leanness strongly suggest the image, and because I think he would have liked it that way, and I chose a darkly silver composition in casting it to suggest all those over- and underexposed snapshots of the thirties.

Of course it was an honor and a joy to have had the chance to do this bust of H.P.L., as it was in my capacity as toastmaster to hand it over to its deserving recipients when the awarding time actually came. I'm proud to know it figured in the First World Fantasy Convention, and hope most sincerely it will continue to do so, year after year, in all the many conventions to come.

THE AWARDS

NOMINEES—LIFE ACHIEVEMENT:

Robert Aickman British author, renowned for his ghost stories

* *Robert Bloch* Youngest professional member of the Lovecraft circle and known for his films and teleplays

Frank Belknap Long A protégé of H. P. Lovecraft's and writer of "scientifantasy" tales for five decades

Donald Wandrei A horror writer who, along with August Derleth, helped found Arkham House, Lovecraft's publisher

Manly Wade Wellman Veteran *Weird Tales* writer, known for half a century of fantasy writing

ROBERT BLOCH/*Life Achievement Award*

Robert Bloch won the Life Achievement Award, and God knows he deserved it. He is the kind of worker who makes lazy good-for-nothings in the field, such as myself, feel pretty rotten. With over four hundred short stories and over a dozen novels to his credit, Bloch is still going strong in print and continuing to pile up a towering list of film and television writing credits as well. There seems to be no end to his output, and a good thing for us all.

I have a number of favorites; it's impossible to narrow the choice down to one. Of his novels, I think *The Kidnapper* is his best, being a really nasty bit of work all around, and I highly recommend it to anyone who doesn't mind his villains looked at square on. But then there is also *Psycho*, of course, and *American Gothic*, which he complains keeps getting put in the wrong racks on account of varying misinterpretations of its title. The short story choice ends up a long list, part of it reading: "The Mannikin," "Black Bargain," "The Man Who Collected Poe," and "Notebook Found in a Deserted House."

For all his many successes, Bloch is a frustrated man because, as a child, possibly a young man, possibly even now, he wanted to become a comedian. Actually he *isn't* very frustrated, come to think of it, because, no matter how increasingly obvious the signs of disapproval are around him, he will continue making all these dreadful jokes.

* Winners are noted by an asterisk.

On receiving his award, for example, he nearly destroyed the solemn dignity of the occasion by stating: "I haven't had so much fun since the rats ate my baby sister."

It's possible the main proof of the man's basic lovability is that people continue to be fond of him, myself included, in spite of those jokes—or, perhaps, because of them.

For this anthology, as a completely inadequate sample of Bloch's work, I've chosen "The Bat Is My Brother," and "Beetles." The first has never been printed in a book (I had to dig it out, literally, from a pile of moldering *Weird Tales*, and then have the thing typed up; its yellowed pages were fragile as a mummy's wrappings), though it should have been, as it's a grand example of what an old pro can do with a classic theme. The second, "Beetles," has been a sentimental favorite of mine since childhood. When I had the good luck, as toastmaster, to introduce Bloch as the guest of honor to the convention, and later to present him with the bust of Lovecraft commemorating his winning the Life Achievement Award, I took the chance to make public something which has always been close to my heart: Robert Bloch is not, to any sensitive cultured human, the shower scene in *Psycho*, Robert Bloch is the last line in "Beetles." Once you've read it, I'm sure you'll agree.

Robert Bloch

THE BAT IS MY BROTHER

I

It began in twilight—a twilight I could not see. My eyes opened on darkness, and for a moment I wondered if I were still asleep and dreaming. Then I slid my hands down and felt the cheap lining of the casket, and I knew that this nightmare was real.

I wanted to scream, but who can hear screams through six feet of earth above a grave?

Better save my breath and try to save my sanity. I fell back, and the darkness rose all around me. The darkness, the cold, clammy darkness of death.

I could not remember how I had come here, or what hideous error had brought about my premature interment. All I knew was that I lived—but unless I managed to escape, I would soon be in a condition horribly appropriate to my surroundings.

Then began that which I dare not remember in detail. The splintering of wood, the burrowing struggle through loosely packed grave earth; the gasping hysteria accompanying my clawing, suffocated progress to the sand surface of the world above.

It is enough that I finally emerged. I can only thank poverty for my deliverance—the poverty which had placed me in a flimsy, unsealed coffin and a pauper's shallow grave.

Clotted with sticky clay, drenched with cold perspiration, racked by utter revulsion, I crawled forth from betwixt the gaping jaws of death.

Dusk crept between the tombstones, and somewhere to my left the moon leered down to watch the shadowy legions that conquered in the name of Night.

The moon saw me, and a wind whispered furtively to brooding trees, and the trees bent low to mumble a message to all those sleeping below their shade. I grew restless beneath the moon's glaring eye, and I wanted to leave this spot before the trees had told my secret to the nameless, numberless dead.

Despite my desire, several minutes passed before I summoned strength to stand erect, without trembling. Then I breathed deeply of fog and faint putridity; breathed, and turned away along the path.

It was at that moment the figure appeared. It glided like a shadow haunting the trees, and as the moonlight fell upon a human face I felt my heart surge in exultation.

I raced toward the waiting figure, words choking in my throat as they fought for prior utterance.

"You'll help me, won't you?" I babbled. "You can see . . . they buried me down there . . . I was trapped . . . alive in the grave . . . out now . . . you'll understand . . . I can't remember how it began, but . . . you'll help me?"

A head moved in silent assent. I halted, regaining composure, striving for coherency.

"This is awkward," I said, more quietly. "I've really no right to ask you for assistance. I don't even know who you are."

The voice from the shadows was only a whisper, but each word thundered in my brain.

"I am a vampire," said the stranger.

Madness. I turned to flee, but the voice pursued me.

"Yes, I am a vampire," he said, "And . . . *so are you!*"

II

I must have fainted then. I must have fainted, and he must have carried me out of the cemetery, for when I opened my eyes once more I lay on a sofa in his house.

The paneled walls loomed high, and shadows crawled across the ceiling beyond the candlelight. I sat up, blinked, and stared at the stranger who bent over me.

I could see him now, and I wondered. He was of medium height, gray-haired, clean-shaven, and clad discreetly in a dark business suit. At first glance he appeared normal enough.

As his face glided toward me, I stared closer, trying to pierce the veil of his seeming sanity, striving to see the madness beneath the prosaic exterior of dress and flesh.

I stared and saw that which was worse than any madness. At close glance his countenance was cruelly illumined by the light. I saw the waxen pallor of his skin, and what was worse than that, the peculiar corrugation. For his entire face and throat was covered by a web of tiny wrinkles, and when he smiled it was with a mummy's grin.

Yes, his face was white and wrinkled; white, wrinkled, and long dead. Only his lips and eyes were alive, and they were red . . . *too* red. A face as white as corpse-flesh, holding lips and eyes as red as blood.

He smelled *musty.*

All these impressions came to me before he spoke. His voice was like the rustle of the wind through a mortuary wreath.

"You are awake? It is well."

"Where am I? And who are you?" I asked the questions but dreaded an answer. The answer came.

"You are in my house. You will be safe here, I think. As for me, I am your guardian."

"Guardian?"

He smiled. I saw his teeth. Such teeth I had never seen, save in the maw of a carnivorous beast. And yet—wasn't *that* the answer?

"You are bewildered, my friend. Understandably so. And that is why you need a guardian. Until you learn the ways of your new life, I shall protect you." He nodded. "Yes, Graham Keene, I shall protect you."

"Graham Keene."

It was my name. I knew it *now*. But how did *he* know it?

"In the name of mercy," I groaned, "tell me what has happened to me!"

He patted my shoulder. Even through the cloth I could feel the icy weight of his pallid fingers. They crawled across my neck like worms, like wriggling white worms—

"You must be calm," he told me. "This is a great shock, I know. Your confusion is a great shock, I know. Your confusion is understandable. If you will just relax a bit and listen, I think I can explain everything."

I listened.

"To begin with, you must accept certain obvious facts. The first being —that you are a vampire."

"But—"

He pursed his lips, his *too* red lips, and nodded.

"There is no doubt about it, unfortunately. Can you tell me how you happened to be emerging from a grave?"

"No, I don't remember. I must have suffered a cataleptic seizure. The shock gave me partial amnesia. But it will come back to me. I'm all right, I must be."

The words rang hollowly even as they gushed from my throat.

"Perhaps. But I think not." He sighed and pointed. "I can prove your condition to you easily enough. Would you be so good as to tell me what you see behind you, Graham Keene?"

"Behind me?"

"Yes, on the wall."

I stared.

"I don't see anything."

"Exactly."

"But—"

"*Where is your shadow?*"

I looked again. There was no shadow, no silhouette. For a moment my sanity wavered. Then I stared at him. "You have no shadow either," I exclaimed, triumphantly. "What does that prove?"

"That I am a vampire," he said, easily. "And so are you."

"Nonsense. It's just a trick of the light," I scoffed.

"Still skeptical? Then explain this optical illusion." A bony hand proffered a shining object.

I took it, held it. It was a simple pocket mirror.

"Look."

I looked.

The mirror dropped from my fingers and splintered on the floor.

"There's no reflection!" I murmured.

"Vampires have no reflections." His voice was soft. He might have been reasoning with a child.

"If you still doubt," he persisted, "I advise you to feel your pulse. Try to detect a heartbeat."

Have you ever listened for the faint voice of hope to sound within you . . . knowing that it alone can save you? Have you ever listened and heard nothing? Nothing but the silence of death?

I knew it then, past all doubt. I was of the Undead . . . the Undead who cast no shadows, whose images do not reflect in mirrors, whose hearts are forever stilled, but whose bodies live on—live, and walk abroad, and take nourishment.

Nourishment!

I thought of my companion's red lips and his pointed teeth. I thought of the light blazing in his eyes. A light of hunger. Hunger for what?

How soon must I share that hunger?

He must have sensed the question, for he began to speak once more.

"You are satisfied that I speak the truth, I see. That is well. You must accept your condition and then prepare to make the necessary adjustments. For there is much you have to learn in order to face the centuries to come.

"To begin with, I will tell you that many of the common superstitions about—people like us—are false."

He might have been discussing the weather, for all the emotion his face betrayed. But I could not restrain a shudder of revulsion at his words.

"They say we cannot abide garlic. That is a lie. They say we cannot cross running water. Another lie. They say that we must lie by day in the earth of our own graves. That's picturesque nonsense.

"These things, and these alone, are true. Remember them, for they are important to your future. We must sleep by day and rise only at sunset.

At dawn an overpowering lethargy bedrugs our senses, and we fall into a coma until dusk. We need not sleep in coffins—that is sheer melodrama, I assure you!—but it is best to sleep in darkness, and away from any chance of discovery by men.

"I do not know why this is so, any more than I can account for other phenomena relative to the disease. For vampirism is a disease, you know."

He smiled when he said it. I didn't smile. I groaned.

"Yes, it is a disease. Contagious, of course, and transmissible in the classic manner, through a bite. Like rabies. What reanimates the body after death no one can say. And why it is necessary to take certain forms of nourishment to sustain existence, I do not know. The daylight coma is a more easily classified medical phenomenon. Perhaps an allergy to the direct actinic rays of the sun.

"I am interested in these matters, and I have studied them.

"In the centuries to come I shall endeavor to do some intensive research on the problem. It will prove valuable in perpetuating my existence, and yours."

The voice was harsher now. The slim fingers clawed the air in excitement.

"Think of that, for a moment, Graham Keene," he whispered. "Forget your morbid superstitious dread of this condition and look at the reality.

"Picture yourself as you were before you awoke at sunset. Suppose you had remained there, inside that coffin, nevermore to awaken! Dead—dead for all eternity!"

He shook his head. "You can thank your condition for an escape. It gives you a new life, not just for a few paltry years, but for centuries. Perhaps—forever!

"Yes, think and give thanks! You need never die, now. Weapons cannot harm you, nor disease, nor the workings of age. You are immortal—and I shall show you how to live like a god!"

He sobered. "But that can wait. First we must attend to our needs. I want you to listen carefully now. Put aside your silly prejudices and hear me out. I will tell you that which needs to be told regarding our nourishment.

"It isn't easy, you know. There aren't any schools you can attend to learn what to do. There are no correspondence courses or books of helpful information. You must learn everything through your own efforts. Everything.

"Even so simple and vital a matter as biting the neck—using the incisors properly—is entirely a matter of personal judgment. Take that little detail, just as an example. You must choose the classic trinity to begin with—the time, the place, and the girl. When you are ready, you must pretend that you are about to kiss her. Both hands go under her ears. That is important, to hold her neck steady, and at the proper angle.

"You must keep smiling all the while, without allowing a betrayal of intent to creep into your features or your eyes. Then you bend your head. You kiss her throat. If she relaxes, you turn your mouth to the base of her neck, open it swiftly, and place the incisors in position.

"Simultaneously—it *must* be simultaneously—you bring your left hand up to cover her mouth. The right hand must find, seize, and pinion her hands behind her back. No need to hold her throat now. The teeth are doing that. Then, and only then, will instinct come to your aid. It must come then, because once you begin, all else is swept away in the red, swirling blur of fulfillment."

I cannot describe his intonation as he spoke, or the unconscious pantomime which accompanied the incredible instructions. But it is simple to name the look that came into his eyes.

Hunger.

"Come, Graham Keene," he whispered. "We must go now."

"Go? Where?"

"To dine," he told me. "To dine!"

III

He led me from the house, and down a garden pathway through a hedge. The moon was high, and as we walked along a windswept bluff, flying figures spun a moving web across the moon's bright face.

My companion shrugged.

"Bats," he said. And smiled.

"They say that—we—have the power of changing shape. That we become bats, or wolves. Alas, it's only another superstition. Would that it were true. For then our life would be easy. As it is, the search for sustenance in mortal form is hard. But you will soon understand."

I drew back. His hand rested on my shoulder in cold command.

"Where are you taking me?" I asked.

"To food."

Irresolution left me. I emerged from nightmare, shook myself into sanity.

"No—I won't!" I murmured. "I can't—"

"You must," he told me. "Do you want to go back to the grave?"

"I'd rather," I whispered. "Yes, I'd rather die."

His teeth gleamed in the moonlight.

"That's the pit of it," he said. "You can't die. You'll weaken without sustenance, yes. And you will appear to be dead. Then, whoever finds you will put you in the grave. But you'll be alive down there. How would you like to lie there undying in the darkness . . . writhing as you decay . . . suffering the torments of red hunger as you suffer the pangs of dissolution? How long do you think that goes on? How long before the brain itself is rotted away? How long must one endure the charnal consciousness of the devouring worm? Does the very dust still billow in agony?"

His voice held horror.

"That is the fate you escaped. But it is still the fate that awaits you unless you dine with me. Besides, it isn't something to avoid, believe me. And I am sure, my friend, that you already feel the pangs of—appetite."

I could not, dared not answer.

For it was true. Even as he spoke, I felt hunger. A hunger greater than any I had ever known. Call it a craving, call it a desire—call it lust. I felt it, gnawing deep within me. Repugnance was nibbled away by the terrible teeth of growing need.

"Follow me," he said, and I followed. Followed along the bluff and down a lonely country road.

We halted abruptly on the highway. A blazing neon sign winked incongruously ahead.

I read the absurd legend. "Danny's Drive-In."

Even as I watched, the sign blinked out.

"Right," whispered my guardian. "It's closing time. They will be leaving now."

"Who?"

"Mr. Danny and his waitress. She serves customers in their cars. They always leave together, I know. They are locking up for the night now. Come along and do as you are told."

I followed him down the road. His feet crunched gravel as he stalked toward the now darkened drive-in stand. My stride quickened in excitement. I moved forward as though pushed by a gigantic hand. The hand of hunger—

He reached the side door of the shack. His fingers rasped the screen. An irritable voice sounded.

"What do you want? We're closing."

"Can't you serve any more customers?"

"Nah. Too late. Go away."

"But we're very hungry."

I almost grinned. Yes, we were *very* hungry.

"Beat it!" Danny was in no mood for hospitality.

"Can't we get anything?"

Danny was silent for a moment. He was evidently debating the point. Then he called to someone inside the stand.

"Marie! Couple customers outside. Think we can fix 'em up in a hurry?"

"Oh, I guess so." The girl's voice was soft, complaisant. Would she be soft and complaisant, too?

"Open up. You guys mind eating outside?"

"Not at all."

"Open the door, Marie."

Marie's high heels clattered across the wooden floor. She opened the screen door, blinked out into the darkness.

My companion stepped inside the doorway. Abruptly, he pushed the girl forward.

"Now!" he rasped.

I lunged at her in darkness. I didn't remember his instructions about smiling at her, or placing my hands beneath her ears. All I knew was that her throat was white and smooth, except where a tiny vein throbbed in her neck.

I wanted to touch her neck there with my fingers—with my mouth—with my teeth. So I dragged her into the darkness, and my hands were over her mouth, and I could hear her heels scraping through the gravel as I pulled her along. From inside the shack I heard a single long moan, and then nothing.

Nothing . . . except the rushing white blur of her neck, as my face swooped toward the throbbing vein . . .

IV

It was cold in the cellar—cold and dark. I stirred uneasily on my couch and my eyes blinked open on blackness. I strained to see, raising myself to a sitting position as the chill slowly faded from my bones.

I felt sluggish, heavy with reptilian contentment. I yawned, trying to grasp a thread of memory from the red haze cloaking my thoughts.

Where was I? How had I come here? What had I been doing?

I yawned again. One hand went to my mouth. My lips were caked with dry, flaking substance. I felt it—then remembrance flooded me.

Last night, at the drive-in, I had feasted. And then—

"No!" I gasped.

"You have slept? Good."

My host stood before me. I arose hastily and confronted him.

"Tell me it isn't true," I pleaded. "Tell me I was dreaming."

"You were," he answered. "When I came out of the shack you lay under the trees, unconscious. I carried you home before dawn and placed you here to rest. You have been dreaming from sunrise to sunset, Graham Keene."

"But last night—?"

"Was real."

"You mean I took that girl and—?"

"Exactly." He nodded. "But come, we must go upstairs and talk. There are certain questions I must ask."

We climbed the stairs slowly and emerged on ground level. Now I could observe my surroundings with a more objective eye. This house was large, and old. Although completely furnished, it looked somehow untenanted. It was as though nobody had lived here for a long time.

Then I remembered who my host was, and what he was. I smiled grimly. It was true. Nobody was *living* in this house now.

Dust lay thickly everywhere, and the spiders had spun patterns of decay in the corners. Shades were drawn against the darkness, but still it crept in through the cracked walls. For darkness and decay belonged here.

We entered the study where I had awakened last night, and as I was seated, my guardian cocked his head toward me in an attitude of inquiry.

"Let us speak frankly," he began. "I want you to answer an important question."

"Yes?"

"What did you do with her?"

"Her?"

"That girl—last night. What did you do with her body?"

I put my hands to my temples. "It was all a blur. I can't seem to remember."

His head darted toward me, eyes blazing. "I'll tell you what you did with her," he rasped. "You threw her body down the well. I saw it floating there."

"Yes," I groaned. "I remember now."

"You fool—why did you do that?"

"I wanted to hide it . . . I thought they'd never know—"

"You *thought!*" Scorn weighted his voice. "You didn't think for an instant. Don't you see, now she will never rise?"

"Rise?"

"Yes, as you rose. Rise to become one of us."

"But I don't understand."

"That is painfully evident." He paced the floor, then wheeled toward me.

"I see that I shall have to explain certain things to you. Perhaps you are not to blame, because you don't realize the situation. Come with me."

He beckoned. I followed. We walked down the hall, entered a large, shelf-lined room. It was obviously a library. He lit a lamp, halted.

"Take a look around," he invited. "See what you make of it, my friend."

I scanned the titles on the shelves—titles stamped in gold on thick, handsome bindings; titles worn to illegibility on ancient, raddled leather. The latest in scientific and medical treatises stood on those shelves, flanked by age-encrusted incunabula. Modern volumes dealt with psychopathology. The ancient lore was frankly concerned with black magic.

"Here is gathered together all that is known, all that has ever been written about—us."

"A library on vampirism?"

"Yes. It took me decades to assemble it completely."

"But why?"

"Because knowledge is power. And it is power I seek."

Suddenly a resurgent sanity impelled me. I shook off the nightmare enveloping me and sought an objective viewpoint. A question crept into my mind, and I did not try to hold it back.

"Just who are you, anyway?" I demanded. "What is your name?"

My host smiled.

"I have no name," he answered.

"No name?"

"Unfortunate, is it not? When I was buired, there were no loving friends, apparently, to erect a tombstone. And when I arose from the grave, I had no mentor to guide me back to a memory of the past. Those were barbaric times in the East Prussia of 1777."

"You died in 1777?" I muttered.

"To the best of my knowledge," he retorted, bowing slightly in mock deprecation. "And so it is that my real name is unknown. Apparently I perished far from my native heath, for diligent research on my part has failed to uncover my paternity, or any contemporaries who recognized me at the time of my—er—resurrection. And so it is that I have no name; or rather, I have many pseudonyms. During the past sixteen decades I have traveled far, and have been all things to all men. I shall not endeavor to recite my history. It is enough to say that slowly, gradually, I have grown wise in the ways of the world. And I have evolved a plan. To this end I have amassed wealth, and brought together a library as a basis for my operations. Those operations I propose will interest you. And they will explain my anger when I think of you throwing the girl's body into the well."

He sat down. I followed suit. I felt anticipation crawling along my spine. He was about to reveal something—something I wanted to hear, yet dreaded. The revelation came, slyly, slowly.

"Have you ever wondered," he began, "why there are not more vampires in the world?"

"What do you mean?"

"Consider. It is said, and it is true, that every victim of a vampire becomes a vampire in turn. The new vampire finds other victims. Isn't it reasonable to suppose, therefore, that in a short time—through sheer mathematical progression—the virus of vampirism would run epidemic throughout the world? In other words, have you ever wondered why the world is not filled with vampires by this time?"

"Well, yes—I never thought of it that way. What is the reason?" I asked.

He glared and raised a white finger. It stabbed forward at my chest— a rapier of accusation.

"Because of fools like you. Fools who cast their victims into wells; fools whose victims are buried in sealed coffins, who hide the bodies or dismember them so no one would suspect their work. As a result, few new recruits join the ranks. And the old ones—myself included—are constantly subject to the ravages of the centuries. We eventually disintegrate, you know. To my knowledge, there are only a few hundred vampires today. And yet, if new victims all were given the opportunity to rise—we would have a vampire army within a year. Within three years there would be millions of vampires! Within ten years we could rule earth! Can't you see that? If there was no cremation, no careless disposal of bodies, no bungling, we could end our hunted existence as creatures of the night—brothers of the bat! No longer would we be a legendary, cowering minority, living each a law unto himself! All that is needed is a plan. And I—I have evolved that plan!"

His voice rose. So did the hairs upon my neck. I was beginning to comprehend, now—

"Suppose we started with the humble instruments of destiny," he suggested. "Those forlorn, unnoticed, ignorant little old men—night watchmen of graveyards and cemeteries."

A smile creased his corpse-like countenance. "Suppose we eliminated them? Took over their jobs? Put vampires in their places—men who would go to the fresh graves and dig up the bodies of each victim they had bitten while those bodies were still warm and pulsing and undecayed? We could save the lives of most of the recruits we make. Reasonable, is it not?"

To me it was madness, but I nodded.

"Suppose that we made victims of those attendants? Then carried them off, nursed them back to reanimation, and allowed them to resume their posts as our allies? They work only at night—no one would know. Just a little suggestion, but so obvious! And it would mean so much!"

His smile broadened.

"All that it takes is organization on our part. I know many of my brethren. It is my desire soon to call them together and present this plan. Never before have we worked cooperatively, but when I show them the possibilities, they cannot fail to respond. Can you imagine it? An earth which we could control and terrorize—a world in which human beings become our property, our cattle? It is so simple, really. Sweep aside your foolish concepts of Dracula and the other superstitious confectionery that masquerades in the public mind as an authentic picture. I admit that we are—unearthly. But there is no reason for us to be stupid, impractical figures of fantasy. There is more for us than crawling around in black cloaks and recoiling at the sight of crucifixes! After all, we are a life-form, a race of our own. Biology has not yet recognized us, but we exist. Our morphology and metabolism have not been evaluated or charted; our actions and reactions never studied. But we exist. And we are superior to ordinary mortals. Let us assert this superiority! Plain human cunning, coupled with our super-normal powers, can create for us a mastery over all living things. For we are greater than Life—we are Life-in-Death!"

I half-rose. He waved me back, breathlessly.

"Suppose we band together and make plans? Suppose we go about, first of all, selecting our victims on the basis of value to our ranks? Instead of regarding them as sources of easy nourishment, let's think in terms of an army seeking recruits. Let us select keen brains, youthfully strong bodies. Let us prey upon the best earth has to offer. Then we shall wax strong and no man shall stay our hand—or teeth!"

He crouched like a black spider, spinning his web of words to enmesh my sanity. His eyes glittered. It was absurd somehow to see this creature of superstitious terror calmly creating a super-dictatorship of the dead.

And yet, I was one of them. It was real. The nameless one would do it, too.

"Have you ever stopped to wonder why I tell you this? Have you ever stopped to wonder why you are my confidant in this venture?" he purred.

I shook my head.

"It is because you are young. I am old. For years I have labored only to this end. Now that my plans are perfected I need assistance. Youth, a modern viewpoint. I know of you, Graham Keene. I watched you before

". . . you became one of us. You were selected for this purpose."

"Selected?" Suddenly it hit home. I fought down a stranglehold gasp as I asked the question. "Then you know who—did this to me? *You know who bit me?*"

Rotting fangs gaped in a smile. He nodded slowly.

"Of course," he whispered. "Why—*I* did!"

V

He was probably prepared for anything except the calmness with which I accepted this revelation. Certainly he was pleased. And the rest of that night, and all the next night, were spent in going over the plans, in detail. I learned that he had not yet communicated with—others—in regard to his ideas.

A meeting would be arranged soon. Then we would begin the campaign. As he said, the times were ripe. War, a world in unrest—we would be able to move unchallenged and find unusual opportunities.

I agreed. I was even able to add certain suggestions as to detail. He was pleased with my cooperation.

Then, on the third night, came hunger. He offered to serve as my guide, but I brushed him aside.

"Let me try my own wings," I smiled. "After all, I must learn sooner or later. And I promise you, I shall be very careful. This time I will see to it that the body remains intact. Then I shall discover the place of burial and we can perform an experiment. I will select a likely recruit, we shall go forth to open the grave, and thus will we test our plan in miniature."

He fairly beamed at that. And I went forth that night, alone.

I returned only as dawn welled out of the eastern sky—returned to slumber through the day. That night we spoke, and I confided my success to his eager ears.

"Sidney J. Garrat is the name," I said. "A college professor, about forty-five. I found him wandering along a path near the campus. The trees form a dark, deserted avenue. He offered no resistance. I left him there. I don't think they'll bother with an autopsy—for the marks on his throat are invisible and he is known to have a weak heart.

"He lived alone without relatives. He had no money. That means a wooden coffin and quick burial at Everest tomorrow. Tomorrow night we can go there."

My companion nodded. "You have done well," he said.

We spent the remainder of the night in perfecting our plans. We would go to Everest, locate the night watchman and put him out of the way, then seek the new grave of Professor Garrat.

And so it was that we re-entered the cemetery on the following evening.

Once again a midnight moon glared from the Cyclopean socket of the sky. Once more the wind whispered to us on our way, and the trees bowed in black obeisance along the path.

We crept up to the shanty of the graveyard watchman and peered through the window at his stooping figure.

"I'll knock," I suggested. "Then when he comes to the door—"

My companion shook his gray head. "No teeth," he whispered. "The man is old, useless to us. I shall resort to more mundane weapons."

I shrugged. Then I knocked. The old man opened the door, blinked out at me with rheumy eyes.

"What is it?" he wheezed, querulously. "Ain't nobuddy suppose' tuh be in uh cemetery this time uh night—"

Lean fingers closed around his windpipe. My companion dragged him forth toward nearby shrubbery. His free arm rose and fell, and a silver arc stabbed down. He had used a knife.

Then we made haste along the path, before the scent of blood could divert us from our mission—and far ahead, on the hillside dedicated to the last slumbers of Poverty, I saw the raw, gaping edges of a new-made grave.

He ran back to the hut, then, and procured the spades we had neglected in our haste. The moon was our lantern and the grisly work began amidst a whistling wind.

No one saw us, no one heard us, for only empty eyes and shattered ears lay far beneath the earth.

We toiled, and then we stooped and tugged. The grave was deep, very deep. At the bottom the coffin lay, and we dragged forth the pine box.

"Terrible job," confided my companion. "Not a professionally dug grave at all, in my opinion. Wasn't filled in right. And this coffin is pine, but very thick. He'd never claw his own way out. Couldn't break through the boards. And the earth was packed too tightly. Why would they waste so much time on a pauper's grave?"

"Doesn't matter," I whispered. "Let's open it up. If he's revived, we must hurry."

We'd brought a hammer from the caretaker's shanty too, and he went down into the pit itself to pry the nails free. I heard the board covering move, and peered down over the edge of the grave.

He bent forward, stooping to peer into the coffin, his face a mask of livid death in the moonlight. I heard him hiss.

"Why—the coffin is empty!" he gasped.

"Not for long!"

I drew the wrench from my pocket, raised it, brought it down with every ounce of strength I possessed until it shattered through his skull.

And then I leaped down into the pit and pressed the writhing, mewing shape down into the coffin, slammed the lid on, and drove the heavy nails into place. I could hear his whimperings rise to muffled screams, but the screams grew faint as I began to heap the clods of earth upon the coffin lid.

I worked and panted there until no sound came from the coffin below. I packed the earth down hard—harder than I had last night when I dug the grave in the first place.

And then, at last, the task was over.

He lay there, the nameless one, the deathless one; lay six feet underground in a stout wooden coffin.

He could not claw his way free, I knew. And even if he did, I'd pressed him into his wooden prison face down. He'd claw his way to hell, not to earth.

But he was past escape. Let him lie there, as he had described it to me —not dead, not alive. Let him be conscious as he decayed, and as the wood decayed and the worms crawled in to feast. Let him suffer until the maggots at last reached his corrupt brain and ate away his evil consciousness.

I could have driven a stake through his heart. But his ghastly desire deserved defeat in this harsher fate.

Thus it was ended, and I could return now before discovery and the coming of dawn—return to his great house which was the only home I knew on the face of the earth.

Return I did, and for the past hours I have been writing this that all might know the truth.

I am not skilled with words, and what I read here smacks of mawkish melodrama. For the world is superstitious and yet cynical—and this account will be deemed the ravings of a fool or madman; worse still, as a practical joke.

So I must implore you; if you seek to test the truth of what I've set down, go to Everest tomorrow and search out the newly dug grave on the hillside. Talk to the police when they find the dead watchman, make them go to the well near Danny's roadside stand.

Then, if you must, dig up the grave and find that which must still writhe and crawl within. When you see it, you'll believe—and in justice, you will relieve the torment of that monstrous being by driving a stake through his heart.

For that stake represents release and peace.

I wish you'd come here, after that—and bring a stake for me . . .

Robert Bloch

BEETLES

When Hartley returned from Egypt, his friends said he had changed. The specific nature of that change was difficult to detect, for none of his acquaintances got more than a casual glimpse of him. He dropped around to the club just once, and then retired to the seclusion of his apartments. His manner was so definitely hostile, so markedly anti-social, that very few of his cronies cared to visit him, and the occasional callers were not received.

It caused considerable talk at the time—gossip rather. Those who remembered Arthur Hartley in the days before his expedition abroad were naturally quite cut up over the drastic metamorphosis in his manner. Hartley had been known as a keen scholar, a singularly erudite fieldworker in his chosen profession of archeology; but at the same time he had been a peculiarly charming person. He had the worldly flair usually associated with the fictional characters of E. Phillips Oppenheim, and a positively devilish sense of humor which mocked and belittled it. He was the kind of fellow who could order the precise wine at the proper moment, at the same time grinning as though he were as much surprised by it all as his guest of the evening. And most of his friends found this air of culture without ostentation quite engaging. He had carried this urbane sense of the ridiculous over into his work; and while it was known that he was very much interested in archeology, and a notable figure in the field, he inevitably referred to his studies as "pottering around with old fossils and the old fossils that discovered them."

Consequently, his curious reversal following his trip came as a complete surprise.

All that was definitely known was that he had spent some eight months on a field trip to the Egyptian Sudan. Upon his return he had immediately severed all connections with the institute he had been associated with. Just what had occurred during the expedition was a matter of excited conjecture among his former intimates. But something had definitely happened; it was unmistakable.

The night he spent at the club proved that. He had come in quietly, too quietly. Hartley was one of those persons who usually made an entrance, in the true sense of the word. His tall, graceful figure, attired in the immaculate evening dress so seldom found outside of the pages of melodramatic fiction; his truly leonine head with its Stokowski-like bristle of gray hair; these attributes commanded attention. He could have passed anywhere as a man of the world, or a stage magician awaiting his cue to step onto the platform.

But this evening he entered quietly, unobtrusively. He wore dinner clothes, but his shoulders sagged, and the spring was gone from his walk. His hair was grayer, and it hung pallidly over his tanned forehead. Despite the bronze of Egyptian sun on his features, there was a sickly tinge to his countenance. His eyes peered mistily from amidst unsightly folds. His face seemed to have lost its mold; the mouth hung loosely.

He greeted no one; and took a table alone. Of course cronies came up and chatted, but he did not invite them to join him. And oddly enough, none of them insisted, although normally they would gladly have forced their company upon him and jollied him out of a black mood, which experience had taught them was easily done in his case. Nevertheless, after a few words with Hartley, they all turned away.

They must have felt it even then. Some of them hazarded the opinion that Hartley was still suffering from some form of fever contracted in Egypt, but I do not think they believed this in their hearts. From their shocked descriptions of the man they seemed one and all to sense the peculiar *alien* quality about him. This was an Arthur Hartley they had never known, an aged stranger, with a querulous voice which rose in suspicion when he was questioned about his journey. Stranger he truly was, for he did not even appear to recognize some of the men who greeted him, and when he did it was with an abstracted manner—a clumsy way of wording it, but what else is there to say when an old friend stares blankly into silence upon meeting, and his eyes seem to fasten on far-off terrors that affright him?

That was the strangeness they all grasped in Hartley. He was afraid. Fear bestrode those sagging shoulders. Fear breathed a pallor into that ashy face. Fear grinned into those empty, far-fixed eyes. Fear prompted the suspicion in the voice.

They told me, and that is why I went round to see Arthur Hartley in his rooms. Others had spoken of their efforts, in the week following his appearance at the club, to gain admittance to his apartment. They said he did not answer the bell, and complained that the phone had been disconnected. But that, I reasoned, was fear's work.

I wouldn't let Hartley down. I had been a rather good friend of his—and I may as well confess that I scented a mystery here. The combination proved irresistible. I went up to his flat one afternoon and rang.

No answer. I went into the dim hallway and listened for footsteps, some sign of life from within. No answer. Complete, utter silence. For a moment I thought crazily of suicide, then laughed the dread away. It was absurd—and still, there had been a certain dismaying unanimity in all the reports I had heard of Hartley's mental state. When the stolidest, most hard-headed of the club bores concurred in their estimate of the man's condition, I might well worry. Still, Suicide . . .

I rang again, more as a gesture than in expectation of tangible results, and then I turned and descended the stairs. I felt, I recall, a little twinge of inexplicable relief upon leaving the place. The thought of suicide in that gloomy hallway had not been pleasant.

I reached the lower door and opened it, and a familiar figure scurried past me on the landing. I turned. It was Hartley.

For the first time since his return I got a look at the man, and in the hallway shadows he was ghastly. Whatever his condition at the club, a week must have accentuated it tremendously. His head was lowered, and as I greeted him he looked up. His eyes gave me a terrific shock. There was a stranger dwelling in their depths—a haunted stranger. I swear he shook when I addressed him.

He was wearing a tattered topcoat, but it hung loosely over his gauntness. I noticed that he was carrying a large bundle done up in brown paper.

I said something, I don't remember what; at any rate, I was at some pains to conceal my confusion as I greeted him. I was rather insistently cordial, I believe, for I could see that he would just as soon have hurried up the stairs without even speaking to me. The astonishment I felt converted itself into heartiness. Rather reluctantly he invited me up.

We entered the flat, and I noticed that Hartley double-locked the door behind him. That, to me, characterized his metamorphosis. In the old days, Hartley had always kept open house, in the literal sense of the word. Studies might have kept him late at the institute, but a chance visitor found his door open wide. And now, he double-locked it.

I turned around and surveyed the apartment. Just what I expected to see I cannot say, but certainly my mind was prepared for some sign of radical alteration. There was none. The furniture had not been moved; the pictures hung in their original places; the vast bookcases still stood in the shadows.

Hartley excused himself, entered the bedroom, and presently emerged after discarding his topcoat. Before he sat down he walked over to the mantle and struck a match before a little bronze figurine of Horus. A second later the thick gray spirals of smoke arose in the approved style of exotic fiction, and I smelt the pungent tang of strong incense.

That was the first puzzler. I had unconsciously adopted the attitude of a detective looking for clues—or perhaps, a psychiatrist ferreting out psychoneurotic tendencies. And the incense was definitely alien to the Arthur Hartley I knew.

"Clears away the smell," he remarked.

I didn't ask "What smell?" Nor did I begin to question him as to his trip, his inexplicable conduct in not answering my correspondence after he left Khartoum, or his avoidance of my company in this week following his return. Instead, I let him talk.

He said nothing at first. His conversation rambled, and behind it all I sensed the abstraction I had been warned about. He spoke of having given up his work, and hinted that he might leave the city shortly and go up to his family home in the country. He had been ill. He was disappointed in Egyptology, and its limitations. He hated darkness. The locust plagues had increased in Kansas.

This rambling was—insane.

I knew it then, and I hugged the thought to me in the perverse delight which is born of dread. Hartley was mad. "Limitations" of Egyptology. "I hate the dark." "The locusts of Kansas."

But I sat silently when he lighted the great candles about the room; sat silently staring through the incense clouds to where the flaming tapers illuminated his twitching features. And then he broke.

"You are my friend?" he said. There was a question in his voice, a puzzled suspicion in his words that brought sudden pity to me. His derangement was terrible to witness. Still, I nodded gravely.

"You are my friend," he continued. This time the words were a statement. The deep breath which followed betokened resolution on his part.

"Do you know what was in that bundle I brought in?" he asked suddenly.

"No."

"I'll tell you. Insecticide. That's what it was. Insecticide!"

His eyes flamed in triumph which stabbed me.

"I haven't left this house for a week. I dare not spread the plague. They follow me, you know. But today I thought of the way—absurdly simple, too. I went out and bought insecticide. Pounds of it. And liquid spray. Special formula stuff, more deadly than arsenic. Just elementary science, really—but its very prosaicness may defeat the Powers of Evil."

I nodded like a fool, wondering whether I could arrange for him to be taken away that evening. Perhaps my friend, Doctor Sherman, might diagnose. . . .

"Now let them come! It's my last chance—the incense doesn't work, and even if I keep the lights burning they creep about the corners. Funny the woodwork holds up; it should be riddled."

What was this?

"But I forgot," said Hartley. "You don't know about it. The plague, I mean. And the curse." He leaned forward and his white hands made octopus-shadows on the wall.

"I used to laugh at it, you know," he said. "Archeology isn't exactly a pursuit for the superstitious. Too much groveling in ruins. And putting curses on old pottery and battered statues never seemed important to me. But Egyptology—that's different. It's human bodies, there. Mummified, but still human. And the Egyptians were a great race—they had scientific secrets we haven't yet fathomed, and of course we cannot even begin to approach their concepts in mysticism."

Ah! There was the key! I listened, intently.

"I learned a lot, this last trip. We were after the excavation job in the new tombs up the river. I brushed up on the dynastic periods, and naturally the religious significance entered into it. Oh, I know all the myths—the Bubatis legend, the Isis resurrection theory, the true names of Ra, the allegory of Set—"

"We found things there, in the tombs—wonderful things. The pottery, the furniture, the bas-reliefs we were able to remove. But the expeditionary reports will be out soon; you can read of it then. We found mummies, too. Cursed mummies."

Now I saw it, or thought I did.

"And I was a fool. I did something I never should have dared to do—for ethical reasons, and for other, more important reasons. Reasons that may cost me my soul."

I had to keep my grip on myself, remember that he was mad, remember that his convincing tones were prompted by the delusions of insanity. Or else, in that dark room I might have easily believed that there was a power which had driven my friend to this haggard brink.

"Yes, I did it, I tell you! I read the Curse of Scarabæus—sacred beetle, you know—and I did it anyway. I couldn't guess that it was true. I was a skeptic; everyone is skeptical enough until things happen. Those things are like the phenomenon of death; you read about it, realize that it occurs to others, and yet cannot quite conceive of it happening to yourself. And yet it does. The Curse of the Scarabæus was like that."

Thoughts of the Sacred Beetle of Egypt crossed my mind. And I remembered, also, the seven plagues. And I knew what he would say. . . .

"We came back. On the ship I noticed them. They crawled out of the corners every night. When I turned the light on they went away, but they always returned when I tried to sleep. I burned incense to keep them off, and then I moved into a new cabin. But they followed me.

"I did not dare tell anyone. Most of the chaps would have laughed, and the Egyptologists in the party wouldn't have helped much. Besides, I couldn't confess my crime. So I went on alone."

His voice was a dry whisper.

"It was pure hell. One night on the boat I saw the black things crawling in my food. After that I ate in the cabin, alone. I dared not see anyone now, for fear they might notice how the things followed me. They did follow me, you know—if I walked in shadow on the deck they crept along behind. Only the sun kept them back, or a pure flame. I nearly went mad trying to account logically for their presence; trying to imagine how they got on the boat. But all the time I knew in my heart what the truth was. They were a sending—the Curse!

"When I reached port I went up and resigned. When my guilt was discovered there would have been a scandal, anyway, so I resigned. I couldn't hope to continue work with those things crawling all over, wherever I went. I was afraid to look anyone up. Naturally, I tried. That one night at the club was ghastly, though—I could see them marching across the carpet and crawling up the sides of my chair, and it took all there was in me to keep from screaming and dashing out.

"Since then I've stayed here, alone. Before I decide on any course for the future, I must fight the Curse and win. Nothing else will help."

I started to interject a phrase, but he brushed it aside and continued desperately.

"No, I couldn't go away. They followed me across the ocean; they haunt me in the streets. I could be locked up and they would still come. They come every night and crawl up the sides of my bed and try to get at my face and I must sleep soon or I'll go mad, they crawl over my face at night, they crawl—"

It was horrible to see the words ooze out between his set teeth, for he was fighting madly to control himself.

"Perhaps the insecticide will kill them. It was the first thing I should have thought of, but of course panic confused me. Yes, I put my trust in the insecticide. Grotesque, isn't it? Fighting an ancient curse with insect-powder?"

I spoke at last. "They're beetles, aren't they?"

He nodded. "Scarabæus beetles. You know the curse. The mummies under the protection of the Scarab cannot be violated."

I knew the curse. It was one of the oldest known to history. Like all legends, it has had a persistent life. Perhaps I could reason.

"But why should it affect you?" I asked. Yes, I would reason with Hartley. Egyptian fever had deranged him, and the colorful curse story had gripped his mind. If I spoke logically, I might get him to understand his hallucination. "Why should it affect you?" I repeated.

He was silent for a moment before he spoke, and then his words seemed to be wrung out of him.

"I stole a mummy," he said. "I stole the mummy of a temple virgin. I must have been crazy to do it; something happens to you under that sun. There was gold in the case, and jewels, and ornaments. And there was the Curse, written. I got them—both."

I stared at him, and knew that in this he spoke the truth.

"That's why I cannot keep up my work. I stole the mummy, and I am cursed. I didn't believe, but the crawling things came just as the inscription said.

"At first I thought that was the meaning of the Curse, that wherever I went the beetles would go, too, that they would haunt me and keep me from men forever. But lately I am beginning to think differently. I think the beetles will act as messengers of vengeance. I think they mean to kill me."

This was pure raving.

"I haven't dared open the mummy-case since. I'm afraid to read the inscription again. I have it here in the house, but I've locked it up and I won't show you. I want to burn it—but I must keep it on hand. In a way, it's the only proof of my sanity. And if the things kill—"

"Snap out of it," I commanded. Then I started. I don't know the exact words I used, but I said reassuring, hearty, wholesome things. And when I finished he smiled the martyred smile of the obsessed.

"Delusions? They're real. But where do they come from? I can't find any cracks in the woodwork. The walls are sound. And yet every night the beetles come and crawl up the bed and try to get at my face. They don't bite, they merely crawl. There are thousands of them—black thousands of silent, crawling things, inches long. I brush them away, but when I fall asleep they come back; they're clever, and I can't pretend. I've never caught one; they're too fast-moving. They seem to understand me—or the Power that sends them understands.

"They crawl up from Hell night after night, and I can't last much longer. Some evening I'll fall completely asleep and they will creep over my face, and then—"

He leaped to his feet and screamed.

"The corner—in the corner now—out of the walls—"

The black shadows were moving, marching.

I saw a blur, fancied I could detect rustling forms advancing, creeping, spreading before the light.

Hartley sobbed.

I turned on the electric light. There was, of course, nothing there. I didn't say a word, but left abruptly. Hartley continued to sit huddled in his chair, his head in his hands.

I went straight to my friend, Doctor Sherman.

2

He diagnosed it as I thought he would: phobia, accompanied by hallucinations. Hartley's feeling of guilt over stealing the mummy haunted him. The visions of beetles resulted.

All this Sherman studded with the mumbo-jumbo technicalities of the professional psychiatrist, but it was simple enough. Together we phoned the institute where Hartley had worked. They verified the story, in so far as they knew Hartley had stolen a mummy.

After dinner Sherman had an appointment, but he promised to meet me at ten and go with me again to Hartley's apartment. I was quite insistent about this, for I felt that there was no time to lose. Of course, this was a mawkish attitude on my part, but that strange afternoon session had deeply disturbed me.

I spent the early evening in unnerving reflection. Perhaps that was the way all so-called "Egyptian curses" worked. A guilty conscience on the part of a tomb-looter made him project the shadow of imaginary punishment on himself. He had hallucinations of retribution. That might explain the mysterious Tut-ankh-ahmen deaths; it certainly accounted for the suicides.

And that was why I insisted on Sherman seeing Hartley that same night. I feared suicide very much, for if ever a man was on the verge of complete mental collapse, Arthur Hartley surely was.

It was nearly eleven, however, before Sherman and I rang the bell. There was no answer. We stood in the dark hallway as I vainly rapped, then pounded. The silence only served to augment my anxiety. I was truly afraid, or else I never would have dared using my skeleton key.

As it was, I felt the end justified the means. We entered.

The living-room was bare of occupants. Nothing had changed since the afternoon—I could see that quite clearly, for all the lights were on, and the guttering candle-stumps still smoldered.

Both Sherman and I smelt the reek of the insecticide quite strongly, and the floor was almost evenly coated with thick white insect powder.

We called, of course, before I ventured to enter the bedroom. It was dark, and I thought it was empty until I turned on the lights and saw the figure huddled beneath the bed-clothes. It was Arthur Hartley, and I needed no second glance to see that his white face was twisted in death.

The reek of insecticide was strongest here, and incense burned; and yet there was another pungent smell—a musty odor, vaguely animal-like.

Sherman stood at my side, staring.

"What shall we do?" I asked.

"I'll get the police on the wire downstairs," he said. "Touch nothing."

He dashed out, and I followed him from the room, sickened. I could not bear to approach the body of my friend—that hideous expression on the face affrighted me. Suicide, murder, heart attack—I didn't even wish to know the manner of his passing. I was heartsick to think that we had been too late.

I turned from the bedroom and then that damnable scent came to my nostrils redoubled, and I knew. "Beetles!"

But how could there be beetles? It was all an illusion in poor Hartley's brain. Even his twisted mind had realized that there were no apertures in the walls to admit them; that they could not be seen about the place.

And still the smell rose on the air—the reek of death, of decay, of ancient corruption that reigned in Egypt. I followed the scent to the second bedroom, forced the door.

On the bed lay the mummy-case. Hartley had said he locked it up in here. The lid was closed, but ajar.

I opened it. The sides bore inscriptions, and one of them may have pertained to the Scarabæus Curse. I do not know, for I stared only at the ghastly, unshrouded figure that lay within. It was a mummy, and it had been sucked dry. It was all shell. There was a great cavity in the stomach, and as I peered within I could see a few feebly-crawling forms—inch-long, black buttons with great writhing feelers. They shrank back in the light, but not before I saw the scarab patterns on the outer crusted backs.

The secret of the Curse was here—the beetles had dwelt within the body of the mummy! They had eaten it out and nested within, and at night they crawled forth. It was true then!

I screamed once when the thought hit me, and dashed back to Hartley's bedroom. I could hear the sound of footsteps ascending the outer stairs; the police were on their way, but I couldn't wait. I raced into the bedroom, dread tugging at my heart.

Had Hartley's story been true, after all? Were the beetles really messengers of a divine vengeance?

I ran into that bedroom where Arthur Hartley lay, stooped over his huddled figure on the bed. My hands fumbled over the body, searching for a wound. I had to know how he had died.

But there was no blood, there was no mark, and there was no weapon beside him. It had been shock or heart attack, after all. I was strangely relieved when I thought of this. I stood up and eased the body back again on the pillows.

I felt almost glad, because during my search my hands had moved over the body while my eyes roved over the room. I was looking for beetles.

Hartley had feared the beetles—the beetles that crawled out of the mummy. They had crawled every night, if his story was to be believed; crawled into his room, up the bed posts, across the pillows.

Where were they now? They had left the mummy and disappeared, and Hartley was dead. Where were they?

Suddenly I stared again at Hartley. There was something wrong with the body on the bed. When I had lifted the corpse it seemed singularly light for a man of Hartley's build. As I gazed at him now, he seemed empty of more than life. I peered into that ravaged face more closely, and then I shuddered. For the cords on his neck moved convulsively, his chest seemed to rise and fall, his head fell sideways on the pillow. He lived—or something inside him did!

And then as his twisted features moved, I cried aloud, for I knew how Hartley had died, and what had killed him; knew the secret of the Scarab Curse and why the beetles crawled out of the mummy to seek his bed. I knew what they had meant to do—what, tonight, they had done. I cried aloud as I saw Hartley's face move, in hopes that my voice would drown that dreadful rustling sound which filled the room and came from *inside Hartley's body.*

I knew that the Scarab Curse had killed him, and I screamed quite wildly as his mouth gaped slowly open. Just as I fainted, I saw Arthur Hartley's dead lips part, allowing a rustling swarm of *black Scarabæus beetles* to pour out across the pillow.

Robert Bloch's Acceptance Speech

Thank you, Gahan . . . I think. You gave me a terrible moment there, you folks in the audience—you stood up, I thought you were going to leave.

About two months ago in London at Coyle's Bookshop, they gave one of their monthly luncheons. This one was in honor of a gentleman I don't think you are aware of—a music hall performer named Arthur (unintelligible). It was the occasion of his seventy-fifth birthday and the publication of his book. Arthur said something which I find strangely apropos at this moment. He looked around the table and said, "This luncheon is not a work of fiction, because everybody at this table is either living or dead." I have much the same feeling.

This is of course formerly the Arkham Hilton, and probably Mr. Lovecraft did spend a night or two here. I know that last night the sounds I heard could have been the inspiration for "The Rats in the Walls." I knew I was in the right place when I came here. I walked into the bar and I heard somebody ordering a gin and Miskatonic.

I must say a few words, for he insisted that I do so, about Gahan Wilson. I was rather surprised at his appearance when I met him (two words unintelligible) when I suddenly realized he had the Innsmouth look—the results of generations of inbreeding. Then I discovered he doesn't have a room at the hotel—he's sleeping in the swimming pool—at the bottom, the surface being covered with green slime. And it bothered me. I began to analyze my reactions to Gahan Wilson. Strange name. Until I realized—I wrote it out—that this is merely Nosliw Nahag spelled backwards. You people who have read the *Necronomicon* all realize who Nosliw Nahag was—a friend of Yog-Sothoth's brother, Irving-Sothoth. You know who Irving-Sothoth was—he went to school with Don Wollhein. The two of them got into the Girl Scouts together—until the teacher found out. So much for Gahan Wilson. Gahan has a tremendous talent as an artist and as a writer. I hate talent. To be quite clear before we leave the subject, I'll tell you that my own name spelled backwards is Trebor Hcolb. If I have a little too much on the nose I can just see myself walking into a room saying, "Hi, I'm Trebor Hcolb!" But I don't do that.

Now, if I may be less serious for a moment, I want to tell you, as Gahan has, what an honor I consider this to be. And I'm not being humble or falsely modest when I say that I really don't think I deserve it, for I realize that I'm in the presence of men here who to my way of thinking are far more equipped to play the role of guest of honor, who have known Howard Phillips Lovecraft personally; they've written of him so brilliantly that all I can say is that I consider this perhaps the most lucky moment of my life. I thank you all for allowing me to be here. In a sense, of course, we're all honored to have been associated with H.P.L. in some way. He has been eulogized here, and rightfully so. I don't believe we could say any more about him as a man, as an artist, as a warm, outgoing personality, of his influence on the field of fantasy. Some of the people here knew him from amateur journals; some knew him because they were his personal friends and colleagues—he knew them in New York. Others knew him because of his assistance in their writing careers. Some of us knew him at the time, or discovered him later, as a writer, but to all of us I think he was a very important influence.

Now, we have heard, because of the number of people who have had a closer association, a great deal of personal reminiscence. At the risk of boring you, I think that I should place myself in that perspective just for a moment.

When I was a kid ten years of age, I was of course greatly influenced by fantasy reading at the time. I had seen fantasy films—I had seen the work of Lon Chaney, Sr. Living in Chicago, one day in the northwest railroad depot, visiting my aunt, she asked, "Would you like a magazine to read on the train?" I said yes. "Any magazine you want." So, with all the naïveté of a ten-year-old, I immediately spotted a magazine with a naked girl on the cover and said, "That's for me!" No, actually, it did not have a naked girl on the cover. But I bought the magazine, read it, and found my first story by Howard Phillips Lovecraft.

Ten years later, during the Depression, I was again reading that magazine. And I must tell you something you younger people are not aware of. *Weird Tales* occupied an unusual position in the 1920s. It called itself the unique magazine, and it was. For those of you who aren't familiar with it, *Weird Tales* was sort of a *Playboy* for psychopaths. The centerfold was the Slaymate of the Month. It printed the works of Lovecraft, Howard, Clark Ashton Smith, Frank Belknap Long, Donald Wandrei, Manny Wade Wellman, H. Warner Munn, and so many others, and we youngsters read these stories with great fascination.

I was living in a suburb of Chicago called (unintelligible) Illinois, for example, and nearby was a place called Heinz Veterans Hospital where veterans of World War I were sequestered, and it had a large field—a field where airplanes could stop. They called them airplanes in those days. Believe it or not, when you heard the sound of a plane overhead you came running out of the house to look at it. None of us could envision that a young man who was working in that field at that time named Charles A. Lindbergh was going to fly the Atlantic in the following year, and I'm sure it didn't occur to most of us, looking up there in the sky, that we would ever ourselves fly in an airplane. It was just inconceivable.

There's this big nostalgia craze now, but to us there was no nostalgia because we lived through it. To us, reading the Tarzan books, there was still a possibility that there might be a Tarzan in Africa because Africa was the Dark Continent, it hadn't been explored, there could be lost cities. When we read Arthur Conan Doyle's *The Lost World,* this was a possibility. There might somewhere in South America be a realm inhabited by prehistoric dinosaurs and Ackerman. Some of us half believed that there was a kindly old physician named Dr. Fu Manchu. And there were, in this world that I imagined, headhunters, cannibals in the South Seas. There were unexplored regions in the Arctic, the Antarctic.

Consequently, the wonders that we read about in WT were not treated entirely in the youthful mind as fantasies, but sometimes as possibilities. Well, nobody treated the wonders that we read about in WT with the grace and style and conviction of H. P. Lovecraft. So *Weird Tales* had a great appeal to us which those of you who were not young in those days couldn't quite understand. The Depression came; the time that I was speaking of, the early 1930s. And those of us who lived through the Depression had other problems. If we enjoyed reading fantasy, well, money was hard to come by. We didn't have it. There were very, very few books of fantasy available. There were no paperbacks. Nothing was reprinted. You read a story in the pulp magazines when it came out, and then it vanished forever. If you saw a film, when it disappeared, it disappeared for good—there was no television to bring it back on "The Late Late Show."

And times were very hard. WT cost twenty-five cents in a day when most pulp magazines cost a dime. I remember that meant a lot to me. I was living at 620 East Knapp Street at the time, and I recall what I'd do. I got an allowance of twenty-five cents a week, and one week's allowance had to be set aside for WT, which generally came on the newsstand the last day of the month or the first day of the following month. And I would get up very, very early on the last day of the month. We had a block away from us a little combination tobacco store-magazine store, and to get to it I would run through the alley. The alley was a grim and forbidding place at six o'clock in the morinng. And over on the left was a huge, ancient, domed edifice called the Wood Dairy. And the thing about this horrible-looking place that looked as if it belonged on Federal

Hill—I suddenly realized that I had never ever seen a single cow in that dairy.

Anyway, I would go through there, rush into this combination tobacco store-magazine store which was run by two spinster ladies, one of whom sold cigars, and the other of whom smoked them, and I would look for WT. I'd get it in my hot little hands, and depending on the nature of the illustration, I would put it under my coat or bring it home openly to my parents, whom I tried to shield from such things. In the letters section I would read references to the stories by H. P. Lovecraft which I'd never been able to see, and which were not then available in back issues which were occasionally offered by WT. And I wanted to get my hands on those stories. So when I was fifteen I sat down and wrote my first fan letter to Lovecraft in care of WT, and asked H. P. Lovecraft where I could read his stories. Many of you know what happened. He answered, and he courteously offered to loan me any or all of the magazines that I requested which contained his stories. He also said, "I'm moving to 10 Barnes Street this month, and I have just catalogued my fantasy library. I'm enclosing a copy of the list of those books, and if there are any of those you'd like to borrow, I'd be happy to loan them."

Now to a fifteen-year-old kid living in the Midwest this came as a (three words unintelligible). It really meant something to me to find myself suddenly corresponding with this great idol of mine, an actual living published professional writer from the mysterious East. So we struck up this correspondence, and along about the third or fourth letter he said, "There's something about your letters that suggest to me that perhaps you might like to try your hand at writing a professional story yourself. Why don't you do so? I'd be glad to look at it and suggest a few criticisms." I did. And H.P.L., God bless him, didn't criticize them. He encouraged me; to the point where I was determined that I was somehow going to do some writing myself.

Not only did he encourage me, but he gave me a list of other writers with whom he was in contact. He said, "Why not drop them a line, get acquainted with the people that are in the field." And some of these people were E. Hoffman Price, Clark Ashton Smith, a fan of his named Bernard Austin Dwyer, Robert Barlow, Frank Belknap Long, Donald Wandrei, August Derleth, and another correspondent named J. Vernon Shea. I remember being very impressed by J. Vernon Shea because he was very much more sophisticated than I was and four years older, and that still holds true in part. He's still much more sophisticated, but now he's ten years older than I am.

So before too long, through my correspondence with Derleth, I was invited to his home in Sauk City, Wisconsin, which was about a hundred and twenty-five miles away. I took the Greyhound bus, went out to Sauk City, and was greeted by Mr. Derleth. And here was this man who acted like something out of *Der Rosenkavalier*. And not only that, but he fulfilled my expectations as a writer by wearing this purple velvet smoking jacket. That impressed me even more because Derleth didn't even smoke. We became friendly, our correspondence went on, and Lovecraft gave me his encouragement. I went down to Chicago and visited Farnsworth Wright, the editor of WT. I met the first WT writer outside of Derleth I ever encountered—Otto Binder. And naturally, being enthusiastic, I tried to proselyte other people. In my English class we were asked to do themes or essays on writers, and I did one on H. P. Lovecraft—got thrown out of class.

Then it was 1934 and I was seventeen when I graduated. The Depression was still going on, and it was a grim picture. You were either in the Civilian Conservation Corps or you starved. Now the Civilian Conservation Corps, again for those of you who weren't around, was a federally endowed chain gang of people who were paid to dig ditches, build bridges, dam rivers, for the princely sum of thirty dollars a month. And that was pretty good pay, until I found out that they sent fifteen bucks home to your parents.

So I had this problem—work or starve. So I thought I'd combine the two and decided to become a writer. Of course I had no expectations of going to college to prepare myself for what I didn't need. But I had Lovecraft. H. P. Lovecraft was my university. So I got myself a secondhand typewriter, put it on a secondhand card table, and went to work. I'd done several items already for the fan press—one story called "Lilies," and one story called "Black Lotus." I figured I'd better do something different or I'd end up as a florist. I wrote a story, and lo and behold, it sold to WT, the same magazine in which my idol was published.

That was a great day. It was an even greater day when I could walk into that cigar store on the first of November 1934 and pick up a copy of that magazine. I'd already fouled myself up by making some disparaging remarks about the Conan stories of the illustrious Robert E. Howard. I alleged as how I much preferred his non-Conan efforts, and this was regarded as very unprofessional conduct. Of course at the time I wrote the letter I was not a professional. But fortunately for me I lucked out. It didn't cause all the readers to turn their backs on me, so I continued to write stories. And it was all due to that man from Providence. I can safely say therefore that I owe my writing career to an act of Providence.

I won't bother to tell you, for you all are aware of the fact, that I wrote a story in which I disposed of Lovecraft, and he wrote a sequel in which he disposed of me, and believe me, beyond all doubt, I don't know anyone else whom I'd rather be killed by. And then, tragically, Lovecraft died in 1937 and part of me died with him, I guess, not only because he was not a god, he was mortal, that is true, but because he had so little recognition in his own lifetime. There were no novels or collections published, no great realization, even here in Providence, of what was lost. And I realized that while he had a following, he hadn't even been WT's most popular author. I don't think that during his lifetime he ever had a cover story in WT.

Then, as you know, August Derleth and Donald Wandrei decided to rectify the omission of his work in hardcovers, and they founded Arkham House and they put out *The Outsider and Others*. We know also that this was not a success at the beginning, but they persevered. And then a series of circumstances started to bring Lovecraft into prominence. There was an Armed Services edition of a reprint of his work that sold several million copies, and a whole new generation of young people became familiar with him. The paperbacks started and have been reprinted, but more important than that was that Lovecraft was discovered by foreign critics. But things looked grim there for a while.

I was doing some research for a little introduction that I wrote for a supernatural story written by Lovecraft acolytes, if we can call them such, and I came across something interesting in a book called *Golden Multitudes* in which were discussed best sellers in this country. In the twenties, by their standards, a good best seller was a book that sold a million or more copies in hardcover, because that's the only way they sold them. Well, 1928 was the year that I knew about. There were no books that fulfilled these qualifications. The most popular books were these—Earl Derr Biggers' *Behind That Curtain*, Viña Delmar's *Bad Girl*, and Ernest Dimnet's *The Art of Thinking*. These were widely reviewed and widely praised. In that same year, the February issue of WT published "The Call of Cthulhu" by H.P.L. There were no reviews of this particular story, and yet today those widely selling and widely acclaimed books are forgotten. Earl Derr Biggers is overshadowed by the character he created, Charlie Chan. Viña Delmar I don't think has attained any great prominence, though I know that she's been reprinted recently. As far as *The Art of Thinking* is concerned, you can tell by looking at the world today what influence that had. And yet that obscure story in an obscure magazine by an obscure writer inaugurated an entire renaissance, an entire cottage industry, you might say, which is now known as the Cthulhu Mythos.

I think one of the reasons it has endured is because Lovecraft created his own new world of legend. There are, of course, in his concept of the universe dominated by the Old Ones various religious parables, and there are some things that have been likened to Jung, the psychiatrist, in which Lovecraft touched the nerve endings which exist in all of us, such as our primordial fears of the unknown and certain paranoid suspicions that there may be forces greater than ourselves which dominate our lives and our thinking. Now, forty-seven years after "The Call of Cthulhu," Howard Phillips Lovecraft, thanks to his rediscovery, and to his critical acclaim, thanks to foreign recognition, his friends, thanks to a whole new generation of readers, is a far more potent literary figure in the field of fantasy than anyone else since the later Edgar Allan Poe. This convention is of course gathered here to honor him for his work in the city where he lived, and where, thirty-six years ago, he died.

Now to those of us who were privileged to know him personally, to those of us who were inspired or influenced by his work, to those of us who owe so much to his kindness, there is a verse he wrote in "The Call of Cthulhu" that I think has great meaning. You remember it—"That is not dead which can eternal lie, and with strange eons even death may die." I say to all of you, H. P. Lovecraft is not dead. He lives forever in our hearts and in our memories. Thank you.

About ROBERT BLOCH

Bob Bloch began his professional writing career at the age of seventeen, selling to pulp magazines. He was a protégé of H. P. Lovecraft's and the youngest member of the Lovecraft circle. Around ten years later, he adapted thirty-nine of his published stories for his own syndicated radio series in 1945, "Stay Tuned for Terror."

In 1958 he won his first Hugo for a short story, and the E. E. Evans Memorial Award the year after that. Following the sale of his novel *Psycho* to Alfred Hitchcock, he moved to Hollywood to write for films and television: *Psycho, The Skull, The Couch, The Cabinet of Caligari, Strait Jacket, The Night Walker, The Psychopath, The Deadly Bees, Torture Garden, The House That Dripped Blood, Asylum,* "Alfred Hitchcock Presents," "Thriller," "Star Trek," "ABC Movie of the Week," etc.

He was guest of honor at conventions in the United States and Canada. He has won the Ann Radcliffe Award for Literature and Television, the Trieste Fantasy Film Festival Award, the Mystery Writers of America Awards, and now the First World Fantasy Award.

Bloch, in talking about his latest collection of suspense stories, said they gave an intimate insight into the "notoriously twisted mind of the author," despite his often quoted disclaimer: "Actually, I have the heart of a small boy. I keep it in a jar, on my desk."

Considering his bent for things gruesome, Bloch has some very gentle hobbies: collecting stamps and books.

NOMINEES—NOVEL:

* THE FORGOTTEN BEASTS OF ELD   *Patricia A. McKillip*
  MERLIN'S RING   *H. Warner Munn*
  A MIDSUMMER TEMPEST   *Poul Anderson*

PATRICIA A. MCKILLIP/*Best Novel*

Although Patricia A. McKillip had written a number of books before *The Forgotten Beasts of Eld*, they were aimed at younger readers. It took this particular book to bring her to the attention of the majority of fantasy fans.

The novel is about Sybel, young daughter and granddaughter of wizards, and her magical beasts: the jewel-hoarding dragon Gyld; the riddle-replying boar Cyrin, the lion Gules, the black swan Terleth, the spell-casting black cat Moriah, and the deadly falcon Ter. Sybel's quest is to tame the fabulous bird Liralen and add it to her menagerie.

However, Sybel knows very little of people and a lot less of men and babies. So she is understandably angry when a handsome young warrior enters her life and leaves an infant prince practically on her doorstep. She overcomes an impulse at first to destroy them, and her anger slowly changes to love for them both.

The poetic language and smoothness with which the story is told caused Fritz Leiber to say, "The story moves on like a dance. The magical beasts revolve as in a ballet." It won high praise from him and from many quarters before it came to Providence and won its prize. Its structure is such—as indeed it should be—that the whole work must really be read before the reach and sweep of it are clear. This excerpt will, at best, only give the reader a taste of it.

Patricia A. McKillip

THE FORGOTTEN BEASTS OF ELD

Prince Tamlorn smiled. "I will come so quietly no one but you, Gules and Cyrin will know I am there. I will come."

"Tam, no," Sybel said helplessly. "You do not realize—" She checked suddenly, her head turned quickly toward a drawling, bubbling wail that ascended, faded and ascended again beyond the closed door. "What—" Gules rumbled beside Tam, rose suddenly and gave a sharp, full-throated growl. Sybel rose. There was a crash beyond the door, and the murmur of men's voices.

"Coren—" she breathed. She turned, flung open the door. Gules Lyon bounded past her, came to a crouch at the fireplace, his gold tail twitching. Coren looked at Sybel over the blades of three swords held at his throat. He was unarmed, backed against the hearthstones. Moriah paced at his feet, wailing at three men who wore the black tunics with the single blood-red star of Drede's service on their breasts. Tam, beside Sybel, said quickly,

"Do not hurt him."

The guards' faces turned slowly to him, their eyes flicking between him and Moriah. One of them said between his teeth, "Prince Tamlorn, this one is of Sirle."

"Do you know them, Tamlorn?" Coren asked. A blade point bit the hollow of his throat, and he closed his mouth.

"Yes. They are my father's guards." His eyes moved back to their tense faces. "I came here to see Sybel. She did not know I was coming. I have talked to her, and I am ready to come home. Let him go."

"This is Coren of Sirle, Norrel's brother—he was at Terbrec—"

"I know, but if you hurt him I do not think you will leave this place alive."

The man glanced at Moriah, then at Gules, his golden eyes full on their faces, rumbling deep in his throat. "The King is half-mad with worry. If we let Coren loose, we will be killed by these beasts. And if Drede knows we let one of Sirle slip through our hands, we might as well be killed by them."

"Are you alone?"

"No. The others are beyond the gate. They will come if we call."

"Then no one but you will need to know that Coren and Sybel were here. I will not tell Drede."

"Prince Tamlorn, he is the King's enemy—your enemy!"

"He is Sybel's husband! And if you want to risk killing him in front of Sybel, Gules and Moriah, go ahead. I can go home by myself like I came."

Moriah screamed again, flat-eared, crouched at Coren's feet, and the blades jumped, winking. One of the guards drew his sword back suddenly. Sybel's flat voice froze the drive of it toward Moriah.

"If you do that, I will kill you."

The guard stared at her still, black eyes, sweat breaking out on his face. "Lady, we will take the Prince and go. I swear it. But how—what guarantee do we have that we will walk alive out of your house, if we let Coren go? What is the surety for our lives?"

Tam's eyes rested a moment speculatively on Coren's face. He came forward and knelt at Coren's feet beneath the swords, and put his arms around Moriah.

"I am. Now let him go."

The swords wavered, winking in the firelight, fell. Coren's breath rose soundlessly and fell.

"Thank you."

Tam looked up at him, stroking Moriah's head. "Think of it as a gift from Drede to Sirle." He rose and said to the guards, "I will come home now. But no one of you is to stay here after me, or follow Sybel and Coren when they leave. No one."

"Prince Tamlorn—we saw nothing of Sybel or Coren."

Tam sighed. "My horse is in the shed—the gray. Get him."

They left quickly, followed by the soft whisperings of Lyon, Boar and Cat. Tam went to Sybel, and she held him a moment, his face hidden in her hair.

"My Tam, you are growing as fearless and wise as Ter."

He drew away from her a little. "No. I am shaking." He smiled at her, and she kissed him quickly. He turned and hugged Gules Lyon tightly, then rose to the sound of hoofbeats at the door.

"Prince Tamlorn," Coren said soberly, "I am very grateful. And I think this gift will be a great embarrassment to the Lord of Sirle."

"I hope he is pleased," Tam said softly. "Good-bye, Sybel. I do not know when I will see you again."

"Good-bye, my Tam."

From a window, she watched him mount, Ter circling above his head, watched his straight figure swallowed by a crowd of dark-cloaked men with their fiery stars, until they had disappeared through the trees. Then she turned and went to Coren, put her arms around him, her face against his breast.

"They might have killed you before I even knew they were in my house, in spite of all my powers. Then what would Rok have said?"

He lifted her face with his hands, a smile creasing his eyes. "That I should not have to depend on my wife to save my skin."

She touched his throat. "You are bleeding."

"I know. You are shaking."

"I know."

"Sybel. Could you have killed that guard? He believed you could, and I was not sure, then, myself."

"I do not know. But if he had killed Moriah, I would have found out." She sighed. "I am glad he did not, for his sake and mine. Coren, I do not think we should stay here long. I do not trust those guards. Let us pack the books and leave."

Coren nodded. He picked up a chair that had overturned, found his sword in a corner and sheathed it. Gules Lyon lay muttering softly by the fire. Moriah prowled back and forth in front of the door. Sybel dropped a soothing hand on the flat, black head. She looked around vaguely at the house and found a strange emptiness that seemed to lie beneath the cool white stones. She said slowly,

"It seems no longer my house . . . It seems to be waiting for another wizard, like Myk or Ogam, to begin his work here in this white silence . . ."

"Perhaps someone will come." He unfolded the big, tough grain sacks they had brought to pack the books in, and added wryly, "I hope he will have gentler memories of it than I ever will."

"I hope so, too." She gave him a tight parting hug, then went out to speak with Gyld and the Black Swan while he packed. The late afternoon turned from gold to silver, and then to ash gray. Coren finished before she returned; he went into the yard, calling her name in the wind. She came to him finally from the trees.

"I was with Gyld. I told him there would be a place for him at Sirle, and he told me he would bring his gold."

"Oh, no. I can see a glittering trail of ancient coin from here to Rok's doorstep."

"Coren, I told him we would see to it somehow . . . he will have to fly by night, when we are ready for him. I hope he does not frighten all of Rok's livestock." She glanced up at the night-scented, ashen sky, and the green-black shapes of trees. "It is getting late. What should we do? I do not think we should even stay at Maelga's house."

"No. Drede would not mind risking a war by killing me if he could trap you, take you to Mondor. If he wants that, they will return tonight to look for us."

"Then what should we do?"

"I have been thinking about that."

"The horses are tired. We cannot go far on them."

"I know."

"Well, what have you been thinking about that has put the smile in your voice?"

"Gyld."

She stared at him. "Gyld? Do you mean—ride him?"

He nodded. "Why not? You could pretend he is the Liralen. Surely he is strong enough."

"But—what would Rok say?"

"What would any man say if a dragon landed in his courtyard? Sybel, we cannot ride the horses far, and this mountain is no safe place for us tonight, wherever we are on it. You can loose the horses, call them back to Sirle when they are rested."

"But there is no place to put Gyld in Sirle."

"I will think of a place. And if I cannot, you can send him back here. Would he be willing?"

She nodded dazedly. "Oh, yes; he loves to fly. But Coren, Rok—"

"Rok would rather see us alive on Gyld than dead on Eld Mountain. If we make a slow journey back with these books, we may be followed. So let us sail home through the sky on Gyld. Sybel, there must be a silence deeper than the silence of Eld between those stars; shall we go listen to it? Come. We will throw all the stars into Sirle, then go and dance on the moon."

A smile, faint and faraway, crept onto her face. "I always wanted to fly . . ."

"So. If you cannot fly the Liralen, then make a fiery night flight on Gyld."

She called Gyld from his winter cave, and he came to her soaring slowly above the trees, a great, dark shape against the stars. She looked deep into his green eyes.

Can you carry a man, a woman and two sacks of books on your back?

She felt a tremor of joy in his mind like a flame springing alive.

Forever.

He waited patiently while Coren secured the books on his back, wound with lengths of rope around the base of his thick neck and wings. He heaved himself up, so Coren could pass and repass the rope beneath him, and his eyes glowed like jewels in the night, and his scales winked, gold-rimmed. Coren placed Sybel between the two bags of books and sat in front of her, holding onto the rope at Gyld's neck. He turned to look at her.

"Are you comfortable?"

She nodded and caught Gyld's mind. *Do the ropes bind you anywhere?*

No.

Then go.

The great wings unfurled, black against the star. The huge bulk lifted slowly, incredibly, away from the cold earth, through the wind-torn, whispering trees. Above the winds struck full force, billowing their cloaks, pushing against them, and they felt the immense play of muscle beneath them and the strain of wing against wind. Then came the full, smooth, joyous soar, a drowning in wind and space, a spiraling descent into darkness that flung them both beyond fear, beyond hope, beyond anything but the sudden surge of laughter that the wind tore from Coren's mouth. Then they rose again, level with the stars, the great wings pulsing, beating a path through the darkness. The full moon, icewhite, soared with them, round and wondering as the single waking eye of a starry beast of darkness. The ghost of Eld Mountain dwindled behind them; the great peak huddled, asleep and dreaming, behind its mists. The land was black beneath them, but for faint specks of light that here and there flamed in a second plane of stars. The winds dropped past Mondor, quieted, until they melted through a silence, a cool, blue-black night that was the motionless night of dreams, dimensionless, startouched, eternal. And at last they saw in the heart of darkness beneath them the glittering torch-lit rooms of the house of the Lord of Sirle.

They came to a gentle rest in his courtyard. A horse, waiting in the yard, screamed in terror. Dogs in the hall howled. Coren dismounted stiffly, his breath catching in a laughter beyond words, and swung Sybel to the ground. She clung to him a moment, stiff with cold, and felt Gyld's mind searching for hers.

Gyld. Be still.

There are men with torches. Shall I—

No. They are friends. They just did not expect us tonight. No one will try to harm us. Gyld, that was a flight beyond hope.

It pleased you.

I am well pleased.

"Rok!" Coren called to his brother's torchlit figure moving toward them down the steps. The dogs swarmed growling between his legs. The children jammed the doors behind him, then scattered in a wave before Ceneth and Eorth. "We have a guest!"

"Coren," Rok said, transfixed by the lucent, inscrutable eyes. "What in the name of the Above and the Below are we going to do with it?"

Coren caught one of the dogs before it nipped at Gyld's wing. "I have thought of that, too," he said cheerfully. "We can store it in the wine cellar."

NOMINEES—SHORT FICTION:

* "Pages from a Young Girl's Journal"   Robert Aickman
"The Events at Poroth Farm"   T. E. D. Klein
"A Father's Tale"   Sterling E. Lanier
"Sticks"   Karl Edward Wagner

ROBERT AICKMAN/*Best Short Work*

I am quite happy to go on record again as stating I believe the best living, breathing author of ghost stories among us, and fortunate, indeed, we are to have him among us, is Robert Aickman. He has completely mastered the classic forms of the *genre* (August Derleth always used to toss around *genre*, so why not?), and he presently amuses himself by flying off from them—*still* classically, mind, no violations of structure—for long distances in unpredictable directions. He has not, as of this writing, managed to sell more than one collection to an American publisher (*Cold Hand in Mine*, Scribner's), but I hope this will soon be corrected.

He has done better in England, having published three anthologies, *Dark Entries, Powers of Darkness*, and *Sub Rosa*.

If you like your horrors stylishly told, and if you don't mind, or even enjoy, the effort of contemplating a chilling, now and then mind-bending insight, I think you'll find any time and money spent in tracking Mr. Aickman's volumes down well spent.

Aickman is, of course, a complicated man, and, like all such, involved at one time or another in a wide variety of activities. He has run both opera and ballet companies, promoted several large festivals, and founded and was chairman of the Inland Waterways Association, an organization which pivotally affected Britain's decision to cancel her plans for destroying her canal system. Some of this and more he set down in an autobiography called *The Attempted Rescue*, which, I am told, sold very well.

When I learned, with considerable pleasure, that he had won the award for best short work, I wrote to Mr. Aickman asking him if he would be kind enough to write a few words concerning his marvelously disturbing fantasies. Did he, to start with, really think they *were* fantasies? And how did he honestly feel about his chief topic, namely ghosts? I remember how fascinated I was to learn at last what Le Fanu and M. R. James really believed concerning the supernatural, and was most curious to find what one of their very few equals felt about the matter.

Speedily and generously Mr. Aickman complied with my request, and here you have his answer. Since it ends by introducing his excellent tale "Pages from a Young Girl's Journal," I'll let it serve that purpose and only make the comment that Mr. Aickman's tales are so detailed and multi-leveled I find they must, all of them, be read at least three times and thought upon between lest the reader cheat himself of the full experience presented.

AN ESSAY

I am greatly touched by Gahan Wilson's request for a few words about my work and inspiration, which may "give the reader something very useful to mull over concerning his own life." This must be taken most seriously, and I begin by standing well back.

I believe that at the time of the Industrial and French revolutions (I am not commenting upon the American one!), mankind took a wrong turning. The beliefs that one day, by application of reason and the scientific method, everything will be known, and every problem and unhappiness solved, seem to me to have led to a situation where, first, we are in imminent danger of destroying the whole world, either with a loud report or by insatiable overconsumption and overbreeding, and where, second, everyone suffers from an existentialist angst, previously confined to the very few. There is a fundamental difference between worrying where one's next meal is coming from and worrying about the quality and reality of one's basic being. The great prophetic work of the modern world is Goethe's *Faust,* so little appreciated among the Anglo-Saxons. Mephistopheles offers Faust unlimited knowledge and unlimited power in exchange for his soul. Modern man has accepted that bargain.

Occultists have long predicted a bimillennium based upon exact knowledge and materialism; rejecting religion, poetry, art, the imagination, and the spirit. Spirit is indefinable, as everything that matters is indefinable; but one can tell the person who has it from the person who has it not. Alternatively, Nostradamus, St. Malachy, and even Mother Shipton concur, from varying distances, at placing "the end of the world" at the end of this century.

Freud, an incomparably greater man than any of his detractors, specified that nine tenths of the human mind was unconscious. It has always seemed to me (possibly with William Blake) that nothing which is worthwhile can be predicted scientifically, let alone brought about, and least of all guaranteed; and that life is mainly a matter of what Kenneth Clark terms "cruel mischances." To bow the head to the will of God, as the Moslems do (or did), seems to me far more in accord with life's observable facts than to attempt ceaselessly to modify the environment, which so often means merely to destroy it, as almost anyone can do. Upon these perceptions (or opinions) my work is based. As Gahan Wilson has so percipiently suggested, I do not regard my work as "fantasy" at all, except, perhaps, for commercial purposes. I try to depict the world as I see it; sometimes artistically exaggerating no doubt ("artistically" is here a descriptive not a qualitative term), and occasionally exaggerating for purposes of parable, as in my story "Growing Boys." I believe in what the Germans term *Ehrfurcht:* reverence for things one cannot understand. Faust's error was an aspiration to understand, and therefore master, things which, by God or by nature, are set beyond the human compass. He could only achieve this at the cost of making the achievement pointless. Once again, it is exactly what modern man has done.

"He says he's seen a ghost. I've never seen a ghost. Why should I believe him?" How often, at the end of my lectures, have I heard that question (sometimes less plainspokenly expressed)! It seems that each individual has a psychic factor which is independent of background, education, sex, race, or even general sensitivity (a burly farmer appears more likely to be strong in it than a tender poet), but which can be almost extinguished, or at least diverted, by conventional processes and assumptions. It seems to me that this psychic factor is likely at least to be alone, if only because ordinary day-to-day living is mainly horrible; so weak at the moment. One reason why we do not wish to survive is that there is no longer anything to survive for. Man does not live by bread alone, if only because ordinary day-to-day living is mainly horrible; so that to think otherwise is a major neurosis—or to think that one thinks otherwise. If life can be justified at all, it is, and always has been, by the belief in, and hope for, "a world elsewhere," as Coriolanus put it; and however the expression is interpreted. We ignore this truth at our utter peril.

This brings me to life after death; though it is only a part of the "world elsewhere," and perhaps not the major part. I believe in life after death, and I decline to particularize upon the meaning of the words, because of all futile and reductionist attempts at definition, this is the most idle. I believe, first, upon the worldwide and almost (though not quite) universal assurances of faith. I believe, second, because I can make no sense otherwise of the tragic lives that people lead; except, perhaps, upon the heretical, though far from illogical, thesis that the world is a construct of a devil: an idea which would be unpopular with many of my readers. I believe, third, upon the evidence of psychic research; thus calling in science to expel the current majority of scientists. I should add that, though I have carried through a small amount of psychic research, including at Borley Rectory, and am a long-standing member of the Ghost Club, yet research evidence and conclusions have influenced my stories only in detail. Most of my stories aim at universal themes, however difficult it may be to attain to them.

I care about the literary art, and I know exactly what the Ancients meant by "the promptings of the Muse." The stories which I consider to be my most successful came to me as if dictated, and in very little need of subsequent correction; as if written in at least a half-trance. Such a story is "Pages from a Young Girl's Journal." As I have so often remarked, the true ghost story is akin to poetry: only in part is it a conscious construction, and when the Muse does not speak, you cannot write it.

Robert Aickman
April 1976

Robert Aickman

PAGES FROM A YOUNG GIRL'S JOURNAL

3rd October. Padua—Ferrara—Ravenna. We've reached Ravenna only four days after leaving that horrid Venice. And all in a hired carriage! I feel sore and badly bitten too. It was the same yesterday, and the day before, and the day before that. I wish I had someone to talk to. This evening, Mamma did not appear for dinner at all. Papa just sat there saying nothing and looking at least two hundred years old instead of only one hundred, as he usually does. I wonder how old he *really* is? But it's no good wondering. We shall never know, or at least I shan't. I often think Mamma *does* know, or very nearly. I wish Mamma were someone I could talk to, like Caroline's Mamma. I often used to think that Caroline and her Mamma were more like sisters together, though of course I could never say such a thing. But then Caroline is pretty and gay, whereas I am pale and quiet. When I came up here to my room after dinner, I just sat in front of the long glass and stared and stared. I must have done it for half an hour or perhaps an hour. I only rose to my feet when it had become quite dark outside.

I don't like my room. It's much too big and there are only two wooden chairs, painted in greeny-blue with gold lines, or once painted like that. I hate having to lie on my bed when I should prefer to sit, and everyone knows how bad it is for the back. Besides, this bed, though it's enormous, seems to be as hard as when the earth's dried up in Summer. Not that the earth's like that here. Far from it. The rain has never stopped since we left Venice. Never once. Quite unlike what Miss Gisborne said before we set out from my dear, dear Derbyshire. This bed really is *huge*. It would take at least eight people my size. I don't like to think about it. I've just remembered: it's the third of the month so that we've been gone exactly half a year. What a lot of places I have been to in that time—or been through! Already I've quite forgotten some of them. I never properly saw them in any case. Papa has his own ideas, and one thing I'm sure of is that they are quite unlike other people's ideas. To me the whole of Padua is just a man on a horse—stone or bronze, I suppose, but I don't even know which. The whole of Ferrara is a huge palace—castle—fortress that simply frightened me, so that I didn't *want* to look. It was as big as this bed—in its own way, of course. And those were two large, famous towns I have visited this very week. Let alone where I was perhaps two months ago! What a farce! as Caroline's Mamma always says. I wish she were here now and Caroline too. No one has ever hugged and kissed me and made things happy as they do.

The Contessa has at least provided me with no fewer than twelve candles. I found them in one of the drawers. I suppose there's nothing else to do but read—except perhaps to say one's prayers. Unfortunately, I finished all the books I brought with me long ago, and it's so difficult to buy any new ones, especially in English. However, I managed to purchase two very long ones by Mrs. Radcliffe before we left Venice. Unfortunately, though there are twelve candles, there are only two candlesticks, both broken, like everything else. Two candles *should* be enough, but all they seem to do is make the room look even larger and darker. Perhaps they are not-very-good foreign candles. I noticed that they seemed very dirty and discolored in the drawer. In fact, one of them looked quite black. That one must have lain in the drawer a very long time. By the way, there is a framework hanging from the ceiling in the middle of the room. I cannot truthfully describe it as a chandelier: perhaps as a ghost of a chandelier. In any case, it is a long way from even the foot of the bed. They do have the most enormous rooms in these foreign houses where we stay. Just as if it were very warm the whole time, which it certainly is not. What a farce!

As a matter of fact, I'm feeling quite cold at this moment, even though I'm wearing my dark-green woolen dress that in Derbyshire saw me through the whole of last winter. I wonder if I should be any warmer *in* bed? It is something I can never make up my mind about. Miss Gisborne always calls me "such a chilly mortal." I see I have used the present tense. I wonder if that is appropriate in the case of Miss Gisborne? Shall I ever see Miss Gisborne again? I mean in *this* life, of course.

Now that six days have passed since I have made an entry in this journal, I find that I am putting down *everything*, as I always do once I made a start. It is almost as if nothing horrid could happen to me as long as I keep on writing. That is simply silly, but I sometimes wonder whether the silliest things are not often the truest.

I write down words on the page, but what do I say? Before we started, everyone told me that, whatever else I did, I *must* keep a journal, a travel journal. I do not think this is a travel journal at all. I find that when I am traveling with Papa and Mamma, I seem hardly to look at the outside world. Either we are lumbering along, with Papa and Mamma naturally in the places from which something can be seen, or at least from which things can be best seen; or I find that I am alone in some great vault of a bedroom for hours and hours and hours, usually quite unable to go to sleep, sometimes for the whole night. I should see so much more if I could sometimes walk about the different cities on my own—naturally, I do not mean at night. I wish that were possible. Sometimes I really hate being a girl. Even Papa cannot hate my being a girl more than I do sometimes.

And when there *is* something to put down, it always seems to be the same thing! For example, here we are in still another of these households to which Papa always seems to have an entree. Plainly it is very wicked of me, but I sometimes wonder *why* so many people should want to know Papa, who is usually so silent and disagreeable, and always so old! Perhaps the answer is simple enough: it is that they never meet him—or Mamma—or me. We drive up, Papa gives us all over to the major-domo or someone, and the family never sets eyes on us, because the family is never at home. These foreign families seem to have terribly many houses and always to be living in another of them. And when one of the family *does* appear, he or she usually seems to be almost as old as Papa and hardly able to speak a word of English. I think I have a pretty voice, though it's difficult to be quite sure, but I deeply wish I had worked harder at learning foreign languages. At least—the trouble is that Miss Gisborne is so bad at teaching them. I must say *that* in my own defense, but it doesn't help much now. I wonder how Miss Gisborne would be faring if she were in this room with me? Not much better than I am, if you ask me.

I have forgotten to say, though, that this is one of the times when we *are* supposed to be meeting the precious family; though, apparently, it consists only of two people, the Contessa and her daughter. Sometimes I feel that I have already seen enough women without particularly wanting to meet any new ones, whatever their ages. There's something rather monotonous about women—unless, of course, they're like Caroline and her Mamma, which none of them are, or could be. So far the Contessa and her daughter have not appeared. I don't know why not, though no doubt Papa knows. I am told that we are to meet them both tomorrow. I expect very little. I wonder if it will be warm enough for me to wear my green satin dress instead of my green woolen dress? Probably not.

And this is the town where the great, the immortal Lord Byron lives in sin and wildness! Even Mamma has spoken of it several times. Not that this melancholy house is actually *in* the town. It is a villa at some little distance away from it, though I do not know in which direction, and I am sure that Mamma neither knows nor cares. It seemed to me that after we passed through the town this afternoon, we traveled on for fifteen or twenty minutes. Still, to be even in the same *region* as Lord Byron must somewhat move even the hardest heart; and my heart, I am very sure, is not hard in the least.

I find that I have been scribbling away for nearly an hour. Miss Gisborne keeps on saying that I am too prone to the insertion of unnecessary hyphens, and that it is a weakness. If a weakness it is, I intend to cherish it.

I know that an hour has passed because there is a huge clock somewhere that sounds every quarter. It must be a *huge* clock because of the noise it makes, and because everything abroad *is* huge.

I am colder than ever and my arms are quite stiff. But I must drag off my clothes somehow, blow out the candles and insinuate my tiny self into this enormous, frightening bed. I do hate the lumps you get all over your body when you travel abroad, and so much hope I don't get many more during the night. Also I hope I don't start feeling thirsty, as there's no water of any kind, let alone water safe to drink.

Ah, Lord Byron, living out there in riot and wickedness! It is impossible to forget him. I wonder what he would think of me? I do hope there are not too many biting things in this room.

4th October. What a surprise! The Contessa has said it will be quite in order for me to go for short walks in the town, provided I have my maid with me; and when Mamma at once pointed out that I had no maid, offered the services of her own! To think of this happening the very day after I wrote down in this very journal that it could never happen! I am now quite certain that it would have been perfectly correct for me to walk about the other towns too. I daresay that Papa and Mamma suggested otherwise only because of the difficulty about the maid. Of course I *should* have a maid, just as Mamma should have a maid too and Papa a man, and just as we should all have a proper carriage of our own, with our crest on the doors! If it was that we were too poor, it would be humiliating. As we are not too poor (I am sure we are not), it is farcical. In any case, Papa and Mamma went on making a fuss, but the Contessa said we had now entered the States of the Church and were, therefore, all living under the special beneficence of God. The Contessa speaks English very well and even knows the English *idioms,* as Miss Gisborne calls them.

Papa screwed up his face when the Contessa mentioned the States of the Church, as I knew he would. Papa remarked several times while we were on the way here, that the Papal States, as he calls them, are the most misgoverned in Europe and that it was not only as a Protestant that he said so. I wonder. When Papa expresses opinions of that kind, they often seem to me to be just notions of his own, like his notions of the best way to travel. After the Contessa had spoken as she did, I felt—very strongly—that it must be rather beautiful to be ruled directly by the Pope and his cardinals. Of course, the cardinals and even the Pope are subject to error, as are our own Bishops and Rectors, all being but men, as Mr. Biggs-Hartley continually emphasizes at home; but, all the same, they simply *must* be nearer to God than the sort of people who rule us in England. I do not think Papa can be depended upon to judge such a question.

I am determined to act upon the Contessa's kind offer. Miss Gisborne says that though I am a pale little thing, I have very much a will of my own. Here will be an opportunity to prove it. There may be certain difficulties because the Contessa's maid can only speak Italian; but when the two of us shall be alone together, it is I who shall be mistress and she who will be maid, and nothing can change that. I have seen the girl. She is a pretty creature, apart from the size of her nose.

Today it has been wet, as usual. This afternoon we drove round Ravenna in the Contessa's carriage: a proper carriage for once, with arms on the doors and a footman as well as the coachman. Papa has paid off our hired coach. I suppose it has lumbered away back to Fusina, opposite to Venice. I expect I can count upon our remaining in Ravenna for a week. That seems to be Papa's usual sojourn in one of our major stopping places. It is not very long, but often it is quite long enough, the way we live.

This afternoon we saw Dante's Tomb, which is simply by the side of the street, and went into a big church with the Throne of Neptune in it, and then into the Tomb of Galla Placidia, which is blue inside, and very beautiful. I was on the alert for any hint of where Lord Byron might reside, but it was quite unnecessary to speculate, because the Contessa almost shouted it out as we rumbled along one of the streets: "The Palazzo Guiccioli. See the netting across the bottom of the door to prevent Lord Byron's animals from straying." "Indeed, indeed," said Papa, looking out more keenly than he had at Dante's Tomb. No more was said, because, though both Papa and Mamma had more than once alluded to Lord Byron's present way of life so that I should be able to understand things that might come up in conversation, yet neither the Contessa nor Papa and Mamma knew how much I might really understand. Moreover, the little Contessina was in the carriage, sitting upon a cushion on the floor at her Mamma's feet, making five of us in all, foreign carriages being as large as everything else foreign; and I daresay *she* knew nothing at all, sweet little innocent.

"Contessina" is only a kind of nickname or *sobriquet*, used by the family and the servants. The Contessina is really a Contessa: in foreign noble familes, if one person is a Duke, then all the other men seem to be Dukes also, and all the women Duchesses. It is very confusing and nothing like such a good arrangement as ours, where there is only one Duke and one Duchess to each family. I do not know the little Contessina's age. Most foreign girls look far older than they really are, whereas most of our girls look younger. The Contessina is *very* slender, a veritable sylph. She has an olive complexion, with no blemish of any kind. People often write about "olive complexions": the Contessina really has one. She has absolutely enormous eyes, the shape of broad beans, and not far off that in color; but she never uses them to look at anyone. She speaks so little and often has such an empty, lost expression that one might think her more than slightly simple; but I do not think she is. Foreign girls are raised quite differently from the way our girls are raised. Mamma frequently refers to this, pursing her lips. I must admit that I cannot see myself finding in the Contessina a friend, pretty though she is in her own way, with feet about half the size of mine or Caroline's.

When foreign girls grow up to become women, they usually continue, poor things, to look older than they are. I am sure this applies to the Contessa. The Contessa has been very kind to me—in the few hours that I have so far known her—and even seems to be a little sorry for me—as, indeed, I am for her. But I do not understand the Contessa. Where was she last night? Is the little Contessina her only child? What has become of her husband? Is it because he is dead that she seems—and looks—so sad? Why does she want to live in such a big house—it is called a Villa, but one might think it a Palazzo—when it is all falling to bits, and much of it barely even furnished? I should like to ask Mamma these questions, but I doubt whether she would have the right answers, or perhaps any answers.

The Contessa did appear for dinner this evening, and even the little Contessina. Mamma was there too, in that frock I dislike. It really is the wrong kind of red—especially for Italy, where *dark* colors seem to be so much worn. The evening was better than last evening; but then it could hardly have been worse. (Mr. Biggs-Hartley says we should never say that: things can *always* be worse.) It was not a *good* evening. The Contessa was trying to be quite gay, despite her own obvious trouble, whatever that is; but neither Papa nor Mamma know how to respond, and I know all too well that I myself am better at thinking about things than at casting a spell in company. What I like most is just a few friends I know really well and whom I can truly trust and love. Alas, it is long since I have had even one such to clasp by the hand. Even letters seem mostly to lose themselves en route, and I can hardly wonder; supposing people are still bothering to write them in the first place, needless to say, which it is difficult to see why they should be after all this time. When dinner was over, Papa and Mamma and the Contessa played an Italian game with both playing cards and dice. The servants had lighted a fire in the Salone and the Contessina sat by it doing nothing and saying nothing. If given a chance, Mamma would have remarked that "the child should have been in bed long ago," and I am sure she should. The Contessa wanted to teach me the game, but Papa said at once that I was too young, which is absolutely farcical. Later in the evening, the Contessa, after playing a quite long time with Papa and Mamma, said that tomorrow she would put her foot down (the Contessa knows so many such expressions that one would swear she must have lived in England) and would *insist* on my learning. Papa screwed his face up and Mamma pursed her lips in the usual way. I had been doing needlework, which I shall never like nor see any point in when servants can always do it for us; and I found that I was thinking many deep thoughts. And then I noticed that a small tear was slowly falling down the Contessa's face. Without thinking, I sprang up; but then the Contessa smiled, and I sat down. One of my deep thoughts was that it is not so much particular disasters that make people cry, but something always there in life itself, something that a light falls on when we are trying to enjoy ourselves in the company of others.

I must admit that the horrid lumps are going down. I certainly do not seem to have acquired any more, which is an advantage when compared with what happened every night in Dijon, that smelly place. But I wish I had a more cheerful room, with better furniture, though tonight I have succeeded in bringing to bed one of our bottles of Mineral Water and even a glass from which to drink it. It is only the Italian Mineral Water, of course, which Mamma says may be very little safer than the ordinary water; but as all the ordinary water seems to come from the dirty wells one sees down the side streets, I think that Mamma exaggerates. I admit, however, that it is not like the bottled water one buys in France. How farcical to have to buy water in a bottle, anyway! All the same, there are some things that I have grown to *like* about foreign countries; perhaps even to prefer. It would never do to let Papa and Mamma hear me talk in such a way. I often wish I were not so sensitive, so that the rooms I am given and things of that kind, did not matter so much. And yet Mamma is more sensitive about the water than I am! I am sure it is not so *important*. It can't be. To me it is *obvious* that Mamma is *less sensitive* than I am, where *important* things are concerned. My entire life is based on that obvious fact! My real life, that is.

I rather wish the Contessa would invite me to share her room, because I think she is sensitive in the same way that I am. But perhaps the little girl sleeps in the Contessa's room. I should not really mind that. I do not *hate* or even dislike the little Contessina. I expect she already has troubles herself. But Papa and Mamma would never agree to it anyway, and now I have written all there is to write about this perfectly ordinary, but somehow rather odd, day. In this big cold room, I can hardly move with chilliness.

5th October. When I went in to greet Mamma this morning, Mamma had the most singular news. She told me to sit down (Mamma and Papa have more chairs in their rooms than I have, and more of other things too), and then said that there was to be a party! Mamma spoke as though it would be a dreadful ordeal, which it was impossible for us to avoid; and she seemed to take it for granted that I should receive the announcement in the same way. I do not know what I really thought about it. It is true that I have never enjoyed a party yet (not that I have been present at many of them); but all day I have been aware of feeling different inside myself, lighter and swifter in some way, and by this evening I cannot but think it is owing to the knowledge that a party lies before me. After all, foreign parties may be different from parties at home, and probably are. I keep pointing that out to myself. This particular party will be given by the Contessa, who, I feel sure, knows more about it than does Mamma. If she does, it will not be the only thing that the Contessa knows more about than does Mamma.

The party is to be the day after tomorrow. While we were drinking our coffee and eating our panini (always very flaky and powdery in Italy), Mamma asked the Contessa whether she was sure there would be time enough for the preparations. But the Contessa only smiled—in a very polite way, of course. It is probably easier to do things quickly in Italy (when one really wants to, that is), because everyone has so many servants. It is hard to believe that the Contessa has much money, but she seems to keep more servants than we do, and, what is more, they behave more like slaves than like servants, quite unlike our Derbyshire keel-the-pots. Perhaps it is simply that everyone is so fond of the Contessa. That I should entirely understand. Anyway, preparations for the party have been at a high pitch all day, with people hanging up banners, and funny smells from the kitchen quarters. Even the Bath House at the far end of the formal garden (it is said to have been built by the Byzantines) has had the spiders swept out and been populated with cooks, perpetrating I know not what. The transformation is quite bewildering. I wonder when Mamma first knew of what lay ahead? Surely it must at least have been before we went to bed last night?

I feel I should be vexed that a new dress is so impracticable. A train of seamstresses would have to work day and night for forty-eight hours, as in the fairy tales. I should like that (who would not?), but I am not at all sure that *I* should be provided with a new dress even if whole weeks were available in which to make it. Papa and Mamma would probably still agree that I had quite enough dresses already even if it were the Pope and his cardinals who were going to entertain me. All the same, I am not really vexed. I sometimes think that I am deficient in proper interest in clothes, as Caroline's Mamma calls it. Anyway, I have learned from experience that new dresses are more often than not thoroughly disappointing. I keep reminding myself of that.

The other important thing today is that I have been out for my first walk in the town with the Contessa's maid, Emilia. I just swept through what Papa had to say on the subject, as I had promised myself. Mamma was lying down at the time, and the Contessa simply smiled her sweet smile and sent for Emilia to accompany me.

I must admit that the walk was not a *complete* success. I took with me our copy of Mr. Grubb's "Handbook to Ravenna and Its Antiquities" (Papa could hardly say No, lest I do something far worse), and began looking places up on the map with a view to visiting them. I felt that this was the best way to start, and that, once started, I could wait to see what life would lay before me. I am often quite resolute when there is a specific situation to be confronted. The first difficulty was the quite long walk into Ravenna itself. Though it was nothing at all to me, and though it was not raining, Emilia soon made it clear that she was unaccustomed to walking a step. This could only have been an affectation, or rather pretense, because everyone knows that girls of that kind come from peasant families, where I am quite sure they have to walk about all day, and much more than merely walk about. Therefore, I took no notice at all, which was made easier by my hardly understanding a word that Emilia actually said. I simply pushed and dragged her forward. Sure enough, she soon gave up all her pretenses and made the best of the situation. There were some rough carters on the road and large numbers of horrid children, but for the most part they stopped annoying us as soon as they saw who we were, and in any case it was as nothing to the roads in Derby, where they have lately taken to throwing stones at the passing carriages.

The next trouble was that Emilia was not in the least accustomed to what I had in mind when we reached Ravenna. Of course people do not go again and again to look at their own local antiquities, however old they may be; and least of all, I suspect, Italian people. When she was not accompanying her mistress, Emilia was used to going to Town only for some precise purpose: to buy something, to sell something, or to deliver a letter. There was that in her attitude which made me think of the saucy girls in the old comedies: whose only work is to fetch and carry billets-doux, and sometimes to take the places of their mistresses, with their mistresses' knowledge or otherwise. I did succeed in visiting another of these Bath Houses, this one a public spectacle and called the Baptistry of the Orthodox, because it fell into Christian hands after the last days of the Romans, who built it. It was, of course, far larger than the Bath House in the Contessa's garden, but in the interior rather dark and with a floor so uneven that it was difficult not to fall. There was also a horrible dead animal inside. Emilia began laughing, and it was quite plain what she was laughing at. She was striding about as if she were back on her mountains, and the kind of thing she seemed to be suggesting was that if I proposed to walk all the way to the very heel or toe of Italy she was quite prepared to walk with me, and perhaps to walk ahead of me. As an English girl, I did not care for this, nor for the complete reversal of Emilia's original attitude, almost suggesting that she has a deliberate and impertinent policy of keeping the situation between us under her own control. So, as I have said, the walk was not a complete success. All the same, I have made a start. It is obvious that the world has more to offer than would be likely to come my way if I were to spend my whole life creeping about with Papa at one side of me and Mamma at the other. I shall think about how best to deal with Emilia now that I better understand her ways. I was not in the least tired when we had walked back to the Villa. I despise girls who get tired, quite as much as Caroline despises them.

Believe it or not, Mamma was still lying down. When I went in, she said that she was resting in preparation for the party. But the party is not until the day after tomorrow. Poor dear Mamma might have done better not to have left England in the first place! I must take great care that I am not like that when I reach the same time of life and am married, as I suppose I shall be. Looking at Mamma in repose, it struck me that she would still be quite pretty if she did not always look so tired and worried. Of course she was once far prettier than I am now. I know that well. I, alas, am not really pretty at all. I have to cultivate other graces, as Miss Gisborne puts it.

I saw something unexpected when I was going upstairs to bed. The little Contessina had left the Salone before the rest of us and, as usual, without a word. Possibly it was only I who saw her slip out, she went so quietly. I noticed that she did not return and supposed that, at her age, she was quite worn out. Assuredly, Mamma would have said so. But then when I myself was going upstairs, holding my candle, I saw for myself what had really happened. At the landing, as we in England should call it, there is in one of the corners an odd little closet or cabinet, from which two doors lead off, both locked, as I know because I have cautiously turned the handles for myself. In this corner, by the light of my candle, I saw the Contessina, and she was being hugged by a man. I think it could only have been one of the servants, though I was not really able to tell. Perhaps I am wrong about that, but I am not wrong about it being the Contessina. They had been there in complete darkness, and, what is more, they never moved a muscle as I came up the stairs and walked calmly along the passage in the opposite direction. I suppose they hoped I should fail to see them in the dimness. They must have supposed that no one would be coming to bed just yet. Or perhaps they were lost to all sense of time, as Mrs. Radcliffe expresses it. I have very little notion of the Contessina's age, but she often looks about twelve or even less. Of course I shall say nothing to anybody.

6th October. I have been thinking on and off all day about the differences between the ways we are supposed to behave and the ways we actually do behave. And both are different from the ways in which God calls upon us to behave, and which we can never achieve whatever we do and however hard we apply ourselves, as Mr. Biggs-Hartley always emphasizes. We seem, every one of us, to be at least three different people. And that's just to start with.

I am disappointed by the results of my little excursion yesterday with Emilia. I had thought that there was so much of which I was deprived by being a girl and so being unable to go about on my own, but now I am not sure that I have been missing anything. It is almost as if the nearer one approaches to a thing, the less it proves to be there, to exist at all. Apart, of course, from the bad smells and bad words and horrid rough creatures from which and from whom we women are supposed to be "shielded." But I am waxing metaphysical; against which Mr. Biggs-Hartley regularly cautions us. I wish Caroline were with us. I believe I might feel quite differently about things if she were here to go about with me, just the two of us. Though, needless to say, it would make no difference to us what the things truly were—or were not. It is curious that things should seem not to exist when visited with one person, and then to exist after all if visited with another person. Of course it is all just fancy, but what (I think at moments like this) is not?

I am so friendless and alone in this alien land. It occurs to me that I must have great inner strength to bear up as I do and to fulfill my duties with so little complaint. The Contessa has very kindly given me a book of Dante's verses, with the Italian on one side and an English translation on the page opposite. She remarked that it would aid me to learn more of her language. I am not sure that it will. I have dutifully read through several pages of the book, and there is nothing in this world that I like more than reading, but Dante's ideas are so gloomy and complicated that

I suspect he is no writer for a woman, certainly not for an English woman. Also his face frightens me, so critical and severe. After looking at his portrait, beautifully engraved at the beginning of the book, I begin to fear that I shall see that face looking over my shoulder as I sit gazing into the looking glass. No wonder Beatrice would have nothing to do with him. I feel that he was quite deficient in the graces that appeal to our sex. Of course one must not even hint such a thing to an Italian, such as the Contessa, for to all Italians Dante is as sacred as Shakespeare or Dr. Johnson is to us.

For once I am writing this during the afternoon. I suspect that I am suffering from ennui and, as that is a sin (even though only a minor one), I am occupying myself in order to drive it off. I know by now that I am much more prone to such lesser shortcomings as ennui and indolence than to such vulgarities as letting myself be embraced and kissed by a servant. And yet it is not that I feel myself wanting in either energy or passion. It is merely that I lack for anything or anyone worthy of such feelings and refuse to spend them upon what is unworthy. But what a "merely" is that! How well I understand the universal ennui that possesses our neighbour, Lord Byron! I, a tiny slip of a girl, feel, at least in this particular, at one with the great poet! There might be consolation in the thought, were I capable of consolation. In any case, I am sure that there will be nothing more that is worth record before my eyes close tonight in slumber.

Later. I was wrong! After dinner tonight, it struck me simply to ask the Contessa whether she had ever *met* Lord Byron. I supposed it might not be a thing she would proclaim unsolicited, either when Papa and Mamma were present, or, for reasons of delicacy, on one of the too rare occasions when she and I were alone; but I thought that I might now be sufficiently simpatica to venture a discreet inquiry.

I fear that I managed it very crudely. When Papa and Mamma had become involved in one of their arguments together, I walked across the room and sat down at the end of the sofa on which the Contessa was reclining; and when she smiled at me and said something agreeable, I simply blurted out my question, quite directly. "Yes, mia cara," she replied, "I have met him, but we cannot invite him to our party because he is too political, and many people do not agree with his politics. Indeed, they have already led to several deaths, which some are reluctant to accept at the hands of a straniero, however eminent." And of course it *was* the wonderful possibility of Lord Byron attending the Contessa's party that *had been* at the back of my thoughts. Not for the first time, the Contessa showed her fascinating insight into the minds of others—or assuredly into my mind.

7th October. The day of the party! It is quite early in the morning and the sun is shining as I have not seen it shine for some time. Perhaps it regularly shines at this time of the day, when I am still asleep? "What you girls miss by not getting up!" as Caroline's Mamma always exclaims, though she is the most indulgent of parents. The trouble is that one *always* awakens early just when it is most desirable that one should slumber longest; as today, with the party before us. I am writing this now because I am *quite certain* that I shall be nothing but a tangle of nerves all day and, after everything is over, utterly spent and exhausted. So, for me, it always is with parties! I am glad that the day after tomorrow will be Sunday.

8th October. I met a man at the party who, I must confess, interested me very much; and, besides that, what matters, as Mrs. Fremlinson enquires in "The Hopeful and the Despairing Heart," *almost* my favorite of all books, as I truly declare?

Who could believe it? Just now, while I was still asleep, there was a knocking at my door, just loud enough to awaken me, but otherwise so soft and discreet, and there was the Contessa *herself*, in the most beautiful negligee, half rose-colored and half mauve, with a tray on which were things to eat and drink, a complete foreign breakfast, in fact! I must acknowledge that at that moment I could well have devoured a complete English breakfast, but what could have been kinder or more thoughtful on the part of the charming Contessa? Her dark hair (but not so dark as with the majority of the Italians) had not yet been dressed, and hung about her beautiful, though sad, face, but I noticed that all her rings were on her fingers, flashing and sparkling in the sunshine. "Alas, mia cara," she said, looking round the room, with its many deficiencies, "the times that were and the times that are." Then she actually bent over my face, rested her hand lightly on the top of my nightgown, and kissed me. "But how pale you look!" she continued. "You are white as a lily on the altar." I smiled. "I am English," I said, "and I lack strong coloring." But the Contessa went on staring at me. Then she said, "The party has quite fatigued you?" She seemed to express it as a question, so I replied, with vigor: "Not in the least, I assure you, Contessa. It was the most beautiful evening of my life." (Which was unquestionably the truth and no more than the truth.) I sat up in the big bed and, so doing, saw myself in the glass. It was true that I did look pale, unusually pale. I was about to remark upon the earliness of the hour, when the

Contessa suddenly seemed to draw herself together with a gasp and turn remarkably pale herself, considering the native hue of her skin. She stretched out her hand and pointed. She seemed to be pointing at the pillow behind me. I looked round, disconcerted by her demeanor; and I saw an irregular red mark upon the pillow, not a very large mark, but undoubtedly a mark of blood. I raised my hands to my throat. "Dio Illustrissimo!" cried out the Contessa. "Ell' e stregata!" I know enough Italian, from Dante and from elsewhere, to be informed of what that means: "She is bewitched." I leapt out of bed and threw my arms around the Contessa before she could flee, as she seemed disposed to do. I besought her to say more, but I was all the time fairly sure that she would not. Italians, even educated ones, still take the idea of "witchcraft" with a seriousness that to us seems unbelievable, and regularly fear even to speak of it. Here I knew by instinct that Emilia and her mistress would be at one. Indeed, the Contessa seemed most uneasy at my mere embrace, but she soon calmed herself, and left the room saying, quite pleasantly, that she must have a word with my parents about me. She even managed to wish me "buon appetito" of my little breakfast.

I examined my face and throat in the looking glass, and there, sure enough, was a small scar on my neck which explained everything—except, indeed, how I had come by such a mark, but for that the novelties, the rigors, and the excitements of last night's party would *entirely* suffice. One cannot expect to enter the tournament of love and emerge unscratched: and it is into the tournament that, as I thrill to think, I verily have made my way. I fear it is perfectly typical of the Italian manner of seeing things that a perfectly natural, and very tiny, mishap should have such a disproportionate effect upon the Contessa. For myself, an English girl, the mark upon my pillow does not even disturb me. We must hope that it does not cast into screaming hysterics the girl whose duty it will be to change the linen.

If I look especially pale, it is partly because the very bright sunlight makes a contrast. I returned at once to bed and rapidly consumed every scrap and drop that the Contessa had brought to me. I seemed quite weak from lack of sustenance, and indeed I have but the slenderest recollection of last night's fare, except that, naturally, I drank far more than on most previous days of my short life, probably more than on *any*.

And now I lie here in my pretty nightgown and nothing else, with my pen in my hand and the sun on my face, and think about *him!* I did not believe such people existed in the real world. I thought that such writers as Mrs. Fremlinson and Mrs. Radcliffe *improved* men, in order to reconcile their female readers to their lot, and to put their less numerous male readers in a good conceit of themselves. Caroline's Mamma and Miss

Gisborne, in their quite different ways, have both indicated as much most clearly; and my own observation hitherto of the opposite sex has confirmed the opinion. But now I have actually met a man at whom even Mrs. Fremlinson's finest creation does but hint! He is an Adonis! an Apollo! assuredly a god! Where he treads, sprouts asphodel!

The first romantic thing was that he was not properly presented to me —indeed, he was not presented at all. I know this was very incorrect, but it cannot be denied that it was very exciting. Most of the guests were dancing an old-fashioned *minuetto*, but as I did not know the steps, I was sitting at the end of the room wih Mamma, when Mamma was suddenly overcome in some way and had to leave. She emphasized that she would be back in only a minute or two, but almost as soon as she had gone, *he* was standing there, quite as if he had emerged from between the faded tapestries that covered the wall or even from the tapestries themselves, except that he looked very far from faded, though later, when more candles were brought in for Supper, I saw that he was older than I had at first supposed, with such a wise and experienced look as I have never seen on any other face.

Of course he had not only to speak to me at once, or I should have risen and moved away, but to *compel* me, with his eyes and words, to remain. He said something pleasant about my being the only rosebud in a garden otherwise autumnal, but I am not such a goose as never to have heard speeches like that before, and it was what he said next that made me fatally hesitate. He said (and never, *never* shall I forget his words): "As we are both visitants from a world that is not this one, we should know one another." It was so exactly what I always feel about myself, as this journal (I fancy) makes clear, that I could not but yield a trifle to his apperceptiveness in finding words for my deepest conviction, extremely irregular and dangerous though I well knew my position to be. *And* he spoke in beautiful English; his accent (not, I think, an Italian one) only making his words the more choice-sounding and delightful!

I should remark here that it was not true that *all* the Contessa's guests were "autumnal," even though most of them certainly were. Sweet creature that she is, she had invited several cavalieri from the local nobility *expressly* for my sake, and several of them had duly been presented to me, but with small conversation resulting, partly because there was so little available of a common tongue, but more because each single cavaliero seemed to me very much what in Derbyshire we call a peg-Jack. It was typical of the Contessa's sympathetic nature that she perceived the unsuccess of these recontres, and made no attempt to fan flames that were never so much as faint sparks. How unlike the matrons of Derbyshire, who, when they have set their minds to the task, will work the bellows in such cases not merely for a whole single evening, but for weeks, months, or on occasion, years! But then it would be unthinkable to apply the word "matron" to the lovely Contessa! As it was, the four cavalieri were left to make what they could of the young Contessina and such other bambine as were on parade.

I pause for a moment seeking words in which to describe him. He is above the average tall, and, while slender and elegant, conveys a wondrous impression of force and strength. His skin is somewhat pallid, his nose aquiline and commanding (though with quivering, sensitive nostrils), his mouth scarlet and (I must apply the word) passionate. Just to look at his mouth made me think of great poetry and wide seas. His fingers are very long and fine, but powerful in their grip: as I learned for myself before the end of the evening. His hair I at first thought quite black, but I saw later that it was delicately laced with grey, perhaps even white. His brow is high, broad, and noble. Am I describing a god or a man? I find it hard to be sure.

As for his conversation I can only say that, indeed, it was not of this world. He proffered none of the empty chatter expected at social gatherings, which, in so far as it has any meaning at all, has a meaning quite different from that which the words of themselves convey—a meaning often odious to me. Everything he said (at least after the first conventional compliment) spoke to something deep within me, and everything I said in reply was what I really wanted to say. I have been able to talk in that way before with no man of any kind, from Papa downwards, and with very few women. And yet I find it difficult to recall what subjects we discussed. I think that may be a *consequence* of the feeling with which we spoke. The feeling I not merely recollect but feel still—all over and through me—deep and warm—transfiguring. The subjects, no. They were life, and beauty, and art, and nature, and myself: in fact, *everything*. Everything, that is, except the very different and very silly things that almost everyone else talks about all the time, chatter and chump without stopping this side of the churchyard. He did once observe that "words are what prevail with women," and I could only smile, it was so true.

Fortunately, Mamma *never* reappeared. As for the rest of them, I daresay they were more relieved than otherwise to find the gauche little English girl off their hands, so to speak, and apparently provided for. With Mamma indisposed, the obligation to watch over me would descend upon the Contessa, but her I saw only in the distance. Perhaps she was resolved not to intrude where *I* should not wish it. If so, it would be what I should expect of her. I do not know.

Then came Supper. Much to my surprise (and chagrin), my friend, if so I may call him, excused himself from participating. His explanation, lack of appetite, could hardly be accepted as sufficient or courteous, but the words he employed, succeeded (as always, I feel, with him) in purging the offense. He affirmed most earnestly that I must sustain myself even though he were unable to escort me, and that he would await my return. As he spoke, he gazed at me so movingly that I could but accept the situation, though I daresay I had as little appetite (for the coarse foods of this world) as he. I perceive that I have so far omitted to refer to the beauty and power of his eyes, which are so dark as to be almost black—at least by the light of candles. Glancing back at him, perhaps a little keenly, it occurred to me that he might be bashful about showing himself in his full years by the bright lights of the Supper tables. It is a vanity *by no means* confined to my own sex. Indeed he seemed almost to be shrinking away from the augmented brightness even at this far end of the room. And this for all the impression of strength which was the most marked thing about him. Tactfully I made to move off. "You will return?" he asked, so anxiously and compellingly. I remained calm. I merely smiled.

And then Papa caught hold of me. He said that Mamma, having gone upstairs, had succumbed totally, as I might have known in advance she would do, and in fact *did* know: and that, when I had supped, I had "better come upstairs also." At that Papa elbowed me through to the tables and started trying to stuff me like a turkey, but, as I have said, I had little gusto for it, so little that I cannot now name a single thing that I ate, or that Papa ate either. Whatever it was, I "washed it down" (as we say in Derbyshire) with an unusual quantity (for me) of the local wine, which people, including Papa, always say is so "light," but which always seems to me no "lighter" than any other, but noticeably "heavier" than some I could name. What is more, I had already consumed a certain amount of it earlier in the evening when I was supposed to be flirting with the local peg-Jacks. One curious thing is that Papa, who never fails to demur at my doing almost anything else, seems to have no objection to my drinking wine quite heavily. I do not think I have ever known him even try to impose a limit. That is material, of course, only in the rare absence of Mamma, to whom this observation does not apply. But Mamma herself is frequently unwell after only two or three glasses. At Supper last night, I was in a state of "trance": eating food was well-nigh impossible, but drinking wine almost fatally facile. Then Papa started trying to push me off to bed again. After all that wine, and with my new friend patiently waiting for me, it was farcical. But I had to dispose of Papa somehow, so I promised him faithfully, and forgot my promise (whatever it was) immediately. Mercifully, I have not so far set eyes upon Papa since that moment.

Or, in reality, upon *anyone* until the Contessa waked me this morning: on anyone but *one*.

There he was quietly awaiting me among the shadows cast by the slightly swaying tapestries and by the flapping bannerets ranged round the walls above us. This time he actually clutched my hand in his eagerness. It was only for a moment, of course, but I felt the firmness of his grip. He said he hoped he was not keeping me from the dance floor, but I replied no, oh, No. In truth, I was barely even capable of dancing at that moment; and I fancy that the measures trod by the musty relics around us were, at the best of times, not for me. Then he said, with a slight smile, that once he had been a great dancer. Oh, I said idly and under the power of the wine; where was that? At Versailles, he replied; and in Petersburg. I must say that, wine or no wine, this surprised me; because surely, as everyone knows, Versailles was burned down by the incendiaries in 1789, a good thirty years ago? I must have glanced at him significantly, because he then said, smiling once more, though faintly: "Yes, I am very, *very* old." He said it with such curious emphasis that he did not seem to demand some kind of a denial, as such words normally do. In fact, I could find nothing immediate to say at all. And yet it was nonsense, and denial would have been sincere. I do not know his age, and find even an approximation difficult, but "very, very old" he most certainly is not, but in all important ways one of the truly youngest people that can be imagined, and one of the most truly ardent. He was wearing the most beautiful black clothes, with a tiny Order of some kind, I am sure *most* distinguished, because so unobtrusive. Papa has often remarked that the flashy display of Honors is no longer correct.

In some ways the most romantic thing of all is that I do not even know his name. As people were beginning to leave the party, not so very late, I suppose, as most of the people were, after all, quite old, he took my hand and this time held it, nor did I even affect to resist. "We shall meet again," he said, "many times," looking so deeply and steadily into my eyes that I felt he had penetrated my inmost heart and soul. Indeed, there was something so powerful and mysterious about my own feelings at that moment that I could only murmur "Yes," in a voice so weak that he could hardly have heard me, and then cover my eyes with my hands, those eyes into which he had been gazing so piercingly. For a moment (it cannot have been longer, or my discomposure would have been observed by others), I sank down into a chair with all about me black and swimming, and when I had recovered myself, he was no longer there, and there was nothing to do but be kissed by the Contessa who said,

"You're looking tired, child," and be hastened to my big bed, immediately.

And though new emotions are said to deprive us of rest (as I have myself been able to confirm on one or two occasions), I seem to have *slept* immediately too, and very deeply, and for a very long time. I know, too, that I dreamed remarkably, but I cannot at all recollect of what. Perhaps I do not need the aid of memory, for surely I can surmise?

On the first occasion since I have been in Italy, the sun is truly very hot. I do not think I shall write any more today. I have already covered pages in my small, clear handwriting, which owes so much to Miss Gisborne's patience and severity, and to her high standards in all matters touching young girlhood. I am rather surprised that I have been left alone for so long. Though Papa and Mamma do not seem to me to accomplish very much in proportion to the effort they expend, yet they are very inimical to "lying about and doing nothing," especially in my case, but in their own cases also, as I must acknowledge. I wonder how Mamma is faring after the excitements of last night? I am sure I should arise, dress, and ascertain; but instead I whisper to myself that once more I feel powerfully drawn towards the embrace of Morpheus.

9th October. Yesterday morning I decided that I had already recorded enough for one single day (though for what wonderful events I had to try, however vainly, to find words!), but there are few private occupations in this world about which I care more than inscribing the thoughts and impressions of my heart in this small, secret journal, which no one else shall ever in this world see (I shall take good care of that), so that I am sure I should again have taken up my pen in the evening, had there been any occurrence sufficiently definite to write about. *That*, I fear, is what Miss Gisborne would call one of my overloaded sentences, but overloaded sentences can be the reflection, I am sure, of overloaded spirits, and even be their only relief and outlet! How well at this moment do I recall Miss Gisborne's moving counsel: Only find the right words for your troubles, and your troubles become half joys. Alas, for me at this hour there can be no right words: in some strange way that I can by no means grasp hold of, I find myself fire and ice in equal parts. I have never before felt so greatly alive and yet I catch in myself an eerie conviction that my days are now closely numbered. It does not frighten me, as one would expect it to do. Indeed, it is very nearly a relief. I have never moved at my ease in this world, despite all the care that has been lavished on me; and if I had never known Caroline, hitherto my dearest friend (and sometimes her Mamma too), by comparison with. . . . Oh, there *are* no words. Also I have not completely recovered from the demands which last night made upon me. This is something I am rather ashamed of and shall admit to no one. But it is true. As well as being torn by emotion, I am worn to a silken thread.

The Contessa, having appeared in my room yesterday morning, then disappeared and was not seen again all day, as on the day we arrived. All the same she seemed to have spoken to Mamma about me, as she had said she would be doing. This soon became clear.

It was already afternoon before I finally rose from my bed and ventured from my sunny room. I was feeling very hungry once more, and I felt that I really must find out whether Mamma was fully recovered. So I went first and knocked at the door of Mamma and Papa's rooms. As there was no answer, I went downstairs, and, though there was no one else around (when it is at all sunny, most Italians simply lie down in the shade), there was Mamma, in full and blooming health, on the terrace overlooking the garden. She had her workbox with her and was sitting in the full sun trying to do two jobs at once, perhaps three, in her usual manner. When Mamma is feeling quite well, she always fidgets terribly. I fear that she lacks what the gentleman we met in Lausanne called "the gift of repose." (I have never forgotten that expression.)

Mamma set about me at once. "Why didn't you dance with even one of those nice young men whom the Contessa had gone to the trouble of inviting simply for your sake? The Contessa is very upset about it. Besides, what have you been doing all the morning? This lovely, sunny day? And what is all this other rubbish the Contessa has been trying to tell me about you? I cannot understand a word of it. Perhaps you can enlighten me? I suppose it is something I ought to know about. No doubt it is a consequence of your Father and Mother agreeing to your going into the town on your own?"

Needless to say, I know by this time how to reply to Mamma when she rants on in terms such as these.

"The Contessa is very upset about it all," Mamma exclaimed again after I had spoken; as if a band of knaves had stolen all the spoons, and I had been privy to the crime. "She is plainly hinting at something which courtesy prevents her putting into words, and it is something to do with you. I should be obliged if you would tell me what it is. Tell me at once," Mamma commanded very fiercely.

Of course I was aware that something had taken place between the Contessa and me that morning, and by now I knew very well what lay behind it: in one way or another the Contessa had divined my recontre of the evening before and had realized something (though how far from the whole!) of the effect it had made upon me. Even to me she had expressed herself in what English people would regard as an overwrought,

Italianate way. It was clear that she had said something to Mamma on the subject, but of a veiled character, as she did not wish actually to betray me. She had, indeed, informed me that she was going to do this, and I now wished that I had attempted to dissuade her. The fact is that I had been so somnolent as to be half without my wits.

"Mamma," I said, with the dignity I have learned to display at these times, "if the Contessa has anything to complain of in my conduct, I am sure she will complain only when I am present." And, indeed, I *was* sure of that; though doubtful whether the Contessa would ever consider complaining about me at all. Her addressing herself to Mamma in the present matter was, I could be certain, an attempt to aid me in some way, even though possibly misdirected, as was almost inevitable with someone who did not know Mamma very well.

"You are defying me, child," Mamma almost screamed. "You are defying your own Mother." She had so worked herself up (surely about nothing? even less than usual?) that she managed to prick herself. Mamma is constantly pricking herself when she attempts needlework, mainly, I always think, because she *will* not concentrate upon any one particular task, and she keeps a wad of lint in her box against the next time it occurs. This time, however, the lint seemed to be missing and she appeared to have inflicted quite a gash. Poor Mamma flapped about like a bird beneath a net, while the blood was beginning to flow quite freely. I bent forward and sucked it away with my tongue. It was really strange to have Mamma's blood in my mouth. The strangest part was that it tasted delightful; almost like an exceptionally delicious sweetmeat! I feel my own blood mantling to my cheek as I write the words now.

Mamma then managed to staunch the miniature wound with her pocket handkerchief: one of the pretty ones she had purchased in Besancon. She was looking at me in her usual critical way, but all she said was: "It is perhaps fortunate that we are leaving here on Monday."

Though it was our usual routine, nothing had been said on the present occasion, and I was aghast. (Here, I suppose, *was* something definite to record yesterday evening!)

"What!" I cried. "Leave the sweet Contessa so soon! Leave, within only a week, the town where Dante walked and wrote!" I smile a little as I perceive how, without thinking, I am beginning to follow the flamboyant Italian way of putting things. I am not really sure that Dante did *write* anything much in Ravenna, but to Italians such objections have little influence upon the choice of words. I realize that it is a habit I must guard against.

"Where Dante walked may be not at all a suitable place for you to walk," rejoined Mamma, uncharitably, but with more sharpness of phrase and thought than is customary with her. She was fondling her injured thumb the while, and had nothing to mollify her acerbity towards me. The blood was beginning to redden the impromptu bandage, and I turned away with what writers call "very mixed feelings."

All the same, I did manage to see some more of the wide world before we leave Ravenna; and on the very next day, this day, Sunday, and even though it is a Sunday. Apparently, there is no English church in Ravenna, so that all we could compass was for Papa to read a few prayers this morning and go through the Litany, with Mamma and me making the responses. The Major-Domo showed the three of us to a special room for the purpose. It had nothing in it but an old table with shaky legs and a line of wooden chairs; all dustier and more decrepit even than other things I have seen in the Villa. Of course all this has happened in previous places when it was a Sunday, but never before under such dispiriting conditions—even, as I felt, *unhealthy* conditions. I was *most* disagreeably affected by the entire experience and *entirely* unable to imbibe the Word of God, as I should have done. I have never felt like that before even at the least uplifting of Family Prayers. Positively *irreverent* thoughts raced uncontrolledly through my little head: for example, I found myself wondering how efficacious God's Word could be for Salvation when droned and stumbled over by a mere uncanonized layman such as Papa—no, I mean, of course, *unordained*, but I have let the first word stand because it is so comic when applied to Papa, who is always denouncing "the Roman Saints" and all they represent, such as frequent days of public devotion in their honor. English people speak so unkindly of the Roman Catholic priests, but at least they have all, including the most unworthy of them, been touched by hands that go back and back and back to Saint Peter and so to the Spurting Fountain of Grace itself. You can hardly say the same for Papa, and I believe that even Mr. Biggs-Hartley's consecrationary position is a matter of dispute. I feel very strongly that the Blood of the Lamb cannot be mediated unless by the Elect or washed in by hands that are not strong and white.

Oh, how can he fulfill his promise that "we shall meet again," if Papa and Mamma drag me, protesting, from the place where we met first? Let alone meet "many times"? These thoughts distract me, as I need not say; and yet I am quite sure that they distract me less than one might expect. For that the reason is simple enough: deep within me I *know* that some wondrous thing, some special election, has passed between him and me, and that meet again we shall in consequence, and no doubt "many times." Distracted about it all though I am, I am simultaneously so sure as to be almost at peace: fire and ice, as I have said. I find I can still sometimes think about other things, which was by no means the case when I fancied, long, long ago, that I was "in love" (perish the thought!) with Mr. Franklin Stobart. Yes, yes, my wondrous friend has brought to my wild soul a measure of peace at last! I only wish I did not feel so tired. Doubtless it will pass when the events of the night before last are more distant (what sadness, though, when they are! What sadness, happen what may!), and, I suppose, this afternoon's tiring walk also. No, *not* "tiring." I refuse to admit the word, and that malapert Emilia returned home "fresh as a daisy," to use the expression her kind of person uses where I come from.

But what a walk it proved to be, none the less! We wandered through the *Pineta di Classe:* a perfectly enormous forest between Ravenna and the sea, with pine trees like very thick, dark, bushy umbrellas, and, so they say, either a brigand or a beast hiding behind each one of them! I have never seen such pine trees before; not in France or Switzerland or the Low Countries, let alone in England. They are more like trees in the Thousand Nights and a Night (not that I have read that work), dense enough at the top and stout-trunked enough for rocs to nest in! And such countless numbers of them, all so old! Left without a guide, I should easily have found myself lost within only a few minutes, so many and so vague are the different tracks among the huge conifers; but I have to admit that Emilia, quite shed now of her bien élevée finicking, strode out almost like a boy, and showed a knowledge of the best routes that I could only wonder at and take advantage of. There is now almost an understanding between me and Emilia, and it is mainly from her that I am learning an amount of Italian that is beginning quite to surprise me. All the time I recall, however, that it is a very simple language: the great poet of "Paradise Lost" (not that I have read that work either) remarked that it was unnecessary to set aside special periods for instruction in Italian, because one could simply pick it up as one went along. So it is proving between me and Emilia.

The forest routes are truly best suited to gentlemen on horseback, and at one place two such emerged from one of the many tracks going off to our left. "Guardi!" cried out Emilia and clutched my arm as if she were my intimate. "Milord Byron and Signor Shelley!" (I do not attempt to indicate Emilia's funny approximation to the English names.) What a moment in my life—or in anyone's life! To see at the same time two persons both so great and famous and both so irrevocably doomed! There was not, of course, time enough for any degree of close observation, though Mr. Shelley seemed slightly to acknowledge with his crop our standing back a little to allow him and his friend free passage; but I fear that my main impression was of both giaours looking considerably older than I had expected and Lord Byron considerably more corpulent (as well as being quite grey-headed, though I believe only at the start of his life's fourth decade). Mr. Shelley was remarkably untidy in his dress and Lord Byron most comical: in that respect at least, the reality was in accord with the report. Both were without hats or caps. They cantered away down the track up which we had walked. They were talking in loud voices (Mr. Shelley's noticeably high in pitch), both together, above the thudding of their horses' hoofs. Neither of them really stopped talking even when slowing in order to wheel, so to speak, round the spot where we stood.

And so I have at length set eyes upon the fabled Lord Byron! A wondrous moment indeed; but how much more wondrous for me if it had occurred before that recent most wondrous of all possible moments! But it would be very wrong of me to complain because the red and risen moon has quite dimmed my universal nightlight! Lord Byron, that child of destiny, is for the whole world and, no doubt, for all time, or at least for a great deal of it! My fate is a different one and I draw it to my breast with a young girl's eager arms!

"Come gentili!" exclaimed Emilia, gazing after our two horsemen. It was not perhaps the most appropriate comment upon Lord Byron, or even upon Mr. Shelley, but there was nothing for me to reply (even if I could have found the Italian words), so on went our walk, with Emilia now venturing so far as to sing, in a quite pretty voice, and me lacking heart to chide her, until in the end the pine trees parted and I got my first glimpse of the Adriatic Sea, and, within a few more paces, a whole wide prospect of it. (The Venetian Lagoon I refuse to take seriously.) The Adriatic Sea is linked with the Mediterranean Sea, indeed quite properly a part or portion of it, so that I can now say to myself that I have "seen the Mediterranean"; which good old Doctor Johnson defined as the true object of all Travel. It was almost as if at long last my own eyes had seen the Holy Grail, with the Redemptive Blood streaming forth in golden splendor; and I stood for whole moments quite lost in my own deep thoughts. The world falls from me once more in a moment as I muse upon that luminous, rapturous flood.

But I can write no more. So unwontedly weary do I feel that the vividness of my vision notwithstanding is something to be marveled at. It is as if my hand were guided as was Isabella's by the distant Traffio in Mrs. Fremlinson's wonderful book; so that Isabella was enabled to leave a record of the strange events that preceded her death—without which record, as it now occurs to me, the book, fiction though it be, could hardly with sense have been written at all. The old moon is drenching my sheets and my nightgown in brightest crimson. In Italy, the moon is always full and always so red.

Oh, when next shall I see my friend, my paragon, my genius!

10th October. I have experienced so sweet and great a dream that I must write down the fact before it is forgotten, and even though I find that already there is almost nothing left that *can* be written. I have dreamed that he was with me; that he indued my neck and breast with kisses that were at once the softest and the sharpest in the world; that that he filled my ears with thoughts so strange that they could have come only from a world afar.

And now the Italian dawn is breaking: all the sky is red and purple. The rains have gone, as if forever. The crimson sun calls to me to take flight before it is once more autumn and then winter. Take flight! Today we are leaving for Rimini! Yes, it is but to Rimini that I am to repair. It is farcical.

And in my dawn-red room there is once again blood upon my person. But this time I know. It is at his embrace that my being springs forth, in joy and welcome; his embrace that is at once the softest and sharpest in the world. How strange that I could ever have failed to recall such bliss!

I rose from my bed to look for water, there being, once more, none in my room. I found that I was so weak with happiness that I all but fainted. But after sinking for a moment upon my bed, I somewhat recovered myself and succeeded in gently opening the door. And what should I find there? Or, rather, whom? In the faintly lighted corridor stood silently none other than the little Contessina, whom I cannot recollect having previously beheld since her Mamma's soirée à danse. She was dressed in some kind of loose dark wrapper, and I may only leave between her and her conscience what she can have been doing. No doubt for some good reason allied therewith, she seemed turned to stone by the sight of *me*. Of course I was in déshabillé even more complete than her own. I had omitted even to cover my nightgown. And upon that there was blood—as if I had suffered an injury. When I walked towards her reassuringly (after all, we are but two young girls and I am not her Judge—nor anyone's), she gave a low croaking scream and fled from me as if I had been the Erl Queen herself, but still almost silently, no doubt for her same good reasons. It was foolish of the little Contessina, because all I had in mind to do was to take her in my arms, and then to kiss her in token of our common humanity and the strangeness of our encounter at such an hour.

I was disconcerted by the Contessina's childishness (these Italians manage to be shrinking bambine and hardened women of the world at one and the same time), and, again feeling faint, leaned against the passage wall. When I stood full on my feet once more, I saw by the crimson light coming through one of the dusty windows that I had reached out to stop myself falling and left a scarlet impression of my hand on the painted plaster. It is difficult to excuse and impossible to remove. How I weary of these règles and conventionalities by which I have hitherto been bound! How I long for the measureless liberty that has been promised me and of which I feel so complete a future assurance!

But I managed to find some water (the Contessa's Villa is no longer of the kind that has servitors alert—or supposedly alert—all night in the larger halls), and with this water I did what I could, at least in my own room. Unfortunately I had neither enough water nor enough strength to do all. Besides, I begin to grow reckless.

11th October. No dear dream last night. Considerable crafty unpleasantness, however, attended our departure yesterday from Ravenna. Mamma disclosed that the Contessa was actually lending us her own carriage. "It's because she wants to see the last of us," said Mamma to me, looking at the cornice. "How can that be, Mamma?" I asked. "Surely, she's hardly seen us at all? She was invisible when we arrived, and now she's been invisible again for days." "There's no connection between those two things," Mamma replied. "At the time we arrived, the Contessa was feeling unwell, as we Mothers often do, you'll learn that for yourself soon. But for the last few days, she's been very upset by your behavior, and now she wants us to go." As Mamma was still looking at the wall instead of at me, I put out the tip of my tongue, only the merest scrap of it, but *that* Mamma did manage to see, and had lifted her hand several inches before she recollected that I was now as good as an adult and so not to be corrected by a simple cuff.

And then when we were all about to enter the draggled old carriage, lo and behold, the Contessa did manage to haul herself into the light, and I caught her actually crossing herself behind my back, or what she no doubt thought was behind my back. I had to clench my hands to stop myself spitting at her. I have since begun to speculate whether she did not really *intend* me to see what she did. I was once so fond of the Contessa, so drawn to her—I can still *remember* that quite well—but *all* is now changed. A week, I find, can sometimes surpass a lifetime; and so, for that matter, can one single indelible night. The Contessa took great care to prevent her eyes once meeting mine, though, as soon as I perceived this, I never for a moment ceased glaring at her like a little basilisk. She apologized to Papa and Mamma for the absence of the Contessina, whom she described as being in bed with screaming megrims or the black cramp or some other malady (I truly cared not what! nor care now!) no doubt incident to girlish immaturity in Italy! And Papa and Mamma made response as if they really minded about the silly little child! Another way of expressing their disapproval of *me*, needless to observe. My considered opinion is that the Contessina and her Mamma are simply two of a kind, but that the Contessa has had time to become more skilled in concealment and duplicity. I am sure that all Italian females are alike, when one really knows them. The Contessa had made me dig my fingernails so far into my palms that my hands hurt all the rest of the day and still look as if I had caught a dagger in each of them, as in Sir Walter Scott's tale.

We had a coachman and a footman on the box, neither of them at all young, but more like two old wiseacres; and, when we reached Classe, we stopped in order that Papa, Mamma, and I could go inside the church, which is famous for its Mosaics, going back, as usual, to the Byzantines. The big doors at the western end were open in the quite hot sunshine and indeed the scene inside did look very pretty, all pale azure, the color of Heaven, and shining gold; but I saw no more of it than that, because as I was about to cross the threshold, I was again overcome by my faintness, and sitting down on a bench, bade Papa and Mamma go in without me, which they immediately did, in the sensible English way, instead of trying to make an ado over me, in the silly Italian way. The bench was of marble, with arms in the shape of lions, and though the marble was worn, and cut, and pockmarked, it was a splendid, heavy object, carved, if I mistake not, by the Romans themselves. Seated on it, I soon felt better once more, but then I noticed the two fat old men on the coach doing something or other to the doors and windows. I supposed they were greasing them, which I am sure would have been very much in order, as would have been a considerable application of paint to the entire vehicle. But when Papa and Mamma at last come out of the church, and we all resumed our places, Mamma soon began to complain of a smell, which she said was, or at least resembled, that of the herb, garlic. Of course when one is abroad, the smell of garlic is *everywhere*, so that I quite understood when Papa merely told Mamma not to be fanciful; but then I found that I myself was more and more affected, so that we completed the journey in almost complete silence, none of us, except Papa, having much appetite for the very crude meal set before us en route at Cesenatico. "You're looking white," said Papa to me, as we stepped from the coach. Then he added to Mamma, but hardly attempting to prevent my hearing, "I can see why the Contessa spoke to you as she did." Mamma merely shrugged her shoulders: something she would never have thought of doing before we came abroad, but which now she does frequently. I nearly said something spiteful. At the end, the Contessa was constantly disparaging my appearance, and indeed I am pale, paler than I once was, though always I have been pale enough, pale as a little phantom; but only I know the reason for the change in me, and no one else shall know it ever, because no one else ever can. It is not so much a "secret." Rather it is a revelation.

In Rimini we are but stopping at the inn; and we are almost the only persons to be doing so. I cannot wonder at this: the inn is a gaunt, forbidding place; the Padrona has what in Derbyshire we call a "harelip"; and the attendance is of the worst. Indeed, no one has so far ventured to come near me. All the rooms, including mine, are very large: and all lead into one another, in the style of two hundred years ago. The building resembles a Palazzo that has fallen upon hard times, and perhaps that is what it is. At first I feared that my dear Papa and Mamma were to be ensconced in the apartment adjoining my own, which would have suited me not at all, but, for some reason, it has not happened, so that between my room and the staircase are two dark and empty chambers, which would once have caused me alarm, but which now I welcome. Everything is poor and dusty. Shall I ever repose abroad in such ease and bien-être as one takes for granted in Derbyshire? Why, no, I shall not: and a chill runs down my back as I inscribe the words; but a chill more of excitement than of fear. Very soon now shall I be entirely elsewhere and entirely above such trivia.

I have opened a pair of the big windows, a grimy and, I fear, a noisy task. I flitted out in the moonlight on to the stone balcony, and gazed down into the Piazza. Rimini seems now to be a very poor town, and there is nothing of the nocturnal uproar and riot which are such usual features of Italian existence. At this hour, all is completely silent—even strangely so. It is still very warm, but there is a mist between the Earth and the Moon.

I have crept into another of these enormous Italian beds. He is winging towards me. There is no further need for words. I have but to slumber, and that will be simple, so exhausted I am.

12th, 13th, 14th October. Nothing to relate but him, and of him nothing that can be related. (I am very tired, but it is tiredness that follows exaltation, not the vulgar tiredness of common life; I noticed today that I no longer have either shadow or reflection.) Fortunately Mamma was quite destroyed (as the Irish simpletons express it) by the journey from Ravenna, and has not been seen since. How many, many hours one's elders pass in retirement! How glad I am never to have to experience such bondage! How I rejoice when I think about the new life which spreads before me into infinity, the new ocean which already laps at my feet, the new vessel with the purple sail and the red oars upon which I shall at any moment embark! When one is confronting so tremendous a transformation, how foolish some words, but the habit of them lingers even when I have hardly strength to hold the pen! Soon, soon, new force will be mine, fire that is inconceivable; and the power to assume any night-shape that I may wish, or to fly through the darkness with none. What love is his! How chosen among all women am I; and I am just a little English girl! It is a miracle, and I shall enter the halls of Those Other Women with pride.

Papa is so beset by Mamma that he has failed to notice that I am eating nothing and drinking only water; that at our horrid, odious meals I am but feigning.

Believe it or not, yesterday we visited, Papa and I, the Tempio Malatestiano. Papa went as an English Visitor: I (at least by comparison with Papa) as a Pythoness. It is a beautiful edifice, among the most beautiful in the world, they say. But for me a special splendor lay in the noble and amorous dead it houses, and in the control over them which I feel increase within me. I was so rent and torn with new power that Papa had to help me back to the inn. Poor Papa, burdened, as he supposes, by two weak invalid women! I could almost pity him.

I wish I had reached the pretty little Contessina and kissed her throat.

15th October. Last night I opened my pair of windows (the other pair resists me, weak—in terms of this world—as I am) and, without quite venturing forth, stood there in nakedness and raised both my arms. Soon a soft wind began to rustle, where all had previously been still as death. The rustling steadily rose to roaring, and the faint chill of the night turned to heat as when an oven door is opened. A great crying out and weeping, a buzzing and screaming and scratching swept in turmoil past the open window, as if invisible (or almost invisible) bodies were turning around and around in the air outside, always lamenting and accusing. My head was split apart by the sad sounds and my body as moist as if I were an ottoman. Then, in an instant, all had passed by. He stood there before me in the dim embrasure of the window. "That," he said, "is Love as the elect of this world know it." "The *elect?*" I besought him, in a voice so low that it was hardly a voice at all (but what matter?). "Why yes," he seemed to reaffirm. "Of this world, the elect."

16th October. The weather in Italy changes constantly. Today once more it is cold and wet.

They have begun to suppose me ill. Mamma, back on her legs for a spell, is fussing like a blowfly round a dying lamb. They even called in a

Medico, after discussing at length in my presence whether an Italian physician could be regarded as of any utility. With what voice I have left, I joined in vigorously that he could not. All the same, a creature made his appearance: wearing fusty black, and, believe it or not, a grey *wig*—in all, a veritable Pantalone. What a farce! With my ever sharper fangs, I had him soon despatched, and yelling like the Old Comedy he belonged to. Then I spat forth his enfeebled, senile lymph, cleaned my lips of his skin and smell, and returned, hugging myself, to my couch.

Janua mortis vita, as Mr. Biggs-Hartley says in his funny Dog Latin. And to think that today is Sunday! I wonder why no one has troubled to pray over me?

17th October. I have been left alone all day. Not that it matters.

Last night came the strangest and most beautiful event of my life, a seal laid upon my future.

I was lying here with my double window open, when I noticed that mist was coming in. I opened my arms to it, but my blood began to trickle down my bosom from the wound in my neck, which of course no longer heals—though I seem to have no particular trouble in concealing the mark from the entire human race, not forgetting learned men with certificates from the University of Sciozza.

Outside in the Piazza was a sound of shuffling and nuzzling, as of sheep being folded on one of the farms at home. I climbed out of bed, walked across, and stepped on to the balcony.

The mist was filtering the moonlight into a silver-grey that I have never seen elsewhere.

The entire Piazza, a very big one, was filled with huge, grizzled wolves, all perfectly silent, except for the small sounds I have mentioned, all with their tongues flopping and lolling, black in the silvery light, and all gazing up at my window.

Rimini is near to the Apennine Mountains, where wolves notoriously abound, and commonly devour babies and small children. I suppose that the coming cold is drawing them into the towns.

I smiled at the wolves. Then I crossed my hands on my little bosom and curtsied. They will be prominent among my new people. My blood will be theirs, and theirs mine.

I forgot to say that I have contrived to lock my door. Now, I am assisted in such affairs.

Somehow I have found my way back to bed. It has become exceedingly cold, almost icy. For some reason I think of all the empty rooms in this battered old Palazzo (as I am sure it once was), so fallen from their former stateliness. I doubt if I shall write any more. I do not think I shall have any more to say.

T. E. D. KLEIN/*The Events at Poroth Farm*

Mr. T. E. D. Klein, also known as Ted Klein, was one of the historic three who originally thought up having a World Fantasy Convention, and one of the heroic Kirby McCauley's mainstays in building and actually putting it on. He is also, as this story shows, a skilled writer of horror stories. I present it to you not just to chill your bones, but to demonstrate the agonizing the judges at the convention had to go through (I was one and I know), for this lovely bit of work was, believe it or not, only a hot contender on the nominee list, and as such is an excellent indication of the level of quality we were dealing with.

I suppose if you must lose it's a comfort to lose to such as Aickman, and of course Klein has another consolation—sooner or later we all know he's going to get that damned prize.

T. E. D. Klein

THE EVENTS AT POROTH FARM

As soon as the phone stops ringing, I'll begin this affidavit. Lord, it's hot in here. Perhaps I should open a window. . . .

Thirteen rings. It has a sense of humor.
I suppose that ought to be comforting.
Somehow I'm not comforted. If it feels free to indulge in these teasing, tormenting little games, so much the worse for me.
The summer is over now, but this room is like an oven. My shirt is already drenched, and this pen feels slippery in my hand. In a moment or two the little drop of sweat that's collecting above my eyebrow is going to splash onto this page.
Just the same, I'll keep that window closed. Outside, through the dusty panes of glass, I can see a boy in red spectacles walking toward the courthouse steps. Perhaps there's a telephone booth in back. . . .
A sense of humor—that's one quality I never noticed in it. I saw only a deadly seriousness and, of course, an intelligence that grew at terrifying speed, malevolent and inhuman. If it now feels itself safe enough to toy with me before doing whatever it intends to do, so much the worse for me. So much the worse, perhaps, for us all.
I hope I'm wrong. Though my name is Jeremy, derived from Jeremiah, I'd hate to be a prophet in the wilderness. I'd much rather be a harmless crank.
But I believe we're in for trouble.
I'm a long way from the wilderness now, of course. Though perhaps not far enough to save me. . . . I'm writing this affidavit in room 2-K of the Union Hotel, overlooking Main Street in Flemington, New Jersey, twenty-five miles south of Gilead. Directly across the street, hippies lounging on its steps, stands the county courthouse where Bruno Hauptmann was tried back in 1935. (Did they ever find the body of that child?) Hauptmann undoubtedly walked down those very steps, now lined with teenagers savoring their last week of summer vacation. Where that boy in the red spectacles sits sucking on his cigarette—did the killer once halt there, police and reporters around him, and contemplate his imminent execution?
For several days now I have been afraid to leave this room.
I have perhaps been staring too often at the ordinary-looking boy on

the steps. He sits there every day. The red spectacles conceal his eyes; it's impossible to tell where he's looking.

I know he's looking at me.

But it would be foolish of me to waste time worrying about executions when I have these notes to transcribe. It won't take long, and then, perhaps, I'll sneak outside to mail them—and leave New Jersey forever. I remain, despite all that's happened, an optimist. What was it my namesake said? "Thou art my hope in the day of evil."

There *is*, surprisingly, some real wilderness left in New Jersey, assuming one wants to be a prophet. The hills to the west, spreading from the southern swamplands to the Delaware and beyond to Pennsylvania, provide shelter for deer, pheasant, even an occasional bear—and hide hamlets never visited by outsiders: pockets of ignorance, some of them, citadels of ancient superstition utterly cut off from news of New York and the rest of the state, religious communities where customs haven't changed appreciably since the days of their settlement a century or more ago.

It seems incredible that villages so isolated can exist today on the very doorstep of the world's largest metropolis—villages with nothing to offer the outsider, and hence never visited, except by the occasional hunter who stumbles on them unwittingly. Yet as you speed down one of the state highways, consider how few of the cars slow down for the local roads. It is easy to pass the little towns without even a glance at the signs—and if there are no signs . . . ? And consider, too, how seldom the local traffic turns off onto the narrow roads that emerge without warning from the woods. And when those untraveled side roads lead into others still deeper in wilderness—and when those in turn give way to dirt roads, deserted for weeks on end. . . . It is not hard to see how tiny rural communities can exist less than an hour from major cities, virtually unaware of one another's existence.

Television will of course link the two—unless, as is often the case, the elders of the community choose to see this distraction as the Devil's tool and proscribe it. Telephones put these outcast settlements into touch with their neighbors—unless they choose to ignore their neighbors. And so in the course of years they are . . . forgotten.

New Yorkers were amazed when in the winter of 1968 the *Times* "discovered" a religious community near New Providence that had existed in its present form since the late 1800's—less than forty miles from Times Square. Agricultural work was performed entirely by hand, women still wore long dresses with high collars, and town worship was held every evening.

I, too, was amazed. I'd seldom traveled west of the Hudson and still thought of New Jersey as some dismal extension of the Newark slums, ruled by gangsters, foggy with swamp gases and industrial waste, a grey land that had surrendered to the city.

Only later did I learn of the rural New Jersey, and of towns whose solitary general stores double as post offices, with one or two gas pumps standing in front. And later still I learned of Baptistown and Quakertown, their old religions surviving unchanged, and of towns like Lebanon, Landsdown, and West Portal, close to Route 22 and civilization but heavy with secrets city folk never dreamed of; Mt. Airy, with its network of hidden caverns, and Mt. Olive, bordering the infamous Budd Lake; Middle Valley, sheltered by dark cliffs, subject of the recent archaeological debate chronicled in *Natural History*, where the wanderer may still find grotesque relics of pagan worship and, some say, may still hear the chants that echo from the cliffs on certain nights; and towns with names like Zion and Zaraphath and Gilead, forgotten communities of bearded men and black-robed women, walled cities too small or obscure for most maps of the state. This was the wilderness into which I traveled, weary of Manhattan's interminable din; and it was outside Gilead where, until the tragedies, I chose to make my home for three months.

Among the silliest of literary conventions is the "town that won't talk" —the Bavarian hamlet where peasants turn away from tourists' queries about "the castle" and silently cross themselves, the New England harbor where fishermen feign ignorance and cast "furtive glances" at the traveler. In actuality, I have found, country people love to talk to the stranger, provided he shows a sincere interest in their anecdotes. Storekeepers will interrupt their activity at the cash register to tell you their theories on a recent murder; farmers will readily spin tales of buried bones and of a haunted house down the road. Rural townspeople are not so reticent as the writers would have us believe.

Gilead, isolated though it is behind its oak forests and ruined walls, is no exception. The inhabitants look with initial suspicion upon all outsiders, but let one demonstrate a respect for their traditional reserve and they will prove friendly enough. They don't approve of modern fashions and look with disfavor on flashy automobiles, but they are hardly to be described as hostile, although that was my original impression.

When asked about the terrible events at Poroth Farm, they will prove more than willing to talk. They will tell you of bad crops and polluted well water, of emotional depression leading to a fatal argument—in short, they will describe a conventional rural murder, and will even volunteer their opinions on the killer's present whereabouts.

But you will learn almost nothing from them—or almost nothing that is true. They don't know what really happened.

I do. I was closest to it.

I had come to spend the summer with Sarr Poroth and his wife. I needed a place where I could do a lot of reading without distraction, and Poroth's farm, secluded as it was even from the village of Gilead six miles down the dirt road, appeared the perfect spot for my studies.

I had seen the Poroths' advertisement in the *Hunterdon County Democrat* on a trip west through Princeton last spring. They advertised for a summer or long-term tenant to live in one of the outbuildings behind the farmhouse. As I soon learned, the building was a long, low cinderblock affair, unpleasantly suggestive of army barracks but clean, new, and cool in the sun; by the start of summer ivy sprouted from the walls and disguised the ugly grey brick. Originally intended to house chickens, it had in fact remained empty for several years until the farm's original owner, a Mr. Baber, sold out last fall to the Poroths, who immediately saw that with the installation of dividing walls, linoleum floors, and other improvements the building might serve as a source of income. I was to be their first tenant.

The Poroths, Sarr and Deborah, were in their early thirties, only slightly older than I, although friends who met them believed the age difference to be greater; their relative solemnity, and the drabness of their clothing, gave them the appearance of greater age, and so did their hair styles: Deborah, though possessing a beautiful length of black hair, wound it all in a tight bun behind her neck, thus pulling the hair back from her face with a severity which looked almost painful, and Sarr maintained a thin fringe of black beard that circled from ears to chin in the manner of the Pennsylvania Dutch, who leave their hair shaggy but refuse to grow moustaches lest they resemble the military class they traditionally despised. Both man and wife were hardworking, grave of expression, and pale despite the time spent laboring in the sun—a pallor accentuated by the inky blackness of their hair. I imagine this unhealthy aspect was partly due to the considerable amount of inbreeding that went on in the area, the Poroths themselves being, I believe, third cousins; on first meeting one might have taken them for brother and sister, two gravely devout children aged in the wilderness.

And yet there was a difference between them and, too, a difference that set them both in contrast to others of their sect. The Poroths were, as far as I could determine, members of a tiny Mennonitic order outwardly related to the Amish, although doctrinal differences were apparently rather profound. It was this order that made up the large part of the community known as Gilead.

I sometimes think the only reason they allowed an infidel like me to live on their property (for my religion was among the first things they inquired about) was because of my name; Sarr was very partial to Jeremiah, and the motto of his order was, "Stand ye in the ways, and see, and ask for the old paths, where is the good way, and walk therein." (VI:16)

Having been raised in no particular religion except a universal skepticism, I began the summer with a hesitancy to raise the topic in conversation, and so I learned comparatively little about the Poroths' beliefs; only toward the end of my stay did I begin to thumb through the Bible in odd moments and take to quoting jeremiads. That was, I suppose, Sarr's influence.

I was able to learn, nonetheless, that for all their conservative aura the Poroths were considered, in effect, young liberals by most of Gilead. Sarr had a bachelor's degree in religious studies from Rutgers, and Deborah had attended a nearby community college for two years, unusual for women of the sect. Too, they had only recently taken to farming, having spent the first year of their marriage near New Brunswick, where Sarr had hoped to find a teaching position and had, when that job situation proved hopeless, worked as a sort of handyman/carpenter. While most inhabitants of Gilead had never left the farm, the Poroths were coming to it late—their families had been merchants for several generations— and so were relatively inexperienced.

The inexperience showed. The farm comprised some ninety acres, but most of that was forest, or fields of weeds too high and thick to walk through. Across the back yard, close to my rooms, ran a small, nameless stream, nearly choked with green scum. A large cornfield to the north lay fallow, but Sarr was planning to seed it this year, using borrowed equipment. His wife spent much of her time indoors, for though she maintained a small vegetable garden she preferred keeping house and looking after the Poroths' great love, their seven cats.

As if to symbolize their broad-mindedness, the Poroths owned a television set, very rare in Gilead; in light of what was to come, however, it is unfortunate they lacked a telephone. (Apparently the set had been received as a wedding present from Deborah's parents, but the monthly expense of a telephone was simply too great.) Otherwise, though, the little farmhouse was "modern" in that it had a working bathroom and gas heat. That they had advertised in the local newspaper was considered remarkable by some of the order's more orthodox members, and indeed a mere subscription to that innocuous weekly had at one time been regarded as a breach of religious conduct.

Though outwardly similar, both of them tall and pale, the Poroths were actually so different as to embody the maxim that "opposites attract." It was that carefully-nurtured reserve that deceived one at first meeting, for in truth Deborah was far more talkative, friendly, and energetic than her husband. Sarr was moody, distant, silent most of the time, with a voice so low that one had trouble following him in conversation. Sitting as stonily as one of his cats, never moving, never speaking, perennially inscrutable, he tended to frighten visitors to the farm until they learned that he was not really sitting in judgment on them; his reserve was not born of surliness, but of shyness.

Where Sarr was catlike, his wife hid beneath the formality of her order the bubbly personality of a kitten. Given the smallest encouragement—say, a family visit—she would plunge into animated conversation, gesticulating, laughing easily, hugging whatever cat was nearby or shouting to guests across the room. When drinking—for both of them enjoyed liquor and, curiously, it was not forbidden by their faith—their innate differences were magnified: Deborah would forget the restraints placed upon women in this Mennonitic order and would eventually dominate the conversation, while her husband would seem to grow increasingly withdrawn, increasingly morose.

Women in the region tended to be submissive to the men, and certainly the important decisions in the Poroths' lives were made by Sarr. Yet I really cannot say who was the stronger of the two. I never saw them quarrel, at least. . . .

Perhaps the best way to tell it is by setting down portions of the journal I kept this summer. Not every entry, of course. Mere excerpts. Just enough to make this affidavit comprehensible to anyone unfamiliar with the incidents at Poroth Farm.

The journal was the only writing I did all summer; my primary reason for keeping it was to record the books I'd read each day, as well as to examine my reactions to relative solitude over a long period of time. All the rest of my energies (as you will no doubt gather from the notes below) were spent reading, in preparation for a course I plan to teach at Trenton State this fall. Or *planned,* I should say, because I don't expect to be anywhere around here come fall.

Where will I be? Perhaps that depends on what's beneath those rose-tinted spectacles.

The course was to cover the Gothic tradition from Shakespeare to Faulkner, from *Hamlet* to *Absalom Absalom!* (And why not view the former as Gothic, with its ghost on the battlements and concern for lost inheritance?) To make the move to Gilead, I'd rented a car for a few days and had stuffed it full of books—only a few of which I ever got to read. But then, I couldn't have known. . . .

How pleasant things were, at the beginning.

June 4

Unpacking day. Spent all morning putting up screens, and a good thing I did. Night now, and a million moths tapping at the windows. One of them as big as a small bird—white—largest I've ever seen. What kind of a caterpillar must it have been? I hope the damned things don't push through the screens.

Had to kill literally hundreds of spiders before moving my stuff in. The Poroths finished doing the inside of this building only a couple of months ago, and already it's infested. Arachnidae—hate the bastards. Why? We'll take that one up with Sigmund someday. Daydreams of Revenge of the Spiders. Writhing body covered with a frenzy of hairy brown legs—"Egad, man, that face! That bloody, torn face! And the missing eyes! It looks like—no! Jeremy!" Killing spiders is supposed to bring bad luck. (Insidious Sierra Club propaganda masquerading as folk myth?) But can't sleep if there's anything crawling around—so what the hell?

Supper with the Poroths. Began to eat, then heard Sarr saying grace. Apologies—but things like that don't embarrass me as much as they used to. (Is that because I'm nearing thirty?)

Chatted about crops, insects, humidity. (Very damp area—band of purplish mildew already around bottom of walls out here.) Sarr told of plans to someday build a larger house when Deborah has a baby, three or four years from now. He wants to build it out of stone. Then he shut up, and I had to keep the conversation going. (Hate eating in silence—animal sounds of mastication, bubbling stomachs.) Deborah joked about cats being her surrogate children. All seven of them hanging around my legs, rubbing against ankles. My nose began running and my eyes itched. Goddamned allergy. Must remember to start treatments this fall, when I get to Trenton State. Deborah sympathetic, Sarr merely watching; she told me my eyes were bloodshot, offered antihistamine. Told them I was glad they at least believe in modern medicine—I'd been afraid she'd offer herbs or mud or something. Sarr said some of the locals still use "snake oil." Asked him how snakes were killed, quoting line from *Vathek*: "The oil of the serpents I have pinched to death will be a pretty present. . . ." We discussed wisdom of pinching snakes. Apparently there's a copperhead out back, near the brook. . . .

The meal was good—lamb and noodles. Not bad for fifteen dollars a week, since I detest cooking. Spice cake for dessert, home-made, of course. Deborah is a good cook. Handsome woman, too.

Still light when I left their kitchen. Fireflies already on the lawn—I've never seen so many. Knelt and watched them a while, listening to the crickets. Think I'll like it here.

Took nearly an hour to arrange my books the way I wanted them. Alphabetical order by authors? No, chronological. . . . But anthologies mess that system up, so back to authors. Why am I so neurotic about my books?

Anyway, they look nice there on the shelves.

Sat up tonight finishing *The Mysteries of Udolpho*. Figure it's best to get the long ones out of the way first. Radcliffe's unfortunate penchant for explaining away all her ghosts and apparitions really a mistake and a bore. All in all, not exactly the most fascinating reading, though a good study in Romanticism. Montoni the typical Byronic hero/villain. But can't demand students read *Udolpho*—too long. In fact, had to keep reminding myself to slow down, have patience with the book. Tried to put myself in frame of mind of 1794 reader with plenty of time on his hands. It works, too—I have plenty of time out here, and already I can feel myself beginning to unwind. What New York does to people. . . .

It's almost two A.M. now, and I'm about ready to turn in. Too bad there's no bathroom in this building—I hate pissing outside at night. God knows what's crawling up your ankles. . . . But it's hardly worth stumbling through the darkness to the farmhouse, and maybe waking up Sarr and Deborah. The nights out here are really pitch-black. . . .

. . . Felt vulnerable, standing there against the night. But what made me even uneasier was the view I got of this building. The lamp on the desk casts the only light for miles, and as I stood outside looking into this room I could see dozens of flying shapes making right for the screens. When you're inside here it's as if you're in a display case—the whole night can see you, but all you can see is darkness. I wish this room didn't have windows on three of the walls—though that does let in the breezes. And I wish the woods weren't so close to my windows by the bed. I suppose privacy is what I wanted—but feel a little unprotected out here.

Those moths are still batting themselves against the screens, but as far as I can see the only things that have gotten in are a few gnats flying around this lamp. The crickets sound good—you sure don't hear them in the city. Frogs are croaking in the brook.

My nose is only now beginning to clear up. Those goddamned cats. Must remember to buy some Contac. Even though the cats are all outside during the day, that farmhouse is full of their scent. But I don't expect to be spending that much time inside the house anyway; this allergy will keep me away from the TV and out here with the books.

Just saw an unpleasantly large spider scurry across the floor near the foot of my bed. Vanished behind the footlocker. Must remember to buy some insect spray tomorrow.

June 11

Hot today, but at night comes a chill. The dampness of this place seems to magnify temperature. Sat outside most of the day finishing the Maturin book, *Melmoth the Wanderer*, and feeling vaguely guilty each time I heard Sarr or Deborah working out there in the field. Well, I've paid for my reading time, so I guess I'm entitled to enjoy it. Though some of these old Gothics are a bit hard to enjoy. The trouble with *Melmoth* is that it wants you to hate. You're especially supposed to hate the Catholics. No doubt this picture of the Inquisition is accurate, but all a book like this can do is put you in an unconstructive rage. Those vicious characters have been dead for centuries, and there's no way to punish them. Still, it's a nice, cynical book for those who like atrocity scenes—starving prisoners forced to eat their girlfriends, delightful things like that. And narratives within narratives within narratives within narratives. I may assign some sections to my class. . . .

Just before dinner, in need of a break, read a story by Arthur Machen. Set in Wales, I believe, like most of his work. It's called "The White People." God, what an experience! I was a little confused by the framing device and all its high-flown talk of "cosmic evil," but the sections from the young girl's notebook were . . . staggering. That air of paganism, the malevolent little faces peeping from the shadows, and those rites she can't dare talk about. . . . It must be the most persuasive horror tale ever written.

Afterward, strolling toward the house, I was moved to climb the old tree in the side yard—the Poroths had already gone in to get dinner ready—and stood upright on a great heavy branch near the middle, making strange gestures and faces that no one could see. Can't say exactly what it was I did, or why. It was getting dark—fireflies below me and a mist rising off the field. I must have looked like a madman's shadow as I made signs to the woods and the moon.

Lamb tonight, and damned good. I may find myself getting fat. Offered, again, to wash the dishes, but apparently Deborah feels that's her role, and I don't care to dissuade her. So talked a while with Sarr about his cats—the usual subject of conversation, especially because, now that summer's coming, they're bringing in dead things every night. Fieldmice, moles, shrews, birds, even a little garter snake. They don't eat them, just lay them out on the porch for the Poroths to see—sort of an offering, I guess. Sarr tosses the bodies in the garbage can, which, as a result, smells indescribably foul. Deborah wants to put bells around their necks; she hates mice but feels sorry for the birds. When she finished the dishes she and Sarr sat down to watch one of their godawful TV programs, so I came out here to read.

Spent the usual ten minutes going over this room, spray can in hand, looking for spiders to kill. Found a couple of little ones, then spent some time spraying bugs that were hanging on the screens hoping to get in. Watched a lot of daddy longlegs curl up and die. . . . Tended not to kill the moths, unless they were making too much of a racket banging against the screen; I can tolerate them okay, but it's only fireflies I really like. I always feel a little sorry when I kill one by mistake and see it hold that cold glow too long. . . . For the dead ones don't wink, they just keep their light on till it fades away.

The insecticide I'm using is made right here in New Jersey, by the Ortho Chemical Company. The label on the can says, "WARNING: For Outdoor Use Only." That's why I bought it—figured it's the most powerful brand available.

Sat in bed reading Algernon Blackwood's witch/cat story, "Ancient Sorceries" (nowhere near as good as Machen, or as his own tale, "The Willows"), and it made me think of those seven cats. The Poroths have around a dozen names for each one of them, which seems a little ridiculous since the creatures barely respond to even *one* name. Sasha, for example, the orange one, is also known as Butch, which comes from Bouche, mouth. And that's short for Eddie La Bouche, so he's also called Ed or Eddie—which in turn comes from some friend's mispronunciation of the cat's original name, Itty, short for Itty Bitty Kitty, which, apparently, he once was. And Zoë, the cutest of the kittens, is also called Bozo and Bisbo. Let's see, how many others can I remember (I'm just learning to tell some of them apart). . . . Felix, or "Flixie," was originally called Paleface, and Phaedra, his mother, is sometimes known as Phuddy, short for Phuddy Duddy.

Come to think of it, the only cat that hasn't got multiple names is Bwada, Sarr's cat. (All the others were acquired after he married Deborah, but Bwada was his pet years before.) She's the oldest of the cats, and the meanest. Fat and sleek, with fine grey fur, darker than silver grey, lighter than charcoal. She's the only cat that's ever bitten anyone—Deborah, as well as friends of the Poroths—and after seeing the way she snarls at the other cats when they get in her way, I decided to keep my distance. Fortunately she's scared of me and retreats whenever I approach. I think being spayed is what's messed her up and given her an evil disposition.

Sounds are drifting from the farmhouse. I can vaguely make out a psalm of some kind. It's late, past eleven, and I guess the Poroths have turned off the TV and are singing their evening devotions. And now all is silence. They've gone to bed. I'm not very tired yet, so I guess I'll stay up a while and read some—

Something odd just happened. I've never heard anything like it. While writing for the past half hour I've been aware, if half-consciously, of the crickets. Their regular chirping can be pretty soothing, like the sound of a well-tuned machine. But just a few seconds ago they seemed to miss a beat! They'd been singing along steadily, ever since the moon came up, and all of a sudden they just *stopped* for a beat—and then they began again, only they were out of rhythm for a moment or two, as if a hand had jarred the record, or there'd been some kind of momentary break in the natural flow. . . .

They sound normal enough now, though. Think I'll start rereading *Otranto* and let that put me to sleep. It may be the foundation of the English Gothics, but I can't imagine anyone actually reading it for pleasure. I wonder how many pages I'll be able to get through before I drop off. . . .

June 12

Slept late this morning, and then, disinclined to read Walpole on such a sunny day, took a walk. Followed the little brook that runs past my building. There's still a lot of that greenish scum clogging one part of it, and if we don't have some rain soon I expect it will get worse. But the water clears up considerably when it runs past the cornfield and through the woods.

Passed Sarr out in the field—he yelled to watch out for the copperhead, which put a pall on my enthusiasm for exploration. . . . But as it happened I never ran into any snakes, and have a fair idea I'd survive even if bitten. Walked around half a mile into the woods, branches snapping in my face. Made an effort to avoid walking into the little yellow caterpillars that hang from every tree. At one point I had to get my feet wet because the trail that runs alongside the brook disappeared and the undergrowth was thick. Ducked under a low arch made by decaying branches and vines, my sneakers sloshing in the water. Found that as the brook runs west it forms a small circular pool with banks of wet sand, surrounded by tall oaks, their roots thrust into the water. Lots of animal tracks in the sand—deer, I believe, and what may be a fox or perhaps some farmer's dog. Obviously a watering place. Waded into the center of the pool—it only came up a little past my ankles—but didn't stand there long because it started looking like rain.

The weather remained nasty all day, but no rain has come yet. Cloudy now, though; can't see any stars.

Finished *Otranto,* began *The Monk.* So far so good—rather dirty, really. Not for today, of course, but I can imagine the sensation it must have caused back at the end of the eighteenth century.

Had a good time at dinner tonight, since Sarr had walked into town and brought back some wine. (Medical note: I seem to be less allergic to cats when mildly intoxicated.) We sat around the kitchen afterward playing poker for matchsticks—very sinful indulgence, I understand; Sarr and Deborah told me, quite seriously, that they'd have to say some extra prayers tonight by the way of apology to the Lord.

Theological considerations aside, though, we all had a good time and Deborah managed to clean us both out. Women's intuition, she says. I'm sure she must have it—she's the type. Enjoy being around her, and not always so happy to trek back outside, through the high grass, the night dew, the things in the soil. . . . I've got to remember, though, that they're a couple, I'm the single one, and I mustn't intrude too long. So left them, tonight, at eleven—or actually a little after that, since their clock has gone off a little. They have this huge grandfather-type clock, a wedding present from Sarr's parents, that has supposedly been keeping perfect time for a century or more. You can hear its ticking all over the house, when everything else is still. Deborah said that last night, just as they were going to bed, the clock seemed to slow down a little, then gave a couple of faster beats and started in as before. Sarr, who's pretty good with mechanical things, examined it, but said he saw nothing wrong. Well, I guess everything's got to wear out a bit, after years and years.

Back to *The Monk.* May Brother Ambrosio bring me pleasant dreams.

June 13

Read a little in the morning, loafed during the afternoon. At 4:30 watched *The Thief of Bagdad*—ruined on TV and portions omitted, but still a great film. Deborah puttered around the kitchen and Sarr spent most of the day outside. Before dinner I went out back with a scissors and cut away a lot of ivy that has tried to grow through the windows of my building. The little shoots fasten onto the screens and really cling.

Beef with rice tonight, and apple pie for dessert. Great. I stayed inside the house after dinner to watch the late news with the Poroths. The announcer mentioned that today was Friday the Thirteenth, and I nearly gasped: not only hadn't I known it was the thirteenth—I hadn't even known it was Friday. That's how much I've lost track of time out here. Fine feeling, really, though at certain times this isolation makes me feel somewhat adrift. I'd been so used to living by the clock and the calendar. . . .

We tried to figure out if anything unlucky happened to any of us today. About the only incident any of us could come up with was Sarr's getting bitten by some animal the cat had left on the porch. The cats had been sitting by the front door waiting to come in for dinner, and when Sarr came in from the fields he was greeted with the usual assortment of dead mice and moles. As he always did, he began gingerly picking the bodies up by the tails and tossing them into the garbage can, meanwhile scolding the cats for being such natural-born killers. There was one body, he told us, that looked different from the others he'd seen: rather like a large shrew, only the mouth was somehow askew, almost as if it were vertical instead of horizontal, with a row of little yellow teeth exposed. He figured that, whatever it was, the cats had pretty well mauled it, which probably accounted for its unusual appearance, it was quite tattered and bloody by this time.

In any case, he'd bent down to pick it up and the thing had bitten him on the thumb. Apparently it had just been feigning death, like an opossum, because as soon as he yelled and dropped it the thing ran off into the grass, with Bwada and the rest in hot pursuit. Deborah had been afraid of rabies—always a real danger round here, rare though it is— but apparently the bite hadn't even pierced the skin. Just a nip, really. Hardly a Friday-the-Thirteenth tragedy.

Lying in bed now listening to sounds in the woods. The trees come really close to my windows on one side and there's always some kind of sound coming from the underbrush in addition to the tapping at the screens. A million creatures out there, after all—most of them insects and spiders, a colony of frogs in the swampy part of the woods, and perhaps even skunks and raccoons. Depending on your mood, you can either ignore the sounds and just go to sleep or—as I'm doing now—remain awake listening to them. When I lie here thinking about what's out there, I feel more protected with the light off. So I guess I'll put away this writing. . . .

June 15

Something really weird happened today. I still keep trying to figure it out.

Sarr and Deborah were gone almost all day. Sunday worship is, I guess, the center of their religious activity; they walked into Gilead early in the morning and didn't return till after four. They'd left, in fact, before I woke up. Last night they'd asked me if I'd like to come along, but I got the impression they'd invited me mainly to be polite, and so I declined. I wouldn't want to make them uncomfortable during services, but perhaps someday I'll accompany them anyway, since I'm curious to see a fundamentalist church in action.

In any case, I was left to share the farm with the Poroths' seven cats and the four hens they'd bought last week. From my window I could see Bwada and Phaedra chasing after something near the barn; lately they'd taken to stalking grasshoppers. As I do every morning, I went into the farmhouse kitchen and made myself some breakfast, leafing through one of the Poroths' religious magazines, and then returned to my rooms out back for some serious reading. I picked up *Dracula* again, which I'd started yesterday, but the soppy Victorian sentimentality began to annoy me; the book had begun so well, on such a frightening note—Jonathan Harker trapped in that Carpathian castle, inevitably the prey of its terrible owner—that when Stoker switched the locale to England and his main characters to women he simply couldn't sustain that initial tension.

With the Poroths gone I felt a little lonely and bored, something I hadn't felt out here yet. Though I'd brought shelves of books to entertain me, I felt restless and wished I owned a car; I'd have gone for a drive, perhaps visited friends at Princeton. As things stood, though, I had nothing to do except watch television or take a walk.

I followed the stream again into the woods and eventually came to the circular pool. There were some new animal tracks in the wet sand and, ringed by oaks, the place was very beautiful, but still I felt bored. Again I waded into the center of the water and looked up at the sky through the trees. Feeling myself alone, I began to make some of the odd signs with face and hands that I had that evening in the tree—but I felt that these movements had been unaccountably robbed of their power. Standing there up to my ankles in water, I felt foolish.

Worse than that, upon leaving it I found a red-brown leech clinging to my right ankle. It wasn't large and I was able to scrape it off with a stone, but it left me with a little round bite that oozed blood and a feeling of—how shall I put it?—physical helplessness. I felt that the woods had somehow become hostile to me and, more important, would forever remain hostile. Something has passed.

I followed the stream back to the farm, and there I found Bwada, lying on her side near some rocks along its bank. Her legs were stretched out as if she were running, and her eyes were wide and astonished-looking. Flies were crawling over them.

She couldn't have been dead for long, since I'd seen her only a few hours before, but she was already stiff. There was foam around her jaws.

I couldn't tell what had happened to her until I turned her over with a stick and saw, on the side that had lain against the ground, a gaping red hole that opened like some new orifice. The skin around it was folded back in little triangular flaps, exposing the pink flesh beneath. I backed off in disgust, but I could see even from several feet away that the hole had been made *from the inside*.

I can't say I was very upset at Bwada's death, because I'd always hated her. What did upset me, though, was the manner of it—I can't figure out what could have done that to her. I vaguely remember reading about a kind of slug that, when eaten by a bird, will bore its way out through the bird's stomach. . . . But I'd never heard of something like this happening with a cat. And far stranger than that, how could . . .

Well, anyway, I saw the body and said, Good riddance. But I didn't know what to do with it. Looking back, of course, I wish I'd buried it right there. . . . But I didn't want to go near it again. I considered walking into town and trying to find the Poroths, because I knew their cats were like children to them, even Bwada, and that they'd want to know right away. But I really didn't feel like running around Gilead asking strange people where the Poroths were—or, worse yet, stumbling into their forbidding-looking church in the middle of a ceremony. . . .

Finally I made up my mind to simply leave the body there and pretend I'd never seen it. Let Sarr discover it himself. I didn't want to have to tell him when he got home that his pet had been killed, for I prefer to avoid unpleasantness. Besides, I felt strangely guilty, the way I often do after someone else's misfortune.

So I spent the rest of the afternoon reading in my room, slogging through the Stoker. I wasn't in the best mood to concentrate. Sarr and Deborah got back after four—they shouted hello and went into the house. When Deborah shouted for dinner, they still hadn't come outside.

All the cats except Bwada were inside having their evening meal when I entered the kitchen, and Sarr asked me if I'd seen her during the day. I lied and said I hadn't. Deborah suggested that occasionally Bwada ignored the supper call because, unlike the other cats, she sometimes ate what she killed and might simply be full. That rattled me a bit, but I had to stick to my lie.

Sarr seemed more concerned than Deborah, and when he told her he intended to search for the cat after dinner (it would still be light), I readily offered my help. I figured I could lead him to the spot where the body lay. . . .

And then, in the middle of our dinner, came that scratching at the door. Sarr got up and opened it. Bwada walked in.

Now I know she was dead. She was *stiff* dead. That wound in her side had been huge, and now it was only . . . a reddish swelling. Hairless. Luckily the Poroths didn't notice my shock; they were busy fussing over her, seeing what was wrong. "Look, she's hurt herself," said Deborah. "She's bumped into something." The animal didn't walk well, and there was a clumsiness in the way she held herself. When Sarr put her down after examining the swelling, she slipped when she tried to walk away.

The Poroths concluded that she had run into a rock or some other object and had badly bruised herself; and now they believe her lack of coordination is due to the shock, or perhaps a pinching of the nerves. That sounds logical enough. Sarr told me before I came out here for the night that if she's worse tomorrow he'll take her to the local vet, even though he'll have trouble paying for treatment. I immediately offered to lend him money, or even pay for the visit myself, because I desperately want to hear a doctor's opinion.

My own conclusion is really not that different from Sarr's. I tend to think now that maybe, just maybe, I was wrong in thinking the cat dead. Maybe what I mistook for rigor mortis was some kind of fit—after all, I know almost nothing about medicine. Maybe she really did run into something sharp, and then went into some kind of shock . . . whose effect hasn't yet worn off. Is this possible?

But I could swear that hole came from inside her.

I couldn't continue dinner and told the Poroths my stomach hurt, which was partly true. We all watched Bwada stumble around the kitchen floor, ignoring the food Deborah put before her as if it weren't there. Her movements were stiff, tentative, like a newborn animal still unsure how to move its muscles. I guess that's the result of her fit.

When I left the house tonight, a little while ago, she was huddled in the corner staring at me. Deborah was crooning over her, but she was staring at me.

Killed a monster of a spider behind my suitcase tonight. That Ortho spray really does a job. When Sarr was in here a few days ago he said the room smelled of spray, but I guess my allergy's too bad for me to smell it.

I enjoy watching the zoo outside my screens. Put my face close and stare the bugs eye to eye. Zap the ones whose faces I don't like with my spray can.

Tried to read more of the Stoker book—but one thing keeps bothering me. The way that cat stared at me. Deborah was brushing its back, Sarr fiddling with his pipe, and that cat just stared at me and never blinked. I stared back, said, "Hey, Sarr? Look at Bwada. That damned cat's not blinking." And just as he looked up, it blinked. Heavily.

Hope we can go to the vet tomorrow, because I want to ask him whether cats can impale themselves on a rock or a stick, and if such an accident might cause a fit of some kind that would make them rigid.

Cold night. Sheets are damp and the blanket itches. Wind from the woods—ought to feel good in the summer, but it doesn't feel like summer.

That damned cat didn't blink till I mentioned it.

Almost as if it understood me.

June 17

. . . Swelling on her side's all healed now. Hair growing back over it. She walks fine, has a great appetite, shows affection to the Poroths. Sarr says her recovery demonstrates how Lord watches over animals, affirms his faith. Says if he'd taken her to a vet he'd just have been throwing away money.

Read some LeFanu. "Green Tea," about the phantom monkey with eyes that glow, and "The Familiar," about the little staring man who drives the hero mad. Not the smartest choice right now, the way I feel, because for all the time that fat grey cat purrs over the Poroths, it just stares at me. And snarls. I suppose the accident may have addled its brain a bit. I mean, if spaying can change a cat's personality, certainly a goring on a rock might. . . .

Spent a lot of time in the sun today. The flies made it pretty hard to concentrate on the stories, but figured I'd get a suntan. I probably have a good tan now (hard to tell because the mirror in here is small and the light dim), but suddenly it occurs to me that I'm not going to be seeing anyone for a long time anyway, except for the Poroths, and so what the hell do I care how I look?

Can hear them singing their nightly prayers now. A rather comforting sound, I must admit, even if I can't share the sentiments.

Petting Felix today—my favorite of the cats, real charm—came away with a tick on my arm which I didn't discover till taking a shower before dinner. As a result, I can still feel imaginary ticks crawling up and down my back. Damned cat.

June 21

. . . Coming along well with the Victorian stuff. Zipped through "The Uninhabited House" and "Monsieur Maurice," both very literate, sophisticated. Deep into the terrible suffering of "The Amber Witch," poor priest and daughter near starvation, when Deborah called me in for dinner. Roast beef, with salad made from garden lettuce. Quite good. And

Deborah was wearing one of the few sleeveless dresses I've seen on her. So she has a body after all. . . . Positively festive!

A rainy night. Hung around the house for a while reading in their living room while Sarr whittled and Deborah crocheted. Rain sounded better from in there than it does out here where it's not so cozy. . . .

At eleven we turned on the news, cats purring around us, Sarr with Zoë on his lap, Deborah petting Phaedra, me sniffling. . . . Halfway through press conference I pointed to Bwada, curled up at my feet, said, "Look at her. You'd think she was watching the news with us." Deborah laughed, leaned over to scratch Bwada behind the ears. As she did so, Bwada turned to look at me.

The rain is letting up slightly. I can still hear the dripping from the trees, leaf to leaf to the dead leaves lining the forest floor. It will probably continue on and off all night. Occasionally I think I hear thrashings in one of the oaks near the barn, but then the sound turns into the falling of the rain.

Mildew higher on the walls of this place. Glad my books are on shelves off the ground. So damp in here my envelopes were ruined—glue moistened, sealing them all shut. Stamps that had been in my wallet are stuck to the dollar bills. At night my sheets are clammy and cold, but each morning I wake up sweating.

Finished "The Amber Witch," really fine. Would that all lives had such happy endings.

June 22

. . . When Poroths returned from church, helped them prepare strips of molding for the upstairs study. Worked out in the tool shed, one of the old wooden outbuildings. I measured, Sarr sawed, Deborah sanded. All in all, hardly felt useful, but what the hell?

While they were busy I sat staring out window. There's a narrow cement walk running from the shed to the main house, and, as was their habit, Minnie and Felix, two of the kittens, were crouched in the middle of it taking in the late afternoon sun. Suddenly Bwada appeared on the house's front porch and began slinking along the cement path in our direction, tail swishing from side to side. When she neared the kittens she gave a snarl—I could see her mouth working—and they leaped to their feet, bristling, and ran off into the grass.

Called this to Poroths' attention. They said, in effect, Yes, we know, she's always been nasty to the kittens, probably because she never could have any of her own. And besides, she's getting old.

When I turned back to the window, Bwada was gone. Asked the Poroths if they didn't think she'd gotten worse lately. Realized that, in speaking, I'd unconsciously dropped my voice, as if someone might be listening through the chinks in the floorboards.

Deborah conceded that, yes, the cat was behaving worse these days toward the others. And not just toward the kittens, as before. Butch, the adult orange male, seemed particularly afraid of her. . . .

Am a little angry at the Poroths. Will have to tell them when I see them tomorrow morning. They claim they never come into these rooms, respect privacy of a tenant, etc. etc., but one of them must have been in here because I've just noticed my can of insect spray is missing. I don't mind their borrowing it, but I like to have it by my bed on nights like this. Went over room looking for spiders just in case; had a fat copy of *American Scholar* in my hand to crush them (only thing it's good for). But found nothing.

Tried to read more of the Bierce, but found my eyes too irritated, watery. Keep scratching them as I write this. Nose pretty clogged, too—the damned allergy's worse tonight. Perhaps because of the dampness. I'll probably have trouble getting to sleep.

June 24

Slept very late this morning because the noise from the woods kept me up late last night. (Come to think of it, the Poroths' praying was unusually loud last night, but that wasn't what bothered me.) I'd been in the middle of writing in this journal—some thoughts on Bierce—when it came. I immediately stopped writing and shut off the light.

At first it sounded like something in the woods near my room—an animal? a child? I couldn't tell, but smaller than a man—shuffling through the dead leaves, kicking them around as if it didn't care who heard it. There was the snapping of branches and, every so often, a silence and then a bump, as if it were hopping over fallen logs. I stood in the dark listening to it, then crept to the window and looked out. Thought I noticed some bushes moving, back there in the undergrowth, but it may have been the wind.

The sound grew farther away. Whatever it was must have been walking directly out into the deepest part of the woods, where the ground gets swampy and treacherous, because, very faintly, I could hear the sucking sounds of feet slogging through that mud.

I stood by the window for almost an hour, occasionally hearing what I thought were movements off there in the swamp, but finally all was quiet except for the crickets and the frogs. I had no intention of going out there with my flashlight in search of the intruder—that's for guys in stories, I'm much too chicken—and I wondered if I should call Sarr. But by this time the noise had stopped and whatever it was had obviously moved on. Besides, I tend to think he'd have been angry if I'd awakened him and Deborah because some stray dog had wandered near the farm. I recalled how annoyed he'd been earlier that day when—maybe not all that tactfully—I'd asked him what he'd done with my bug spray. (Must remember to walk into town tomorrow and pick up a can. Still can't figure out where I misplaced mine.)

I went over to the windows on the other side and watched the moonlight on the barn for a while; my nose probably looked crosshatched from pressing against the screen. In contrast to the woods, the grass looked peaceful under the full moon. Then I lay in bed, but had a hard time falling asleep. Just as I was getting relaxed the sounds started again. High-pitched wails and caterwauls, from deep within the woods. Even after thinking about it all today, I still don't know whether the noise was human or animal. There were no actual words, of that I'm certain, but nevertheless there was the impression of *singing*. In a crazy, tuneless kind of way the sound seemed to carry the same solemn rhythm of the Poroths' prayers earlier that night.

The noise only lasted a minute or two, but I lay awake till the sky began to get lighter. Probably should have read a little more Bierce, but was reluctant to turn on the lamp. Slept all morning and, in the afternoon, followed the road the opposite direction from Gilead, seeking anything of interest. But the road gets muddier and muddier till it disappears altogether by the ruins of an old homestead—rocks and cement covered with moss—and it looked so much like poison ivy around there I didn't want to risk tramping through.

At dinner (pork chops, home-grown stringbeans, and pudding—quite good) mentioned the noise of last night. Sarr acted very concerned and went to his room to look up something in one of his books; Deborah and I discussed the matter at some length and concluded that the shuffling sounds weren't necessarily related to the wailing. The former were almost definitely those of a dog—dozens in the area, and they love to prowl around at night, exploring, hunting coons—and as for the wailing . . . well, it's hard to say. She thinks it may have been an owl or whippoorwill, while I suspect it may have been that same stray dog. I've heard the howl of wolves and I've heard hounds baying at the moon, and both have the same element of, I suppose, *worship* in them that these did.

Sarr came back downstairs and said he couldn't find what he'd been looking for. Said that when he moved into this farm he'd had "a fit of piety" and had burned a lot of old books he'd found in the attic; now he wishes he hadn't.

Looked up something on my own after leaving the Poroths. *Mammals*

(Golden Nature Guide) lists both red and grey foxes and, believe it or not, coyotes as surviving here in New Jersey. No wolves left, though—but the guide might be wrong.

Then, on a silly impulse, opened another reference book, Barbara Byfield's *Glass Harmonica*. (Beautiful woman, beautiful book.) Sure enough, my hunch was right: looked up June 23rd and it said, "St. John's Eve. Sabbats likely."

I'll stick to the natural explanation. Still, I'm glad Mrs. Byfield lists nothing for tonight; I'd like to get some sleep. There is, of course, a beautiful full moon—werewolf weather, as Maria Ouspenskaya might have said. But then, there are no wolves left in New Jersey. . . . Which reminds me, I really must read some Frederick Marryat. But only after *Northanger Abbey;* my course always comes first.

June 25

. . . After returning from town, the farm looked very lonely. Wish they'd had a library in Gilead with more than religious tracts. Or a stand that sold the *Times*. (Though it's strange how, after a week or two, you no longer miss it.)

Overheated from walk—am I getting out of shape? Or is it just the hot weather? Took a cold shower. When I opened the bathroom door I accidentally let Bwada out—I'd wondered why the chair was propped against it. She raced into the kitchen, pushed open the screen door by herself, and I had no chance to catch her. (Wouldn't have attempted to anyway; her claws are wicked.) I apologized later when Deborah came in from the fields. She said Bwada had become vicious toward the other cats and that Sarr had confined her to the bathroom as punishment. The first time he'd shut her in there, Deborah said, the cat had gotten out; apparently she's smart enough to turn the doorknob by swatting at it a few times. Hence the chair.

Sarr came in carrying Bwada, both obviously out of temper. He'd seen a streak of orange running through the field toward him, followed by a grey blur. Butch had stopped at his feet and Bwada had pounced on him, but before she could do any damage Sarr had grabbed her around the neck and had carried her back here. He'd been bitten once and scratched a lot on his hands, but not badly; maybe the cat still likes him best. He threw her back in the bathroom and shoved the chair against the door, then sat down and asked Deborah to join him in some silent prayer. I thumbed uneasily through a religious magazine till they were done and we sat down to dinner.

I apologized again but he said he wasn't mad at me, that the Devil had gotten into his cat. It was obvious he meant that quite literally. During dinner (omelet—the hens have been laying well) we heard a grating sound from the bathroom, and Sarr ran in to find her almost out the window; we can't figure out how, but somehow she was strong enough to slide it up partway. She seemed so placid, though, when Sarr pulled her down from the sill—he'd been expecting another fight—that he let her out into the kitchen. At this she simply curled up near the stove and went to sleep, so I guess she'd worked off her rage for the day. The other cats gave her a wide berth, though.

Watched a couple of hours of television with the Poroths. They may have gone to college, but the shows they find interesting . . . God! I'm ashamed of myself for sitting there like a cretin in front of that box. I won't even mention what shows we watched, lest history record the true abysmality of my tastes.

And yet I find the TV draws us closer together, as if we were having an adventure together. Shared experience, really. Like knowing the same people or going to the same school.

But there's a lot of duplicity in those Poroths—and I don't mean just religious hypocrisy, either. Came out here after watching the news, and though I hate to accuse anyone of spying on me, there's no doubt that Sarr or Deborah has been inside this room today. I began tonight's entry with great irritation because I found my desk in disarray; this journal wasn't even put back in the right drawer. I keep all my pens on one side, all my pencils on another, ink and erasers in the middle, etc., and when I sat down tonight I saw that everything was out of place. Thank God I haven't included anything too personal in here. . . . What I assume happened was that Deborah came in to wash the mildew off the walls—she's mentioned doing so several times, and she knew I'd be in town part of the day—and got sidetracked into reading this, thinking it must be some kind of secret diary. (I'm sure she was disappointed to find that it's merely a literary journal, with nothing about her in it.)

What bugs me is the difficulty of broaching the subject. I can't just walk in and charge Deborah with being a sneak—Sarr is moody enough as it is—and even if I hint at "someone messing up my desk" they'll know what I mean and perhaps get angry. Whenever possible I prefer to avoid unpleasantness. I guess the best thing to do is simply hide this book under my mattress from now on and say nothing. If it happens again, though, I'll definitely move out of here.

. . . I've been reading some *Northanger Abbey*. Really quite witty, as all her stuff is, but it's obvious the mock-Gothic bit isn't central to the story. I'd thought it was going to be a real parody. . . . Love stories always tend to bore me, and normally I'd be asleep right now, but my damned nose is so clogged tonight that it's hard to breathe when I lie back. Usually being out here clears it up. I've used this goddamned inhaler a dozen times in the past hour, but within a few minutes I sneeze and have to use it again. Wish Deborah'd gotten around to cleaning off the mildew instead of wasting her time looking in here for True Confessions and deep dark secrets. . . .

Think I hear something moving outside. Best to shut off my light.

June 30

Slept late. Read some Shirley Jackson stories over breakfast, but got so turned off at her view of humanity I switched to old Aleister Crowley, who at least keeps a sunny disposition. For her, people in the country are callously vicious, those in the city are callously vicious, husbands are (of course) callously vicious, and children are merely sadistic. The only ones with feelings are her put-upon middle-aged heroines, with whom she obviously identifies. I guess if she didn't write so brilliantly the stories wouldn't sting so.

Inspired by Crowley, walked back to the pool in the woods. Had visions of climbing a tree, swinging on vines, anything to commemorate his exploits. . . . Saw something dead floating in the center of the pool and ran back to the farm. Copperhead? Caterpillar? It had somehow opened up. . . .

Joined Sarr chopping stakes for tomatoes. Could hear his ax all over the farm. Told me Bwada hadn't come home last night and no sign of her this morning. Good riddance, as far as I'm concerned. Helped him chop some stakes, while he was busy peeling off bark. That ax can get heavy fast! My arm hurt after three lousy stakes, and Sarr had already chopped fifteen or sixteen. Must start exercising. But I'll wait till my arm's less tired. . . .

July 2

Unpleasant day. Two A.M. now and still can't relax.

Sarr woke me up this morning—stood at my window calling "Jeremy . . . Jeremy . . ." over and over very quietly. (Civilized.) He had his .22 in one hand. Asked me to help with a burial.

Last night, after he and Deborah had gone to bed, they'd heard noise of kitchen door opening and someone entering house. They both assumed it was me, come to use the bathroom, but then they heard the cats screaming. Sarr ran down, switched on light in time to see Bwada on top of Butch, claws in his side, fangs buried in back of neck. From the way he described it, sounds almost sexual in reverse. Butch had stopped struggling and Minnie, the orange kitten, was already dead. The door was partly open, and when Bwada saw Sarr, she ran out.

Sarr and Deborah hadn't followed her, had spent night praying over bodies of Minnie and Butch. I *thought* I'd heard their voices late last night, but that's all I heard, probably because I'd been been playing my radio. (Something I rarely do—you can't hear noises from woods with it on.)

Poroths took deaths the way they'd take the death of a child. Regular little funeral service over by the unused pasture, with Sarr and Deborah dressed in mourning (though they always dress close to that). I must say I didn't fell particularly involved—my allergy's never permitted me to take much interest in cats, though I'm fond of Felix—but I tried to act concerned: when Sarr asked, appropriately, "Is there no balm in Gilead? Is there no physician there?" (Jeremiah VIII:22), I nodded gravely. Read passages out of Deborah's Bible (Sarr seemed to know all by heart), said amen when they did, knelt when they knelt, and tried to comfort Deborah when she cried. Asked her if cats could go to heaven, received a tearful "Of course." But Sarr added that Bwada would burn in hell.

What concerned me, apparently a lot more than it did either of them, was how the damned thing could get into the house. Sarr gave me this stupid, earnest answer: "She was always a smart cat." Like an outlaw's mother, still proud of her baby. . . .

Yet he and I looked all over the land for her so he could kill her. Barns, tool shed, old stables, garbage dump, etc. He called her and pleaded with her, swore to me she hadn't always been like this.

We could hardly check every tree on the farm—unfortunately—and the woods are a perfect hiding place even for animals larger than a cat. So naturally we found no trace of her. But we did try; even walked up the road as far as the ruined homestead.

But for all that, we could have stayed much closer to home. . . .

We returned for dinner, and I stopped at my room to change clothes. My door was open. Nothing inside was ruined, everything was in its place and as it should be, except the bed. The sheets were in tatters right down to the mattress, and the pillow had been ripped to shreds. Feathers were all over the floor. There were even claw marks on my blanket.

At dinner the Poroths demanded they be allowed to pay for the damage—nonsense, they have enough to worry about—and Sarr suggested I sleep downstairs in their living room. Explained to him that, no problem, I've got lots more sheets; but he said no, he didn't mean that: he meant for my own protection. He believes the thing is particularly inimical, for some reason, toward me.

It seemed so absurd at the time . . . I mean, nothing but a big fat grey cat. But now, sitting out here, a few feathers still scattered on the floor around my bed, I wish I were back inside the house. I did give in to Sarr when he insisted I take his ax with me. . . . But what I'd rather have is simply a room without windows.

I don't think I want to go to sleep tonight, which is one reason I'm continuing to write this. Just sit up all night on my new bedsheets, my back against the Poroths' pillow, leaning against the wall behind me, the ax beside me on the bed, this journal on my lap. . . . The thing is, I'm rather tired out from all the walking I did today. Not used to that much exercise.

I'm pathetically aware of every sound. At least once every five minutes some snapping of a branch or rustling of leaves makes me jump. . . . "Thou art my hope in the day of evil." At least that's what the man said. . . .

July 3

Woke up this morning with the journal and the ax cradled in my arms. What awakened me was the trouble I had breathing—nose all clogged, sneezing a lot. Down the center of one of my screens, facing the woods, was a huge slash. . . .

July 15

Pleasant day, St. Swithin's Day—and yet, my birthday. Thirty years old, lordy lordy lordy. Today I am a man. First dull thoughts on waking: "Damnation. Thirty today." But another voice inside me, smaller but more sensible, spat contemptuously at such an artificial way of charting time. "Ah, don't give it another thought," it said. "You've still got plenty of time to fool around." Advice I took to heart.

Weather today? Actually, somewhat nasty. And thus the weather for the next forty days, since "If rain on St. Swithin's Day, forsooth, no summer drouthe," or something like that. My birthday predicts the weather. It's even mentioned in *The Glass Harmonica*.

As one must, took a critical self-assessment. First area for improvement; flabby body. Second? Less bookish, perhaps? Nonsense—I'm satisfied with the progress I've made. "And seekest thou great things for thyself? Seek them not." (Jeremiah XLV:5) So I simply did what I remembered from the RCAF exercise series and got good and winded. Flexed my stringy muscles in the shower, certain I'll be a Human Dynamo by the end of the summer. Simply a matter of willpower.

Was so ambitious I trimmed the ivy around my windows again. It's begun to block the light, and someday I may not be able to get out the door.

Read Ruthven Todd's *Lost Traveller*. Merely the narrative of a dream turned to nightmare, and illogical as hell. Wish, too, that there'd been more than merely a few hints of sex. On the whole, rather unpleasant; that gruesome ending is so inevitable. . . . Took me much of the afternoon. And then, came upon an incredible essay by Lafcadio Hearn, something entitled "Gaki," detailing the curious Japanese belief that insects are really demons, or the ghosts of evil men. Uncomfortably convincing!

Dinner late because Deborah, bless her, was baking me a cake. Had time to walk into town and phone my parents. Happy birthday, happy birthday. Both voiced first worry—am I not getting bored out here? Assured them I still had plenty of books and did not grow tired of reading. "But it's so . . . *secluded* out there," Mom said. "Don't you get lonely?"

Ah, she hadn't reckoned on the inner resources of a man of thirty. How can I get lonely, I asked, when there's still so much to read? Besides, there are the Poroths to talk to.

Then the kicker: Dad wanted to know about the cat. Last time I'd spoken to them it had sounded like a very real danger. "Are you still sleeping inside the farmhouse, I hope?" No, really, I only had to do that for a few days, while it was prowling around at night. Yes, it had killed some chickens—a hen every night, in fact. But there were only four hens, and then it stopped. We haven't had a sign of it in more than a week.

"But what it did to your sheets . . . If you'd been sleeping . . . Such savagery." Yes, that was unfortunate, but there's been no trouble since. Honest. It was only an animal, after all, just a housecat gone a little wild. It posed the same kind of threat as a . . . (I was going to say, logically, wildcat. But for Mom said) nasty little dog. Like Doug Miller's bull terrier. Besides, it's probably miles and miles away by now. Or dead.

They offered to drive out with packages of food, books, a television, but I made it clear I needed nothing. Getting too fat, actually.

Still light when I got back. Deborah had finished the cake, Sarr brought up some wine, and we had a nice little celebration. The two of them being over thirty, they were happy to welcome me to the fold.

It's nice out here. The wine has relaxed me and I keep yawning. It was good to talk to Mom and Dad again. Just as long as I don't dream of *The Lost Traveller*, I'll be content. And happier still if I don't dream at all. . . .

July 30

Well, Bwada is dead—this time for sure. We'll bury her tomorrow. Deborah was hurt, just how badly I can't say, but she managed to fight

Bwada off. Tough woman, though she seems a little shaken. And with good reason.

It happened this way: Sarr and I were in the tool shed after dinner, building more shelves for the upstairs study. Though the fireflies were out, there was still a little daylight left. Deborah had gone up to bed after doing the dishes; she's been tired a lot lately, falls asleep early every night while watching TV with Sarr. He thinks it may be something in the well water.

It had begun to get dark but we were still working. Sarr dropped a box of nails and, while we were picking them up, he thought he heard a scream. Since I hadn't heard anything, he shrugged and was about to start sawing again when—fortunately—he changed his mind and ran off to the house. I followed him as far as the porch, not sure whether to go upstairs, until I heard him pounding on their bedroom door and calling Deborah's name. As I ran up the stairs I heard her say, "Wait a minute. Don't come in. I'll unlock the door . . . soon." Her voice was extremely hoarse, practically a croaking. We heard her rummaging in the closet—finding her bathrobe, I guess—and then she opened the door.

She looked absolutely white. Her long hair was in tangles and her robe buttoned incorrectly. Around her neck she had wrapped a towel, but we could see patches of blood soaking through it. Sarr gasped and carried her over to the bed, shouting at me to bring up some bandages from the bathroom.

When I returned Deborah was lying in bed, still pressing the towel to her throat. I asked Sarr what had happened; it almost looked as if the woman had tried suicide.

He didn't say anything, just pointed to the floor on the other side of the bed. I stepped around for a look. A crumpled grey shape was lying there, half covered by the bedclothes. It was Bwada, a wicked-looking wound in her side. On the floor next to her lay an umbrella. Deborah had killed her with it.

She told us she'd been asleep when she felt something crawl heavily over her face. It had been like a bad dream. She'd tried to sit up, and suddenly Bwada was at her throat, digging in. Luckily Deborah had had the presence of mind to tear the animal off and dash to the closet, where the first weapon she saw was the umbrella. Just as the cat sprang at her again, Deborah said, she'd raised the weapon and lunged. Remarkable woman! The rest sounds incredible to me, but it's probably the sort of crazy thing that happens in moments like this: somehow the cat had impaled itself on the umbrella.

Her voice, as she spoke, was barely more than a whisper. Sarr had to persuade her to remove the towel from her throat; she kept protesting that she wasn't hurt that badly, that the towel had stopped the bleeding. Sure enough, when Sarr finally lifted the cloth from her neck, the wounds proved relatively small, the slash marks already clotting. Thank God that thing didn't really get its teeth in. . . .

My guess—only a guess—is that it had been weakened from days of living in the woods; it was obviously incapable of feeding itself adequately, as I think was proved by the fact that it didn't eat the hens it had killed, just left them dead on the nests. While Sarr dressed Deborah's wounds I pulled back the bedclothes and took a closer look at the animal's body. The fur was matted and patchy. Odd that an umbrella could make a puncture like that—it seemed to come more from inside, as if the skin had been pushed outward. The explanation is simple, of course: it was Deborah's extraordinary good luck to have jabbed the animal precisely in its old wound, which had reopened. Naturally I didn't mention this to Sarr.

He made dinner for us tonight—soup, actually, because he thought that was best for Deborah. Her voice sounded so bad he told her not to strain it any more by talking, at which she nodded and smiled. We both had to help her downstairs, as she was a little weak from shock.

In the morning Sarr will have the doctor out to check for rabies. He'll have to examine the cat, too, so we put the body in the freezer, to preserve it as well as possible. Afterward we'll bury it.

Deborah seemed okay when I left. Sarr was reading through some medical books, and she was just lying on the living room couch gazing at her husband with a look of gratitude—not moving, not saying anything, not even blinking.

I feel quite relieved. God knows how many nights I've lain here thinking every sound I heard was Bwada. I'll feel more relieved, of course, when that demon's safely underground; but I think I can say, at the risk of being melodramatic, that the reign of terror is over.

Hmm, I'm still a little hungry—used to more than soup for dinner. These daily push-ups do burn up energy. I'll probably dream of hamburgers and chocolate layer cakes.

July 31

. . . The doctor collected scrapings from Bwada's teeth and scolded us for doing a poor job of preserving the body. Said storing it in the freezer was a sensible idea (Sarr's) but that we should have done so sooner, since it was already decomposing. The dampness, I imagine, must act fast on dead flesh.

He pronounced Deborah in excellent condition—the marks on her throat are, remarkably, almost healed—but said her reflexes were a little off. Sarr invited him to stay for the burial, but (quite correctly) he declined. He's not a member of their order, doesn't live in the area, and apparently doesn't get along that well with the people of Gilead, many of whom mistrust modern science. (Not that the old geezer sounded very representative of modern science. When I asked him for some good exercises, he said "chopping wood and running down deer.")

Standing under the heavy clouds, Sarr looked like a revivalist minister. His sermon was from Jeremiah XXII:19, "He shall be buried with the burial of an ass." The burial took place far from the graves of Bwada's two victims, and closer to the woods. We sang one song, Deborah just mouthing the words (still mustn't strain throat muscles), Sarr solemnly asked the Lord to look mercifully upon all His creatures, and I muttered an "amen." Then we walked back to the house, Deborah leaning on Sarr's arm; she's still a little stiff.

It was grey the rest of the day and I sat in my room reading *The King in Yellow*. Well, not really *that* book, of course (would that I could): Chambers made up that title himself, didn't he? But that's what the collection is called. . . . That single gimmick—masterful, I admit—seems to be his sole inspiration.

I was disappointed that dinner was again made by Sarr; Deborah was upstairs resting, he said. He sounded concerned, felt there were things wrong with her the doctor had overlooked. We ate our meal in silence, and I came back here immediately after washing the dishes. Feel very drowsy and, for some reason, also rather depressed. It may be the gloomy weather—we are, after all, just animals, more affected by the sun and the seasons than we like to admit. More likely it was the absence of Deborah tonight. Hope she feels better.

Note: The freezer still smells of the cat's body; opened it tonight and got a strong whiff of decay.

August 1

Writing this, breaking habit, in early morning. Went to bed early last night after finishing the entry above, but was awakened around two by sounds coming from the woods. Wailing, deeper than before, followed by a low, guttural monologue. No words, at least that I could distinguish. If frogs could talk . . . For some reason I fell asleep before the sounds ended, so I don't know what followed.

Could very well have been an owl of some kind, and later a large bullfrog. But I quote, without explanation, from *The Glass Harmonica:* "July 31: Lammas Eve. Sabbats likely."

August 4

Little energy to write tonight, and even less to write about. (Come to think of it, I slept most of the day: woke up at eleven, later took an afternoon nap. Alas, senile at thirty!)

Haven't had the energy to clean this place, either. (Writing about work is better than doing it.) The ivy's beginning to cover the windows again, and the mildew's been climbing steadily up the walls. It's like a dark green band that keeps widening. Soon it will reach my books. . . .

Speaking of which, note: Opened M. R. James at lunch today—*Ghost Stories of an Antiquary*—and a silverfish slithered out. Omen?

Played a little game with myself this evening—

I just had one hell of a shock. While writing the above I heard a soft tapping, like nervous fingers drumming on a table, and discovered an enormous spider, biggest of the summer, crawling only a few inches from my ankle. It must have been living behind this desk. . . .

When you can hear a spider walk across the floor, you *know* it's time to keep your socks on. Thank God for insecticide.

Oh, yeah, that game—the What If game. I probably play it too often. (Vain attempt to enlarge realm of the possible? Heighten my own sensitivity? Or merely work myself into an icy sweat?) I pose unpleasant questions for myself, e.g., what if this glorified chicken coop is sinking into quicksand? (Wouldn't be at all surprised.) What if the Poroths are tired of me? What if I woke up inside my own coffin?

What if I never see New York again?

What if some stories in the horror collections aren't fiction? If Machen sometimes told the truth? If there *are* White People, malevolent little faces peering out of the moonlight? Whispers in the grass? Poisonous things in the woods? Hate and evil in the world?

Enough of this foolishness. Time for bed.

August 9

. . . Read some Hawthorne in the morning and, over lunch, reread this week's *Hunterdon County Democrat* for the dozenth time. Sarr and Deborah were working somewhere in the fields and I felt I ought to get some physical activity myself; but the thought of starting my exercises again after more than a week's laziness just seemed too unpleasant. . . .

I took a walk down the road a little way, but only as far as a smashed-up cement culvert half buried in the woods. I was bored, but Gilead just seemed too far away.

Was going to cut the ivy away from my windows when I got back, but decided the place looks more artistic covered in vines. Rationalization?

Chatted with Poroths about politics, The World Situation, a little cosmology, blah blah blah. Dinner wasn't very good, probably because I'd been looking forward to it all day. The lamb was underdone and the beans were cold. Still, I'm always the gentleman, and was almost pleased when Deborah agreed to my offer to do the dishes. I've been doing them a lot lately.

I didn't have much interest in reading tonight and would have been up for some television, but Sarr's gotten into one of his religious kicks lately and began mumbling prayers to himself immediately after dinner. (Deborah, more human, wanted to watch the TV news. She seems to have an insatiable curiosity about world events—yet she claims the isolation here appeals to her.) Absorbed in his chanting, Sarr made me uncomfortable—I didn't like his face—and so after doing the dishes I left.

I've been listening to the radio for the last hour or so. . . . I recall days when I'd have gotten uptight at having wasted an hour—but out here I've lost all track of time. Feel adrift—a little disconcerting, but healthy, I'm sure.

. . . Shut the radio off a moment ago and now realize my room is filled with crickets. Up close their sound is hardly pleasant—cross between a radiator and a tea-kettle, very shrill. They'd been sounding off all night but I'd thought it was interference on the radio.

Now I notice them; they're all over the room. A couple of dozen, I should think. Hate to kill them, really—they're one of the few insects I can stand, along with ladybugs and fireflies. But they make such a racket!

Wonder how they got in. . . .

August 14

Played with Felix all morning—mainly watching him chase insects, climb trees, doze in the sun. Spectator sport. After lunch went back to my room to look up something in Lovecraft, and discovered my books were out of order. This is definitely one of the Poroths' doing; I'm always careful to put them back in alphabetical order by author. Pissed they didn't mention coming in here, but also a little surprised they have any interest in this stuff.

Arranged them correctly and then sat down to reread Lovecraft's essay on "Supernatural Horror in Literature." It upset me to see how little I've actually read, how far I still have to go. So many obscure authors, so many books I've never come across. . . . Left me feeling depressed and tired, so I took a nap for the rest of the afternoon.

Over dinner—vegetable omelet, rather tasteless—Deborah continued to question us on current events. It's getting to be like junior high school, with daily newspaper quizzes. . . . Don't know how she got started on this, or why the sudden interest, but it obviously annoys the hell out of Sarr.

Sarr used to be a sucker for her little-girl pleadings—I remember how he used to carry her upstairs, becoming pathetically tender, the moment she'd say, "Oh, honey, I'm so tired"—but now he just becomes angry. Often he goes off morose and alone to pray, and the only time he laughs is when he watches television.

Tonight, thank God, he was in a mood to forego the prayers, and so after dinner we all watched a lot of offensively ignorant TV programs. I was disturbed to find myself laughing along with the canned laughter, but I have to admit the TV helps us get along better together. Came back here after the news.

Not very tired after sleeping part of the afternoon, so began to read John Christopher's *The Possessors;* but good though it was, my mind began to wander to all the books I *haven't* yet read, and I got so depressed I turned on the radio. Find it takes my mind off things.

August 19

Slept long into the morning, then walked down to the brook, scratching groggily. Deborah was kneeling in front of it daydreaming, and I was embarrassed because I'd come upon her talking to herself. We exchanged a few insincere words and she went back toward the house.

Sat by some rocks, throwing blades of grass into the water. The sun on my head felt almost painful, as if my brain were growing too large for my skull. I turned and looked at the farmhouse. In the distance it looked like a picture at the other end of a large room; the grass was the carpet. Deborah was stroking a cat, then seemed to grow angry when it struggled from her arms; I could hear the screen door slam as she went into the kitchen, but the sound reached me so long after the visual image that the whole scene struck me as, somehow, fake. I gazed up at the oaks behind me and they seemed trees out of a cheap postcard, the kind in which thinly colored paint is dabbed over a black-and-white photograph. If you look closely at them you can see that the green in the trees is not merely in the leaves, but rather floats as a vapor over leaves, branches, parts of the sky. . . . The trees behind me seemed the productions of a poor painter, the color and shape not quite meshing. Parts of the sky were green. . . . Pieces of the green seemed to float away from my vision, no matter how hard I tried I couldn't follow them.

Far down the stream I could see something small and kicking, a black beetle, legs in the air borne swiftly along in the current. Then it was gone.

Thumbing through the Bible while I ate my lunch—mostly cookies. By late afternoon I was playing word games while I lay on the grass near my room. The shrill twitter of the birds, I would say, the birds singing in the sun. . . . And inexorably I'd continue with the sun dying in the moonlight, the moonlight falling on the floor, the floor sagging to the cellar, the cellar filling with water, the water seeping into the ground, the ground twisting into smoke, the smoke staining the sky, the sky burning in the sun, the sun dying in the moonlight, the moonlight falling on the floor . . . Thus the melancholy progressions that held my mind like a whirlpool.

Sarr woke me for dinner; I had dozed off, and my clothes were damp from the grass. As we walked up to the house together he whispered that, earlier in the day, he'd come upon his wife bending over me, peering into my sleeping face. "Her eyes were wide," he said. "Like Bwada's." I said I didn't understand why he was telling me this.

"Because," he recited in a whisper, gripping my arm, "the heart is deceitful above all things, and desperately wicked: who can know it?"

I recognized that. Jeremiah XVII:9.

Dinner was especially uncomfortable; the two of them sat picking at their food, occasionally raising their eyes to one another like children in a staring contest. I longed for the conversations of our early days, inconsequential though they must have been, and wondered where things had first gone wrong.

The meal was dry and unappetizing, but the dessert looked delicious—chocolate mousse, made from an old family recipe. Deborah had served it earlier in the summer and knew both Sarr and I loved it. This time, however, she gave none to herself, explaining that she had to watch her weight.

"Then we'll not eat any!" Sarr shouted, and with that he snatched my dish from in front of me, grabbed his own, and hurled them both against the wall, where they splattered like mudballs.

Deborah was very still; she said nothing, just sat there watching us. She didn't look particularly afraid of this madman, I was happy to see—but *I* was. He may have read my thoughts, because as I got up from my seat he said much more gently, in the soft voice normal to him. "Sorry, Jeremy. I know you hate scenes. We'll pray for each other, all right?"

"Are you okay?" I asked Deborah. "I'm going out now, but I'll stay if you think you'll need me for anything." She stared at me with a slight smile and shook her head. I raised my eyebrows and nodded toward her husband, and she shrugged.

"Things will work out," she said. I could hear Sarr laughing as I shut the door.

When I snapped on the light out here I took off my shirt and stood in front of the little mirror. It had been nearly a week since I'd showered, and I'd become used to the smell of my body. My hair had wound itself into greasy brown curls, my beard was at least two weeks old, and my eyes . . . well, the eyes that stared back at me looked like those of an old man. The whites were turning yellow, like old teeth. I looked at my chest and arms, flabby at thirty, and I thought of the frightening alterations in my friend Sarr, and I knew I'd have to get out of here.

It's now quite late at night. Two-thirty (just glanced at my watch). I've been packing my things.

August 20

I woke about an hour ago and continued packing. Lots of books to put away, but I'm just about done. It's not even nine A.M. yet, much earlier than I normally get up; but I guess the thought of leaving here fills me with a new energy.

The first thing I saw on rising was a garden spider whose body was as big as some of the mice the cats have killed. It was sitting on the ivy that grows over my windowsill—fortunately, on the other side of the screen. Apparently it had had good hunting all summer, preying on the insects that live in the leaves. Concluding that nothing so big and fearsome has a right to live, I held the spray can against the screen and doused the creature with poison. It struggled halfway up the screen, then stopped, arched its legs, and dropped backwards into the ivy.

I plan to walk into town this morning and telephone the office in Flemington where I rented my car. If they can have one ready today I'll hitch there to pick it up; otherwise I'll spend tonight here and pick it up tomorrow. I'll be leaving a little early in the season, but the Poroths already have my month's rent, so they shouldn't be too offended.

And anyway, how could I be expected to stick around here with all that nonsense going on, never knowing when my room might be ransacked, having to put up with Sarr's insane suspicions and Deborah's moodiness?

Before I go into town, though, I really must shave and shower for the good people of Gilead. I've been sitting inside here waiting for some sign the Poroths are up, but as yet—it's almost nine—I've heard nothing. I wouldn't care to barge in on them while they're still having breakfast or, worse, just getting up. . . . So I'll just wait here by the window till I see them.

. . . Ten o'clock now, and they still haven't come out. Perhaps they're making preserves or something. I'll give them half an hour more, then I'm going in.

Here my journal ends. Until today, almost a week later, I have not cared to set down any of the events that followed. But here in the temporary safety of this hotel room, protected by a heavy brass travel-lock I had sent up from the hardware store down the street, watched over by the good people of Flemington—and, perhaps, by something not good—I can continue my narrative.

The first thing I noticed as I approached the house was that the shades were drawn, even in the kitchen. Had they decided to sleep late this morning? I wondered. Throughout my thirty years I have come to associate drawn shades with a foul smell, the smell of a sickroom, of shamefaced poverty and food gone bad, of people lying too long beneath blankets; but I was not ready for the stench of decay that met me when I opened the kitchen door and stepped into the darkness. Something had died in that room—and not recently.

At the moment the smell first hit, four little shapes scrambled across the linoleum toward me and out into the daylight. The Poroths' cats.

By the other wall a lump of shadow moved, a pale face caught light penetrating the shades. Sarr's voice, its habitual softness exaggerated to a whisper: "Jeremy. I thought you were still asleep."

"Can I—

"No. Don't turn on the light." He got to his feet, a black form towering against the window. Fiddling nervously with the kitchen door—the tin doorknob, the rubber bands stored around it, the fringe at the bottom of the drawn window shade—I opened it wider and let in more light. It fell on the dark thing at his feet, over which he had been crouching: Deborah, the flesh of her throat torn and wrinkled like the skin of an old apple.

Her clothing lay in a heap beside her. She appeared long dead. The eyes were shriveled, sunken into sockets black as a skull's.

I think I may have staggered at that moment, because he came toward me. His steady, unblinking gaze looked so sincere—but *why was he smiling?* "I'll make you understand," he was saying, or something like that; even now I feel my face twisting into horror as I try to write of him. "I had to kill her. . . ."

"You—"

"She tried to kill me," he went on, silencing all questions. "The same thing that possessed Bwada . . . possessed her."

My hand played behind my back with the bottom of the window shade. "But her throat—"

"That happened a long time ago. Bwada did it. I had nothing to do with . . . that part." Suddenly his voice rose. "Look, I had to kill her. She tried to stab me with the bread knife." He turned, stooped over and, clumsy in the darkness, began feeling about him on the floor. "Where is that thing?" he was mumbling. "I'll show you. . . ." As he crossed a beam of sunlight something gleamed like a silver handle on the back of his shirt.

Thinking, perhaps, to help him search, I pulled gently on the window shade, then released it; it snapped upward like a gunshot, flooding the room with light. From deep within the center of his back protruded the dull wooden haft of the bread knife, buried almost completely but for an inch or two of gleaming steel.

He must have heard my intake of breath—even as I write this today my hand shakes as I picture that sight, and it is difficult to compose my thoughts—he must have heard me, because immediately he stood, his back to me, and reached up behind himself toward the knife, his arm stretching in vain, his fingers curling around nothing. The blade had been planted in a spot he couldn't reach.

He turned toward me and shrugged in embarrassment, a child caught in a foolish error. "Oh, yeah," he said, grinning at his own weakness, "I forgot it was there."

Suddenly he thrust his face into mine, fixing me in a gaze that never wavered, his eyes wide with candor. "It's easy for us to forget things," he explained—and then, still smiling, still watching, volunteered that last trivial piece of information, that final message whose words released me from inaction and left me free to dash from the room, to sprint in panic down the road, pursued by what had once been the farmer Sarr Poroth.

It serves no purpose here to dwell on my flight down that dirt road, breathing in such deep gasps that I was soon moaning with every breath; how, with my enemy racing behind me, not even winded, his steps never flagging, I veered into the woods; how I finally lost him, perhaps from the inexperience of whatever thing now controlled his body, and was able to make my way back to the road, only to come upon him again as he rounded a bend; his laughter as he followed me, and how it continued long after I had evaded him a second time; and how, after hiding until nightfall in the old cement culvert, I ran the rest of the way in pitch-darkness, stumbling in the ruts, torn by vines, nearly blinding myself when I ran into a low branch, until I arrived in Gilead filthy, exhausted, and almost incoherent.

Suffice to say that my escape was largely a matter of luck, a physical wreck fleeing something oblivious to pain or fatigue; but that, beyond mere luck, I had been impelled by a sense of almost cosmic dread produced by his last words to me, that last communication from an alien face smiling inches from my own, and which I chose to take as his final warning:

"Sometimes we forget to blink."

You can read the rest in the newspapers. The *Hunterdon County Democrat* covered most of the story, though its man wrote it up as merely another lunatic wife-slaying, the result of loneliness, religious mania, and a mysteriously tainted well. (Traces of insecticide were found, among other things, in the water.) The *Somerset Reporter* took a different slant, implying that I had been the third member of an erotic triangle and that Sarr had murdered his wife in a fit of jealousy.

Needless to say, I was by this time past caring what was written about me. I was too haunted by visions of that lonely, abandoned farmhouse, the wails of its hungry cats, and by the sight of Deborah's corpse, discovered by the police, protruding from that hastily dug grave beyond the cornfield.

Accompanied by state troopers, I returned to my ivy-covered outbuilding. A bread knife had been plunged deep into its door, splintering the wood on the other side. The blood on it was Sarr's.

My journal had been hidden under my mattress, and so was untouched, but (I look at them now, piled in cardboard boxes beside my suitcase) my precious books had been thrown onto the floor, their bindings slashed.

My summer is over, and now I sit inside here all day listening to the radio, waiting for the next report. Sarr—or his corpse—has not been found.

I should think the evidence was clear enough to corroborate my story, but I suppose I should have expected the reception it received from the police. They didn't laugh at my theory of "possession"—not to my face, anyway—but they ignored it in obvious embarrassment. Some see a nice young bookworm gone slightly deranged after contact with a murderer; others believe my story to be the desperate fabrication of an adulterer trying to avoid the blame for Deborah's death.

I can understand their reluctance to accept my explanation of the events, for it's one that goes a little beyond the "natural," a little beyond the scientific considerations of motive, *modus operandi,* and fingerprints.

But I find it very unnerving that at least one official—an assistant district attorney, I think, though I'm afraid I'm very ignorant of these matters—believes I am guilty of murder.

There has, of course, been no arrest; still, I've been given the time-honored instructions against leaving town.

The theory proposing my own complicity in the events is, I must admit, rather ingenious—and so carefully worked out that it will surely gain more adherents than my own. This police official is going to try to prove that I killed poor Deborah in a fit of passion and, immediately afterward, disposed of Sarr. He points out that their marriage had been an observably happy one until I arrived, a disturbing influence from the city. My motive, he says, was simple lust—unrequited, to be sure—aggravated by boredom. The heat, the insects, and, most of all, the oppressive loneliness—all constituted an environment alien to any I'd been accustomed to, and all worked to unhinge my reason.

I have no cause to fear, however, for this affidavit will certainly establish my innocence. Surely no one can ignore the evidence of my journal (though I can imagine an antagonistic few proclaiming that I wrote the journal not at the farm but here in the Union Hotel, this very week).

What galls me is not the suspicions of a few detectives, but the predicament their suspicions place me in. Quite simply, *I cannot run away*. I am compelled to remain locked up in this room, potential prey to whatever the thing that was Sarr Poroth has now become—the thing that was once a cat, and once a woman, and once . . . what? A large white moth? A serpent? A shrewlike thing with wicked teeth?

A police chief? A President? A boy with eyes of blood that sits beneath my window?

Lord, who will believe me?

It was that night that started it all, I'm convinced of it now. The night I made those strange signs in the tree. The night the crickets missed a beat.

I'm not a philosopher, and I can supply no ready explanation for why this new evil has been released into the world. I'm only a poor scholar, a bookworm, and I must content myself with mumbling a few phrases that keep running through my mind, phrases out of books read long ago when I thought there was hope for me. I am haunted by scraps from the Pandora's Box myth, and by a semantic discussion I once read comparing "unnatural" and "supernatural."

And something about "a tiny rent in the fabric of the universe. . . ."

Just large enough to let something in. Something not of nature, and hard to kill.

Ironically, the police may be right. Perhaps it was my visit to Gilead that brought about the deaths. Perhaps I had a hand in letting loose the force that has killed two people and will soon kill more.

I've just checked. He hasn't moved from the steps of the courthouse; and even when I look out my window, the rose spectacles never waver. Who knows where the eyes beneath them point? Who knows if they remember to blink?

Lord, this heat is sweltering. My shirt is sticking to my skin, and droplets of sweat are rolling down my face dripping onto this page, making the ink run.

My hand is tired from all this writing, and I think it's time to end this affidavit.

If, as I now believe possible, I inadvertently called down evil from the sky and began the events at Poroth Farm, my death will only be fitting. And after my death, many more. We are all, I'm afraid, in danger. Please, then, forgive this prophet of doom, old at thirty, his last jeremiad: "The harvest is past, the summer is ended, and we are not saved."

STERLING E. LANIER/ *A Father's Tale*

Despite the P. G. Wodehousian flavor of his name, Brigadier Ffellowes is by no means a comic figure. There is nothing of the gentle bumbler about him, he is all skill, full of crafty knowledge, and is in all ways a fit and proper opponent for the terrifying array of fiends and monsters which Sterling E. Lanier has been unkind enough to pit against him through the years.

These stories can be enjoyed with reasonable regularity in the pages of *Fantasy and Science Fiction,* and have been collected in *The Peculiar Exploits of Brigadier Ffellowes,* published by Walker and Company. I hope the following introduction will convince you to further your acquaintance through those channels with this delightfully stalwart soldier.

Sterling E. Lanier

A FATHER'S TALE

"You certainly seem to like the tropics, sir," said a younger member. It was one of the dull summer evenings in the club. The outside fetor in New York City was unbelievable. Heat, accumulated off the sidewalks, hung in the air. Manhattan was hardly a Summer Holiday, despite the claims of its mayor. It was simply New York. The City, a place one had to work in or probably die in.

"I suppose you have a point there," Ffellowes answered. The library was air-conditioned, but all of us who recently had come in from the streets were sweating, with one exception. Our British member was utterly cool, though he had come in after most of us.

"Heat," said Ffellowes, as he took a sip of his Scotch, "is, after all, relative, especially in case. Rela*tives*. I should say."

"But many of your tales, if you'll pardon me, in fact most of them, have been, well—set in the tropics," the young member kept on.

Ffellowes stared coldly at him. "I was not aware, young man, that I had told any *tales*."

At this point, Mason Williams, the resident irritant, who could not let the brigadier alone, exploded. "Hadn't told any tales! Haw-haw, haw-haw!"

To my amazement, and, I may add, to the credit of the new election committee, this piece of rudeness was quashed at once, and by the same younger fellow who had started the whole thing.

He turned on Williams, stared him in the eye, and said, "I don't believe you and I were speaking, sir. I was waiting for Brigadier Ffellowes to comment." Williams shut up like a clam. It was beautiful.

Ffellowes smiled quietly. His feelings about Williams were well-known, if equally unexpressed. A man who'd been in all of Her Majesty's Forces, seemingly including all the intelligence outfits, is hardly to be thrown off gear by a type like Williams. But the defense pleased him.

"Yes," he confessed, "I *do* like the tropics. Always go there when I can. But—and I stress this—it was a certain hereditary bias. I acquired it, one might say, in the genes. You see, my father, and for that matter his, had it as well."

Again the young member stuck his neck out. Those of us, the old crowd, who were praying that we would get a story, simply kept on praying. Ffellowes was not mean, or petty, but he hated questions. But the boy plugged on.

"My God, sir," he bored in, "you mean your father had some of the same kind of weird experiences you've had?"

I don't know to this day why the brigadier, ordinarily the touchiest of men, was so offbeat this evening. But he didn't either dummy up or leave. Maybe, just maybe, he was getting so fed up with Williams he didn't want to let the young fellow down. Anyway, those of us who knew him leaned forward. Of course, Mason Williams did too. He hated Ffellowes but never enough to miss a story, which is, I suppose, an indication that he isn't completely mindless.

"If you care to hear this particular account, gentlemen," began Ffellowes, "you will have to take it second-hand, as it were. I wasn't there myself, and all I know comes from my father. However—he *was* there, and I may say that I will strongly resent [here he did not quite look at Williams] any imputation that he spoke to me anything but the absolute truth." There was silence. Total. Williams had lost too many encounters.

Said Ffellowes, "The whole thing started off the west coast of Sumatra. My father had been doing a spell of service with old Brooke of Sarawak, the second of the so-called White Rajahs, C.V. that would be. Anyway, Dad was on vacation, leave, or what have you. The Brookes, to whom he'd been 'seconded,' as the saying goes, from the Indian Army, were most generous to those who served them. And my father wanted to see a few new areas and get about a bit. This was in the fall of 1881, mind you, when things were different.

"So there he was, coming down the Sumatran coast, in one of Brooke's own private trading *prahus*, captained by old *Dato Burung*, picked crew and all that, when the storm hit.

"It was a bad one, that storm, but he had a largish craft, as those things went, a big *Prau Mayang*, a sort of merchant ship of those waters. No engine, of course, but a sturdy craft, sixty feet long, well capable of taking all the local weathers, save perhaps for a real typhoon, which this was not. They all battened down to ride out the storm. They had no trouble.

"Surely enough, the next morning was calm and clear. And off the lee side, within sight of the green west Sumatran coast, was a wreck. It wasn't much, but the remnants of another *prau*, a *prau bedang*, the local light craft used for fishing, smuggling, and what have you. Ordinarily, this much smaller vessel would have carried two modified lateen sails, or local variants, but now both masts were gone, snapped off at the deck, obviously by the previous night's storm. The fragile hulk was wallowing in the deep milky swells, which were the only trace of the earlier wind.

"My father's ship bore down on her. He had given no orders, but a ship in trouble in these waters was fair game for anyone. Occasionally, hapless folk were even rescued. Dad stood on the quarterdeck in his whites, and that was quite enough to make sure there would be no throat cutting. Forbidding anything else would have been silly. Next to him stood his personal servant, old Umpa. This latter was a renegade Moro from the Sulus, but a wonderful man. He was at least sixty, but as lean and wiry as a boy. Whatever my father did was all right with him, and anything anyone else did was wrong, just so long as my father opposed it, mind you.

"To his surprise, as the bigger craft wore, to come up under the wreck's lee, a hand was raised. Beaten down though the little craft had been, there was someone still left alive. Dad's vessel launched a rowing boat, and in no time the sole survivor of the wreck was helped up to the poop and placed before him. To his further amazement, it was not a Sundanese fisherman who confronted him, but a Caucasian.

"The man was dressed quite decently, in tropical whites, and even had the remnants of a celluloid collar. Aside from the obvious ravages of the sea, it was plain that some time must have passed since the other had known any amenities of civilization. His whites, now faded, were torn at the knees, badly stained with green slime and ripped at various places. His shoes were in an equally parlous condition, almost without soles. Yet, the man still had an air about him. He was tall, a youngish man, sallow and aquiline in feature, with a hawk nose. Despite his rags, he bore himself as a person of consequence. His beard was only a day or two grown.

"'Captain Ffellowes, Second Rajput Rifles, very much at your service,' said my father, as this curious piece of human flotsam stared at him. 'Can I be of some service?'

"The answer was peculiar. 'Never yet, sir, have I failed in a commission. I should not like this occasion to be the first. With your permission, we will go below.' With that, this orphan of the gale fell flat on his face, so quickly that not even my father or the ship's captain could catch him as he slumped.

"They bent, both of them, quickly enough when the man fell. As my father reached down to take his head, the grey eyes opened.

"'At all costs, watch for Matilda Briggs,' said the unknown, in low and quite even tones. The lids shut and the man passed into total and complete unconsciousness. It was obvious to my father that he had only been sustaining himself by an intense effort of will. What the last piece of nonsense meant was certainly obscure. Who on earth was Matilda Briggs, and why should she be sought? As they carried the man below to my father's cabin, he had decided the chap was simply delirious. On the other hand, he was obviously a man of education, and his precise speech betrayed the university graduate. One can be excused of snobbery at this point. There were not so many of this type about in the backwaters of the world in those days, you know, despite what Kipling may have written on the subject. Most educated Englishmen in Southeast Asia had jobs and rather strictured ones at that. The casual drifter or 'remittance man' was a later type than one found in the 1880s, and had to wait for Willie Maugham to portray him.

"Well, my father took his mystery man below; the crew looted the remnants of the little *prau* (and found nothing, I may say, including any evidence of anyone else; they told the skipper that the mad *Orang Blanda* must have taken her out alone); and the White Rajah's ship set sail and continued on her way down the Sumatran coast.

"Dad looked after the chap as best he could. Westerners, Europeans, if you like, though my father would have jibbed at the phrase since he thought that sort of thing began at Calais, did this sort of thing without much thinking then. There were so few of them, you see, surrounded by the great mysterious mass of Asia. Outside the British fief, as the Old Man said, one felt A.C.I., or Asia Closing In. No doubt the feeling of the average G.I. in Viet Nam a few years ago. I know what they meant, having spent enough time out in those regions.

"First, the chap was, as I have said, a lean, tough-looking creature. As he lay there on my father's bed in the stern cabin, even in utter exhaustion and repose, his sharp features were set in commanding lines. His clothes, or rather their remains, which the native servants stripped off at my father's orders, revealed nothing whatsoever of their owner's past. Yet, as the ragged coat was pulled off the tattered shirt, something fell to the cabin deck with a tinkle and a glitter. My father picked it up at once and found himself holding a man's heavy gold ring, set with an immense sapphire of the purest water. Was this the unknown's? Had he stolen it? No papers, and my father made it plain that he felt no compunction in looking for them, were on the castaway's person. Save for the ring, and his rags, he appeared to own nothing.

"For a day, as the *prau* ran slowly down the coast, my father nursed the stranger as tenderly as a woman could have done. There was no fever, but the man's life had almost run out, nonetheless. It was simple exhaustion carried to the nth degree. Whatever the derelict had been doing, he had almost, as you chaps say, 'burned himself out' in the doing of it. Dad sponged and swabbed him, changed his personal linen, and directed the servants he had with him, as they all fought for the man's life. The ship's cook, an inspired Buginese, wrought mightily with the stores at his command, and nourishing soups were forced down the patient's lips, even though he lay in total unconsciousness.

"On the second day, my father was sitting by the man's bed, turning over in his hand the sapphire ring, when he was startled to hear a voice. Looking up, he saw that the patient was regarding both him and also what he held.

"'I once refused an emerald of rather more value,' was the unknown's comment. 'I can assure you, for whatever my assurances are worth, that object that you hold is indeed my personal property and not the loot of some native temple.' The man turned his head and looked out the nearest of the cabin ports within reach. Through it, one could discern the green shoreline in the near distance. He turned back to my father and smiled, though in a curiously icy way.

"'The object you hold, sir, is a recompense for some small services, of the reigning family currently responsible for the archipelago which we appear to be skirting. I should be vastly obliged for its return since it has some small sentimental value.'

"Having no reason to do otherwise, Dad instantly surrendered the ring.

"'My thanks,' was the languid comment. 'I assume that I also have you to thank for my treatment on board this somewhat piratical vessel?'

"The question was delivered in such an insolent tone that my father rose to his feet, ready to justify himself at length. He was waved back to his cushion by a commanding arm. After a pause, the unknown spoke.

"'As an Englishman, and presumably a patriot, I have some small need of your assistance.' The face seemed to brood for a moment, before the man spoke again; then he stared in a glacial way directly at my father, running his gaze from top to toe before speaking again. His words appeared addressed to himself, a sort of soliloquy.

"'Hmm, English, an officer, probably Sandhurst—Woolwich gives one rather less flexibility—on leave, or else extended service; speaks fluent Malay; seconded to some petty ruler as a guide into civilization, perhaps; at any rate, tolerably familiar with the local scene.'

"At this cold-blooded, and quite accurate appraisal (my family has indeed sent its males to Sandhurst for some time), my father continued to sit, waiting for the next comment from his bizarre guest.

"'Sir,' said the other, sitting up as he spoke, and fixing my father with a steely glare, 'you are in a position to assist all of humanity. I flatter myself that never have I engaged in a problem of more importance, and, furthermore, one with no precedents whatsoever. Aside from one vaguely analogous occurrence in Recife, in '77, we are breaking fresh ground.'

"As he delivered this cryptic series of remarks, the man clapped, yes, actually clapped his hands, while his eyes, always piercing, lit up with glee, or some similar emotion. My father decided on the spot that the chap was deranged, if not under the influence of one of those subtle illnesses in which the East abounds. But he was brought back at once by the next question, delivered in the same piercing, almost strident, voice.

"'What is our latitude, sir? How far south have we been taken since I was picked up?' Such was the immense authority conveyed by the strange voyager's personality, that my father had no thought of not answering. Since he himself took the sights with a sextant every dawn, he was able to give an accurate reply at once. The other lay back, obviously in thought.

"Rousing himself after a moment, he seemed to relax, and his chiseled features broke into a pleasant smile as he stared at my father.

"'I fear you think me mad,' he said simply, 'or else ill. But I assure you that I am neither. The Black Formosa Corruption has never touched me, nor yet Tapanuli Fever. I am immune, I fancy, to the miasmas of this coast, though I take no credit for the status. In fact, I believe it to be hereditary. If the world would pay more attention to that forgotten Bohemian monk, Mendel, we should be in a position to learn much . . . but I digress.' Once more he stared keenly at my father, then seemed to come to some private decision.

"'Would you, sir, be good enough to place yourself under my orders for the immediate future? I can promise you danger, great danger, little or no reward, but—and you have my word, which I may say has never yet been called into question—you would be serving your country and indeed all of humanity in aiding me. If what I learnt is any evidence, the entire world, and I am not given to idle speculation, is in the gravest of perils.' He paused again. 'Moreover, I can not at this point take you into my full confidence. It would mean, for the moment, that you would have to follow my instructions without question. Is this prospect of any attraction?'

"My father was somewhat taken aback by this sudden spate of words. Indeed, he was both irritated and impressed, at one and the same time, by the masterful way the stranger played upon him.

"'I should be happy, sir, or rather happier, if I had your name,' he said stiffly. To his complete surprise, the other clapped his hands again and fell back on his couch, laughing softly.

"'Oh, perfect!' The man was genuinely amused. 'Of course, my name would solve everything.' He ceased laughing and sat up in the bed with a quick motion, and once he did so, all humor left the scene.

"'My name is—well, call me Verner. It is the name of a distant connection and bluntly speaking—not my own. But it will serve. As to any other *bona fides*, I fear you will have to forgive me. I simply cannot say more. Again, what do you say to my proposal?'

"My father was somewhat disconcerted by his guest's manners, but—and I stress this—one cannot realize what the circumstances were unless one had been there."

As Ffellowes spoke, and perhaps because he spoke, we *were* there, in the quiet waters off Sumatra, long, long ago. The silence of the library in the club became the silence of the East. Honking taxis, bawling doormen, straining buses, all the normal New York noises heard through our shuttered windows, were gone. Instead, with quickened breathing, we heard the tinkle of *gamilans* and the whine of tropic mosquitoes, the shift of the tide over the reefs, and smelled the pungent scent of frangipani blossoms. I stole one look at Mason Williams and then relaxed. He had his mouth open and was just as hung up as the rest of us. The brigadier continued.

"'I am astounded, sir, at your presumption,' my father said. 'Here you are a—'

"'—veritable castaway and runagate, no doubt the sweepings of some Asian gutter,' finished the other in crisp tones, putting my father's unspoken words into life. 'Nevertheless, what I have said to you is so deadly in earnest that if you will not agree to aid me, I must ask that you put me afoot at once, on yonder inhospitable shore, from whence, as you must have discerned, I have recently fled.' He stared again at my father's face, his piercing eyes seeming to probe beyond the mere skin. 'Come, man, give me your decision. I cannot idle away the hours in your yacht's saloon, no matter how luxurious. Either aid me, on my terms, mind you, or let me go!'

"'What do you need then?' It was my father's tentative capitulation. I can only say in his defense, if he should need one, that as he told me the story, Verner's manner was such as somehow did not brook any opposition.

"'Hah,' said Verner. 'You are with me. Trust the Bulldog.' My father professed to misunderstand the man, though the unedifying implications were plain.

"'I wish all of your maps, at once, particularly of this coast,' was Verner's next remark. 'I have not been in these waters at all. I need the very best charts you possess.'

"My father bustled about, found all the maps he had, and as he had made something of a study of the area, he had all the best Dutch naval charts and whatnot. He brought them down into the big stern cabin. There, he found that in his absence, there had been a palace revolution of sorts. His captain, *Dato* Ali Burung, was on his knees before Mr. Verner, beating his head on the carpet, or rather, the straw matting.

"When the Asian arose, sensing my father's arrival, he had no shame on his flat features. 'We are going to help the *Tuan Vanah, Tuan,* are we not?' was what the chap said. Really, as my father put it, it wasn't enough that the strange traveler had seduced *him:* he had also somehow had the same effect on the toughest native skipper in the South China Sea! Whoever and whatever he was, Mr. Verner had, as you fellows put it, 'control.'

"'I am tentatively prepared to assist you in your quest, Mr. Verner.' My Old Man had given his commitment, and beyond 'unbelievable, but utterly true to type,' he heard no further particulars from his uninvited guest, who relapsed into silence.

"The next morning, they stood in to the coast. Western Sumatra in those days was much as it is today, I expect. They were well north of the *Mentawi* isles at the time, and just a bit south of the *Butus*. In there were, and no doubt still are, a thousand little anchorages. My father, or rather, old *Dato* Burung, found one of them. It was a tiny river, flowing into the sea under nipa palms, which almost arched over the entrance. It was the sort of place a Westerner wouldn't expect to launch a log canoe, but from which they had been turning out big seagoing vessels since well before the Christian era.

"There was even a small village, a *kampong*, as they say in those parts. The people thought they were pirates, my father said, and turned out the town for the ship. But Mr. Verner wanted nothing from them. He had ascertained that my father had a number of Martini-Henry rifles aboard, perhaps from old Burung. Even in those days, this was hardly the latest thing, but in any of the backwaters of Asia, a breechloading rifle, even the old Martini, was a thing of rare worth. At any rate, Verner had taken control of the arms locker and twelve of the skipper's prize thugs were armed and standing guard on the beach.

"I daresay you wonder what my father was doing, to let himself and his ship be commandeered in this casual way. All I can give you is the story he told me. Verner, whoever he was, had simply 'taken over.' Dad told me that he violently resented everything the man suggested, but could not raise any objection, at least beyond commonplaces. He simply was no longer in charge, and somehow he had come to accept it.

"'Where are we going?' said Verner in answer to a question. 'Where I

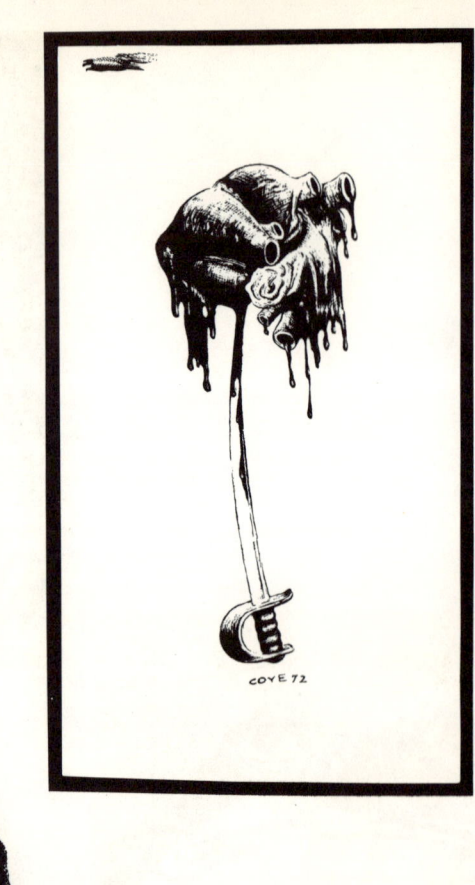

LEE BROWN COYE: A SELF-PORTRAIT

tell you, which is, as the crow is supposed to reckon matters, some twenty miles due north. There, hopefully, we will find a certain ship. This latter, we may or may not board. In any case, my orders are final. Is that quite understood?'

"The fellow's commands to the natives were delivered, I may say, in excellent Coast Malay. The timid folk of the local village came out and gave everyone garlands of flowers. No doubt, it was not the first time it had happened, but invaders who wanted nothing beyond food, and even paid for that, were something new. Yet, in retrospect, there may have been other reasons. . . .

"Verner, as if he had nothing to do with it at all, stood on the beach among the mangroves, waiting for my father to give all the orders. Finally, Dad asked him what he wanted next. He confessed to me in after years, that the man was so much in charge, that if he had said 'jump in the river,' the crew would have done so despite the abundant knobs of salt-water crocodiles, imitating tree stumps on every shallow bank and bar.

"The guest of the sea was now wearing one of my father's linen suits although he refused a *Solah Topee* and went hatless. His ruined boots had been replaced by sandals, but the fact was, as Dad put it, Verner could have worn a loincloth, or some sort of sarong, and still have been as much in charge as if he had been the supreme Rajah of Bandung. One simply gave up arguing when around him. You tolerated his presence because the only alternative was killing him!

"'We must have food for two days and two nights,' said Verner to my father. 'We shall be going north along the coast for about that distance. Would you be good enough to order your remaining ship's people to remain in these parts for some four days. No, better five. Some mischance may delay us. After that, they may head north, until they either meet us—or do not.'

"Since the orders appeared already to have been given, and since the twelve toughest members of the crew of my father's *prau*, all armed to the teeth with not only their native cutlery but with rifles from my father's arms locker as well, were waiting, this latter would appear to have been only courtesy. But it was not. Verner himself made that plain.

"'Captain Ffellowes, I much regret the outward appearance of these matters,' he told my father. 'While I personally have no doubt of your trustworthiness, the simple folk you command feel rather more strongly concerning my mission. In fact, though you might attempt to divert them from their purpose, and, be it said, mine as well, you would do little more than present them with your carcass as a species of local signpost. Possibly, indeed, probably, impaled as well, on bamboo shoots. Should you desire this new impalement on your coat of arms (ghastly pun, really), you have only to urge my immediate arrest.'

"Frankly, as my father put it to me, the man was becoming an incubus, and he seemed to have no sense at all of what was due a fellow Englishman. Although my father was allowed his pistols, Colt's matched Bisleys as it happens, on his belt, two of the twelve hearties from the crew flanked him at all times. It was more than clear that he was along on sufferance. Twice, Verner came to a halt as they crawled through the vile coastal scrub behind the mangroves, but it was not my father whom he consulted, but rather old Burung, the skipper of the *prau*. The man himself seemed to feel somewhat abashed by this insolent favoritism of a native, and at one of the rest stops, he actually spoke to my father in some terms of apology. 'See here, Captain,' he said, 'it is a capital mistake not to accept the best local information one can get.' My father was by this time too affronted by Verner's behavior to pay him much heed. Yet—the man, by his very presence, somehow brooked no interference. Dad simply nodded. He felt, he told me later, it was as if he were in a dream, or suspended in space. The whole thing, from the arrival on board his vessel of Verner and all that had happened subsequently, seemed to be a walking nightmare. He wondered, how could all this be happening? The only rock in a failing world was his personal man, Umpa, who trudged sturdily along beside him. He, at least, seemed faithful to his master.

"Have I failed to mention the heat? It was bad enough at sea, off the coast, but here it was almost unbearable. The party was following a winding trail along the shore, though somewhat back from it, which wound through green coco palms, jackfruit plantations gone wild, rambutan and pure jungle. Sometimes they were under dank shade, with great tropical hardwoods towering overhead, shutting off the sun; the next moment they would break out into heavy yellowish rattan and lantana brush growth and the saber-edged grasses of the coast. This would be hacked through by the advance guard with their myriad steel weapons. The next instant they would be in slippery mud under the giant trees again. Leeches and ticks fell upon their necks at every instant; gnats and mosquitoes assaulted them continuously, but they kept moving through innumerable muddy bogs and across many small tidal creeks as well.

"As if this were not bad enough, Burung, as well as some of the other natives and Verner too, were constantly stooping over patches of mud, in order to see what appeared to be quite ordinary traces of game. Once, late in the afternoon, they called my father over and showed him, in high glee, some daub or other which seemed important to them.

"'Look here, Captain,' said Verner. 'This can hardly fail to interest an old *shikari*, such as yourself!'

"My father looked and saw some spoor or other of an animal, large enough to be sure, in the bank mud of one of the many small estuaries through which they had just stumbled. The trace had four clawed footprints and was otherwise without meaning. It was indeed wet, that is, recent, with the water oozing in around the rim of the track, but beyond being the trace of some no doubt harmless creature, probably distorted by expansion, it appeared to have no significance whatever.

"My father's attitude seemed to annoy Verner a great deal, and without any further argument the man signaled to the others that they must press on. As they did so, Dad heard Verner say, as if to himself, 'Microcephalous! A case of simian survival!' The meaning of these phrases escaped him.

"At length, even Verner, who seemed made of iron, had to call a halt. He spoke to *Dato* Burung in low tones, and a camp was set up. My father, now stumbling with fatigue and insect-bitten to the limit, was gently passed along the line of marchers, until placed in the circle formed around the tiny fire they had lit. At this point, he related, he would not have cared much if they had told him that he was the main course in the evening meal.

"He roused himself, though, when he saw Verner seated next to him on the same rotting log. The fellow was almost as cool-looking as he had been on the *prau* after his recovery and, to my father's amazement, was in the act of fitting a clean paper collar to his very tattered shirt. God knows where he got them.

"At my father's gaze, something must have penetrated this strange person's subconscious mind. He finished dealing with his collar and without any affectation laid his hand on my father's knee.

"'I fear that you are still in doubt, my dear chap,' he said in vibrant tones. 'We are now far enough from the hue and cry so that one may elaborate without any fear of indiscretion. Pray tell me how I can serve you. Is there any matter on your mind?' The tones were as soft and caressing as those of a woman, and the man's whole attitude so charged with sympathy that my father almost wept. Exhausted and bemused as he was by what had transpired around him in the last twenty-four hours, he nevertheless retained enough energy to ask why this extraordinary jaunt through a trackless wilderness was necessary?

"'The matter is quite plain,' returned his singular congener. 'We are going to call upon a local ruler who is apparently dead, a native people who, though certainly native, are not people, and a ship due to be charged with more misery than any vessel that ever floated on this planet's seas. Finally we shall, I trust, destroy the scientific works of one Van Ouisthoven, who has been seemingly dead for fifteen years.'

"This flood of lunacy was too much for my father, who had been both physically and mentally taxed almost beyond endurance. He fell asleep, slumped over his own rotting log, even as he heard the final words of Verner's explanation. Yet the words stayed in his memory, so much so that even at his life's end, he could still recite them to me.

"It was not, however, to be a sleepless night. The noises of the great tropical rain forest were no doubt designed to make newcomers uncomfortable, but my father was an old stager at this sort of thing. Yet the cries of the civet cats, the hooting of the fish owls, the usual noises of insect and tree frog, none of these would have been sufficient to wake Dad. Suddenly, as he recollected, about 1 A.M., Verner and old Burung shook him awake. 'Listen,' hissed Verner, who actually grasped him by the collar.

"At first, my father heard nothing. There were the normal tropic sounds, the night wind in the great trees, the innumerable insects, locusts and such, the faraway cry of a sleepy gibbon, and that was all. But Verner's grip remained tight on his collar, and so—he listened. He could smell the reek of old Burung on the other side, full of garlic and menace, but the silence and the attention of the two finally got to him as well.

"Then he heard it. Over all the normal night noises, he heard the chatter of a squirrel. No one can mistake that nasty, scolding sound, and it came first from one side of the camp and then the other. The sound is the same in the Temperate Zone as it is in the tropics. But—and mind you, my father was an old tropic hand and a noted *shikari*—squirrels are not animals of the night. No scientist to this day has found anything but the flying squirrels active at night. And they are silent, or almost so. Also, this was deeper in pitch.

"Mixed with the chattering was a gruff, snarling bark, though that seemed to come only at intervals. Anything else he might have thought was shaken out of him by Verner. 'That is the enemy, Captain. They have already taken one sentry. Do you now feel my precautions to be unnecessary?'

"If this were not enough, the next thing was a sort of strangled choking noise from the other side of camp. Verner darted off like a flash, and came back almost as quickly. 'Another gone,' he said. 'We must move on in the morning, or they will pick us off like so many flies on a side of beef.' My father roused himself long enough to see that two more of the crew were detailed to stand sentry go, and then he relapsed once more into exhausted slumber. But, as he lay down, he was very conscious that something out in the great black forest was a hideous danger, clear and present. He fell asleep with dread on his soul.

"My father remembered nothing until he was roughly shaken in the first light of morning. He felt, and was, filthy, as well as being still tired, confused and angry at the way Verner had somehow pirated the loyalty of his men. Then he remembered the incidents of the night. He looked over and saw the very man himself, bent over a log which he was using as a table, in deep converse with my father's, or Rajah Brooke's, own captain, Burung. Ignoring the native crewman who was trying to give him sustenance in the form of cold rice, my father lurched over to the duo, who were his captors as he then felt.

"Verner looked up coldly at first, then seeing who had caused the interruption, smiled. It was the same glacial smile, to be sure, a mere rictus, but the strange man actually rose from his seat, and, as if by osmosis, so did *Dato* Burung.

"'Just the man we wanted,' said Verner. 'My dear chap, do come and look at this map. It purports to be the mouth of the river *Lubuk Rajah*. I fear you will be disappointed to learn that it was once considered by some to be the Biblical Ophir. The whole idea is, of course, beyond any reasoned belief. I, myself, when in the *Mekran*, found that. . . . Still, a most interesting and primitive area, geologically speaking. There is a young Dutch physician in these islands, Dubois, I believe, who is laying the ground for some splendid work on human origins. He is unknown to you? Strange how the body controls the mind, in terms of limitation, that is.'

"My father, who was, on his own admission to me given many years later on, only half awake, ignored this rambling and stared at the map which had been spread out on the rude table before him. There was indeed a river mouth and a small harbor. As an officer of the British Army, he was familiar with planes and gradients of the landscape, but here were other things on this map. There were lines, in various colors, extending around a central area. This central part appeared to be a settlement of some sort. In short, it looked like any typical village on any Southeast Asian coast, as observed and recorded by a European cartographer. Except for the odd lines, that is.

"He next heard his mentor, for so Verner had come to seem, in the same tone, but in excellent *Malay*, state the following: "Those are their lines. They have an inner and an outer defensive circuit. We shall have to somehow go between them. Do you have any suggestions?"

"'Look here, Verner,' said my father. 'What the Hell are you planning to do?' Nothing but fatigue, he told me, would have made him use language of this degree of coarseness.

"'I had thought it would have been apparent to any child with even a board school education,' said Verner, turning back to stare at him with those strange eyes. 'I propose to destroy this entire village, root and branch, females, young, the whole—as our American cousins put it—shebang. All at once. And I fear that I am compelled to ask for your direct assistance in the matter.'

"My father stared at him. He was, after all, a British officer, charged with spreading our native virtues, *Pax Britannica* and all that it implied in those days. He was told now that he was to assist in totally obliterating some native village in a foreign colonial possession! It was fantastic! Do please remember this was long before genocide became a word in the English language.

"*Dato* Burung said something to Verner in Malay, but so fast and low that my father totally failed to grasp it.

"'Quite so,' said Verner, 'but we have none and should we seek a prisoner, we stand the risk of further alerting all the others. No, I think the *Tuan*, captain, will have to sleep. Then, perhaps he and I may make the trail together, and once and for all see what Van Ouisthoven's work has come to. Strange that this whole matter should have grown from a simple assessment of mining machinery.' This last sentence was in English.

"My father was at this point, utterly out of his wits, strength, and did indeed fall silent. His next memories as he listened were those of hearing Verner say, in his clipped tones, and musingly in English, 'There are strange rhythms in world events, yet none stranger than that of unpaid businessmen!'

"They were now on the march in the usual blazing dawn. They had wound, in the previous day's journey, much closer to the coast than he had thought. Only a few mangroves and giant Java plums kept them from the glare of light, which now burst over the hills to the east. The day brought with it the inevitable cloud of insect horrors to replace the night's mosquitoes. His face puffed up and his eyes swollen, my father faced Verner—the man had the same catlike neatness, despite their march—at a trail fork and demanded to know who was in charge.

"He looked at my father coolly enough. His first words cut off anything my father was impelled to say, quite short.

"'Do you know, Captain, anything about general assurance companies? No? I rather thought not. Then you will have heard nothing of Messrs. Morrison, Morrison and Dodd. You will be pleased to know that a highly respectable firm, of Mincing Lance, no less, is the cause of your present discomfort.' On receiving nothing but the blankest of looks from Dad, he continued in the same light, jocular vein, obviously amused to make some mystery of his remarks, as though, Dad said, they were not mysterious enough already.

"'All I know, sir,' interrupted my father, 'is that you have mishandled me in the most outrageous fashion, suborned and subverted my officers and men, the employees of His Highness, the Rajah of Sarawak, and finally taken us away on some dubious journey for an unnamed purpose. I insist, sir, that you tell me what—' At this point my father fell silent, for as his voice rose, a wave of Verner's hand had caused a cloth to be thrown over his mouth by one of the burliest of his own crewmen, and despite his struggles, he was flung back upon a nearby tree trunk in the most compelling way. During all this, Verner continued to regard him in the most placid manner. When he had waited, as my father was compelled to admit, for his struggles to cease, he again waved his hand and the swaddling was removed. Meanwhile, Dad had seen old Umpa, his faithful servant, sworn to guard him with his life, quietly picking his teeth across the way!

"'Captain,' said Verner, leaning forward and staring into my father's eyes, 'behave yourself!'

"It was the rebuke one gives a child, and, my father was free to state, entirely successful. He sat quietly; the gag was withdrawn, and he stood in silence while listening to his interlocutor.

"'In a short time, Captain,' said the cold voice, 'we are going to carry out a murderous assault, by stealth, upon what appears to be a peaceful village. I cannot, even at this date, take you entirely into my confidence. However, I give you a few morsels of thought to mull over. Your men, starting with the captain, are the picked officers of the *Rajah Muda* of Sarawak. Think, man! Would they be likely to go over to a complete stranger such as myself, a castaway of no known antecedents, without the most compelling of reasons? Your own servant, that Moro savage, is with us. Do you dare exclude yourself?'"

There was a silence in the club library at this, and Ffellowes, who had lit a cigar, pulled on it gently before resuming. We were all so caught up that he could have said almost anything, but, even so, this was a point most of us had missed. Why indeed had the faithful crew of his Rajah's vessel turned coat so fast over to this wandering stranger?

"'The answer is simple, as are indeed most answers,' resumed Verner to my father. 'They believe most strongly in what I am doing. Why do you not ask them?'

"'*Dato* Burung,' said Dad to the old Bajau skipper. 'Why do you obey the strange *Tuan*? Why do you guard me as a prisoner?' He looked into the old man's jet eyes for the first time, seeing him not as a part of the ship, but as a *man*.

"'*Tuan*,' the old man spoke most respectfully. 'We have heard in the islands for many moons, and some few suns, that there will come a time when we will all rule ourselves. But, *Tuan*, not through those who are Not-men. We go now, under this strange *Tuan's* orders, to kill the Not-men. Only men should rule men. The *Orang Blanda*, even the great ones, are silly, but—you are *men*, of whatever strange, mad country. But —never Not-men, this is against the Law of the Prophet. These are *Efreets*, something not to be born. They must be killed.' The old pirate sighed and caressed his long drooping mustaches. 'It is quite simple, really.'

"This last piece of lunacy, as Dad told me, should have convinced any sane man that he had no chance. Instead, maddeningly, it swung him completely over to the other side. You see, he *knew* old Burung, and trusted him; had now for over a year served with him and his crew. Then there was Umpa, his Moro servant. He had been saved from execution by Dad's personal intervention. And he was a *Hadji*, had made the Mecca pilgrimage. He now stared at my father and nodded his head. If these men believed. . . .

"My father's response rather startled Verner in fact, if anything could startle a man as much in control of himself as that cold fish.

"'I'm your man,' Dad said simply, stretching out his hand. 'What do we do next?'

"Verner stared at him for a moment, then a lean hand clasped his. 'Thank you, Captain,' he said, and nothing more. 'Now—I badly need your help. The innermost grounds of this place are unknown to me. I escaped, more by luck than anything else, from what seems to be the outer perimeter. As you must have guessed, we are not too far from the place off which I was so fortunate as to have you encounter me. There is a ship in the harbor there which must at any hazard be prevented from leaving. She must in fact be destroyed. She is the *Matilda Briggs*, of American registry, out of Tampa in the state of Florida, I think. Her charter is under grave suspicion. A bark of some 700 tons. No ship in the world has ever carried such a cargo of future misery in the history of the human race. I repeat, she must be destroyed, *at all costs*.'

"'Of what does this cargo consist?' my father asked.

"'Females and infants in arms, in all probability,' was the cool answer. The man's face was grave, however, and it was evident that he was not in jest. My father could say no more. He was now committed, on the sole basis of common trust.

"'Now,' continued Verner, in his usual icy manner, but speaking Malay. 'Let us plan our next move.' The six remaining crewmen moved in closer. They obviously knew something portended. The other two had been made guards, to watch both trails, north and south.

"'See here,' cried Verner, pointing to the map. 'This is the weak point, here at this juncture of slopes. It is very plain that here is where we must strike.' Then he said a curious thing, almost an aside, a remark baffling to my father. 'May God defend the right. If it *is* the right.' The comment was so unlike Verner's usual detached attitude that it stuck in Dad's memory.

"'We shall be well off enough if the *Dolfjin* does not play us false,' continued the master of the expedition. He seemed to be talking to himself as much as anyone else. 'She's only 250 tons, but she carried two 12 pounders. And yet my last message may not have got through.'

"With no more remarks, Verner proceeded to dispose of the whole party. Two men, the crewmen with the best edged weapons, were sent on ahead to act as an advance guard. The two sentries were called in and made a rear party. The remaining four, including old Burung, plus my father and Verner, made up the central column. Dad loosened his revolvers in their holsters. He had been in some rough work more than once; yet he felt somehow that this business would take rank with the best of them. Verner seemed to carry no weapon at all, beyond a straight stick of some heavy wood he had cut.

"They were now on an obvious trail. It was early morning and the light was fair, despite the oppressive heat, even under the dark overhang of the giant trees. Moreover, the party was now heading inland, a bit away from the sea, in a northeasterly direction. Suddenly, as if by some species of legerdemain, they were confronted with an open area. The jungle simply stopped, and before them lay, in the morning light, a European village. Allowing for the tropics, there were fenced, brush-bordered fields, low peak-roof houses, chimneys curling with smoke, and in the middle distance a large structure, hard to see through the morning mist, but also peak-roofed, which might have served as the headquarters of the squire, or what have you, with no trouble. Anything less likely on the Sumatran coast than this rustic view would be hard to imagine. It was as if a segment of Bavaria, or perhaps Switzerland, had been removed bodily to the tropics. To make the scene complete, off to the left was a tiny harbor, empty save for a three-masted bark at anchor. She was surrounded by boats.

"'They have learned well,' said Verner in cryptic tones. 'Come on, you men. We should have had some opposition by now. They must be leaving and we can afford no wait. There lies the *Matilda Briggs*.'

"Even as he spoke, they were surrounded. My father was a man of few words at the best of times, and in this description (I may say," said Ffellowes at this point, "I was a child of my father's old age) he always became somewhat incoherent.

"There were many of them, all larger than man-size. Their pointed faces were drawn back from the great yellow chisel teeth, which snapped and chattered as they came on. They barked, too, like giant dogs. They had been hiding in the growth at the edge of the fields, and now they rushed in upon the small party, their clawed hands, yes, *hands*, clutching great crooked knives and other edged tools. The early morning air was still, no wind or even a shadow of a breath; and as my father put it, their stink, an acrid bitter reek, came on before them. It was inconceivable, but it was happening. Even the stumpy, naked tails that flailed the air behind them as they scuttered forward on their hind legs seemed to add no more unbelievability to the whole scene. It was monstrous, incredible, impossible—and it was happening!

"Then, the Nineteenth Century, as my father put it, justified itself. All of the crew, as any of Brooke's men had to, knew how to shoot. The sharp crack of the Martinis rang out in the muggy air.

"The men could see the harbor, even as they fought. There was a stream of small boats putting out to the ship at anchor, shuttling back and forth. In between pauses in fighting, each side drew breath, so to speak. Had they not had the advantage of firearms, my father told me, I venture to say that the small party of ten would have been overwhelmed in an instant. Even so, the courage of the creatures, or ferocity, rather, was astonishing. They removed their dead and wounded after each onslaught, and as fast as this was done, returned to the attack. Automatically, Verner took one flank and my father the other. *Dato* Burung, the old scoundrel, stayed with the center. Between them, somehow or other, they managed to hold the tiny line. More than once the monsters came to close quarters, but each time they were beaten back with cold steel. Verner, using only his heavy stick, disabled at least two of them personally, the stick revolving in a curious pinwheel manner, of point and side, that my father declared to be miraculous in its effect. But the attacks never ceased. There was, even though my father could not grasp the whole of the matter, an element of desperation about the way the creatures behaved, which was almost suicidal. Despite their immense strength, and the fact that their bulk much exceeded that of a man, they were clumsy with their weapons, and not only unskillful, but seemingly untrained in their usage. Save for a few barks and snarls at the outset, they were utterly silent.

"The whole affair could not have exceeded a quarter hour, but when it was over, my father felt that it had been going on for most of the morning. As suddenly as they had come, the monstrous enemy vanished, drawing off into the rice fields and the scrub which lined them. He was astonished to note the same placid harbor below and the small craft plying busily to and from the ship at anchor, so quick had been the onslaught.

"'Now,' said Verner, breaking in on his thoughts abruptly. 'We have two objectives, Captain. Yonder largish building, which abuts on the hill slope, is surely the central situation of these inimical creatures and must have been Van Ouisthoven's headquarters. As you can see, there are open-faced mine workings behind it, and a conduit as well. This it indeed must be, the *point d'appui*, of your section. I, on the other hand, will have to deal with the vessel in the harbor and attempt to ensure its total destruction. Am I clear?'

"If he was not clear, he had at least given orders; and a British officer, once he has accepted a superior, obeys orders, or did in those benighted days, before all this crapulous nonsense about morality came into the picture." (I have got to say here that this is the only time I ever heard Ffellowes do any "bitching," and he told me afterward that he simply was repeating what his father had said.)

"The idea of a 'section,' which in the British Army implied the use of a company or more, was laughable. My father," said Ffellowes, "found his first amusement at Verner's misuse of military language somehow consoling. The man was not God, after all, and did not know everything. This was a military operation and had best be run on military lines. Of the eight 'lower ranks' who had begun the fight, three were incapacitated, one being in point of fact—dead; the other two, badly wounded and in no condition to move at all. Of the remainder, all had cuts and bruises, including both Umpa and old Burung, who had bound a great flap of cut skin, blood and all, back under his turban. But they could go on.

"In the upshot, my father took three men, Verner two.

"'Should we not meet again, my thanks for your support,' said Verner in his chilly manner. 'It may comfort you to know that you have been involved in a matter far beyond the normal purlieu of the average Indian Army officer.' A cheery farewell, indeed! In addition, ammunition was running low. Each man had no more than twenty-five rounds for his rifle, and my father no more than that for his two revolvers. He mentioned this latter to Verner and was dismissed with a wave of the hand.

"'Pray rendezvous at the harbor, my dear Ffellowes,' was all he got in response. With that, the man was off, his grubby white suit soon vanishing around the lower end of the forest. To do the man justice, my father never thought him a coward. And he still carried only his heavy stick.

"There was nothing left to do but head for the central building, the transplanted seat of the local squirearchy, or whatever. It seemed, through the morning haze, to sit in the center of the fields, against the hill behind; and as Verner had said, there was the scar on the green slope beyond it, the red earth visible in the morning sun, which clearly showed that something or other was being worked. Indeed, there was even a glitter of twin rails. My father was in the infantry, not the engineers, but he could see a railway if it were thrust at him. Some dim meaning of the horror that Verner had hinted at now came upon him. Something monstrous and inchoate, in terms of the world at large, lay before him. The busy little boats, shuttling out to the ship, the placid harbor, the frenzied attack by the great, tool-wielding beasts, all began to fall into a dreadful pattern. The sight of those shining rails, leading from the central building to the mine on the hill, crystallized it, into a fear which must at some time haunt the dreams of every thinking person.

"When I tell you that my father was a convinced antievolutionist, who thought Darwin a moral degenerate, the matter may become clearer still. Or may not.

"A narrow path led downslope through the fields, or rather paddies, for rice seemed to be the crop grown. Dense brush of the usual rattan and other thorny plants lined it, and the party tensed themselves for an attack. But none came. In the morning heat, so hot that a mist obscured the hills in the distance, only faint chittering cries and barks came from far away. Each moment the little party of blood-stained, ragged men tensed as they rounded a curve between banks of thick scrub. The men could no longer see the harbor and sometimes could see no more than a few feet ahead. Yet the hideous things appeared to have withdrawn, at least for the time.

"Nevertheless, the trace they followed seemed to lead in the direction of the large building, and once or twice they caught a glimpse of the raw face of the hill which lay behind it, over the tops of the fringing shrubbery.

"At length, when my father estimated that they must have covered a mile or more, Umpa, his old servant, who was in the lead, held up a hand in warning. They froze, and then Umpa signaled to my father to join them. As Dad stole up and as he crouched beside the old savage, an amazing sight met his eyes.

"Before them rose a gentle slope, of clipped grass, rising for a hundred yards to the veranda of the large building they had seen in the distance.

The path, which was almost a tunnel under the overhanging scrub, debouched onto this lawn, for it was nothing less, quite abruptly; and as my father looked about, he could see other openings of a similar nature all around the fringe of the brush.

"But the building itself was even more startling. Minus the broad veranda, it was nothing more than a Dutch farmhouse, of the sort one can still see in Zeeland, though much larger than most. There was the peaked roof, the stuccoed walls, with wooden beams set between the stucco as facing, and even wooden shutters on the high-arched windows. Small balconies held massive urns full of bright flowers, and near the door were set large geometric flower beds, also bright with scarlet blooms. The only thing missing was a blonde maid in starched cap and wooden shoes, chevying hens away from the stoop. A more unlikely edifice under the circumstances would be hard to envisage.

"No smoke curled from the high brick chimneys though, and there was no sign of life. My father could make nothing of this, but he had his orders, and he waved to the men to follow him. Half crouching, half running, they raced across the lawn, all of them trying to see in every direction at once, waiting for an attack from any or all sides to overwhelm them. They were a little more than halfway when the big front door opened suddenly. Every weapon went up as one, and they all halted in their tracks. Yet no one fired.

"Before them stood an old bearded gentleman, his ruddy face and snowy hair making him look like a tropical version of Saint Nick, a conceit not much accentuated by his costume, which consisted of a rather soiled duck jacket and equally dirty sarong. Old as he obviously was, there was no mistaking his urgency. His sharp blue eyes had nothing senile about them, and he waved them forward to him with a gesture of both command and urgency, peering about as he did so in a way that made his meaning plain, as plain indeed as his silence. My father also waved the others on, and in an instant they were in the hall of the house and the heavy door was shut and bolted behind them.

"The old chap addressed my father in sharp tones. When he saw that his Dutch gutturals were unintelligible, he switched to good, though accented, English. 'Are there no more of you? This is madness! We need at least a regiment to deal with my Folk. Did not my messages make this plain? And now they are *leaving!* You are too late!' His despair would have been comic had my father not seen what he had just seen.

"'Who the deuce are you, old chap,' he asked, 'and what on earth are you doing here?' He wanted to know much more, such as how the old man was still alive and a few other obvious things like that.

"His question seemed to stun the old gentleman. 'Who am I? I am Van

Ouisthoven. This is my place, *Kampong De Kan*, my house, my laboratory. Who else should I be?'

"My father had an excellent memory. This was the name Verner had twice mentioned, that of a man 'dead for fifteen years.' Verner then, did not possess the key to all knowledge, despite his air of omniscience. But the old man was clutching my father's sleeve.

"'Did you not come in answer to my messages? Don't you know what has been happening? You have been fighting—you have met the Folk, that is obvious. Why are you here, then, if not to stop them? And, God help us, why so *few?*'

"In a few sentences, my father told the history of the past few days. The old chap was sharp as a needle, and he listened intently.

"'So—I see. Maybe a message did get through, maybe not. But, anyway, this other Englishman comes and he knows or guesses something. There was a disturbance some four days ago, and Grixchox (or something like that) would tell me nothing. So he gets away from them then; a brave man to come here alone to face the Folk! And you find him, and he, how to put it, takes over you and your ship.' His eyes grew thoughtful, then focused.

"'Listen. Everything rests on that ship out there. It must *not* get out, you understand me! I have been a prisoner here for a long while. But they do not kill me. They still remember that I taught *them!* But they do not know all my secrets. When they begin to learn, they scare me; I get just a few things in. But them—they are clever, they made me *not* nervous, they make me think I am their God, and all the time—among themselves—they plot. When the day comes, they kill all my Javanese boys quickly, yes, and their women and the little ones too. Only me they save. I can still teach them something, and—they do not forget that without me, they never *be!* Now, come fast. We have things to get. They are all down at the boat; that is why you got here alive, my friend. Come.'

"With no more words, he led them to the interior of the house, which went way back into the hill and was far larger than it appeared from the outside. The place was beautifully kept, by the way, old pictures on the walls, the floor spotless, rattan carpets here and there, and so on.

"Finally, Van Ouisthoven stopped at what was to outward appearances a blank section of wall between two large doors. Murmuring to himself in soft tones, the old man ran his fingers over the wall, an inlaid one of varicolored native woods. Then he gave a gasp of satisfaction and pressed hard. Silently, a great panel slid aside, and there before them lay a snug closet, perhaps ten feet deep and as much high and wide. In it were various shapes, covered with heavy canvas. The old Hollander flung this aside, and from my father and the others came gasps in their turn.

"Oiled and gleaming on its tripod base, funnel hopper feed mechanism seated in place, sat the fat brass cylinder of a Gatling gun! It was the small model, invented for the use of your New York police, I believe; but there were enough of them in service in the British and Indian Army that my father was fully conversant with its operation. Behind lay a stack of boxes, wrapped in brown oilskin, which could be nothing but its ammunition. A stand of Martini rifles and more ammunition stood next to it.

"'Get it out, at once,' shouted Van Ouisthoven, 'we get it down to the harbor and those ungrateful *schlems* learn something they didn't learn yet. But hurry! That crook Yankee what skippers the *Matilda Briggs*, he'll take them all off yet if we don't hurry! They have been giving him my gold for years!'

"In a few words, my father told the others what he wanted. One man carried four boxes of ammunition for the gun. The other two took the weapon itself, one being Umpa, who carried the tripod and another box. My father slung two rifles and gave the old Dutchman another, at the same time taking a pouch of rifle cartridges. They were all laden, but not so much so that they could not make good time. The urgency of what they were doing—though, to be sure, even my father only half understood it—somehow communicated itself to all of them.

"As they left the front door, my father was amazed to see the old man take a large box of wax vestas from his jacket pocket and calmly light a tall bamboo screen just inside the door. As it took fire, Van Ouisthoven turned to my father and said sadly, 'It must go. The whole thing. If some should survive, they must have nothing to come back to. All must go. And it is suitable. Here it started.' There was nothing in his eyes as he spoke but grim determination, and Dad could only begin to grasp what it must have cost the old chap. But he knew his history, and he remembered the men who cheeerfully flooded their Dutch countryside in 1587 to turn back the Prince of Parma's Spanish Army.

"With no more words, the five of them set off down across the lawn and into another trail, this time headed for the harbor. Behind them a plume of black smoke came out the open door and began to rise in the heat of the steaming tropic mists.

"As they entered the new track, clear through the morning air, came the distant sound of a rifle shot, followed by others. With no word spoken, they all began to run, their various loads seeming light as they did. Van Ouisthoven's age was a mystery to my father, but he kept up gamely, his white beard jutting forward and his rifle at the ready.

"The trail they were on was a goodish bit broader than the narrow trace on which they had first approached the house, beaten smooth with much use, and presenting no obstruction to movement. They kept alert, the two Europeans guarding the flanks and moving first. The rifle fire continued in the distance, and grew louder as they advanced. How long they ran would be impossible to estimate, but suddenly they came into the open and saw a panorama which stayed riveted in their memories. My father could describe it, after a fifth glass of port, as if it had been only the day before.

"The tiny bay lay before them, a broad stretch of yellow sand skirting a calm blue lagoon. Some hundreds of yards offshore lay the bark at anchor, a shabby enough craft, her brown hull paint peeling, patched sails half up but idle in the almost windless air. Between her and the shore, boats, three of them, none large, plied steadily with paddles, all heading for the ship.

"Directly in front of my father and his group, Verner and his three seamen fronted the monsters. It was a curious situation. The three seamen, including Burung, were prone, firing at intervals, in unison, and only when there was a rush. Their ammunition must have been almost exhausted. Behind them, Verner leaned on his crude cane, somehow conveying an air of casual urbanity, as if bored by the whole proceedings, his shabby garments even now appearing neat, despite their rips and tatters. My father, who disliked the man intensely, was always careful to aver, nevertheless, that he carried himself in a very gentlemanly manner at all times.

"There were bodies on the sand between Verner's people and the Folk. Huge bodies covered with yellow-brown fur, great ivory chisel teeth fixed in death grimaces, strange hairy hands still clutching their crude knives. Behind them, in turn, were the rest of the Folk, the great males, in a circle, their horrid faces turned toward their enemies, their gruff barking notes and shriller chatter filling the air. Even as my father saw them, they were massing for another rush. In back of the ring of raging creatures were a mass of smaller brutes, many of them no larger than children. The Folk, or at least some of them, had been brought to bay, and their females and young were the cause."

As we heard this story, those of us who knew Ffellowes saw something we had seldom seen, I mean the man was *feeling!* As he told the final moments of this tale, the man was really moved. He illustrated his story with jerky hand motions, and there was actual sweat on his forehead! Whatever the truth of his yarns, and I have long since suspended judgment on them, there is no doubt about one thing, in this one anyway. The guy felt it! And it was supposed to have happened to his *father* back long before any of us were born!

He went on. "My father wasted no time. Several crisp orders and the Gatling was set up, with Dad holding the yoke bars. Old Umpa was the ammunition loader and emptied the first box of shells into the hopper feed.

"'Get down, Verner, get down flat!' Dad bellowed. Verner, whose back was to them, fell as if struck dead. The others being prone already, a clear field of fire was possible. Dad began to turn the crank.

"The bellow of the Gatling drowned out all other noises, and my father traversed it back and forth as coldly as if he had been on a target range. Old Umpa, his dark, scarred visage expressionless, broke open the boxes and emptied cartridges into the hopper as calmly as if he were shelling nuts. The result was appalling. The great furry brutes went down like nine-pins, and as fast as those in front fell, the others behind followed. It was over in five minutes.

"My father stopped firing and the bluish smoke drifted in the faint breeze. The water at the beach edge was red, and so too were the sands. It looked like a slaughterhouse. The bulky carcasses lay in their gory death like so many shot muskrats, which indeed they resembled, save in size.

"Verner rose from the sand and dusted himself off in precise, almost mincing way. His three trusties also got up, old Burung in the lead, and walked over to us.

"'You have justified my belief in you, Captain,' he said in his usual icy tones. 'These dangerous vermin were tolerably close to terminating a career which has not been without some small distinction. And who is this, pray tell?'

"It was a considerable pleasure for my father to introduce Van Ouisthoven to Mr. Verner, though the latter was, to be sure, as imperturbable as usual.

"'I see that the reports of your death, *Mynjheer*, have been considerably exaggerated.' Verner's voice was even chiller than its normal wont. 'You have much to answer for, sir. You have imperiled the entire human race by your meddling in matters better left to Providence.'

"His rebuke, however, went unnoticed. For even Verner had forgot the ship. Now, with a cry, the old Hollander pointed, and we all remembered her. Under easy sail, square sails set on the two foremasts, and gaff on the mizzen, the *Matilda Briggs* was standing out to sea. The three small boats which had been plying to and from shore drifted on the tide.

"It was a beautiful scene, really. There was the brown ship, as lovely as only a sailing vessel can be, the azure waters, the fringe of *nipa* and coco palms on the shore, and then the open sea beyond the harbor's mouth. But it was horror! One thing had been made plain to my father; that the ship must not escape. And here she was, stealing out to sea, and they were helpless. The Gatling, though unparalleled at close range, was useless beyond two hundred yards, and the ship was thrice that already. Everyone stood in numb silence, and simply watched her go. And saw her end.

"Around the corner of the northern point of the bay, came the bow of a small black steamer with white upper works. And as she appeared, she began to fire, first the bow gun and then the stern, as soon as they could bear upon target. She was not large, but on her staff she wore the blue, red and white of the navy of Holland. In silence the little crowd on the beach watched the annihilation of the *Matilda Briggs*. The two guns the gunboat used were not of great caliber, but the bark was a fragile thing, wood-built, old and hard-used. Her masts fell in seconds, and the fires kindled by the exploding shells were all over her in another instant. Ceaselessly, remorselessly, the warship fired. When she stopped and the echoes of her guns no longer resounded in one's ears, there was nothing on the surface of the lagoon, nothing but a smear of oily muck, some oily smoke, a litter of wood scraps, and the dark fins of countless sharks.

"'The *Dolfjin* has just justified the Dutch naval estimates indeed those of the entire mass of all the world's navies,' came the didactic comment of Verner over my father's shoulder. 'A curious reflection on the rise of modern fleets, that one minute gunboat should prove the probable savior of the human race. She came only just in time,' he added.

"But my father was not really listening to Verner. He was watching Van Ouisthoven instead. The old man was walking slowly down the beach to the pile of bodies where the Folk lay, the males in front of their females and young. For some reason, my father followed him as he skirted the fringe of the mass of dead creatures and advanced slowly and with head bent on the last heap at the water's edge.

"While my father stood silent behind him, the old fellow began to pull the bodies apart in the last heap, the one nearest the water, ignoring the warm blood that stained his arms and clothing. Persistently, he tugged and hauled, shoving the great carcasses aside, until at last he was rewarded.

"Something moved under his hands, and his motions grew more excited. My father drew one of his revolvers and stood waiting, poised for any eventuality.

"A blunt-nosed head appeared from under one of the larger shapes, and into the bright sun of noon wiggled a small furry creature, no more than three feet high. In one arm it clutched something flat, but the other hand it held out to Van Ouisthoven, squeaking plaintively as it did so.

The man whom it addressed stood silent, his shoulders seeming to stoop even more, if possible. Then in the same absence of sound, Van Ouisthoven held out one hand—to my father. In the same bleak silence, as if no other noise could be allowed, my father handed over the revolver he held. He saw tears pouring down Van Ouisthoven's face. There was a shot. My father confessed he had his eyes closed at this juncture. Then a second shot.

"When Dad could bear to look again, two figures were clasped together. The old Hollander lay hugging the small shape of the last of the Folk, a bullet in his own brain. Beside them on the sand lay the object which the little thing had been holding so tightly. My father stirred it with his foot. It was a Dutch primer, brightly illustrated in color, with pictures of children in Holland at play.

"The next scene of the drama, or what have you, took place in the captain's cabin of His Netherlandish Majesty's ship, the *Dolfjin*. They were headed down the coast to pick up my father's *prau*. The Dutch naval officer had ceased his questions, and the interminable voice of Verner had taken up the tale. Through a fog of fatigue blended with irritation, my father tried to follow what the man was saying. His comprehensive dislike of the fellow's personality was palliated only by a genuine admiration of the man's attainments and perseverance.

"'It becomes quite clear, I think, to all present, that no report of this affair must reach any but the few constituted authorities, those who are cognizant to some extent, that is, of the problem. Were the facts to be made plain, I fear, some scientific rascals would be able to reproduce the late Van Ouisthoven's work. While he had a good degree from Leyden, he was hardly, save in sheer persistence, a genius, and it is highly possible. . . .'

"Here, my father, who could not forget the old man's death, made some ejaculation or even swore, though this was most unlike him.

"'My dear Ffellowes,' said Verner, his voice losing some of its habitual *sang-froid*. 'No one is more cognizant than myself of that unfortunate man's dilemma. He must, perforce, destroy the very thing he had created. His last moments, which I also observed, were charged with remorse and grief. Yet, what choice had he? Or, indeed, any of us? His final actions, awful though they may appear to an observer, gave him rank with the leaders of the human race. He raised Caliban from the depths and to the depths he dispatched him.'

"My father said nothing. He was too sunk in weariness and sadness to venture further. Yet—for one moment, Verner's wiry hand had pressed his shoulder, and he felt the unspoken sympathy which the other could not express in any other way, both to the dead, and to himself. There was a silence.

"'To resume,' Verner continued, his high querulous voice cutting off any debate, 'the facts are indeed singular. They stem, in fact, from the unpaid bills of a Manchester firm of machinery manufacturers. These people, whose name is in the highest degree inconsequential to this story, retained in turn, my employers. Messrs. Morrison, Morrison and Dodd, who act only as appraisers of various mechanical artifices and manufacturers, but also, in a subsidiary vein, as assurers of the same. Thus are great affairs put in train! The bills of the original company were not being paid! A steady and reliable account had ceased payment, without prior notice! An outrage, in the ordered community of business! What transpired? Morrison, Morrison and Dodd were called in and found themselves at sea, literally and figuratively. The account was in the great Dutch island of Sumatra. Some ten thousands of pounds sterling were owed. The Dutch, when appealed to, could give no assistance.

"'The area in question was remote and feverish, on the so-called Tapanuli coast. Few ships called there. In any case, the Hollands Government could hardly prosecute a bankrupt on behalf of an English firm. They declined action. So the matter stood. But do not undervalue the persistence of the English man of business. He will follow a bad debt to the end. Hence my appearance in this matter, brought about by devious means and my own desires, let it be said.

"'When the matter was first put to me, I was at first totally disinterested. It seemed to have little of consequence, and less of any noteworthy quality about it. I was resistant to the idea of my services being engaged. Yet, I made a few preliminary moves. One of these was to frequent the numerous haunts in the areas of the London docks, where information on this part of the world might be ascertained, if patience were applied.

"'My patience was rewarded. Some mouthings of a dying lascar seaman in a den of the vilest description caused me to accept the commission. What the fellow said was vague and in the highest degree inconclusive. Nevertheless, it brought me out here to the East. For, in speaking of the very area of coast in which we now find ourselves, he said something of great interest.

"'Do not go there,' he choked out. 'That is the land of Not-men. Men like you and me, we are killed on sight!'

"'So, by strange methods, including enlisting persons so lofty in stature they may not be mentioned on this vessel, through a previous indebtedness to my humble person, I secured the right to go anywhere in these islands. And also to ask for the aid of such Dutch naval craft as might be available. In fact, I could tell my colleague here to sink anything he saw moving on this coast.

"'And so by circuitous means,' continued Verner, 'I came to one Cornelius Van Ouisthoven, the original bad debtor of my employers. The man was presumed dead. Not one relative in his family had heard from him for many years. But—and a large BUT it was—he had ordered mining machinery, railway machinery, all sorts of machinery, and had not paid for it, that is, after a certain point in time.

"'I found myself with a curious and unsolvable equation, involving this hitherto unknown Dutch gentleman, whose background I was at some pains to look into. Added to him there was some unpaid-for machinery, and finally, as I drew closer to the area in question, more and more rumors about a land where *men* were not welcome!

"'So curious were all these circumstances that I felt I must investigate in person. I did so, and the results were as you know. I found myself the prisoner of these creatures the old gentleman chose to call "the Folk."

"'I managed to escape and even flee the harbor in one of the native craft whose previous owners, no doubt innocent fishermen, the Folk had slain. These vessels, which were beyond their management, were left drawn up on the beach.

"'I have not been so fortunate as to secure Van Ouisthoven's notes, but I rather fancy I can piece together the main *membra*.

"'Briefly, the old man was a biologist, and one of extraordinary patience. He bred some native rodent, almost certainly *Rhizomys sumatrensis*, the local so-called, "bamboo rat" to extraordinary size. In my dissecting days at Barts, various genera of the *Rodentia* were exposed to me, and I well remember noting that this particular species had very well-developed paws, quite resembling hands, in fact.

"'Hands come before brains, you know. This is the most recent opinion. Without grasping organs, our peculiar human brains would be worthless. So, the old recluse went on with his work. And, from what you tell me, Ffellowes, he succeeded.

"'Brain is an inevitable increment of size at this rate. These vermin are quite clever enough as it is. Someone at the British Museum has deduced that there are four thousand species of rodents on the planet already. But if we are to be supplanted, let it be in due course. Even the old man agreed with that at the end.'

"And there," said Ffellowes, extinguishing his cigar, "my story, or 'tale' if you like, Williams, ends. My father was returned to his own vessel, he contined his cruise through the islands, and no report of any of this exists anywhere, unless it be in some hidden archives of the Kingdom of the Netherlands. That is all."

There was a longer silence this time. It was broken by the younger member who had brought on the whole business in the first place.

"But, Brigadier, with all respect, sir, there is something vaguely familiar about all this. Who was this man, Verner, or whatever he called himself? He sounds like some creature of fiction himself."

Ffellowes' answer was—well—typical. He stared at the young man coldly, but not in anger.

"Possible, no doubt. Since I never read sensational literature, I fear that I am in no position to give an answer. I have nothing to go on, you understand, but my father's unsupported word. I have always felt that sufficient!"

After a much longer silence, the brigadier was found to have gone, as silently as always. And, as usual, no one else seemed to have anything to say.

BRITISH FANTASY AWARD

KARL EDWARD WAGNER/*Sticks*

Since we share a common language, and a common affection for the fantastic, Britain was represented at the festivities. And, in a "hands across the sea" gesture, which will be a permanent feature of the World Fantasy Conventions, Britain presented its *own* award—wisely, I think—to the already nominated short story "Sticks" by Karl Edward Wagner.

The British award is in honor of August Derleth, and in the beginning scrolls of merit were given out. The award has evolved into a chilling little figurine of a cowled being (human, possibly) and was bestowed upon "Sticks."

Karl Wagner's story first appeared in America in *Whispers,* a magazine devoted to supernatural horror and edited by Stuart Schiff. The story grew out of a sort of melding of Wagner's imagination and the peculiar sticks which artist Lee Brown Coye is now and then wont to have floating mysteriously in his drawings.

Karl Edward Wagner

STICKS

I

The lashed together framework of sticks jutted from a small cairn alongside the stream. Colin Leverett studied it in perplexment—half a dozen odd lengths of branch, wired together at cross angles for no fathomable purpose. It reminded him unpleasantly of some bizarre crucifix, and he wondered what might lie beneath the cairn.

It was the spring of 1942—the kind of day to make the War seem distant and unreal, although the draft notice waited on his desk. In a few days Leverett would lock his rural studio, wonder if he would see it again—be able to use its pens and brushes and carving tools when he did return. It was goodby to the woods and streams of upstate New York, too. No fly rods, no tramps through the countryside in Hitler's Europe. No point in putting off fishing that troutstream he had driven past once, exploring back roads of the Otselic Valley.

Mann Brook—so it was marked on the old Geological Survey map—ran southeast of DeRuyter. The unfrequented country road crossed over a stone bridge old before the first horseless carriage, but Leverett's Ford eased across and onto the shoulder. Taking fly rod and tackle, he included pocket flask and tied an iron skillet to his belt. He'd work his way downstream a few miles. By afternoon he'd lunch on fresh trout, maybe some bullfrog legs.

It was a fine clear stream, though difficult to fish as dense bushes hung out from the bank, broken with stretches of open water hard to work without being seen. But the trout rose boldly to his fly, and Leverett was in fine spirits.

From the bridge the valley along Mann Brook began as fairly open pasture, but half a mile downstream the land had fallen into disuse and was thick with second growth evergreens and scrub-apple trees. Another mile, and the scrub merged with dense forest, which continued unbroken. The land here, he had learned, had been taken over by the state many years back.

As Leverett followed the stream he noted the remains of an old railroad embankment. No vestige of tracks or ties—only the embankment itself, overgrown with large trees. The artist rejoiced in the beautiful drywall culverts spanning the stream as it wound through the valley. To his mind it semed eerie, this forgotten railroad running straight and true through virtual wilderness.

He could imagine an old wood-burner with its conical stack, steaming along through the valley dragging two or three wooden coaches. It must be a branch of the old Oswego Midland Rail Road, he decided, abandoned rather suddenly in the 1870s. Leverett, who had a memory for detail, knew of it from a story his grandfather told of riding the line in 1871 from Otselic to DeRuyter on his honeymoon. The engine had so labored up the steep grade over Crumb Hill that he got off to walk alongside. Probably that sharp grade was the reason for the line's abandonment.

When he came across a scrap of board nailed to several sticks set into a stone wall, his darkest thought was that it might read "No Trespassing." Curiously, though the board was weathered featureless, the nails seemed quite new. Leverett scarcely gave it much thought, until a short distance beyond he came upon another such contrivance. And another.

Now he scratched at the day's stubble on his long jaw. This didn't make sense. A prank? But on whom? A child's game? No, the arrangement was far too sophisticated. As an artist, Leverett appreciated the craftsmanship of the work—the calculated angles and lengths, the designed intricacy of the maddeningly inexplicable devices. There was something distinctly uncomfortable about their effect.

Leverett reminded himself that he had come here to fish and continued downstream. But as he worked around a thicket he again stopped in puzzlement.

Here was a small open space with more of the stick lattices and an arrangement of flat stones laid out on the ground. The stones—likely taken from one of the many dry-wall culverts—made a pattern maybe twenty by fifteen feet, that at first glance resembled a ground plan for a house. Intrigued, Leverett quickly saw that this was not so. If the ground plan for anything, it would have to be for a small maze.

The bizarre lattice structures were all around. Sticks from trees and bits of board nailed together in fantastic array. They defied description; no two seemed alike. Some were only one or two sticks lashed together in parallel or at angles. Others were worked into complicated lattices of dozens of sticks and boards. One could have been a child's tree house—it was built in three planes, but was so abstract and useless that it could be nothing more than an insane conglomeration of sticks and wire. Sometimes the contrivances were stuck in a pile of stones or a wall, maybe thrust into the railroad embankment or nailed to a tree.

It should have been ridiculous. It wasn't. Instead it seemed somehow sinister—these utterly inexplicable, meticulously constructed stick lattices spread through a wilderness where only a tree-grown embankment or a forgotten stone wall gave evidence that man had ever passed through. Leverett forgot about trout and frog legs, instead dug into his pockets for a notebook and stub of pencil. Busily he began to sketch the more intricate structures. Perhaps someone could explain them; perhaps there was something to their insane complexity that warranted closer study for his own work.

Leverett was roughly two miles from the bridge when he came upon the ruins of a house. It was an unlovely colonial farmhouse, box-shaped and gambrel-roofed, fast falling into the ground. Windows were dark and empty; the chimneys on either end looked ready to topple. Rafters showed through open spaces in the roof, and the weathered boards of the walls had in places rotted away to reveal hewn timber beams. The foundation was stone and disproportionately massive. From the size of the unmortared stone blocks, its builder had intended the foundation to stand forever.

The house was nearly swallowed up by undergrowth and rampant lilac bushes, but Leverett could distinguish what had been a lawn with imposing shade trees. Farther back were gnarled and sickly apple trees and an overgrown garden where a few lost flowers still bloomed—wan and serpentine from years in the wild. The stick lattices were everywhere— the lawn, the trees, even the house were covered with the uncanny structures. They reminded Leverett of a hundred misshapen spider webs— grouped so closely together as to almost ensnare the entire house and clearing. Wondering, he sketched page on page of them, as he cautiously approached the abandoned house.

He wasn't certain just what he expected to find inside. The aspect of the farmhouse was frankly menacing, standing as it did in gloomy desolation where the forest had devoured the works of man—where the only sign that man had been here in this century were these insanely wrought latticeworks of sticks and board. Some might have turned back at this point. Leverett, whose fascination for the macabre was evident in his art, instead was intrigued. He drew a rough sketch of the farmhouse and the grounds, overrun with the enigmatic devices, with thickets of hedges and distorted flowers. He regretted that it might be years before he could capture the eeriness of this place on scratchboard or canvas.

The door was off its hinges, and Leverett gingerly stepped within, hoping that the flooring remained sound enough to bear even his sparse frame. The afternoon sun pierced the empty windows, mottling the decaying floorboards with great blotches of light. Dust drifted in the sunlight. The house was empty—stripped of furnishings other than indistinct tangles of rubble mounded over with decay and the drifted leaves of many seasons.

Someone had been here, and recently. Someone who had literally covered the mildewed walls with diagrams of the mysterious lattice structures. The drawings were applied directly to the walls, crisscrossing the rotting wallpaper and crumbling plaster in bold black lines. Some of vertiginous complexity covered an entire wall like a mad mural. Others were small, only a few crossed lines, and reminded Leverett of cuneiform glyphics.

His pencil hurried over the pages of his notebook. Leverett noted with fascination that a number of the drawings were recognizable as schematics of lattices he had earlier sketched. Was this then the planning room for the madman or educated idiot who had built these structures? The gouges etched by the charcoal into the soft plaster appeared fresh—done days or months ago, perhaps.

A darkened doorway opened into the cellar. Were there drawings there as well? And what else? Leverett wondered if he should dare it. Except for streamers of light that crept through cracks in the flooring, the cellar was in darkness.

"Hello?" he called. "Anyone here?" It didn't seem silly just then. These stick lattices hardly seemed the work of a rational mind. Leverett wasn't enthusiastic with the prospect of encountering such a person in this dark cellar. It occurred to him that virtually anything might transpire here, and no one in the world of 1942 would ever know.

And that in itself was too great a fascination for one of Leverett's temperament. Carefully he started down the cellar stairs. They were stone and thus solid, but treacherous with moss and debris.

The cellar was enormous—even more so in the darkness. Leverett reached the foot of the steps and paused for his eyes to adjust to the damp gloom. An earlier impression recurred to him. The cellar was too big for the house. Had another dwelling stood here originally—perhaps destroyed and rebuilt by one of lesser fortune? He examined the stonework. Here were great blocks of gneiss that might support a castle. On closer look they reminded him of a fortress—for the dry-wall technique was startlingly Mycenaean.

Like the house above, the cellar appeared to be empty, although without light Leverett could not be certain what the shadows hid. There seemed to be darker areas of shadow along sections of the foundation wall, suggesting openings to chambers beyond. Leverett began to feel uneasy in spite of himself.

There was something here—a large table-like bulk in the center of the cellar. Where a few ghosts of sunlight drifted down to touch its edges, it seemed to be of stone. Cautiously he crossed the stone paving to where it loomed—waist-high, maybe eight feet long and less wide. A roughly shaped slab of gneiss, he judged, and supported by pillars of unmortared stone. In the darkness he could only get a vague conception of the object. He ran his hand along the slab. It seemed to have a groove along its edge.

His groping fingers encountered fabric, something cold and leathery and yielding. Mildewed harness, he guessed in distaste.

Something closed on his wrist, set icy nails into his flesh.

Leverett screamed and lunged away with frantic strength. He was held fast, but the object on the stone slab pulled upward.

A sickly beam of sunlight came down to touch one end of the slab. It was enough. As Leverett struggled backward and the thing that held him heaved up from the stone table, its face passed through the beam of light.

It was a lich's face—desiccated flesh tight over its skull. Filthy strands of hair were matted over its scalp, tattered lips were drawn away from broken yellowed teeth, and sunken in their sockets eyes that should be dead were bright with hideous life.

Leverett screamed again, desperate with fear. His free hand clawed the iron skillet tied to his belt. Ripping it loose, he smashed at the nightmarish face with all his strength.

For one frozen instant of horror the sunlight let him see the skillet crush through the mould-eaten forehead like an axe—cleaving the dry flesh and brittle bone. The grip on his wrist failed. The cadaverous face fell away, and the sight of its caved-in forehead and unblinking eyes from between which thick blood had begun to ooze would awaken Leverett from nightmare on countless nights.

But now Leverett tore free and fled. And when his aching legs faltered as he plunged headlong through the scrub-growth, he was spurred to desperate energy by the memory of the footsteps that had stumbled up the cellar stairs behind him.

II

When Colin Leverett returned from the War, his friends marked him a changed man. He had aged. There were streaks of gray in his hair; his springy step had slowed. The athletic leanness of his body had withered to an unhealthy gauntness. There were indelible lines to his face, and his eyes were haunted.

More disturbing was an alteration of temperament. A mordant cynicism had eroded his earlier air of whimsical asceticism. His fascination with the macabre had assumed a darker mood, a morbid obsession that his old acquaintances found disquieting. But it had been that kind of a war, especially for those who had fought through the Apennines.

Leverett might have told them otherwise, had he cared to discuss his nightmarish experience on Mann Brook. But Leverett kept his own counsel, and when he grimly recalled that creature he had struggled with in the abandoned cellar, he usually convinced himself it had only been a derelict—a crazy hermit whose appearance had been distorted by the poor light and his own imagination. Nor had his blow more than glanced off the man's forehead, he reasoned, since the other had recovered quickly enough to give chase. It was best not to dwell upon such matters, and this rational explanation helped restore sanity when he awoke from nightmares of that face.

Thus Colin Leverett returned to his studio, and once more plied his pens and brushes and carving knives. The pulp magazines, where fans had acclaimed his work before the War, welcomed him back with long lists of assignments. There were commissions from galleries and collectors, unfinished sculptures and wooden models. Leverett busied himself.

There were problems now. *Short Stories* returned a cover painting as "too grotesque." The publishers of a new anthology of horror stories sent back a pair of his interior drawings—"too gruesome, especially the rotted, bloated faces of those hanged men." A customer returned a silver figurine, complaining that the martyred saint was too thoroughly martyred. Even *Weird Tales,* after heralding his return to its ghoul-haunted pages, began returning illustrations they considered "too strong, even for our readers."

Leverett tried halfheartedly to tone things down, found the results vapid and uninspired. Eventually the assignments stopped trickling in. Leverett, becoming more the recluse as years went by, dismissed the pulp days from his mind. Working quietly in his isolated studio, he found a living doing occasional commissioned pieces and gallery work, from time to time selling a painting or sculpture to major museums. Critics had much praise for his bizarre abstract sculptures.

III

The War was twenty-five years history when Colin Leverett received a letter from a good friend of the pulp days—Prescott Brandon, now editor-publisher of Gothic House, a small press that specialized in books of the weird-fantasy genre. Despite a lapse in correspondence of many years, Brandon's letter began in his typically direct style:

"The Eyrie/Salem, Mass./Aug. 2
To the Macabre Hermit of the Midlands:
Colin, I'm putting together a deluxe 3 volume collection of H. Kenneth

Allard's horror stories. I well recall that Kent's stories were personal favorites of yours. How about shambling forth from retirement and illustrating these for me? Will need 2-color jackets and a dozen line interiors each. Would hope that you can startle fandom with some especially ghastly drawings for these—something different from the hackneyed skulls and bats and werewolves carting off half-dressed ladies.

Interested? I'll send you the materials and details, and you can have a free hand. Let us hear—Scotty"

Leverett was delighted. He felt some nostalgia for the pulp days, and he had always admired Allard's genius in transforming visions of cosmic horror into convincing prose. He wrote Brandon an enthusiastic reply.

He spent hours rereading the stories for inclusion, making notes and preliminary sketches. No squeamish sub-editors to offend here; Scotty meant what he said. Leverett bent to his task with maniacal relish.

Something different, Scotty had asked. A free hand. Leverett studied his pencil sketches critically. The figures seemed headed in the right direction, but the drawings needed something more—something that would inject the mood of sinister evil that pervaded Allard's work. Grinning skulls and leathery bats? Trite. Allard demanded more.

The idea had inexorably taken hold of him. Perhaps because Allard's tales evoked that same sense of horror; perhaps because Allard's visions of crumbling Yankee farmhouses and their depraved secrets so reminded him of that spring afternoon at Mann Brook . . .

Although he had refused to look at it since the day he had staggered in, half-dead from terror and exhaustion, Leverett perfectly recalled where he had flung his notebook. He retrieved it from the back of a seldom used file, thumbed through the wrinkled pages thoughtfully. These hasty sketches reawakened the sense of foreboding evil, the charnel horror of that day. Studying the bizarre lattice patterns, it seemed impossible to Leverett that others would not share his feeling of horror that the stick structures evoked in him.

He began to sketch bits of stick latticework into his pencil roughs. The sneering faces of Allard's degenerate creatures took on an added shadow of menace. Leverett nodded, pleased with the effect.

IV

Some months afterward a letter from Brandon informed Leverett he had received the last of the Allard drawings and was enormously pleased with the work. Brandon added a postscript:

"For God's sake Colin—What is it with these insane sticks you've got poking up everywhere in the illos! The damn things get really creepy after awhile. How on earth did you get onto this?"

Leverett supposed he owed Brandon some explanation. Dutifully he wrote a lengthy letter, setting down the circumstances of his experience at Mann Brook—omitting only the horror that had seized his wrist in the cellar. Let Brandon think him eccentric, but not madman and murderer.

Brandon's reply was immediate:

"*Colin—Your account of the Mann Brook episode is fascinating—and incredible! It reads like the start of one of Allard's stories! I have taken the liberty of forwarding your letter to Alexander Stefroi in Pelham. Dr. Stefroi is an earnest scholar of this region's history—as you may already know. I'm certain your account will interest him, and he may have some light to shed on the uncanny affair.*

Expect 1st volume, Voices from the Shadow, *to be ready from the binder next month. The proofs looked great. Best—Scotty*"

The following weeks brought a letter postmarked Pelham, Massachusetts:

"*A mutual friend, Prescott Brandon, forwarded your fascinating account of discovering curious sticks and stone artifacts on an abandoned farm in upstate New York. I found this most intriguing, and wonder if you recall further details? Can you relocate the exact site after 30 years? If possible, I'd like to examine the foundations this spring, as they call to mind similar megalithic sites of this region. Several of us are interested in locating what we believe are remains of megalithic construction dating back to the Bronze Age, and to determine their possible use in rituals of black magic in colonial days.*

Present archeological evidence indicates that ca. 1700–2000 BC there was an influx of Bronze Age peoples into the Northeast from Europe. We know that the Bronze Age saw the rise of an extremely advanced culture, and that as sea-farers they were to have no peers until the Vikings. Remains of a megalithic culture originating in the Mediterranean can be seen in the Lion Gate in Mycenae, in the Stonehenge, and in dolmens, passage graves and barrow mounds throughout Europe. Moreover, this seems to have represented far more than a style of architecture peculiar to the era. Rather, it appears to have been a religious cult whose adherents worshipped a sort of earth-mother, served her with fertility rituals and sacrifices, and believed that immortality of the soul could be secured through interment in megalithic tombs.

That this culture came to America cannot be doubted from the hundreds of megalithic remnants found—and now recognized—in our region. The most important site to date is Mystery Hill in N.H., comprising a great many walls and dolmens of megalithic construction—most notably the Y Cavern barrow mound and the Sacrificial Table (see postcard). Less spectacular megalithic sites include the group of cairns and carved stones at Mineral Mt., subterranean chambers with stone passageways such as at Petersham and Shutesbury, and uncounted shaped megaliths and buried "monk's cells" throughout this region.

Of further interest, these sites seem to have retained their mystic aura for the early colonials, and numerous megalithic sites show evidence of having been used for sinister purposes by colonial sorcerers and alchemists. This became particularly true after the witchcraft persecutions drove many practitioners into the western wilderness—explaining why upstate New York and western Mass. have seen the emergence of so many cultist groups in later years.

Of particular interest here is Shadrach Ireland's "Brethren of the New Light," who believed that the world was soon to be destroyed by sinister "Powers from Outside" and that they, the elect, would then attain physical immortality. The elect who died beforehand were to have their bodies preserved on tables of stone until the "Old Ones" came forth to return them to life. We have definitely linked the megalithic sites at Shutesbury to later unwholesome practices of the New Light cult. They were absorbed in 1781 by Mother Ann Lee's Shakers, and Ireland's putrescent corpse was hauled from the stone table in his cellar and buried.

Thus I think it probable that your farmhouse may have figured in similar hidden practices. At Mystery Hill a farmhouse was built in 1826 that incorporated one dolmen in its foundations. The house burned down ca. 1848–55, and there were some unsavory local stories as to what took place there. My guess is that your farmhouse had been built over or incorporated a similar megalithic site—and that your "sticks" indicate some unknown cult still survived there. I can recall certain vague references to lattice devices figuring in secret ceremonies, but can pinpoint nothing definite. Possibly they represent a development of occult symbols to be used in certain conjurations, but this is just a guess. I suggest you consult Waite's Ceremonial Magic or such to see if you can recognize similar magical symbols.

Hope this is of some use to you. Please let me hear back.

Sincerely, Alexander Stefroi"

There was a postcard enclosed—a photograph of a 4½ ton granite slab, ringed by a deep groove with a spout, identified as the Sacrificial Table at Mystery Hill. On the back Stefroi had written:

"You must have found something similar to this. They are not rare—we have one in Pelham removed from a site now beneath Quabbin Reservoir. They were used for sacrifice—animal and human—and the groove is to channel blood into a bowl, presumably."

Leverett dropped the card and shuddered. Stefroi's letter reawakened the old horror, and he wished now he had let the matter lie forgotten in his files. Of course, it couldn't be forgotten—even after thirty years.

He wrote Stefroi a careful letter, thanking him for his information and adding a few minor details to his account. This spring, he promised, wondering if he would keep that promise, he would try to relocate the farmhouse on Mann Brook.

v

Spring was late that year, and it was not until early June that Colin Leverett found time to return to Mann Brook. On the surface, very little had changed in three decades. The ancient stone bridge yet stood, nor had the country lane been paved. Leverett wondered whether anyone had driven past since his terror-sped flight.

He found the old railroad grade easily as he started downstream. Thirty years, he told himself—but the chill inside him only tightened. The going was far more difficult than before. The day was unbearably hot and humid. Wading through the rank underbrush raised clouds of black flies that savagely bit him.

Evidently the stream had seen severe flooding in the past years, judging from piled logs and debris that blocked his path. Stretches were scooped out to barren rocks and gravel. Elsewhere gigantic barriers of uprooted trees and debris looked like ancient and mouldering fortifications. As he worked his way down the valley, he realized that his search would yield nothing. So intense had been the force of the long ago flood that even the course of the stream had changed. Many of the dry-wall culverts no longer spanned the brook, but sat lost and alone far back from its present banks. Others had been knocked flat and swept away, or were buried beneath tons of rottings logs.

At one point Leverett found remnants of an apple orchard groping through weeds and bushes. He thought that the house must be close by, but here the flooding had been particularly severe, and evidently even those ponderous stone foundations had been toppled over and buried beneath debris.

Leverett finally turned back to his car. His step was lighter.

A few weeks later he receive a response from Stefroi to his reported failure:

"Forgive my tardy reply to your letter of 13 June. I have recently been pursuing inquiries which may, I hope, lead to the discovery of a previously unreported megalithic site of major significance. Naturally I am disappointed that no traces remained of the Mann Brook site. While I tried not to get my hopes up, it did seem likely that the foundations would have survived. In searching through regional data, I note that

there were particularly severe flashfloods in the Otselic area in July 1942 and again in May 1946. Very probably your old farmhouse with its enigmatic devices was utterly destroyed not very long after your discovery of the site. This is weird and wild country, and doubtless there is much we shall never know.

I write this with a profound sense of personal loss over the death two nights ago of Prescott Brandon. This was a severe blow to me—as I am sure it was to you and to all who knew him. I only hope the police will catch the vicious killers who did this senseless act—evidently thieves surprised while ransacking his office. Police believe the killers were high on drugs from the mindless brutality of their crime.

I had just received a copy of the third Allard volume, Unhallowed Places. A superbly designed book, and this tragedy becomes all the more insuperable with the realization that Scotty will give the world no more such treasures. In Sorrow, Alexander Stefroi"

Leverett stared at the letter in shock. He had not received news of Brandon's death—had only a few days before opened a parcel from the publisher containing a first copy of Unhallowed Places. A line in Brandon's last letter recurred to him—a line that seemed amusing to him at the time:

"Your sticks have bewildered a good many fans, Colin, and I've worn out a ribbon answering inquiries. One fellow in particular—a Major George Leonard—has pressed me for details, and I'm afraid that I told him too much. He has written several times for your address, but knowing how you value your privacy I told him simply to permit me to forward any correspondence. He wants to see your original sketches, I gather, but these overbearing occult-types give me a pain. Frankly, I wouldn't care to meet the man myself."

VI

"Mr. Colin Leverett?"

Leverett studied the tall lean man who stood smiling at the doorway of his studio. The sports car he had driven up in was black and looked expensive. The same held for the turtleneck and leather slacks he wore, and the sleek briefcase he carried. The blackness made his thin face deathly pale. Leverett guessed his age to be late 40 by the thinning of his hair. Dark glasses hid his eyes, black driving gloves his hands.

"Scotty Brandon told me where to find you," the stranger said.

"Scotty?" Leverett's voice was wary.

"Yes, we lost a mutual friend, I regret to say. I'd been talking with him just before . . . But I see by your expression that Scotty never had time to write."

He fumbled awkwardly. "I'm Dana Allard."

"Allard?"

His visitor seemed embarrassed. "Yes—H. Kenneth Allard was my uncle."

"I hadn't realized Allard left a family," mused Leverett, shaking the extended hand. He had never met the writer personally, but there was a strong resemblance to the few photographs he had seen. And Scotty had ben paying royalty checks to an estate of some sort, he recalled.

"My father was Kent's half-brother. He later took his father's name, but there was no marriage, if you follow."

"Of course." Leverett was abashed. "Please find a place to sit down. And what brings you here?"

Dana Allard tapped his briefcase. "Something I'd been discussing with Scotty. Just recently I turned up a stack of my uncle's unpublished manuscripts." He unlatched the briefcase and handed Leverett a sheaf of yellowed paper. "Father collected Kent's personal effects from the state hospital as next-of-kin. He never thought much of my uncle, or his writing. He stuffed this away in our attic and forgot about it. Scotty was quite excited when I told him of my discovery."

Leverett was glancing through the manuscript—page on page of cramped handwriting, with revisions pieced throughout like an indecipherable puzzle. He had seen photographs of Allard manuscripts. There was no mistaking this.

Or the prose. Leverett read a few passages with rapt absorption. It was authentic—and brilliant.

"Uncle's mind seems to have taken an especially morbid turn as his illness drew on," Dana hazarded. "I admire his work very greatly but I find these last few pieces . . . Well, a bit *too* horrible. Especially his translation of his mythical *Book of Elders*."

It appealed to Leverett perfectly. He barely noticed his guest as he pored over the brittle pages. Allard was describing a megalithic structure his doomed narrator had encountered in the crypts beneath an ancient churchyard. There were references to "elder glyphics" that resembled his lattice devices.

"Look here," pointed Dana. "These incantations he records here from Alorri-Zrokros's forbidden tome: 'Yogth-Yugth-Sut-Hyrath-Yogng'—Hell, I can't pronounce them. And he has pages of them."

"This is incredible!" Leverett protested. He tried to mouth the alien syllables. It could be done. He even detected a rhythm.

"Well, I'm relieved that you approve. I'd feared these last few stories and fragments might prove a little too much for Kent's fans."

"Then you're going to have them published?"

Dana nodded. "Scotty was going to. I just hope those thieves weren't searching for this—a collector would pay a fortune. But Scotty said he was going to keep this secret until he was ready for announcement." His thin face was sad.

"So now I'm going to publish it myself—in a deluxe edition. And I want you to illustrate it."

"I'd feel honored!" vowed Leverett, unable to believe it.

"I really liked those drawings you did for the trilogy. I'd like to see more like those—as many as you feel like doing. I mean to spare no expense in publishing this. And those stick things . . ."

"Yes?"

"Scotty told me the story on those. Fascinating! And you have a whole notebook of them? May I see it?"

Leverett hurriedly dug the notebook from his file, returned to the manuscript.

Dana paged through the book in awe. "These things are totally bizarre—and there are references to such things in the manuscript, to make it even more fantastic. Can you reproduce them all for the book?"

"All I can remember," Leverett assured him. "And I have a good memory. But won't that be overdoing it?"

"Not at all! They fit into the book. And they're utterly unique. No, put everything you've got into this book. I'm going to entitle it *Dwellers in the Earth*, after the longest piece. I've already arranged for its printing, so we begin as soon as you can have the art ready. And I know you'll give it your all."

VII

He was floating in space. Objects drifted past him. Stars, he first thought. The objects drifted closer.

Sticks. Stick lattices of all configurations. And then he was drifting among them, and he saw that they were not sticks—not of wood. The lattice designs were of dead-pale substance, like streaks of frozen starlight. They reminded him of glyphics of some unearthly alphabet—complex, enigmatic symbols arranged to spell . . . what? And there *was* an arrangement—a three-dimensional pattern. A maze of utterly baffling intricacy . . .

Then somehow he was in a tunnel. A cramped, stone-lined tunnel through which he must crawl on his belly. The dank, moss-slimed stones pressed close about his wriggling form, evoking shrill whispers of claustrophobic dread.

And after an indefinite space of crawling through this and other stone-lined burrows, and sometimes through passages whose angles hurt his eyes, he would creep forth into a subterranean chamber. Great slabs of granite a dozen feet across formed the walls and ceiling of this buried chamber, and between the slabs other burrows pierced the earth. Altar-like, a gigantic slab of gneiss waited in the center of the chamber. A spring welled darkly between the stone pillars that supported the table. Its outer edge was encircled by a groove, sickeningly stained by the substance that clotted in the stone bowl beneath its collecting spout.

Others were emerging from the darkened burrows that ringed the chamber—slouched figures only dimly glimpsed and vaguely human. And a figure in a tattered cloak came toward him from the shadow—stretched out a claw-like hand to seize his wrist and draw him toward the sacrificial table. He followed unresistingly, knowing that something was expected of him.

They reached the altar and in the glow from the cuneiform lattices chiseled into the gneiss slab he could see the guide's face. A mouldering corpse-face, the rotted bone of its forehead smashed inward upon the foulness that oozed forth . . .

And Leverett would awaken to the echo of his screams . . .

He'd been working too hard, he told himself, stumbling about in the darkness, getting dressed because he was too shaken to return to sleep. The nightmares had been coming every night. No wonder he was exhausted.

But in his studio his work awaited him. Almost fifty drawings finished now, and he planned another score. No wonder the nightmares.

It was a grueling pace, but Dana Allard was ecstatic with the work he had done. And *Dwellers in the Earth* was waiting. Despite problems with typesetting, with getting the special paper Dana wanted—the book only waited on him.

Though his bones ached with fatigue, Leverett determinedly trudged through the graying night. Certain features of the nightmare would be interesting to portray.

VIII

The last of the drawings had gone off to Dana Allard in Petersham, and Leverett, fifteen pounds lighter and gut-weary, converted part of the bonus check into a case of good whiskey. Dana had the offset presses rolling as soon as the plates were shot from the drawings. Despite his precise planning, presses had broken down, one printer quit for reasons not stated, there had been a bad accident at the new printer—seemingly innumerable problems, and Dana had been furious at each delay. But the production pushed along quickly for all that. Leverett wrote that the book was cursed, but Dana responded that a week would see it ready.

Leverett amused himself in his studio constructing stick lattices and trying to catch up on his sleep. He was expecting a copy of the book when he received a letter from Stefroi:

"*Have tried to reach you by phone last few days, but no answer at your house. I'm pushed for time just now, so must be brief. I have indeed uncovered an unsuspected megalithic site of enormous importance. It's located on the estate of a long-prominent Mass. family—and as I cannot receive authorization to visit it, I will not say where. Have investigated secretly (and quite illegally) for a short time one night and was nearly caught. Came across reference to the place in collection of 17th century letters and papers in a divinity school library. Writer denouncing the family as a brood of sorcerers and witches, references to alchemical activities and other less savory rumors—and describes underground stone chambers, megalithic artifacts etc. which are put to "foul usage and diabolic praktise." Just got a quick glimpse but his description was not exaggerated. And Colin—in creeping through the woods to get to the site, I came across dozens of your mysterious "sticks!" Brought a small one back and have it here to show you. Recently constructed and exactly like your drawings. With luck, I'll gain admittance and find out their significance—undoubtedly they have significance—though these cultists can be stubborn about sharing their secrets. Will explain my interest is scientific, no exposure to ridicule—and see what they say. Will get a closer look one way or another. And so—I'm off! Sincerely, Alexander Stefroi*"

Leverett's bushy brows rose. Allard had intimated certain dark rituals in which the stick lattices figured. But Allard had written over thirty years ago, and Leverett assumed the writer had stumbled onto something similar to the Mann Brook site. Stefroi was writing about something current.

He rather hoped Stefroi would discover nothing more than an inane hoax.

The nightmares haunted him still—familiar now, for all that its scenes and phantasms were visited by him only in dream. Familiar. The terror that they evoked was undiminished.

Now he was walking through forest—a section of hills that seemed to be close by. A huge slab of granite had been dragged aside, and a pit yawned where it had lain. He entered the pit without hesitation, and the rounded steps that led downward were known to his tread. A buried stone chamber, and leading from it stone-lined burrows. He knew which one to crawl into.

And again the underground room with its sacrificial altar and its dark spring beneath, and the gathering circle of poorly glimpsed figures. A knot of them clustered about the stone table, and as he stepped toward them he saw they pinned a frantically writhing man.

It was a stoutly built man, white hair disheveled, flesh gouged and filthy. Recognition seemed to burst over the contorted features, and he wondered if he should know the man. But now the lich with the caved-in skull was whispering in his ear, and he tried not to think of the unclean things that peered from that cloven brow, and instead took the bronze knife from the skeletal hand, and raised the knife high, and because he could not scream and awaken, did with the knife as the tattered priest had whispered . . .

And when after an interval of unholy madnss, he at last did awaken, the stickiness that covered him was not cold sweat, nor was it nightmare the half-devoured heart he clutched in one fist.

IX

Leverett somehow found sanity enough to dispose of the shredded lump of flesh. He stood under the shower all morning, scrubbing his skin raw. He wished he could vomit.

There was a news item on the radio. The crushed body of noted archeologist, Dr. Alexander Stefroi, had been discovered beneath a fallen granite slab near Whately. Police speculated the gigantic slab had shifted with the scientist's excavations at its base. Identification was made through personal effects.

When his hands stopped shaking enough to drive, Leverett fled to Petersham—reaching Dana Allard's old stone house about dark. Allard was slow to answer his frantic knock.

"Why, good evening, Colin! What a coincidence your coming here just now! The books are ready. The bindery just delivered them."

Leverett brushed past him. "We've got to destroy them!" he blurted. He'd thought a lot since morning.

"Destroy them?"

"There's something none of us figured on. Those stick lattices—there's a cult, some damnable cult. The lattices have some significance in their rituals. Stefroi hinted once they might be glyphics of some sort, I don't know. But the cult is still alive. They killed Scotty . . . they killed Stefroi. They're onto me—I don't know what they intend. They'll kill you to stop you from releasing this book!"

Dana's frown was worried, but Leverett knew he hadn't impressed him the right way. "Colin, this sounds insane. You really have been overextending yourself, you know. Look, I'll show you the books. They're in the cellar."

Leverett let his host lead him downstairs. The cellar was quite large, flagstoned and dry. A mountain of brown-wrapped bundles awaited them.

"Put them down here where they wouldn't knock the floor out," Dana explained. "They start going out to distributors tomorrow. Here, I'll sign your copy."

Distractedly Leverett opened a copy of *Dwellers in the Earth*. He gazed at his lovingly rendered drawings of rotting creatures and buried stone chambers and stained altars—and everywhere the enigmatic latticework structures. He shuddered.

"Here." Dana Allard handed Leverett the book he had signed. "And to answer your question, they *are* elder glyphics."

But Leverett was staring at the inscription in its unmistakable handwriting: "For Colin Leverett, Without whom this work could not have seen completion—H. Kenneth Allard."

Allard was speaking. Leverett saw places where the hastily applied flesh-toned makeup didn't quite conceal what lay beneath. "Glyphics symbolic of alien dimensions—inexplicable to the human mind, but essential fragments of an evocation so unthinkably vast that the 'pentagram' (if you will) is miles across. Once before we tried—but your iron weapon destroyed part of Althol's brain. He erred at the last instant—almost annihilating us all. Althol had been formulating the evocation since he fled the advance of iron four millennia past.

"Then you reappeared, Colin Leverett—you with your artist's knowledge and diagrams of Althol's symbols. And now a thousand new minds will read the evocation you have returned to us, unite with our minds as we stand in the Hidden Places. And the Great Old Ones will come forth from the earth, and we, the dead who have steadfastly served them, shall be masters of the living."

Leverett turned to run, but now they were creeping forth from the shadows of the cellar, as massive flagstones slid back to reveal the tunnels beyond. He began to scream as Althol came to lead him away, but he could not awaken, could only follow.

AFTERWORD

Some readers may note certain similarities between characters and events in this story and the careers of real-life figures, well known to fans of this genre. This was unavoidable, and no disrespect is intended. For much of this story *did* happen, though I suppose you've heard that one before.

In working with Lee Brown Coye on Wellman's *Worse Things Waiting*, I finally asked him why his drawings so frequently included sticks in their design. Lee's work is well known to me, but I had noticed that the "sticks" only began to appear in his work for Ziff-Davis in the early '60s. Lee finally sent me a folder of clippings and letters, far more eerie than this story—and factual.

In 1938 Coye *did* come across a stick-ridden farmhouse in the desolate Mann Brook region. He kept this to himself until fall of 1962, when John Vetter passed the account to August Derleth and to antiquarian-archeologist Andrew E. Rothovius. Derleth intended to write Coye's adventure as a Lovecraft novelette, but never did so. Rothovius discussed the site's possible megalithic significance with Coye in a series of letters and journal articles on which I have barely touched. In June 1963 Coye returned to the Mann Brook site and found it obliterated. It is a strange region, as HPL knew.

Coye's fascinating presentation of their letters appeared in five weekly installments of his "Chips and Shavings" column in the *Mid-York Weekly* from August 22 to September 26, 1963. Rothovius, whose research into the New England megaliths has been published in many journals, wrote an excellent and disquieting summary of his research in Arkham House's *The Dark Brotherhood,* to which the reader is referred.

NOMINEES—BEST BOOK—SINGLE AUTHOR
COLLECTION OR ANTHOLOGY:

From Evil's Pillow—Basil Copper   a collection of ghost stories from England

°*Worse Things Waiting*—Manly Wade Wellman   a retrospective of fifty years of fantasy writing

MANLY WADE WELLMAN/*Single Author Collection*

I had, in a way, dreaded meeting Manly Wellman at the convention. I was afraid Manly Wade Wellman wouldn't turn out to be Manly Wade Wellman. You know what I mean—that the warm, complicated, and kindly personality which had shown through his work, and of which I had become so fond through the years, might turn out to have been all along some kind of misconception; a bad guess.

I need not have worried, because Manly Wellman is just what you hope he'll be, reader, and maybe even better. He has the South/Southwest accent you often hear rolling out at you from the stories, easy ways (but he places himself carefully), strong hands that have known a lot of work, and gentle eyes that don't miss much.

He won his Single Author Collection Award for *Worse Things Waiting*, published by Carcosa, handsomely illustrated by Lee Brown Coye, and now a collector's prize. The book doesn't contain any of the John the Balladeer stories, those being well assembled in his *Who Fears the Devil?*, nor does it have any of his John Thunstone stories, particular favorites of mine, which Wellman says will be gathered into a book, and I say the sooner the better. But it does assemble the best of his other work and is, therefore, a treasure. Go forth and track it down, as the following two samples from it, "Come into my Parlor," a monster story I think you'll find quite unique, and "Fearful Rock," a robust demonstration of the relative powers of good and evil, are just good indications of what a delight the whole book is. Wellman has written me of the two stories that they are "Both of them founded on what people tell as fact, here in the jumbled lights and shadows of the South."

Mr. Wellman always knows how to give you a good scare.

Manly Wade Wellman

COME INTO MY PARLOR

Between Henry and myself exist almost perfect mutual respect and understanding. I do not presume ordinarily to advise him about how he administers the yard, the shrubbery, the orchard or the vegetable garden; he refrains ordinarily from commenting on my tastes and enthusiasms. But on that morning he straightened up from the bean-bed, hoe in huge dented fist, and turned his broad, black proud old face full toward me.

"You really goin' that swamp, seh?" he demanded. "Seems like all I int'rested in is plants we can eat; all you int'rested in is plants can eat us."

"Not unless they grow bigger than anything I've collected so far, Henry," I temporized, making my expression as solemn as his. "Pitcher plants eat only insects."

"They maybe grow bigger'n you seen," he persisted. "I live down here longer'n you done. I seen lots o' things. Some of 'em don't do no good. You let me tell you, seh."

I generally let him tell me. There had been his stubborn attitude about planting according to the "signs." Stars and moon indicated "good days" for various crops. During our first association in Carolina I had sometimes scoffed, not very gently, and overrode his suggestions. The maddening sequel was that the sowings by "signs" had prospered, and those less astrologically conditioned were skimpy. I had yielded the point, telling myself lamely that I did so to spare my gardener's feelings. Thereafter Henry's planting was uniformly fruitful. But this morning I differed once again.

"I'll be all right, Henry. I know there are snakes in the swamp, but I'll wear wading boots. The pitcher plants—they're what I want to write about for a paper. For what they call a botanical journal."

"Then go some other swamp 'sides that'n," he almost pleaded. "That the Gardinel Swamp. Call it that 'cause they's a gardinel there."

"Gardinel?" The term was new to me. "What's a gardinel, Henry? Something alive?"

He pondered. "Can't rightly say it's alive or not, seh. But it ain't goin' do you no good, I mean to say."

"Come on, tell me," I urged him. "Tell me about gardinels. What are they?"

"Not what you goin' think they is," he replied darkly. "Now, that all I goin' say. 'Cause if I told you, first thing you won't believe me. Next thing, you'll halfway believe and go lookin'. And I ain't goin' have you look too close to no gardinel."

"You mean that the swamp's haunted," I teased him. "What are gardinels, Henry? Ghosts? Witches?"

He shook his head slowly and reproachfully. I mused that if Henry were stripped to a loin-cloth, with plumes bound to his brow and a spear and shield in his big hands, he would look like a warrior chief of some proud and dangerous African tribe. "Listen me," he said deeply and carefully. "I don't make no ign'ant talk. I ain't believe in nothin' about plat-eyes nor witches nor them things, not since I was just a chap. But that Gardinel Swamp, seh, it ain't goin' do you no good." He cocked an eye upward. "Goin' rain, anyhow."

In weather predictions, too, Henry was almost always right; but the sky was blue and hot with the heat of late Carolina spring, and I did not bother even to speak my confidence of a sunny day. "I'll see you later, Henry, and tell you everything."

"I do hopes so," he said pessimistically, and I left him to the gardening and walked back around the house to where my car stood under the dogwoods. I got into the front seat, already stacked with iron bucket, trowel and machete, and drove away.

I had not far to drive, though most of the way was over excessively bad dirt roads. Bucking and bouncing my car over ruts and rocks, I comforted myself with the thought that this meant the swamp would be comparatively untouched. Fishermen would go elsewhere, likewise botanists. Four grim miles my car and I toiled. Five. I came to what must be the place described to me by the plausible tea-tinted house boy Henry never seemed to like—the point where the mutilated trail dipped sharply down between groves of jack oak and long-leaf pine, then rose again beyond. At the lowest stretch were close-thronged trees, matted between with vines and weeds, and through them a flashing hint of water.

I pulled my wading boots up to my thighs and took pail, trowel and machete. Through the thickets led a suggestion of an old foot path. As I entered it I had to slash away the thickest of the tangle. Something slithered away underfoot—one of the snakes which, I tried to convince Henry and myself, I did not fear. Mud and shallow water tugged at my boot soles. Ahead of me sang legions of frogs, in voices of varied pitch, tempo and inflection. As I advanced, they grew discreetly silent around me, then resumed their chant on my back trail. I labored up a low bank of sandy clay, and looked at the lake.

It was quiet, deep, and fairly extensive. Well under the water, tinted yellow-green with leaf mould, I could see masses of ancient trunks and branches, the trees that were drowned when the lake was created by the dam on which I stood. Who had built that dam, and what had become of the builder? The house boy could not tell me. If Henry knew, he had not said. But at the far end I could see the tops of dead trees that stood above water level, where the channel of the old stream would still exist. Along its soggy margins would be pitcher plants. I tramped away, pausing once to see a big whiteheaded bird—I thought it might be an eagle—drop down like a divebomber, splash violently in the water, and soar away with a struggling shiny something in its talons. I walked half a mile. Another snake, fat and black and even more nervous than I, wriggled from before me. The trees grew closer to the water, and their leaves made me a canopy against the sun's blaze. Under them led the trail, faint and partially grown over, as though unused to feet. Following it, I came to what I wanted.

In the juicy waterside loam they grew, belt beyond belt, lifting their yellow blooms like signal lanterns above their arrays of leaf-tubes, the pitcher plants. Inside me bloomed a satisfying warmth, as I gazed all alone on beds and clusters of them, mine for the easy troweling.

At my first glimpse I could see thirty or forty among the roots and fallen boughs, but I picked my way carefully among them; I would have trod as soon on the toes of my sweetheart. These were a common sort, as much as any pitcher plant can be common—*Sarracenia flava*, with umbrella-like blooms and upright tubular leaves, each furnished with a frilly lidlike tip above the upper opening. But I was entranced. "*Sarracenia flava*," I said aloud, enjoying the Latin term, and wondered if I were not developing into a bore and fanatic, a hobbyist gone to seed.

Well back in the mass stood the largest of all. It had several huge leaves, the tallest rising chest-high to me and as large round its upper bulge as my two hands could span. Approaching my face, I caught a whiff of rotten stench. Gingerly I lifted the canopy-tip and peered in; the hollow was almost full of insect corpses, stacked to within short inches of the top. No wonder the leaf had grown and stretched. I studied the bright red tracery of lines upon the deep green, so like a network of blood vessels. Was this color a lure to flying gnats and beetles, or could it be something akin to animal blood, sucked from many victims? I peered into a smaller tube, and saw in the dim jade-filtered light of the interior a frothy something, like spittle. Spittle—it must be notably close to just that, or digestive juice. I had read about it. Its particular nature was that its molecules did not adhere, as in so many liquids. An exploring insect, attracted by the honey-dew of the tube's upper reaches and then forced to crawl downward by the earth-pointing hairs, would fall into that mess, and sink and become digested.

Beyond, the *Sarracenia flava* thinned out, but where a tiny stagnant arm of the stream ran across the soft muck I found at a rockside another pet study of mine; a clump of sundew. Like a cluster of tiny sea anemones it seemed, its leaves making a muster of round, fuzzy red blobs; and like sea anemones those blobs welcomed in their prey. Where the Venus flytrap is like two hands clapping shut upon the victim, these were like single palms outstretched and greedy. Beyond was a smaller, paler clump; the stronger one, exuding a more plentiful supply of dew-bait, was clutching the greater share of swamp insects. I was disposed to be sympathetic. After a failure or two, I caught one of the gnats that buzzed around my perspiring face, and carefully dropped it upon a pleading leaf of the weaker sundew. If any plant had the wit and character to recognize charity and be grateful, it would be such a vegetable carnivore.

Something of a scientific question was clarifying itself in my mind as I stepped across the little run of water and came beyond to yet other trove for a man of my inclinations. More *Sarracenia*, and this time *Sarracenia purpurea*. The dentral umbrella-bloom was deep maroon here, and the pitchers true pitchers in form—squat and plump, and the frill on each served, not as a canopy to force flying prey down, but as a lip to bring crawling prey in. These lay low on the damp earth, soliciting ground insects as the leaves of the *flava* reached high after winged ones. But the red veinlike traceries were notably similar, and the wetness within contained its melancholy messes of dead and half-dissolved ants and midges. I knelt on one rubber-sheathed knee and began to trowel out a good specimen. My impulse was shaping itself into articulate plan.

These plants ate animals. Everybody, scientist and layman, knew that. In some countries men even nurtured them indoors to keep down clouds of flies and mosquitoes. But to what extent did pitcher plants, sundews and their kin depend upon meat? I tried to hark back to my first interest in the subject—my fourth grade at grammar school, and a fascinating sentence written on the blackboard for us to parse:

The pitcher plant is sometimes called the monkey-cup, because apes will often lift the lids and drink the water when they can find no springs to quench their thirst.

I could remember it, and repeat it perfectly. I doubted its truth as scientific pronouncement; no fastidious monkey, however parched, would be apt to drink of the mingled putrescence and stickiness contained in a vegetable pitcher. But the drama of the sentence had fired at once my boyish interest. I had even tried to draw a picture of a monkey at his alleged potations, and the teacher had seen and accused me of caricaturing her own rather simian features. From that day forward, pitcher plants and other meat-eaters of the vegetable world had been my enthusiasm.

What I would do now would be to take specimens from this swamp—many specimens, gathered on trip after trip. I would grow them, with much water and leaf mould, at my own house. I would test them with animal food, trapped insects and shreds of beef and pork from my icebox. I would feed some plentifully others sparingly, others not at all. The response, in growth or languishing, might interest the world of science. Even Henry, for all his sage and practical concentration on food plants, could hardly help but be interested. Growing things were his work. If he would join me in caring for my planned garden of pitcher plants—

The rain began, and even as I straightened up it became a downpour.

Once again Henry had been right about the weather. Admitting that, I felt as if I were doing him a favor in the admission. As to that, never had he been more right; the rain drenched my clothes almost on the instant, hammered my hat savagely, and trickled down my trouser legs into my wading boots. I wanted to get away from there, and turned back the way I had come; but then, as though it had been waiting to see what I would do, the wind arrived. It swept a flood of rain, almost horizontal, into my face. So hard and unexpected was the impact of driven water that I gave back before it, putting out my hand for support. I seized only a big rising tube-leaf of *Sarracenia flava*, that broke under my grasp.

I stooped for my bucket and machete, and turned my back to the tempest, mule-fashion. Before me showed the half-hidden trail. It crawled on among the pitcher plants, as thick here as some sort of grotesque lawn—I knew it must lead somewhere. And anywhere would naturally be better than this. I let the gale and the rain drive me along.

It seemed to me that the plants grew bigger and yet bigger as I tramped between them and past them. The *flava* rose like green posts, and the lower-lying, heavier receptacles of the *purpurea* swelled here and there almost to pint-size, and quivered under the rain-beat as though with life and sense. I hoped for a tree under which to stand, and there were trees, but no foliage could deny that storm. On I plodded, and on, so wet now that I could not get wetter, through mud that sucked up over my insteps and tried to tug my boots from my feet. There came a curve in the trail, around a specimen of *flava* so high and luxuriant as to be almost a clumpy shrub. Then, beyond, I saw what brightened my spirits inside my soggy clothing and water-hammered skin.

It was a house. Not a big house nor, as seen through the veil of rain, a particularly handsome one. But it was a house, and inside would be shelter.

I staggered the last few steps toward it. Its shape seemed solid but irregular, as though it had been built by someone who did not know rule nor plumb-line. It looked gray and coarse-grainy, as though sheathed in plaster, and its conical-seeming roof was brown and apparently made of thick, untidy thatching. Toward the trail faced a doorway, dark and wide, and to either side of this a window, like eyes in a gray old face. Those windows had a glassy shine to them, and beyond them flickering lights, as though there were an open fire within. I made my way toward the door, pausing once with my hand hooked upon a low branch of a tree in the front yard, holding myself erect under that incessant rain that was like the stream of a fire hose played upon me by a malevolent practical joker. I gazed at the doorway. It had no panel, but there were curtains of a sort, drawn together from inside; leather-brown curtains sturdy enough not to be blown or swept aside by the rain that assailed them.

"Hey!" I yelled the universal Carolina greeting, hoping to be heard above the tumult.

The light-flickers at the windows seemed to rise, then to fall. That was all the response. Letting go of the branch I plodded closer through marshy mud. "May I come in?" I yelled, more loudly. I pounded at the edge of the doorway. It made a muffled sound, as if on wet earth. "Is anybody home?" I tried again, feeling like the traveler in Walter de la Mare's poem.

Nobody answered. I gazed at the curtains. They were somehow laced or hooked together from top to bottom. Determinedly I lectured myself that hospitality in this case was obligation as well as virtue. If nobody would admit me, I would go in anyway. Perhaps the house-dweller was away, caught somewhere else in the tempest. If he begrudged me shelter, he would be selfish and evil to the last degree.

But first I fought my way back to the tree, and drove into it the point of my machete. I could hardly trespass, even in my need, with so formidable-seeming a blade naked in my hand. On the haft of the machete I hung my bucket, noticing that the rain had filled it almost to the halfway point. Then I returned and pushed against the curtains. They parted, slowly and springily, and I could see that their fastening was an ingenious one. Each inner edge bore a fringe of incurved spines or clamps, made perhaps of whalebone. When the curtains were drawn, these projections would interlace like clasped fingers. They bent inward before my pressure, and let me pass through. Then the curtains snapped together behind me, as if they were of strong elastic.

I stood panting and dripping, wondering where the fire was. The interior was dark. The air, which I gulped in wearily, seemed heavy, tepid, dull. "Hello!" I called, and my voice sounded muffled, as though I spoke in a soundproof chamber with walls curtained against echoes. Nothing answered me.

I took another step, sidewise this time, groping to right and left. My boots moved something light on the floor, but I could touch no furniture. I strained my eyes, trying to accustom them to the blackness. But it remained superlatively dark, as dark, I mentally repeated in terms of the old cliche, as the inside of a cow. As dark, probably, as Jonah found the belly of the sea monster that gulped him down. Gulped him down! That brought back to my mind the curtain that had sprung behind me like closing jaws, and its edges fringed with what might be compared to whalebone.

But I could barely hear the downpour of rain without. "It may rain outdoors if it chooses," I paraphrased Tweedledee and Tweedledum aloud, for the comfort of hearing a voice, even my own. I turned around, and the toes of my boots stirred something again. Firewood? I thought of the gleam I had seen through the windows. If the fire had died so suddenly, I would build it up again.

I probed my pockets, and touched a wet briar pipe, then a pouch and a match-safe. These last were water-proof, and thoughts of tobacco made my mouth water. In the dark I zipped open the pouch, filled the pipe, then produced a match. I struck it on the roughened edge of the safe and lifted the flame toward the bowl of the pipe.

By the tiny light I saw something of the chamber I had invaded. My first impression was of a feeble pinkness, and of an inner shape without corners or planes, a sort of egg-shaped hollow. Odd what illusions assail one's first glance, I philosophized as I kindled the tobacco and drew a lungful of smoke. Then I held the match high for a second and better examination.

It had been no illusion. The room was egg-shaped indeed, and its tinted surface seemed rough and porous, like the plaster outside. I stepped toward the nearest partition to touch it, and abruptly drew my hand away again. The substance of the wall was elastic and clammy, like dead meat. I backed away, still holding the flaming splinter of wood. My heel touched something that rolled aside from the pressure, and I glanced down.

The thing was round and pale, about the size of a small melon, and seemed to gaze up at me blankly with two shadowy eyes. Beyond it was another, among jumbled scatterings like loosened faggots of sticks, also pale and smooth. I studied the nearest roundness, and saw that it looked so much like a human skull because that was what it was.

And the nearby round thing was another skull. Farther off lay a third. The sticks—they were bones. Ribs, femurs, shins. At that instant the match burned down to my fingertips, and I dropped it. The darkness jumped in around me again.

"This isn't any good," I said, again aloud, and my words were almost those of Henry. "My host seems to collect skeletons—probably with violence. I was a fool to leave my machete outside."

I struck a second match and turned to seek the curtained doorway. Better the bath of rain than this baleful shelter.

For a moment I thought the door was gone. Then I made out the clasped spines, like giant stitching running from floor to a point above my head. The inner surface of the curtains matched the walls in color and texture, and was not at once identifiable. I held the match high and with my other hand pried at the projections that held the curtain-edges together.

At first touch they were yielding, then seemed abruptly to grow stiff and stubborn. Too, they were somehow twined together, like splicing of wire—had they done that when I came in, or were they doing it now? My matchlight danced on them, and I hoped my eyes and fancy were not playing me tricks. I stopped trying to conquer the clamps, and pushed hard to one side, hoping to force the curtains apart in that manner.

My hand slipped a little. The surface was slightly wet—no; copiously wet. I dropped my second match, shakily kindled a third, and studied the place. Sweatlike moisture had sprung out where I had touched the fleshy-seeming material, a patch the size and shape of my open hand. And there, at least the expanse was not porous, but seemed to be covered with bristly hair, the dead pinkness of the rest of the compartment. I investigated with a fingertip, and pulled it back with a cry.

The hairs had seemed to dart at that fingertip, and it ran blood. A drop fell at my feet, another. In panic and desperation, I doubled my fist and struck at where the curtains must be. My fist bounded back—it, too, dripped blood. More hairs had greeted its impact. Hairs seemed to sprout everywhere, to creep forth from the thick-sprinkled pores.

I shook my bleeding hand, and more drops flew from it. They splashed audibly on the floor, to which I looked again. It was damp around my feet. A little frothy pool, like sea foam, had sprung up there. As I stepped clear of it, more seeped into view around the new position of my boot soles. One of the ribs lying at hand stirred in the deepening liquid.

Again I wished for my machete. Taking another match from the safe, I lighted it at the dying one, and then felt in my pocket for my claspknife. It was slim and pearl-handled, heartbreakingly inadequate as weapon or tool, but I made shift to open it. My hands shook like autumn leaves in a wind, and the knife dropped from my fingers. I stooped for it, groping in the frothy liquid at my feet. The stuff burned my skin like acid, and I pulled my hand out of it with a loud and frightened oath. My current matchlight showed my fingers tinted angry-rosy, with blisters burgeoning upon them. I struck another match. I had to.

Now the confining chamber-walls showed stirring and quivering. They were bushy and horrent with pale bristles, erect as porcupine quills, all rhythmically a-tremble, all pointing toward me as if to focus some dreadful attention. Between them foamed and dripped forth more juice, cascading down. I sloshed toward the center of the floor, to a point equidistant from all touches of that grisly lining. The flood of liquid was rising more swiftly, now to my ankles, then to my shins. It rippled and rolled, and the bones danced in its wavelets. Yet again my light went out, and I did not renew it.

My mind clung to a few points of logic, as a man in a hurricane clings to the branches of a tree, trying to keep himself from being borne away. Henry's half-forgotten words came clearly back into my memory. To my scoffing assurance that pitcher plants eat nothing larger than insects he had said, "They maybe grow bigger'n you seen." Of gardinels, "Not what you goin' think they is." To my promise to return, "I do hopes so."

Against this disaster he had tried vainly to warn me. He had not told me everything because he knew I would reject the full truth. I had walked of my own will into a trap as deadly as were the hollow leaves of *Sarracenia* to mosquitoes. Like those pitcher-snares, this tight-closed interior was now exuding something that would digest comfortably the dinner it had taken in. My boots alone had saved me so far, their stout waterproof construction had baffled the gnawings of the flood of secretion. But that flood was rising, with greedy swiftness. It was at my knees now. Soon it would reach my unprotected upper legs. Even if I stayed on my feet . . .

But I would not be able to manage even that. The chamber was filling with a steamy-sour smell that drove itself into my nostrils, and beyond into all of me. My head swam, my brain seemed to shrink small and drowsy within it. I felt my knees waver. I tried to plant my feet apart to keep my balance, and they slid and almost lost their grip on the slippery floor beneath the liquid. I shut my eyes in the dark, but some appearance of lightning flashed within them, and my ears rang and roared as with the sound of giant waterfalls. Every joint of my body, every sinew, slowly relaxed, as if gratefully seeking rest. That odor was drugging me. One more lungful of it, two more at most, and I would collapse into the pool that rose around me, and it would sting me with corrosive agony just once, briefly, not enough to keep me awake.

Then the universe vibrated around me. I opened my eyes, and fancied that light gleamed before me, a greatening patch of gray clarity, across which darker shadows struggled. I heard a voice, deep and commanding, call me by my name. This would be the ultimate illusion, some little surviving crumb of my wits told me. I stepped involuntarily toward that light, and it was strong enough to show me a huge bare arm, plum-black like some rich tropical fruit, extended toward me. It opened a broad hand as though to seize me.

"Come!" roared that compelling voice. "Come quick!"

The great lighted space grew. Its confining border of darkness fell away, before the edge of something bright and powerful, like the flaming sword of an angel. Another plum-black hand wielded that hewing weapon, with a strength and fury beyond my dream of what mortal hand could do. Was this the coming of death himself, I asked, terribly embodied as epic poets had written him? Or only some vague symbolism in my perishing consciousness?

I swayed nearer the great arm, or it reached more insistently toward me, and its hand fastened upon my shoulder as the jaws of a beast clutch a fainting prey. Half dragging, half lifting, the hand drew me toward the light and up into it, and then I must have fallen, though I did not feel the impact of any surface.

But when my eyes and brain cleared, I lay on damp earth, gazing up past shiny-wet leaves into a sky where plum clouds broke away from the high-climbing sun. A face pushed itself into my range of vision. It was a broad, black face, with tense lines around its mouth and anxiety in its intent eyes.

"Henry," I mumbled, "what are you doing here?"

He shook his head slowly. "I come after you, seh. When you wouldn't set no store by what I say, I come after you. Just about time I did, too."

I sat up, supporting myself with spread hands on the mud. "But where—" I began shakily, and broke off. I tried again. "The last thing I remember, I was inside—"

"That's the truth, seh. Inside the gardinel. The trail show me the way you go. I hear you sloshin' around in there, and stuck outside in a tree I find this." He lifted his big hand to show my machete. "I chop through that curtain-thing and snake you out there, I mean to say."

He dropped the machete, fished a bandana from the pocket of his dungarees, and roughly but capably wiped my face. "I tell you," he admonished me mildly, "that thing don't do you no good."

I looked around me. With his help I got to my feet. "Where is it?"

"Long ways from here, seh. I carry you here. Don't pay no mind to where it find itself now. Gardinels, they hide when they want to. Never know where they pop up. Anyways, I ain't takin' you back to look—I scared worse'n I ever been since I wasn't no bigger'n a rabbit."

"Scared," I repeated. "You were scared. I don't blame you. But you got me out."

"Yes, seh, I get you out." He smiled then, a great ivory-studded slash across his face. "Thankful as can be I can do that. I guess maybe you the only man ever been inside a gardinel and come out to tell."

"I saw the bones of other men," I remembered, much against my will.

"I reckon so. Way I always hear it, gardinels don't eat nothin' less good'n man meat."

"As pitcher plants eat insects," I suggested.

"Just like them. Those plant-things put up somethin' bugs like, sort of honey-tastin' stuff. Gardinels—I don't figger is they plants, or animals, or somethin' else not either—but they put up what a man might want. They fix theyself to look like a house near as they can. Man go in, man don't come out no more. He perish to death in there. Savin' only yourself."

"Like the mimicry of the pitcher plants," I pondered out loud. "Not protective mimicry, it's predatory mimicry. I wouldn't have believed—"

"Didn't I say just like that this mornin'?" reminded Henry. "If you don't b'lieve me then, who goin' b'lieve you now you fix to tell about it?" He chopped reflectively at a bush-top with the machete, then studied me. "You feel like you can walk back to the car?"

"I can," I said. "I'm going home. I'll destroy every pitcher plant I have."

"Yes, seh. And I'll help you destroy them, seh."

Manly Wade Wellman

FEARFUL ROCK

1. *The Sacrifice*

Enid Mandifer tried to stand up under what she had just heard. She managed it, but her ears rang, her eyes misted. She felt as if she were drowning.

The voice of Persil Mandifer came through the fog, level and slow, with the hint of that foreign accent which nobody could identify:

"Now that you know that you are not really my daughter, perhaps you are curious as to why I adopted you."

Curious . . . was that the word to use? But this man who was not her father after all, he delighted in understatements. Enid's eyes had grown clearer now. She was able to move, to obey Persil Mandifer's invitation to seat herself. She saw him, half sprawling in his rocking-chair against the plastered wall of the parlor, under the painting of his ancient friend Aaron Burr. Was the rumor true, she mused, that Burr had not really died, that he still lived and planned ambitiously to make himself a throne in America? But Aaron Burr would have to be an old, old man—a hundred years old, or more than a hundred.

Persil Mandifer's own age might have been anything, but probably he was nearer seventy than fifty. Physically he was the narrowest of men, in shoulders, hips, temples and legs alike, so that he appeared distorted and compressed. White hair, like combed thistledown, fitted itself in ordered streaks to his high skull. His eyes, dull and dark as musket-balls, peered expressionlessly above the nose like a stiletto, the chin like the pointed toe of a fancy boot. The fleshlessness of his legs was accentuated by tight trousers, strapped under the insteps. At his throat sprouted a frill of lace, after a fashion twenty-five years old.

At his left, on a stool, crouched his enormous son Larue. Larue's body was a collection of soft-looking globes and bladders—a tremendous belly, round-kneed short legs, puffy hands, a gross bald head between fat shoulders. His white linen suit was only a shade paler than his skin, and his loose, faded-pink lips moved incessantly. Once Enid had heard him talking to himself, had been close enough to distinguish the words. Over and over he had said: "I'll kill you. I'll kill you. I'll kill you."

These two men had reared her from babyhood, here in this low, spacious manor of brick and timber in the Ozark country. Sixteen or eighteen years ago there had been Indians hereabouts, but they were gone, and the few settlers were on remote farms. The Mandifers dwelt alone with their slaves, who were unusually solemn and taciturn for Negroes.

Persil Mandifer was continuing: "I have brought you up as a gentleman would bring up his real daughter—for the sole and simple end of making her a good wife. That explains, my dear, the governess, the finishing-school at St. Louis, the books, the journeys we have undertaken to New Orleans and elsewhere. I regret that this distressing war between the states," and he paused to draw from his pocket his enameled snuff-box, "should have made recent junkets impracticable. However, the time has come, and you are not to be despised. Your marriage is now to befall you."

"Marriage," mumbled Larue, in a voice that Enid was barely able to hear. His fingers interlaced, like fat white worms in a jumble. His eyes were for Enid, his ears for his father.

Enid saw that she must respond. She did so: "You have—chosen a husband for me?"

Persil Mandifer's lips crawled into a smile, very wide on his narrow blade of a face, and he took a pinch of snuff. "Your husband, my dear, was chosen before ever you came into this world," he replied. The smile grew broader, but Enid did not think it cheerful. "Does your mirror do you justice?" he teased her. "Enid, my foster-daughter, does it tell you truly that you are a beauty, with a face all lustrous and oval, eyes full of tender fire, a cascade of golden-brown curls to frame the whole?" His gaze wandered upon her body, and his eyelids drooped. "Does it convince you, Enid, that your figure combines rarely those traits of fragility and rondure that are never so desirable as when they occur together? Ah, Enid, had I myself met you, or one like you, thirty years ago——"

"Father!" growled Larue, as though at sacrilege. Persil Mandifer chuckled. His left hand, white and slender with a dark cameo upon the forefinger, extended and patted Larue's repellent bald pate, in superior affection.

"Never fear, son," crooned Persil Mandifer. "Enid shall go a pure bride to him who waits her." His other hand crept into the breast of his coat and drew forth something on a chain. It looked like a crucifix.

"Tell me," pleaded the girl, "tell me, fa——" She broke off, for she could not call him father. "What is the name of the one I am to marry?"

"His name?" said Larue, as though aghast at her ignorance.

"His name?" repeated the lean man in the rocking-chair. The crucifix-like object in his hands began to swing idly and rhythmically, while he paid out chain to make its pendulum motion wider and slower. "He has no name."

Enid felt her lips grow cold and dry. "He has no——"

"He is the Nameless One," said Persil Mandifer, and she could discern the capital letters in the last two words he spoke.

"Look," said Larue, out of the corner of his weak mouth that was nearest his father. "She thinks that she is getting ready to run."

"She will not run," assured Persil Mandifer. "She will sit and listen, and watch what I have here in my hand." The object on the chain seemed to be growing in size and clarity of outline. Enid felt that it might not be a crucifix, after all.

"The Nameless One is also ageless," continued Persil Mandifer. "My dear, I dislike telling you all about him, and it is not really necessary. All you need know is that we—my fathers and I—have served him here, and in Europe, since the days when France was Gaul. Yes, and before that."

The swinging object really was increasing in her sight. And the basic cross was no cross, but a three-armed thing like a capital T. Nor was the body-like figure spiked to it; it seemed to twine and clamber upon that T-shape, like a moneky on a bracket. Like a monkey, it was grotesque, disproportionate, a mockery. That climbing creature was made of gold, or of something gilded over. The T-shaped support was as black and bright as jet.

Enid thought that the golden creature was dull, as if tarnished, and that it appeared to move; an effect created, perhaps, by the rhythmic swinging on the chain.

"Our profits from the association have been great," Persil Mandifer droned. "Yet we have given greatly. Four times in each hundred years must a bride be offered."

Mist was gathering once more, in Enid's eyes and brain, a thicker mist than the one that had come from the shock of hearing that she was an adopted orphan. Yet through it all she saw the swinging device, the monkey-like climber upon the T. And through it all she heard Mandifer's voice:

"When my real daughter, the last female of my race, went to the Nameless One, I wondered where our next bride would come from. And so, twenty years ago, I took you from a foundling asylum at Nashville."

It was becoming plausible to her now. There was a power to be worshipped, to be feared, to be fed with young women. She must go— no, this sort of belief was wrong. It had no element of decency in it, it was only beaten into her by the spell of the pendulum-swinging charm. Yet she had heard certain directions, orders as to what to do.

"You will act in the manner I have described, and say the things I have repeated, tonight at sundown," Mandifer informed her, as though from a great distance. "You will surrender yourself to the Nameless One, as it was ordained when first you came into my possession."

"No," she tried to say, but her lips would not even stir. Something had crept into her, a will not her own, which was forcing her to accept defeat. She knew she must go—where?

"To Fearful Rock," said the voice of Mandifer, as though he had heard and answered the question she had not spoken. "Go there, to that house where once my father lived and worshipped, that house which, upon the occasion of his rather mysterious death, I left. It is now our place of devotion and sacrifice. Go there, Enid, tonight at sundown, in the manner I have prescribed. . . ."

2. The Cavalry Patrol

Lieutenant Kane Lanark was one of those strange and vicious heritage-anomalies of one of the most paradoxical of wars—a war where a great Virginian was high in Northern command, and a great Pennsylvanian stubbornly defended one of the South's principal strongholds; where the two presidents were both born in Kentucky, indeed within scant miles of each other; where father strove against son, and brother against brother, even more frequently and tragically than in all the jangly verses and fustian dramas of the day.

Lanark's birthplace was a Maryland farm, moderately prosperous. His education had been completed at the Virginia Military Institute, where he was one of a very few who were inspired by a quiet, bearded professor of mathematics who later became the Stonewall of the Confederacy, perhaps the continent's greatest tactician. The older Lanark was strongly for state's rights and mildly for slavery, though he possessed no Negro chattels. Kane, the younger of two sons, had carried those same attitudes with him as much as seven miles past the Kansas border, whither he had gone in 1861 to look for employment and adventure.

At that lonely point he met with Southern guerrillas, certain loose-shirted, weapon-laden gentry whose leader, a gaunt young man with large, worried eyes, bore the craggy name of Quantrill and was to be called by a later historian the bloodiest man in American history. Young Kane Lanark, surrounded by sudden leveled guns, protested his sympathy with the South by birth, education and personal preference. Quantrill replied, rather sententiously, that while this might be true, Lanark's horse and money-belt had a Yankee look to them, and would be taken as prisoners of war.

After the guerrillas had galloped away, with a derisive laugh hanging in the air behind them, Lanark trudged back to the border and a little settlement, where he begged a ride by freight wagon to St. Joseph, Missouri. There he enlisted with a Union cavalry regiment just then in the forming, and his starkness of manner, with evidences about him of military education and good sense, caused his fellow recruits to elect him a sergeant.

Late that year, Lanark rode with a patrol through southern Missouri, where fortune brought him and his comrades face to face with Quantrill's guerrillas, the same that had plundered Lanark. The lieutenant in charge of the Federal cavalry set a most hysterical example for flight, and died of six Southern bullets placed accurately between his shoulder blades; but Lanark, as ranking non-commissioned officer, rallied the others, succeeded in withdrawing them in order before the superior force. As he rode last of the retreat, he had the fierce pleasure of engaging and sabering an overzealous guerrilla, who had caught up with him. The patrol rejoined its regiment with only two lost, the colonel was pleased to voice congratulations and Sergeant Lanark became Lieutenant Lanark, vice the slain officer.

In April of 1862, General Curtis, recently the victor in the desperately fought battle of Pea Ridge, showed trust and understanding when he gave Lieutenant Lanark a scouting party of twenty picked riders, with orders to seek yet another encounter with the marauding Quantrill. Few Union officers wanted anything to do with Quantrill, but Lanark, remembering his harsh treatment at those avaricious hands, yearned to kill the guerrilla chieftain with his own proper sword. On the afternoon of April fifth, beneath a sun bright but none too warm, the scouting patrol rode down a trail at the bottom of a great, trough-like valley just south of the Missouri-Arkansas border. Two pairs of men, those with the surest-footed mounts, acted as flanking parties high on the opposite slopes, and a watchful corporal by the name of Googan walked his horse well in advance of the main body. The others rode two and two, with Lanark at the head and Sergeant Jaeger, heavy-set and morosely keen of eye, at the rear.

A photograph survives of Lieutenant Kane Lanark as he appeared that very spring—his breadth of shoulder and slimness of waist accentuated by the snug blue cavalry jacket that terminated at his sword-belt, his ruddy, beak-nosed face shaded by a wide black hat with a gold cord. He wore a mustache, trim but not gay, and his long chin alone of all his command went smooth-shaven. To these details be it added that he rode his bay gelding easily, with a light, sure hand on the reins, and that he had the air of one who knew his present business.

The valley opened at length upon a wide level platter of land among high, pine-tufted hills. The flat expanse was no more than half timbered, though clever enemies might advance unseen across it if they exercised caution and foresight enough to slip from one belt or clump of trees to the next. Almost at the center of the level, a good five miles from where Lanark now halted his command, stood a single great chimney or finger of rock, its lean tip more than twice the height of the tallest tree within view.

To this geologic curiosity the eyes of Lieutenant Lanark snapped at once.

"Sergeant!" he called, and Jaeger sidled his horse close.

"We'll head for that rock, and stop there," Lanark announced. "It's a natural watch-tower, and from the top of it we can see everything, even better than we could if we rode clear across flat ground to those hills. And if Quantrill is west of us, which I'm sure he is, I'd like to see him coming a long way off, so as to know whether to fight or run."

"I agree with you, sir," said Jaeger. He peered through narrow, puffy lids at the pinnacle, and gnawed his shaggy lower lip. "I shall lift up mine eyes unto the rocks, from whence cometh my help," he misquoted reverently. The sergeant was full of garbled Scripture, and the men called him "Bible" Jaeger behind that wide back of his. This did not mean that he was soft, dreamy or easily fooled; Curtis had chosen him as sagely as he had chosen Lanark.

Staying in the open as much as possible, the party advanced upon the rock. They found it standing above a soft, grassy hollow, which in turn ran eastward from the base of the rock to a considerable ravine, dark and full of timber. As they spread out to the approach, they found something else; a house stood in the hollow, shadowed by the great pinnacle.

"It looks deserted, sir," volunteered Jaeger, at Lanark's bridle-elbow. "No sign of life."

"Perhaps," said Lanark. "Deploy the men, and we'll close in from all sides. Then you, with one man, enter the back door. I'll take another and enter the front."

"Good, sir." The sergeant kneed his horse into a faster walk, passing from one to another of the three corporals with muttered orders. Within sixty seconds the patrol closed upon the house like a twenty-fingered hand. Lanark saw that the building had once been pretentious—two stories, stoutly made of good lumber that must have been carted from a distance, with shuttered windows and a high peaked roof. Now it was a paint-starved gray, with deep veins and traceries of dirty black upon its clapboards. He dismounted before the piazza with its four pillar-like posts, and threw his reins to a trooper.

"Suggs!" he called, and obediently his own personal orderly, a plump blond youth, dropped out of the saddle. Together they walked up on the resounding planks of the piazza. Lanark, his ungloved right hand swinging free beside his holster, knocked at the heavy front door with his left fist. There was no answer. He tried the knob, and after a moment of shoving, the hinges creaked and the door went open.

They walked into a dark front hall, then into a parlor with dust upon the rug and the fine furniture, and rectangles of pallor upon the walls where pictures had once hung for years. They could hear echoes of their every movement, as anyone will hear in a house to which he is not accustomed. Beyond the parlor, they came to an ornate chandelier with crystal pendants, and at the rear stood a sideboard of dark, hard wood. Its drawers all hung half open, as if the silver and linen had been hastily removed. Above it hung plate-racks, also empty.

Feet sounded in a room to the rear, and then Jaeger's voice, asking if his lieutenant were inside. Lanark met him in the kitchen, conferred; then together they mounted the stairs is the front hall.

Several musty bedrooms, darkened by closed shutters, occupied the second floor. The beds had dirty mattresses, but no sheets or blankets.

"All clear in the house," pronounced Lanark. "Jaeger, go and detail a squad to reconnoiter in that little ravine east of here—we want no rebel sharpshooters sneaking up on us from that point. Then leave a picket there, put a man on top of the rock, and guards at the front and rear of this house. And have some of the others police up the house itself. We may stay here for two days, even longer."

The sergeant saluted, then went to bellow his orders, and troopers dashed hither and thither to obey. In a moment the sound of sweeping arose from the parlor. Lanark, to whom it suggested spring cleaning, sneezed at thought of the dust, then gave Suggs directions about the care of his bay. Unbuckling his saber, he hung it upon the saddle, but his revolver he retained. "You're in charge, Jaeger," he called, and sauntered away toward the wooded cleft.

His legs needed the exercise; he could feel them straightening by degrees after their long clamping to his saddle-flaps. He was uncomfortably dusty, too, and there must be water at the bottom of the ravine. Walking into the shade of the trees, he heard, or fancied he heard, a trickling sound. The slope was steep here, and he walked fast to maintain an easy balance upon it, for a minute and then two. There was water ahead, all right, for it gleamed through the leafage. And something else gleamed, something pink.

That pinkness was certainly flesh. His right hand dropped quickly to his revolver-butt, and he moved forward carefully. Stooping, he took advantage of the bushy cover, at the same time avoiding a touch that might snap or rustle the foliage. He could hear a voice now, soft and rhythmic.

Lanark frowned. A woman's voice? His right hand still at his weapon, his left caught and carefully drew down a spray of willow. He gazed into an open space beyond.

It was a woman, all right, within twenty yards of him. She stood ankle-deep in a swift, narrow rush of brook-water, and her fine body was nude, every graceful curve of it, with a cascade of golden-brown hair falling and floating about her shoulders. She seemed to be praying, but her eyes were not lifted. They stared at a hand-mirror, that she held up to catch the last flash of the setting sun.

3. *The Image in the Cellar*

Lanark, a young, serious-minded bachelor in an era when women swaddled themselves inches deep in fabric, had never seen such a sight before; and to his credit be it said that his first and strongest emotion was proper embarrassment for the girl in the stream. He had a momentary impulse to slip back and away. Then he remembered that he had ordered a patrol to explore this place; it would be here within moments.

Therefore he stepped into the open, wondering at the time, as well as later, if he did well.

"Miss," he said gently. "Miss, you'd better put on your things. My men——"

She stared, squeaked in fear, dropped the mirror and stood motionless. Then she seemed to gather herself for flight. Lanark realized that the trees beyond her were thick and might hide enemies, that she was probably a resident of this rebel-inclined region and might be a decoy for such as himself. He whipped out his revolver, holding it at the ready but not pointing it.

"Don't run," he warned her sharply. "Are those your clothes beside you? Put them on at once."

She caught up a dress of flowered calico and fairly flung it on over her head. His embarrassment subsided a little, and he came another pace or two into the open. She was pushing her feet—very small feet they were—into heelless shoes. Her hands quickly gathered up some underthings and wadded them into a bundle. She gazed at him apprehensively, questioningly. Her hastily-donned dress remained unfastened at the throat, and he could see the panicky stir of her heart in her half-bared bosom.

"I'm sorry," he went on, "but I think you'd better come up to the house with me."

"House?" she repeated fearfully, and her dark, wide eyes turned to look beyond him. Plainly she knew which house he meant. "You—live there?"

"I'm staying there at this time."

"You—came for me?" Apparently she had expected someone to come.

But instead of answering, he put a question of his own. "To whom were you talking just now? I could hear you."

"I—I said the words. The words my fath——" She broke off, wretchedly, and Lanark was forced to think how pretty she was in her confusion. "The words that Persil Mandifer told me to say." Her eyes on his, she continued softly: "I came to meet the Nameless One. Are you the—Nameless One?"

"I am certainly not nameless," he replied. "I am Lieutenant Lanark, of the Federal Army of the Frontier, at your service." He bowed slightly, which made it more formal. "Now, come along with me."

He took her by the wrist, which shook in his big left hand. Together they went back eastward through the ravine, in the direction of the house.

Before they reached it, she told him her name, and that the big natural pillar was called Fearful Rock. She also assured him that she knew nothing of Quantrill and his guerrillas; and a fourth item of news shook Lanark to his spurred heels, the first non-military matter that had impressed him in more than a year.

An hour later, Lanark and Jaeger finished an interview with her in the parlor. They called Suggs, who conducted the young woman up to one of the bedrooms. Then lieutenant and sergeant faced each other. The light was dim, but each saw bafflement and uneasiness in the face of the other.

"Well?" challenged Lanark.

Jaeger produced a clasp-knife, opened it, and pared thoughtfully at a thumbnail. "I'll take my oath," he ventured, "that this Miss Enid Mandifer is telling the gospel truth."

"Truth!" exploded Lanark scornfully. "Mountain-folk ignorance, I call it. Nobody believes in those devil-things these days."

"Oh, yes, somebody does," said Jeager, mildly but definitely. "I do." He put away his knife and fumbled within his blue army shirt. "Look here, Lieutenant."

It was a small book he held out, little more than a pamphlet in size and thickness. On its cover of gray paper appeared the smudged woodcut of an owl against a full moon, and the title:

John George Hohman's
POW-WOWS
or
LONG LOST FRIEND

"I got it when I was a young lad in Pennsylvania," explained Jaeger, almost reverently. "Lots of Pennsylvania people carry this book, as I do." He opened the little volume, and read from the back of the title page:

"'Whosoever carries this book with him is safe from all his enemies, visible or invisible; and whoever has this book with him cannot die without the holy corpse of Jesus Christ, nor drown in any water nor burn up in any fire, nor can any unjust sentence be passed upon him.'"

Lanark put out his hand for the book, and Jaeger surrendered it, somewhat hesitantly. "I've heard of supposed witches in Pennsylvania," said the officer. "Hexes, I believe they're called. Is this a witch book?"

"No, sir. Nothing about black magic. See the cross on that page? It's a protection against witches."

"I thought that only Catholics used the cross," said Lanark.

"No. Not only Catholics."

"Hmm." Lanark passed the thing back. "Superstition, I call it. Nevertheless, you speak this much truth: that girl is in earnest, she believes what she told us. Her father, or stepfather, or whoever he is, sent her up here on some ridiculous errand—perhaps a dangerous one." He paused. "Or I may be misjudging her. It may be a clever scheme, Jaeger—a scheme to get a spy in among us."

The sergeant's big bearded head wagged negation. "No, sir. If she was telling a lie, it'd be a more believable one, wouldn't it?" He opened his talisman book again. "If the lieutenant please, there's a charm in here, against being shot or stabbed. It might be a good thing, seeing there's a war going on—perhaps the lieutenant would like me to copy it out?"

"No, thanks." Lanark drew forth his own charm against evil and nervousness, a leather case that contained cheroots. Jaeger, who had convictions against the use of tobacco, turned away disapprovingly as his superior bit off the end of a fragrant brown cylinder and kindled a match.

"Let me look at that what-do-you-call-it book again," he requested, and for a second time Jaeger passed the little volume over, then saluted and retired.

Darkness was gathering early, what with the position of the house in the grassy hollow, and the pinnacle of Fearful Rock standing between it and the sinking sun to westward. Lanark called for Suggs to bring a candle, and, when the orderly obeyed, directed him to take some kind of supper upstairs to Enid Mandifer. Left alone, the young officer seated himself in a newly dusted armchair of massive dark wood, emitted a cloud of blue tobacco smoke, and opened the *Long Lost Friend*.

It had no publication date, but John George Hohman, the author, dated his preface from Berks County, Pennsylvania, on July 31, 1819. In the secondary preface filled with testimonials as to the success of Hohman's miraculous cures, was included the pious ejaculation: "The Lord bless the beginning and the end of this little work, and be with us, that we may not misuse it, and thus commit a heavy sin!"

"Amen to that!" said Lanark to himself, quite soberly. Despite his assured remarks to Jaeger, he was somewhat repelled and nervous because of the things Enid Mandifer had told him.

Was there, then, potentiality for such supernatural evil in this enlightened Nineteenth Century, even in the pages of the book he held? He read further, and came upon a charm to be recited against violence and danger, perhaps the very one Jaeger had offered to copy for him. It began rather sonorously: "The peace of our Lord Jesus Christ be with me. Oh shot, stand still! In the name of the mighty prophets Agtion and Elias, and do not kill me. . . ."

Lanark remembered the name of Elias from his boyhood Sunday schooling, but Agtion's identity, as a prophet or otherwise, escaped him. He resolved to ask Jaeger; and, as though the thought had acted as a summons, Jaeger came almost running into the room.

"Lieutenant, sir! Lieutenant!" he said hoarsely.

"Yes, Sergeant Jaeger?" Lanark rose, stared questioningly, and held out the book. Jaeger took it automatically, and as automatically stowed it inside his shirt.

"I can prove, sir, that there's a real devil here," he mouthed unsteadily.

"What?" demanded Lanark. "Do you realize what you're saying, man? Explain yourself."

"Come, sir," Jaeger almost pleaded, and led the way into the kitchen. "It's down in the cellar."

From a little heap on a table he picked up a candle, and then opened a door full of darkness.

The stairs to the cellar were shaky to Lanark's feet, and beneath him was solid black shadow, smelling strongly of damp earth. Jaeger, stamping heavily ahead, looked back and upward. That broad, bearded face, that had not lost its full-blooded flush in the hottest fighting at Pea Ridge, had grown so pallid as almost to give off sickly light. Lanark began to wonder if all this theatrical approach would not make the promised devil seem ridiculous, anticlimactic—the flutter of an owl, the scamper of a rat, or something of that sort.

"You have the candle, sergeant," he reminded, and the echo of his voice momentarily startled him. "Strike a match, will you?"

"Yes, sir." Jaeger had raised a knee to tighten his stripe-sided trousers. A snapping scrape, a burst of flame, and the candle glow illuminated them both. It revealed, too, the cellar, walled with stones but floored with clay. As they finished the descent, Lanark could feel the soft grittiness of that clay under his bootsoles. All around them lay rubbish—boxes, casks, stacks of broken pots and dishes, bundles of kindling.

"Here," Jaeger was saying, "here is what I found."

He walked around the foot of the stairs. Beneath the slope of the flight lay a long, narrow case, made of plain, heavy boards. It was unpainted and appeared ancient. As Jaeger lowered the light in his hand, Lanark saw that the joinings were secured with huge nails, apparently forged by hand. Such nails had been used in building the older sheds on his father's Maryland estate. Now there was a creak of wooden protest as Jaeger pried up the loosened lid of the coffin-like box.

Inside lay something long and ruddy. Lanark saw a head and shoulders, and started violently. Jaeger spoke again:

"An image, sir. A heathen image." The light made grotesque the sergeant's face, one heavy half fully illumined, the other secret and lost in the black shadow. "Look at it."

Lanark, too, stooped for a closer examination. The form was of human length, or rather more; but it was not finished, was either divided into legs below nor extended into arms at the roughly shaped shoulders. The head, too, had been molded without features, though from either side, where the ears should have been it sprouted up-curved horns like a bison's. Lanark felt a chill creep upon him, whence he knew not.

"It's Satan's own image," Jaeger was mouthing deeply. "'Thou shalt not make unto thee any graven image——'"

With one foot he turned the coffin-box upon its side. Lanark took a quick stride backward, just in time to prevent the ruddy form from dropping out upon his toes. A moment later, Jaeger had spurned the thing. It broke, with a crashing sound like crockery, and two more trampling kicks of the sergeant's heavy boots smashed it to bits.

"Stop!" cried Lanark, too late. "Why did you break it? I wanted to have a good look at the thing."

"But it is not good for men to look upon the devil's works," responded Jaeger, almost pontifically.

"Don't advise me, sergeant," said Lanark bleakly. "Remember that I am your officer, and that I don't need instruction as to what I may look at." He looked down at the fragments. "Hmm, the thing was hollow, and quite brittle. It seems to have been stuffed with straw—no, excelsior. Wood shavings, anyway." He investigated the fluffy inner mass with a toe. "Hullo, there's something inside of the stuff."

"I wouldn't touch it, sir," warned Jaeger, but this time it was he who spoke too late. Lanark's boot-toe had nudged the object into plain sight, and Lanark had put down his gauntleted left hand and picked it up.

"What is this?" he asked himself aloud. "Looks rather like some sort of strong-box—foreign, I'd say, and quite old. Jaeger, we'll go upstairs."

In the kitchen, with a strong light from several candles, they examined the find quite closely. It was a dark oblong, like a small dispatch-case or, as Lanark had commented, a strong-box. Though as hard as iron, it was not iron, nor any metal either of them had ever known.

"How does it open?" was Lanark's next question, turning the case over in his hands. "It doesn't seem to have hinges on it. Is this the lid—or this?"

"I couldn't say." Jaeger peered, his eyes growing narrow with perplexity. "No hinges, as the lieutenant just said."

"None visible, nor yet a lock." Lanark thumped the box experimentally, and proved it hollow. Then he lifted it close to his ear and shook it. There was a faint rustle, as of papers loosely rolled or folded. "Perhaps," the officer went on, "this separate slice isn't a lid at all. There may be a spring to press, or something that slides back and lets another plate come loose."

But Suggs was entering from the front of the house. "Lieutenant, sir! Something's happened to Newton—he was watching on the rock. Will the lieutenant come? And Sergeant Jaeger, too."

The suggestion of duty brought back the color and self-control that Jaeger had lost. "What's happened to Newton?" he demanded at once, and hurried away with Suggs.

Lanark waited in the kitchen for only a moment. He wanted to leave the box, but did not want his troopers meddling with it. He spied, beside the heavy iron stove, a fireplace, and in its side the metal door to an old brick oven. He pulled that door open, thrust the box in, closed the door again, and followed Suggs and Jaeger.

They had gone out upon the front porch. There, with Corporal Gray and a blank-faced trooper on guard, lay the silent form of Newton, its face covered with a newspaper.

Almost every man of the gathered patrol knew a corpse when he saw one, and it took no second glance to know that Newton was quite dead.

4. The Mandifers

Jaeger, bending, lifted the newspaper and then dropped it back. He said something that, for all his religiosity, might have been an oath.

"What's the matter, sergeant?" demanded Lanark.

Jaeger's brows were clamped in a tense frown, and his beard was actually trembling. "His face, sir. It's terrible."

"A wound?" asked Lanark, and lifted the paper in turn. He, too, let it fall back, and his exclamation of horror and amazement was unquestionably profane.

"There ain't no wound on him, Lieutenant Lanark," offered Suggs, pushing his wan, plump face to the forefront of the troopers. "We heard Newton yell—heard him from the top of the rock yonder."

All eyes turned gingerly toward the promontory.

"That's right, sir," added Corporal Gray. "I'd just sent Newton up, to relieve Josserand."

"You heard him yell," prompted Lanark. "Go on, what happened?"

"I hailed him back," said the corporal, "but he said nothing. So I climbed up—that north side's the easiest to climb. Newton was standing at the top, standing straight up with his carbine at the ready. He must have been dead right then."

"You mean, he was struck somehow as you watched?"

Gray shook his head. "No, sir. I think he was dead as he stood up. He didn't move or speak, and when I touched him he sort of coiled down—like an empty coat falling off a clothesline." Gray's hand made a downward-floating gesture in illustration. "When I turned him over I saw his face, all twisted and scared-looking, like—like what the lieutenant has seen. And I sung out for Suggs and McSween to come up and help me bring him down."

Lanark gazed at Newton's body. "He was looking which way?"

"Over yonder, eastward." Gray pointed unsteadily. "Like it might have been beyond the draw and them trees in it."

Lanark and Jaeger peered into the waning light, that was now dusk. Jaeger mumbled what Lanark had already been thinking—that Newton had died without wounds, at or near the moment when the horned image had been shattered upon the cellar floor.

Lanark nodded, and dismissed several vague but disturbing inspirations. "You say he died standing up, Gray. Was he leaning on his gun?"

"No, sir. He stood on his two feet, and held his carbine at the ready. Sounds impossible, a dead man standing up like that, but that's how it was."

"Bring his blanket and cover him up," said Lanark. "Put a guard over him, and we'll bury him tomorrow. Don't let any of the men look at his face. We've got to give him some kind of funeral." He turned to Jaeger. "Have you a prayer book, sergeant?"

Jaeger had fished out the *Long Lost Friend* volume. He was reading something aloud, as though it were a prayer: ". . . and be and remain with us on the water and upon the land," he pattered out. "May the Eternal Godhead also—"

"Stop that heathen nonsense," Lanark almost roared. "You're supposed to be an example to the men, sergeant. Put that book away."

Jaeger obeyed, his big face reproachful. "It was a spell against evil spirits," he explained, and for a moment Lanark wished that he had waited for the end. He shrugged and issued further orders.

"I want all the lamps lighted in the house, and perhaps a fire out here in the yard," he told the men. "We'll keep guard both here and in that gulley to the east. If there is a mystery, we'll solve it."

"Pardon me, sir," volunteered a well-bred voice, in which one felt rather than heard the tiny touch of foreign accent. "I can solve the mystery for you, though you may not thank me."

Two men had come into view, were drawing up beside the little knot of troopers. How had they approached? Through the patroled brush of the ravine? Around the corner of the house? Nobody had seen them coming, and Lanark, at least, started violently. He glowered at this new enigma.

The man who had spoken paused at the foot of the porch steps, so that lamplight shone upon him through the open front door. He was skeleton-gaunt, in face and body, and even his bones were small. His eyes burned forth from deep pits in his narrow, high skull, and his clothing was that of a dandy of the forties. In his twig-like fingers he clasped bunches of herbs.

His companion stood to one side in the shadow, and could be seen only as a huge coarse lump of a man.

"I am Persil Mandifer," the thin creature introduced himself. "I came here to gather from the gardens," and he held out his handfuls of leaves and stalks. "You, sir, you are in command of these soldiers, are you not? Then know that you are trespassing."

"The expediencies of war," replied Lanark easily, for he had seen Suggs and Corporal Gray bring their carbines forward in their hands. "You'll have to forgive our intrusion."

A scornful mouth opened in the emaciated face, and a soft, superior chuckle made itself heard. "Oh, but this is not my estate. I am allowed here, yes—but it is not mine. The real Master——" The gaunt figure shrugged, and the voice paused for a moment. The bright eyes sought Newton's body. "From what I see and what I heard as I came up to you, there has been trouble. You have transgressed somehow, and have begun to suffer."

"To you Southerners, all Union soldiers are trespassers and transgressors," suggested Lanark, but the other laughed and shook his fleshless white head.

"You misunderstand, I fear. I care nothing about this war, except that

I am amused to see so many people killed. I bear no part in it. Of course, when I came to pluck herbs, and saw your sentry at the top of Fearful Rock—" Persil Mandifer eyed again the corpse of Newton. "There he lies, eh? It was my privilege and power to project a vision up to him in his loneliness that, I think, put an end to his part of this puerile strife."

Lanark's own face grew hard. "Mr. Mandifer," he said bleakly, "you seem to be enjoying a quiet laugh at our expense. But I should point out that we greatly outnumber you, and are armed. I'm greatly tempted to place you under arrest."

"Then resist that temptation," advised Mandifer urbanely. "It might be disastrous to you if we became enemies."

"Then be kind enough to explain what you're talking about," commanded Lanark. Something swam into the forefront of his consciousness. "You say that your name is Mandifer. We found a girl named Enid Mandifer in the gulley yonder. She told us a very strange story. Are you her stepfather? The one who mesmerized her and——"

"She talked to you?" Mandifer's soft voice suddenly shifted to a windy roar that broke Lanark's questioning abruptly in two. "She came, and did not make the sacrifice of herself? She shall expiate, sir, and you with her!"

Lanark had had enough of this high-handed civilian's airs. He made a motion with his left hand to Corporal Gray, whose carbine-barrel glinted in the light from the house as it leveled itself at Mandifer's skull-head.

"You're under arrest," Lanark informed the two men.

The bigger one growled, the first sound he had made. He threw his enormous body forward in a sudden leaping stride, his gross hands extended as though to clutch Lanark. Jaeger, at the lieutenant's side, quickly drew his revolver and fired from the hip. The enormous body fell, rolled over and subsided.

"You have killed my son!" shrieked Mandifer.

"Take hold of him, you two," ordered Lanark, and Suggs and Josserand obeyed.

The gaunt form of Mandifer achieved one explosive struggle, then fell tautly motionless with the big hands of the troopers upon his elbows.

"Thanks, Jaeger," continued Lanark. "That was done quickly and well. Some of you drag this body up on the porch and cover it. Gray, tumble upstairs and bring down that girl we found."

While waiting for the corporal to return. Lanark ordered further that a bonfire be built to banish a patch of the deepening darkness. It was beginning to shoot up its bright tongues as the corporal ushered Enid Mandifer out upon the porch.

She had arranged her disordered clothing, and even contrived to put up her hair somehow, loosely but attractively. The firelight brought out a certain strength of line and angle in her face, and made her eyes shine darkly. She was manifestly frightened at the sight of her stepfather and the blanket-covered corpses to one side; but she faced determinedly a flood of half-understandable invectives from the emaciated man. She answered him, too; Lanark did not know what she meant by most of the things she said, but gathered correctly that she was refusing, finally and completely, to do something.

"Then I shall say no more," gritted out the spidery Mandifer, and his bared teeth were of the flat, chalky white of long-dead bone. "I place this matter in the hands of the Nameless One. He will not forgive, will not forget."

Enid moved a step toward Lanark, who put out a hand and touched her arm reassuringly. The mounting flame of the bonfire lighted up all who watched and listened—the withered, glaring mummy that was Persil Mandifer, the frightened but defiant shapeliness of Enid in her flower-patterned gown, Lanark in his sudden attitude of protection, the ring of troopers in their dusty blue blouses. With the half-lighted front of the weathered old house like a stage set behind them, and alternate red lights and sooty shadows playing over all, they might have been a tableau in some highly melodramatic opera.

"Silence," Lanark was grating. "For the last time, Mr. Mandifer, let me remind you that I have placed you under arrest. If you don't calm down immediately and speak only when you're spoken to, I'll have my men tie you flat to four stakes and put a gag in your mouth."

Mandifer subsided at once, just as he was on the point of hurling another harsh threat at Enid.

"That's much better," said Lanark. "Sergeant Jaeger, it strikes me that we'd better get our pickets out to guard this position."

Mandifer cleared his throat with actual diffidence. "Lieutenant Lanark —that is your name, I gather," he said in the soft voice which he had employed when he had first appeared. "Permit me, sir, to say but two words." He peered as though to be sure of consent. "I have it in my mind that it is too late, useless, to place any kind of guard against surprise."

"What do you mean?" asked Lanark.

"It is all of a piece with your offending of him who owns this house and the land which encompasses it," continued Mandifer. "I believe that a body of your enemies, mounted men of the Southern forces, are upon you. That man who died upon the brow of Fearful Rock might have seen them coming, but he was brought down sightless and voiceless, and nobody was assigned in his place."

He spoke truth. Gray, in his agitation, had not posted a fresh sentry. Lanark drew his lips tight beneath his mustache.

"Once more you feel that it is a time to joke with us, Mr. Mandifer," he growled. "I have already suggested gagging you and staking you out."

"But listen," Mandifer urged him.

Suddenly hoofs thundered, men yelled a double-noted defiance, high and savage—"*Yee-hee!*"

It was the rebel yell.

Quantrill's guerrillas rode out of the dark and upon them.

5. *Blood in the Night*

Neither Lanark nor the others remembered that they began to fight for their lives; they only knew all at once that they were doing it. There was a prolonged harsh rattle of gun-shots like a blast of hail upon hard wood; Lanark, by chance or unconscious choice, snatched at and drew his sword instead of his revolver.

A horse's flying shoulder struck him, throwing him backward but not down. As he reeled to save his footing, he saved also his own life; for the rider, a form all cascading black beard and slouch hat, thrust a pistol almost into the lieutenant's face and fired. The flash was blinding, the ball ripped Lanark's cheek like a whiplash, and then the saber in his hand swung, like a scythe reaping wheat. By luck rather than design, the edge bit the guerrilla's gun-wrist. Lanark saw the hand fly away as though on wings, its fingers still clutching the pistol, all agleam in the firelight. Blood gushed from the stump of the rider's right arm, like water from a fountain, and Lanark felt upon himself a spatter as of hot rain. He threw himself in, clutched the man's legs with his free arm and, as the body sagged heavily from above upon his head and shoulder, he heaved it clear out of the saddle.

The horse was plunging and whinnying, but Lanark clutched its reins and got his foot into the stirrup. The bonfire seemed to be growing strangely brighter, and the mounted guerrillas were plainly discernible, raging and trampling among his disorganized men. Corporal Gray went down, dying almost under Lanark's feet. Amid the deafening drum-roll of shots, Sergeant Jeager's bull-like voice could be heard: "Stop, thieves and horsemen, in the name of God!" It sounded like an exorcism, as though the Confederate raiders were devils.

Lanark had managed to climb into the saddle of his captured mount. He dropped the bridle upon his pommel, reached across his belly with his left hand, and dragged free his revolver. At a little distance, beyond the tossing heads of several horses, he thought he saw the visage of Quantrill, clean-shaven and fierce. He fired at it, but he had no faith in his own left-handed snap-shooting. He felt the horse frantic and unguided, shoving and striving against another horse. Quarters were too close for a saber-stroke, and he fired again with his revolver. The guerrilla spun out of the saddle. Lanark had a glimpse he would never forget, of great bulging eyes and a sharp-pointed mustache.

Again the rebel yell, flying from mouth to bearded mouth, and then an answering shout, deeper and more sustained; some troopers had run out of the house and, standing on the porch, were firing with their carbines. It was growing lighter, with a blue light. Lanark did not understand that.

Quantrill did not understand it, either. He and Lanark had come almost within striking distance of each other, but the guerrilla chief was gazing past his enemy, in the direction of the house. His mouth was open, with strain-lines around it. His eyes glowed. He feared what he saw.

"Remember me, you thieving swine!" yelled Lanark, and tried to thrust with his saber. But Quantrill had reined back and away, not from the sword but from the light that was growing stronger and bluer. He thundered an order, something that Lanark could not catch but which the guerrillas understood and obeyed. Then Quantrill was fleeing. Some guerrillas dashed between him and Lanark. They, too, were in flight. All the guerrillas were in flight. Somebody roared in triumph and fired with a carbine—it sounded like Sergeant Jaeger. The battle was over, within moments of its beginning.

Lanark managed to catch his reins, in the tips of the fingers that held his revolver, and brought the horse to a standstill before it followed Quantrill's men into the dark. One of his own party caught and held the bits, and Lanark dismounted. At last he had time to look at the house.

It was afire, every wall and sill and timber of it, burning all at once, and completely. And it burnt deep blue, as though seen through the glass of an old-fashioned bitters-bottle. It was falling to pieces with the consuming heat, and they had to draw back from it. Lanark stared around to reckon his losses.

Nearest the piazza lay three bodies, trampled and broken-looking. Some men ran in and dragged them out of danger; they were Persil Mandifer, badly battered by horses' feet, and the two who had held him. Josserand and Lanark's orderly, Suggs. Both the troopers had been shot through the head, probably at the first volley from the guerrillas.

Corporal Gray was stone-dead, with five or six bullets in him, and three more troopers had been killed, while four were wounded, but not critically. Jeager, examining them, pronounced that they could all ride if the lieutenant wished it.

"I wish it, all right," said Lanark ruefully. "We leave first thing in the morning. Hmm, six dead and four hurt, not counting poor Newton, who's there in the fire. Half my command—and, the way I forgot the first principles of military vigilance, I don't deserve as much luck as that. I think the burning house is what frightened the guerrillas. What began it?"

Nobody knew. They had all been fighting too desperately to have any idea. The three men who had been picketing the gulley, and who had dashed back to assault the guerrillas on the flank, had seen the blue flames burst out, as it were from a hundred places; that was the best view anybody had.

"All the killing wasn't done by Quantrill," Jaeger comforted his lieutenant. "Five dead guerrillas, sir—no, six. One was picked up a little way off, where he'd been dragged by his foot in the stirrup. Others got wounded, I'll be bound. Pretty even thing, all in all."

"And we still have one prisoner," supplemented Corporal Googan.

He jerked his head toward Enid Mandifer, who stood unhurt, unruffled almost, gazing raptly at the great geyser of blue flame that had been the house and temple of her stepfather's nameless deity.

It was a gray morning, and from the first streaks of it Sergeant Jaeger had kept the unwounded troopers busy, making a trench-like grave halfway between the spot where the house had stood and the gulley to the east. When the bodies were counted again, there were only twelve; Persil Mandifer's was missing, and the only explanation was that it had been caught somehow in the flames. The ruins of the house, that still smoked with a choking vapor as of sulfur gas, gave up a few crisped bones that apparently had been Newton, the sentry who had died from unknown causes; but no giant skeleton was found to remind one of the passing of Persil Mandifer's son.

"No matter," said Lanark to Jaeger. "We know that they were both dead, and past our worrying about. Put the other bodies in—our men at this end, the guerrillas at the other."

The order was carried out. Once again Lanark asked about a prayer book. A lad by the name of Duckin said that he had owned one, but that it had been burned with the rest of his kit in the blue flame that destroyed the house.

"Then I'll have to do it from memory," decided Lanark.

He drew up the surviving ten men at the side of the trench. Jaeger took a position beside him, and, just behind the sergeant, Enid Mandifer stood.

Lanark self-consciously turned over his clutter of thoughts, searching for odds and ends of his youthful religious teachings. "'Man that is born of woman hath but short time to live, and is full of misery'," he managed to repeat. "'He cometh up, and is cut down, like a flower'." As he said the words "cut down," he remembered his saber-stroke of the night before, and how he had shorn away a man's hand. That man, with his heavy black beard, lay in this trench before them, with the severed hand under him. Lanark was barely able to beat down a shudder. "'In the midst of life'," he went on, "'we are in death'."

There he was obliged to pause. Sergeant Jaeger, on inspiration, took one pace forward and threw into the trench a handful of gritty earth.

"'Ashes to ashes, dust to dust'," remembered Lanark. "'Unto Almighty God we commit these bodies'"—he was sure that that was a misquotation worthy of Jaeger himself, and made shift to finish with one more tag from his memory: "'. . . in sure and certain hope of the Resurrection unto eternal life'."

He faced toward the file of men. Four of them had been told to fall in under arms, and at his order they raised their carbines and fired a volley into the air. After that, the trench was filled in.

Jaeger then cleared his throat and began to give orders concerning horses, saddles and what possessions had been spared by the fire. Lanark walked aside, and found Enid Mandifer keeping pace with him.

"You are going back to your army?" she asked.

"Yes, at once. I was sent here to see if I could find and damage Quantrill's band. I found him, and gave at least as good as I got."

"Thank you," she said, "for everything you've done for me."

He smiled deprecatingly, and it hurt his bullet-burnt cheek.

"I did nothing," he protested, and both of them realized that it was the truth. "All that has happened—it just happened."

He drew his eyes into narrow gashes, as if brooding over the past twelve hours.

"I'm halfway inclined to believe what your stepfather said about a supernatural influence here. But what about you, Miss Mandifer?"

She tried to smile in turn, not very successfully.

"I can go back to my home. I'll be alone there."

"Alone?"

"I have a few servants."

"You'll be safe?"

"As safe as anywhere."

He clasped his hands behind him. "I don't know how to say it, but I have begun to feel responsible for you. I want to know that all will be well."

"Thank you," she said a second time. "You owe me nothing."

"Perhaps not. We do not know each other. We have spoken together only three or four times. Yet you will be in my mind. I want to make a promise."

"Yes?"

They had paused in their little stroll, almost beside the newly filled grave trench. Lanark was frowning, Enid Mandifer nervous and expectant.

"This war," he said weightily, "is going to last much longer than people thought at first. We—the Union—have done pretty well in the West here, but Lee is making fools of our generals back East. We may have to fight for years, and even then we may not win."

"I hope, Mr.—I mean, Lieutenant Lanark," stammered the girl, "I hope that you will live safely through it."

"I hope so, too. And if I am spared, if I am alive and well when peace comes, I swear that I shall return to this place. I shall make sure that you, too, are alive and well."

He finished, very certain that he could not have used stiffer, more stupid words; but Enid Mandifer smiled now, radiantly and gratefully.

"I shall pray for you, Lieutenant Lanark. Now, your men are ready to leave. Go, and I shall watch."

"No," he demurred. "Go yourself, get away from this dreadful place."

She bowed her head in assent, and walked quickly away. At some distance she paused, turned, and waved her hand above her head.

Lanark took off his broad, black hat and waved in answer. Then he faced about, strode smartly back into the yard beside the charred ruins. Mounting his bay gelding, he gave the order to depart.

6. Return

It was spring again, the warm, bright spring of the year 1866, when Kane Lanark rode again into the Fearful Rock country.

His horse was a roan gray this time; the bay gelding had been shot under him, along with two other horses, during the hard-fought three days at Westport, the "Gettysburg of the West," when a few regulars and the Kansas militia turned back General Sterling Price's raid through Missouri. Lanark had been a captain then, and a major thereafter, leading a cavalry expedition into Kentucky. He narrowly missed being in at the finish of Quantrill, whose death by the hand of another he bitterly resented. Early in 1865 he was badly wounded in a skirmish with Confederate horsemen under General Basil Duke. Thereafter he could ride as well as ever, but when he walked he limped.

Lanark's uniform had been replaced by a soft hat and black frock coat, his face was browner and his mustache thicker, and his cheek bore the jaggedly healed scar of the guerrilla pistol-bullet. He was richer, too; the death of his older brother, Captain Douglas Lanark of the Confederate artillery, at Chancellorsville, had left him his father's only heir. Yet he was recognizable as the young lieutenant who had ridden into this district four years gone.

Approaching from the east instead of the north, he came upon the plain with its grass-levels, its clumps of bushes and trees, from another and lower point. Far away on the northward horizon rose a sharp little finger; that would be Fearful Rock, on top of which Trooper Newton had once died, horrified and unwounded. Now, then, which way would lie the house he sought for? He idled his roan along the trail, and encountered at last an aged, ragged Negro on a mule.

"Hello, uncle," Lanark greeted him, and they both reined up. "Which way is the Mandifer place?"

"Mandifuh?" repeated the slow, high voice of the old man. "Mandifuh, suh, cap'n? Ah doan know no Mandifuh."

"Nonsense, uncle," said Lanark, but without sharpness, for he liked Negroes. "The Mandifer family has lived around here for years. Didn't you ever know Mr. Persil Mandifer and his stepdaughter, Miss Enid?"

"Puhsil Mandifuh?" It was plain that the old fellow had heard and spoken the name before, else he would have stumbled over its unfamiliarities. "No, suh, cap'n. Ah doan nevah heah tella such gemman."

Lanark gazed past the mule and its tattered rider. "Isn't that a little house among those willows?"

The kinky head turned and peered. "Yes, suh, cap'n. Dat place b'long to Pahson Jaguh."

"Who?" demanded Lanark, almost standing up in his stirrups in his sudden interest. "Did you say Jaeger? What kind of man is he?"

"He jes a pahson—Yankee pahson," replied the Negro, a trifle nervous at this display of excitement. "Big man, suh, got red face. He Yankee. You ain' no Yankee, cap'n, suh. Whaffo you want Pahson Jaguh?"

"Never mind," said Lanark, and thrust a silver quarter into the withered brown palm. He also handed over one of his long, fragrant cheroots. "Thanks, uncle," he added briskly, then spurred his horse and rode on past.

Reaching the patch of willows, he found that the trees formed an open curve that faced the road, and that within this curve stood a rough but snug-looking cabin, built of sawn, unpainted planks and home-split shingles. Among the brush to the rear stood a smaller shed, apparently a stable, and a pen for chickens or a pig. Lanark reined up in front, swung out of his saddle, and tethered his horse to a thorny shrub at the trailside. As he drew tight the knot of the halter-rope, the door of heavy boards opened with a creak. His old sergeant stepped into view.

Jaeger was a few pounds heavier, if anything, than when Lanark had last seen him. His hair was longer, and his beard had grown to the center of his broad chest. He wore blue jeans tucked into worn old cavalry boots, a collarless checked shirt fastened with big brass studs, and leather suspenders. He stared somewhat blankly as Lanark called him by name and walked up to the doorstep, favoring his injured leg.

"It's Captain Lanark, isn't it?" Jaeger hazarded. "My eyes——" He paused, fished in a hip pocket and produced steel-rimmed spectacles. When he donned them, they appeared to aid his vision. "Indeed it is Captain Lanark! Or Major Lanark—yes, you were promoted——"

"I'm Mr. Lanark now," smiled back the visitor. "The war's over, Jaeger. Only this minute did I hear of you in the country. How does it happen that you settled in this place?"

"Come in, sir." Jaeger pushed the door wide open, and ushered Lanark into an unfinished front room, well lighted by windows on three sides. "It's not a strange story," he went on as he brought forward a well-mended wooden chair for the guest, and himself sat on a small keg. "You will remember, sir, that the land hereabouts is under a most unhallowed influence. When the war came to an end, I felt strong upon me the call to another conflict—a crusade against evil." He turned up his eyes, as though to subpoena the powers of heaven as witnesses to his devotion. "I preach here, the gospels and the true godly life."

"What is your denomination?" asked Lanark.

Jaeger coughed, as though abashed. "To my sorrow, I am ordained of no church; yet might this not be part of heaven's plan? I may be here to lead a strong new movement against hell's legions."

Lanark nodded as though to agree with this surmise, and studied Jaeger anew. There was nothing left in manner or speech to suggest that here had been a fierce fighter and model soldier, but the old rude power was not gone. Lanark then asked about the community, and learned that there were but seven white families within a twenty-mile radius. To these Jaeger habitually preached of a Sunday morning, at one farm home or another, and in the afternoon he was wont to exhort the more numerous Negroes.

Lanark had by now the opening for his important question. "What about the Mandifer place? Remember the girl we met, and her stepfather?"

"Enid Mandifer!" breathed Jaeger huskily, and his right hand fluttered up. Lanark remembered that Jaeger had once assured him that not only Catholics warded off evil with the sign of the cross.

"Yes, Enid Mandifer." Lanark leaned forward. "Long ago, Jaeger, I made a promise that I would come and make sure that she prospered. Just now I met an old Negro who swore that he had never heard the name."

Jaeger began to talk, steadily but with a sort of breathless awe, about what went on in the Fearful Rock country. It was not merely that men died—the death of men was not sufficient to horrify folk around whom a war had raged. But corpses, when found, held grimaces that nobody cared to look upon, and no blood remained in their bodies. Cattle, too, had been slain, mangled dreadfully—perhaps by the strange, unidentifiable creatures that prowled by moonlight and chattered in voices that sounded human. One farmer of the vicinity, who had ridden with Quantrill, had twice met strollers after dusk, and had recognized them for comrades whom he knew to be dead.

"And the center of this devil's business," concluded Jaeger, "is the farm that belonged to Persil Mandifer." He drew a deep, tired-sounding breath. "As the desert and the habitation of dragons, so is it with that farm. No trees live, and no grass. From a distance, one can see a woman. It is Enid Mandifer."

"Where is the place?" asked Lanark directly.

Jaeger looked at him for long moments without answering. When he did speak, it was an effort to change the subject. "You will eat here with me at noon," he said. "I have a Negro servant, and he is a good cook."

"I ate a very late breakfast at a farmhouse east of here," Lanark put him off. Then he repeated, "Where is the Mandifer place?"

"Let me speak this once," Jaeger temporized. "As you have said, we are no longer at war—no longer officer and man. We are equals, and I am able to refuse to guide you."

Lanark got up from his chair. "That is true, but you will not be acting the part of a friend."

"I will tell you the way, on one condition." Jaeger's eyes and voice pleaded. "Say that you will return to this house for supper and a bed, and that you will be within my door by sundown."

"All right," said Lanark. "I agree. Now, which way does that farm lie?"

Jaeger led him to the door. He pointed. "This trail joins a road beyond, an old road that is seldom used. Turn north upon it, and you will come to a part which is grown up in weeds. Nobody passes that way.

Follow on until you find an old house, built low, with the earth dry and bare around it. That is the dwelling-place of Enid Mandifer."

Lanark found himself biting his lip. He started to step across the threshold, but Jaeger put a detaining hand on his arm. "Carry this as you go."

He was holding out a little book with a gray paper cover. It had seen usage and trouble since last Lanark had noticed it in Jaeger's hands; its back was mended with a pasted strip of dark cloth, and its edges were frayed and gnawed-looking, as though rats had been at it. But the front cover still said plainly:

John George Hohman's
POW-WOWS
or
LONG LOST FRIEND

"Carry this," said Jaeger again, and then quoted glibly: "'Whoever carries this book with him is safe from all his enemies, visible or invisible; and whoever has this book with him cannot die without the holy corpse of Jesus Christ, nor drown in any water, nor burn up in any fire, nor can any unjust sentence be passed upon him.'"

Lanark grinned in spite of himself and his new concern. "Is this the kind of a protection that a minister of God should offer me?" he inquired, half jokingly.

"I have told you long ago that the *Long Lost Friend* is a good book, and a blessed one." Jaeger thrust it into Lanark's right-hand coat pocket. His guest let it remain, and held out his own hand in friendly termination of the visit.

"Good-bye," said Lanark. "I'll come back before sundown, if that will please you."

He limped out to his horse, untied it and mounted. Then, following Jaeger's instructions, he rode forward until he reached the old road, turned north and proceeded past the point where weeds had covered the unused surface. Before the sun had fallen far in the sky, he was come to his destination.

It was a squat, spacious house, the bricks of its trimming weathered and the dark brown paint of its timbers beginning to crack. Behind it stood unrepaired stables, seemingly empty. In the yard stood what had been wide-branched trees, now leafless and lean as skeleton paws held up to a relentless heaven. And there was no grass. The earth was utterly sterile and hard, as though rain had not fallen since the beginning of time.

Enid Mandifer had been watching him from the open door. When she saw that his eyes had found her, she called him by name.

7. The Rock Again

Then there was silence. Lanark sat his tired roan and gazed at Enid, rather hungrily, but only a segment of his attention was for her. The silence crowded in upon him. His unconscious awareness grew conscious —conscious of that blunt, pure absence of sound. There was no twitter of birds, no hum of insects. Not a breath of wind stirred in the leafless branches of the trees. Not even echoes came from afar. The air was dead, as water is dead in a still, stale pond.

He dismounted then, and the creak of his saddle and the scrape of his bootsole upon the bald earth came sharp and shocking to his quiet-filled ears. A hitching-rail stood there, old-seeming to be in so new a country as this. Lanark tethered his horse, pausing to touch its nose reassuringly —it, too, felt uneasy in the thick silence. Then he limped up a gravel-faced path and stepped upon a porch that rang to his feet like a great drum.

Enid Mandifer came through the door and closed it behind her. Plainly she did not want him to come inside. She was dressed in brown alpaca, high-necked, long-sleeved, tight above the waist and voluminous below. Otherwise she looked exactly as she had looked when she bade him good-bye beside the ravine, even to the strained, sleepless look that made sorrowful her fine oval face.

"Here I am," said Lanark. "I promised that I'd come, you remember."

She was gazing into his eyes, as though she hoped to discover something there. "You came," she replied, "because you could not rest in another part of the country."

"That's right," he nodded, and smiled, but she did not smile back.

"We are doomed, all of us," she went on, in a low voice. "Mr. Jaeger— the big man who was one of your soldiers——"

"I know. He lives not far from here."

"Yes. He, too, had to return. And I live—here." She lifted her hands a trifle, in hopeless inclusion of the dreary scene. "I wonder why I do not run away, or why, remaining, I do not go mad. But I do neither."

"Tell me," he urged, and touched her elbow. She let him take her arm and lead her from the porch into the yard that was like a surface of tile. The spring sun comforted them, and he knew that it had been cold, so near to the closed front door of Persil Mandifer's old house.

She moved with him to a little rustic bench under one of the dead trees. Still holding her by the arm, he could feel at the tips of his fingers the shock of her footfalls, as though she trod stiffly. She, in turn, quite evidently was aware of his limp, and felt distress; but, tactfully, she did not inquire about it. When they sat down together, she spoke.

"When I came home that day," she began, "I made a hunt through all of my stepfather's desks and cupboards. I found many papers, but nothing that told me of the things that so shocked us both. I did find money, a small chest filled with French and American gold coins. In the evening I called the slaves together and told them that their master and his son were dead.

"Next morning, when I wakened, I found that every slave had run off, except one old woman. She, nearly a hundred years old and very feeble, told me that fear had come to them in the night, and they they had run like rabbits. With them had gone the horses, and all but one cow."

"They deserted you!" cried Lanark hotly.

"If they truly felt the fear that came here to make its dwelling-place!" Enid Mandifer smiled sadly, as if in forgiveness of the fugitives. "But to resume; the old aunty and I made out here somehow. The war went on, but it seemed far away. We watched the grass die before June, the leaves fall, the beauty of this place vanish."

"I am wondering about that death of grass and leaves," put in Lanark. "You connect it, somehow, with the unholiness at Fearful Rock; yet things grow there."

"Nobody is being punished there," she reminded succinctly. "Well, we had the chickens and the cow, but no crops would grow. If they had, we needed hands to farm them. Last winter aunty died, too. I buried her myself, in the back yard."

"With nobody to help you?"

"I found out that nobody cared or dared to help." Enid said that very slowly, and did not elaborate upon it. "One Negro, who lives down the road a mile, has had some mercy. When I need anything, I carry one of my gold pieces to him. He buys for me, and in a day or so I seek him out and get whatever it is. He keeps the change for his trouble."

Lanark, who had thought it cold upon the porch of the house, now mopped his brow as though it were a day in August. "You must leave here," he said.

"I have no place to go," she replied, "and if I had I would not dare."

"You would not dare?" he echoed uncomprehendingly.

"I must tell you something else. It is that my stepfather and Larue—his son—are still here."

"What do you mean? They were killed," Lanark protested. "I saw them fall. I myself examined their bodies."

"They were killed, yes. But they are here, perhaps within earshot."

It was his turn to gaze searchingly into her eyes. He looked for madness, but he found none. She was apparently sane and truthful.

"I do not see them," she was saying, "or, at most, I see only their sliding shadows in the evening. But I know of them, just around a corner or behind a chair. Have you never known and recognized someone just behind you, before you looked? Sometimes they sneer or smile. Have you," she asked, "ever felt someone smiling at you, even though you could not see him?"

Lanark knew what she meant. "But stop and think," he urged, trying to hearten her, "that nothing has happened to you—nothing too dreadful —although so much was promised when you failed to go through with that ceremony."

She smiled, very thinly. "You think that nothing has happened to me? You do not know the curse of living here, alone and haunted. You do not understand the sense I have of something tightening and thickening about me; tightening and thickening inside of me, too." Her hand touched her breast, and trembled. "I have said that I have not gone mad. That does not mean that I shall never go mad."

"Do not be resigned to any such idea," said Lanark, almost roughly, so earnest was he in trying to win her from the thought.

"Madness may come—in the good time of those who may wish it. My mind will die. And things will feed upon it, as buzzards would feed upon my dead body."

Her thin smile faded away. Lanark felt his throat growing as dry as lime, and cleared it noisily. Silence was still dense around them. He asked her, quite formally, what she found to do.

"My stepfather had many books, most of them old," was her answer. "At night I light one lamp—I must husband my oil—and sit well within its circle of light. Nothing ever comes into that circle. And I read books. Every night I read also a chapter from a Bible that belonged to my old aunty. When I sleep, I hold that Bible against my heart."

He rose nervously, and she rose with him. "Must you go so soon?" she asked, like a courteous hostess.

Lanark bit his mustache. "Enid Mandifer, come out of here with me."

"I can't."

"You can. You shall. My horse will carry both of us."

She shook her head, and the smile was back, sad and tender this time. "Perhaps you cannot understand, and I know that I cannot tell you. But if I stay here, the evil stays here with me. If I go, it will follow and infect the world. Go away alone."

She meant it, and he did not know what to say or do.

"I shall go," he agreed finally, with an air of bafflement, "but I shall be back."

Suddenly he kissed her. Then he turned and limped rapidly away, raging at the feeling of defeat that had him by the back of the neck. Then, as he reached his horse he found himself glad to be leaving the spot, even though Enid Mandifer remained behind, alone. He cursed with a vehemence that made the roan flinch, untied the halter and mounted. Away he rode, to the magnified clatter of hoofs. He looked back, not once but several times. Each time he saw Enid Mandifer, smaller and smaller, standing beside the bench under the naked tree. She was gazing, not along the road after him, but at the spot where he had mounted his horse. It was as though he had vanished from her sight at that point.

Lanark damned himself as one who retreated before an enemy, but he felt that it was not as simple as that. Helplessness, not fear, had routed him. He was leaving Enid Mandifer, but again he promised in his heart to return.

Somewhere along the weed-teemed road, the silence fell from him like a heavy garment slipping away, and the world hummed and sighed again.

After some time he drew rein and fumbled in his saddlebag. He had lied to Jaeger about his late breakfast, and now he was grown hungry. His fingers touched and drew out two hardtacks—they were plentiful and cheap, so recently was the war finished and the army demobilized—and a bit of raw bacon. He sandwiched the streaky smoked flesh between the big square crackers and ate without dismounting. Often, he considered, he had been content with worse fare. Then his thoughts went to the place he had quitted, the girl he had left there. Finally he skimmed the horizon with his eye.

To north and east he saw the spire of Fearful Rock, like a dark threatening finger lifted against him. The challenge of it was too much to ignore.

He turned his horse off the road and headed in that direction. It was a longer journey than he had thought, perhaps because he had to ride slowly through some dark swampground with a smell of rotten grass about it. When he came near enough, he slanted his course to the east, and so came to the point from which he first approached the rock and the house that had then stood in its shadow.

A crow flapped overhead, cawing lonesomely. Lanark's horse seemed to falter in its stride, as though it had seen a snake on the path, and he had to spur it along toward its destination. He could make out the inequalities of the rock, as clearly as though they had been sketched in with a pen, and the new spring greenery of the brush and trees in the gulley beyond to the westward; but the tumbledown ruins of the house were somehow blurred, as though a gray mist or cloud hung there.

Lanark wished that his old command rode with him, at least that he had coaxed Jaeger along; but he was close to the spot now, and would go in, however uneasily, for a closer look.

The roan stopped suddenly, and Lanark's spur made it sidle without advancing. He scolded it in an undertone, slid out of the saddle and threaded his left arm through the reins. Pulling the beast along, he limped toward the spot where the house had once stood.

The sun seemed to be going down.

8. *The Grapple by the Grave*

Lanark stumped for a furlong or more, to the yard of the old house, and the horse followed unwillingly—so unwillingly that had there been a tree or a stump at hand, Lanark would have tethered and left it. When he paused at last, under the lee of the great natural obelisk that was Fearful Rock, the twilight was upon him. Yet he could see pretty plainly the collapsed, blackened ruins of the dwelling that four years gone had burned before his eyes in devil-blue flame.

He came close to the brink of the foundation-hollow, and gazed narrowly into it. Part of the chimney still stood, broken off at about a level with the surface of the ground, the rubbish that had been its upper part lying in jagged heaps about its base. Chill seemed to rise from that littered depression, something like the chill he had guessed at rather than felt when he had faced Enid Mandifer upon her porch. The chill came slowly, almost stealthily, about his legs and thighs, creeping snake-like under his clothing to tingle the skin upon his belly. He shuddered despite himself, and the roan nuzzled his shoulder in sympathy. Lanark lifted a hand and stroked the beast's cheek, then moved back from where the house had stood.

He gazed westward, in the direction of the gulley. There, midway between the foundation-hollow and the natural one, was a much smaller opening in the earth, a pit filled with shadow. He remembered ordering a grave dug there, a grave for twelve men. Well, it seemed to be open now, or partially open.

He plodded toward it, reached it and gazed down in the fading light. He judged that the dead of his own command still lay where their comrades had put them, in a close row of six toward the east. It was the westward end of the trench that had been dug up, the place where the guerrillas had been laid. Perhaps the burial had been spied upon, and the Southerners had returned to recover their fallen friends.

Yet there was something below there, something pallid and flabby-looking. Lanark had come to make sure of things, and he stooped, then climbed down, favoring his old wound. It was darker in the ditch than above; yet he judged by the looseness of earth under his feet that in one spot, at least, there had been fresh digging—or, perhaps, some other person walking and examining. And the pallid patch was in reality two pallid patches, like discarded cloaks or jackets. Still holding the end of his horse's bridle, he put down his free hand to investigate.

Human hair tickled his fingers, and he snatched them back with an exclamation. Then he dug in his pocket, brought out a match, and snapped it aglow on the edge of his thumbnail.

He gazed downward for a full second before he dropped the light. It went out before it touched the bottom of the hole. But Lanark had seen enough.

Two human skins lay there—white, empty human skins. The legs of them sprawled like discarded court stockings, the hands of them like forgotten gauntlets. And tousled hair covered the collapsed heads of them. . . .

He felt light-headed and sick. Frantically he struggled up out of that grave, and barely had he come to his knees on the ground above, when his horse snorted and jerked its bridle free from his grasp. Lanark sprang up, tingling all over. Across the trench, black and broad, stood a human —or semi-human—figure.

Lanark felt a certain draining cold at cheek and brow. Yet his voice was steady as he spoke, challengingly:

"What do you want?"

The creature opposite stooped, then bent its thick legs. It was going to jump across the ditch. Lanark took a quick backward step toward his horse—an old Colt's revolver was tucked into his right saddlebag.

But the sudden move on his part was too much for the jangled nerves of the beast. It whickered, squealed, and jerked around. A moment later it bolted away toward the east.

At the same time, the form on the other side of the open grave lunged forward, cleared the space, and came at Lanark.

But it was attacking one who had been in close fights before, and emerged the victor. Lanark, though partially a cripple, had lost nothing of a cavalryman's toughness and resolution. He sprang backward, let his assailant's charge slow before it reached him, then lashed out with his left fist. His gloved knuckles touched soft flesh at what seemed to be the side of the face, flesh that gave under them. Lanark brought over his right, missed with it, and fell violently against the body of the other. For a moment he smelled corruption, and then found his feet and retreated again.

The black shape drew itself stoopingly down, as though to muster and concentrate its volume of vigor. It launched itself at Lanark's legs, with two arms extended. The veteran tried to dodge again, this time sidewise, but his lameness made him slow. Hands reached and fastened upon him, one clutching his thigh, the other clawing at the left-hand pocket of his coat.

But in the moment of capture, the foul-smelling thing seemed to shudder and snatch itself away, as though the touch of Lanark had burned it. A moan came from somewhere in its direction. The crouched body straightened, the arms lifted in cringing protection of the face. Lanark, mystified but desperately glad, himself advanced to the attack. As he came close he threw his weight. It bowled the other backward and over, and he fell hard upon it. His own hands, sinewy and sure, groped quickly upon dank, sticky-seeming garments, found a rumpled collar and then a throat.

That throat appeared to be muddy, or at any rate slippery and foul. With an effort Lanark sank his fingertips into it, throttling grimly and with honest intention to kill. There was no resistance, only a quivering of the body under his knee. The arms that screened the face fell quivering away to either side. At that moment a bright moon shimmered from behind a passing veil of cloud. Lanark gazed down into the face of his enemy.

A puffy, livid, filth-clotted face—but he knew it. Those spiked mustaches, those bulging eyes, the shape, contour and complexion. . . .

"You're one of Quantrill's——" accused Lanark between clenched teeth. Then his voice blocked itself, and his hands jerked away from their stranglehold. His mouth gaped open.

"*I killed you once!*" he cried.

Between him and the body he had pinned down there drifted a wild whirl of vision. He saw again the fight in the blue fireglow, the assailant who spurred against him, the flash of his own revolver, the limp collapse of the other. He saw, too, the burial next morning—blue-coated troopers shoveling loam down upon a silent row of figures; and, ere clods hid it, a face peeping through a disarranged blanket, a face with staring eyes and mustaches like twin knife-points.

Then his eyes were clear again, and he was on his feet and running. His stiff leg gave him pain, but he slackened speed no whit. Once he looked back. A strange blueness, like a dim reflection of the fire long ago, hung around the base of Fearful Rock. In the midst of it, he saw not one but several figures. They were not moving—not walking, anyway—but he could swear that they gazed after him.

Something tripped him, a root or a fallen branch. He rose, neither quickly nor confidently, aching in all his limbs. The moon had come up, he took time to realize. Then he suddenly turned dizzy and faint all over, as never in any battle he had seen, not even Pea Ridge and Westport; for something bulky and dark was moving toward and against him.

Then it whinnied softly, and his heart stole down from his throat—it was his runaway horse.

Lanark was fain to stand for long seconds, with his arm across the saddle, before he mounted. Then he turned the animal's head southward and shook the bridle to make it walk. At last he was able to examine himself for injuries.

Though winded, he was not bruised or hurt, but he was covered with earth and mold, and his side pocket had been almost ripped from his coat. That had happened when the—the creature yonder had tried to grapple him. He wondered how it had been forced to retreat so suddenly. He put his hand in the pocket.

He touched a little book there, and drew it forth.

It was Jaeger's *Long Lost Friend*.

A good hour later, Lanark rode into the yard of his ex-sergeant. The moon was high, and Jaeger was sitting upon the front stoop.

Silently the owner of the little house rose, took Lanark's bridle rein and held the horse while Lanark dismounted. Then he led the beast around to the rear yard, where the little shed stood. In front of this he helped Lanark unbridle and unsaddle the roan.

A Negro boy appeared, diffident in his mute offer of help, and Jaeger directed him to rub the beast down with a wisp of hay before giving it water or grain. Then he led Lanark to the front of the house.

Jaeger spoke at the threshold: "I thank God you are come back safely."

9. *Debate and Decision*

Jaeger's Negro servant was quite as good a cook as promised. Lanark, eating chicken stew and biscuits, reflected that only twice before had he been so ravenous—upon receiving the news of Lee's surrender at Appomattox, and after the funeral of his mother. When he had finished, he drew forth a cheroot. His hand shook as he lighted it. Jaeger gave him one of the old looks of respectful disapproval, but did not comment. Instead he led Lanark to the most comfortable chair in the parlor and seated himself upon the keg. Then he said: "Tell me."

Lanark told him, rather less coherently than here set down, the adventures of the evening. Again and again he groped in his mind for explanations, but not once found any to offer.

"It is fit for the devil," pronounced Jaeger when his old commander had finished. "Did I not say that you should have stayed away from that woman? You're well out of the business."

"I'm well into it you mean," Lanark fairly snapped back. "What can you think of me, Jaeger, when you suggest that I might let things stand as they are?"

The frontier preacher massaged his shaggy jowl with thoughtful knuckles. "You have been a man of war and an officer of death," he said heavily. "God taught your hands to fight. Yet your enemies are not those who perish by the sword." He held out his hand. "You say you still have the book I lent you?"

From his torn pocket Lanark drew Hohman's *Long Lost Friend*. Jaeger took it and stared at the cover. "The marks of fingers," he muttered, in something like awe. He examined the smudges closely, putting on his spectacles to do so, then lifted the book to his nose. His nostrils wrinkled, as if in distaste, and he passed the thing back. "Smell it," he directed.

Lanark did so. About the slimy-looking prints on the cover hung a sickening odor of decayed flesh.

"The demon that attacked you, that touched this book, died long ago," went on Jaeger. "You know as much—you killed him with your own hand. Yet he fights you this very night."

"Maybe you have a suggestion," Lanark flung out, impatient at the assured and almost snobbish air of mystery that colored the manner of his old comrade in arms. "If this is a piece of hell broke loose, perhaps you did the breaking. Remember that image—that idol-thing with horns—that you smashed in the cellar? You probably freed all the evil upon the world when you did that."

Jaeger frowned, but pursued his lecture. "This very book, this *Long Lost Friend*, saved you from the demon's clutch," he said. "It is a notable talisman and shield. But with the shield one must have a sword, with which to attack in turn."

"All right," challenged Lanark. "Where is your sword?"

"It is a product of a mighty pen," Jaeger informed him sententiously. He turned in his seat and drew from a box against the wall a book. Like the *Long Lost Friend*, it was bound in paper, but of a cream color. Its title stood forth in bold black letters:

THE SECRETS
OF
ALBERTUS MAGNUS

"A translation from the German and the Latin," explained Jaeger. "Printed, I think, in New York. This book is full of wisdom, although I wonder if it is evil, unlawful wisdom."

"I don't care if it is." Lanark almost snatched the book. "Any weapon must be used. And I doubt if Albertus Magnus was evil. Wasn't he a churchman, and didn't he teach Saint Thomas Aquinas?" He leafed through the beginning of the book. "Here's a charm, Jaeger, to be spoken in the name of God. That doesn't sound unholy."

"Satan can recite scripture to his own ends," misquoted Jaeger. "I don't remember who said that, but——"

"Shakespeare said it, or something very like it," Lanark informed him. "Look here, Jaeger, farther on. Here's a spell against witchcraft and evil spirits."

"I have counted at least thirty such in that book," responded the other. "Are you coming to believe in them, sir?"

Lanark looked up from the page. His face was earnest and, in a way, humble.

"I'm constrained to believe in many unbelievable things. If my experience tonight truly befell me, then I must believe in charms of safety. Supernatural evil like that must have its contrary supernatural good."

Jaeger pushed his spectacles up on his forehead and smiled in his beard. "I have heard it told," he said, "that charms and spells work only when one believes in them."

"You sound confident of that, at least," Lanark smiled back. "Maybe you will help me, after all."

"Maybe I will."

The two gazed into each other's eyes, and then their hands came out, at the same moment. Lanark's lean fingers crushed Jaeger's coarser ones.

"Let's be gone," urged Lanark at once, but the preacher shook his head emphatically.

"Slowly, slowly," he temporized. "Cool your spirit, and take council. He that ruleth his temper is greater than he that taketh a city." Once more he put out his hand for the cream-colored volume of Albertus Magnus, and began to search through it.

"Do you think to comfort me from that book?" asked Lanark.

"It has more than comfort," Jaeger assured him. "It has guidance." He found what he was looking for, pulled down his spectacles again, and read aloud:

"'Two wicked eyes have overshadowed me, but three other eyes are overshadowing me—the one of God the Father, the second of God the Son, the third of God the Holy Spirit; they watch my body and soul, my blood and bone; I shall be protected in the name of God.'"

His voice was that of a prayerful man reading Scripture, and Lanark felt moved despite himself. Jaeger closed the book gently and kept it in his hand.

"Albertus Magnus has many such charms and assurances," he volunteered. "In this small book, less than two hundred pages, I find a score and more of ways for punishing and thwarting evil spirits, or those who summon evil spirits." He shook his head, as if in sudden wrath, and turned up his spectacled eyes. "O Lord!" he muttered. "How long must devils plague us for our sins?"

Growing calmer once more, he read again from the book of Albertus Magnus. There was a recipe for invisibility, which involved the making of a thumb-stall from the ear of a black cat boiled in the milk of a black cow; an invocation to "Bedgoblin and all ye evil spirits"; several strange rituals, similar to those Lanark remembered from the *Long Lost Friend*, to render one immune to wounds received in battle; and a rime to speak while cutting and preparing a forked stick of hazel to use in hunting for water or treasure. As a boy, Lanark had once seen water "witched," and now he wondered if the rod-bearer had gained his knowledge from Albertus Magnus.

"'Take an earthen pot, not glazed,'" Jaeger was reading on, "'and yarn spun by a girl not seven years old'——"

He broke off abruptly, with a little inarticulate gasp. The book slammed shut between his hands. His eyes were bright and hot, and his face pale to the roots of his beard. When he spoke, it was in a hoarse whisper:

"That was a spell to control witches, in the name of Lucifer, king of hell. Didn't I say that this book was evil?"

"You must forget that," Lanark counseled him soberly. "I will admit that the book might cause sorrow and wickedness, if it were in wicked hands; but I do not think that you are anything but a good man."

"Thank you," said Jaeger simply. He rose and went to his table, then returned with an iron inkpot and a stump of a pen. "Let me have your right hand."

Lanark held out his palm, as though to a fortune-teller. Upon the skin Jaeger traced slowly, in heavy capital letters, a square of five words:

```
S A T O R
A R E P O
T E N E T
O P E R A
R O T A S
```

Under this, very boldly, three crosses:

X X X

"A charm," the preacher told Lanark as he labored with the pen. "These mystic words and the crosses will defend you in your slumber, from all wicked spirits. So says Albertus Magnus, and Hohman as well."

"What do they mean?"

"I do not know that." Jaeger blew hotly upon Lanark's palm to dry the ink. "Will you now write the same thing for me, in my right hand?"

"If you wish." Lanark, in turn, dipped in the inkpot and began to copy the diagram. "*Opera* is a word I know," he observed, "and *tenet* is another. *Sator* may be some form of the old pagan word, *satyr*—a kind of horned human monster——"

He finished the work in silence. Then he lighted another cigar. His hand was as steady as a gun-rest this time, and the match did not even flicker in his fingertips. He felt somehow stronger, better, more confident.

"You'll give me a place to sleep for the night?" he suggested.

"Yes. I have only pallets, but you and I have slept on harder couches before this."

Within half an hour both men were sound asleep.

10. *Enid Mandifer Again*

The silence was not so deadly the following noon as Lanark and Jaeger dismounted at the hitching-rack in front of Enid Mandifer's; perhaps this was because there were two horses to stamp and snort, two bridles to jingle, two saddles to creak, two pairs of boots to spurn the pathway toward the door.

Enid Mandifer, with a home-sewn sunbonnet of calico upon her head, came around the side of the house just as the two men were about to step upon the porch. She called out to them, anxiously polite, and stood with one hand clutched upon her wide skirt of brown alpaca.

"Mr. Lanark," she ventured, "I hoped that you would come again. I have something to show you."

It was Jaeger who spoke in reply: "Miss Mandifer, perhaps you may remember me. I'm Parson Jaeger, I live south of here. Look." He held out something—the *Long Lost Friend* book. "Did you ever see anything of this sort?"

She took it without hesitation, gazing interestedly at the cover. Lanark saw her soft pink lips move, silently framing the odd words of the title. Then she opened it and studied the first page. After a moment she turned several leaves, and a little frown of perplexity touched her bonnet-shaded brow. "These are receipts—recipes—of some kind," she said slowly. "Why do you show them to me, Mr. Jaeger?"

The ex-sergeant had been watching her closely, his hands upon his heavy hips, his beard thrust forward and his head tilted back. He put forth his hand and received back the *Long Lost Friend*.

"Excuse me, Miss Mandifer, if I have suspected you unjustly," he said, handsomely if cryptically. Then he glanced sidewise at Lanark, as though to refresh a memory that needed no refreshing—a memory of a living-dead horror that had recoiled at very touch of the little volume.

Enid Mandifer was speaking once more: "Mr. Lanark, I had a dreadful night after you left. Dreams . . . or maybe not dreams. I felt things come and stand by my bed. This morning, on a bit of paper that lay on the floor——"

From a pocket in the folds of her skirt, she produced a white scrap. Lanark accepted it from her. Jaeger came close to look.

"Writing," growled Jaeger. "In what language is that?"

"It's English," pronounced Lanark, "but set down backward—from right to left, as Leonardo da Vinci wrote."

The young woman nodded eagerly at this, as though to say that she had already seen as much.

"Have you a mirror?" Jaeger asked her, then came to a simpler solution. He took the paper and held it up to the light, written side away from him. "Now it shows through," he announced. "Will one of you try to read? I haven't my glasses with me."

Lanark squinted and made shift to read:

"'Any man may look lightly into heaven, to the highest star; but who dares require of the bowels of Earth their abysmal secrets?'"

"That is my stepfather's handwriting," whispered Enid, her head close to Lanark's shoulder.

He read on: "'The rewards of Good are unproven; but the revenges of Evil are great, and manifest on all sides. Fear will always vanquish love.'"

He grinned slightly, harshly. Jaeger remembered having seen that grin in the old army days, before a battle.

"I think we're being warned," Lanark said to his old sergeant. "It's a challenge, meant to frighten us. But challenges have always drawn me."

"I can't believe," said Enid, "that fear will vanquish love." She blushed suddenly and rosily, as if embarrassed by her own words. "That is probably beside the point," she resumed. "What I began to say was that the sight of my stepfather's writing—why is it reversed like that?—the sight, anyway, has brought things back into my mind."

"What things?" Jaeger demanded eagerly. "Come into the house, Miss Mandifer, and tell us."

"Oh, not into the house," she demurred at once. "It's dark in there—damp and cold. Let's go out here, to the seat under the tree."

She conducted them to the bench whither Lanark had accompanied her the day before.

"Now," Jaeger prompted her, and she began:

"I remember of hearing him, when I was a child, as he talked to his son Larue and they thought I did not listen or did not comprehend. He told of these very things, these views he has written. He said, as if teaching Larue, 'Fear is stronger than love; where love can but plead, fear can command.'"

"A devil's doctrine!" grunted Jaeger, and Lanark nodded agreement.

"He said more," went on Enid. "He spoke of 'Those Below,' and of how they 'rule by fear, and therefore are stronger than Those on High, who rule by weak love.'"

"Blasphemy," commented Jaeger, in his beard.

"Those statements fit what I remember of his talk," Lanark put in. "He spoke, just before we fought the guerrillas, of some great evil to come from flouting Those Below."

"I remember," nodded Jaeger. "Go on, young woman."

"Then there was the box."

"The box?" repeated both men quickly.

"Yes. It was a small case, of dark gray metal, or stone—or something. This, too, was when I was little. He offered it to Larue, and laughed when Larue could not open it."

Jaeger and Lanark darted looks at each other. They were remembering such a box.

"My stepfather then took it back," Enid related, "and said that it held his fate and fortune; that he would live and prosper until the secret writing within it should be taken forth and destroyed."

"I remember where that box is," Lanark said breathlessly to Jaeger. "In the old oven, at—"

"We could not open it, either," interrupted the preacher.

"He spoke of that, too," Enid told them. "It would never open, he told Larue, save in the 'place of the Nameless One'—that must be where the house burned—and at midnight under a full moon."

"A full moon!" exclaimed Lanark.

"There is a full moon tonight," said Jaeger.

11. Return of the Sacrifice

Through the cross-hatching of new-leafed branches the full moon shone down from its zenith. Lanark and Enid Mandifer walked gingerly through the night-filled timber in the gulley beyond which, they knew, lay the ruins of the house where so much repellent mystery had been born.

"It's just eleven o'clock," whispered Lanark, looking at his big silver watch. He was dressed in white shirt and dark trousers, without coat, hat or gloves. His revolver rode in the front of his waistband, and as he limped along, the sheath of Jaeger's old cavalry saber thumped and rasped his left boot-top. "We must be almost there."

"We are there," replied Enid. "Here's the clearing, and the little brook of water."

She was right. They had come to the open space where first they had met. The moonlight made the ground and its new grass pallid, and struck frosty-gold lights from the runlet in the very center of the clearing. Beyond, to the west, lay menacing shadows.

Enid stooped and laid upon the ground the hand-mirror she carried. "Stand to one side," she said, "and please don't look."

Lanark obeyed, and the girl began to undress.

The young man felt dew at his mustache, and a chill in his heart that was not from dew. He stared into the trees beyond the clearing, trying to have faith in Jaeger's plan. "We must make the devils come forth and face us," the sergeant-preacher had argued. "Miss Mandifer shall be our decoy, to draw them out where we can get at them. All is very strange, but this much we know—the unholy worship did go on; Miss Mandifer was to be sacrificed as part of it; and, when the sacrifice was not completed, all these evil things happened. We have the hauntings, the blue fire of the house, the creature that attacked Mr. Lanark, and a host of other mysteries to credit to these causes. Let us profit by what little we have found out, and put an end to the Devil's rule in this country."

It had all sounded logical, but Lanark, listening, had been hesitant until Enid herself agreed. Then it was that Jaeger, strengthening his self-assumed position of leadership, had made the assignments. Enid would make the journey, as before, from her house to the gulley, there strip and say the words with which her stepfather had charged her four springs ago. Lanark, armed, would accompany her as guard. Jaeger himself would circle far to the east and approach the ruins from the opposite direction, observing, and, if need be, attacking.

These preparations Lanark reviewed mentally, while he heard Enid's bare feet splashing timidly in the water. It came to him, a bit too late, that the arms he bore might not avail against supernatural enemies. Yet Jaeger had seemed confident. . . . Enid was speaking, apparently repeating the ritual that was supposed to summon the unnamed god-demon of Persil Mandifer:

"A maid, alone and pure, I stand, not upon water nor on land; I hold a mirror in my hand, in which to see what Fate may send. . . ."
She broke off and screamed.

Lanark whipped around. The girl stood, misty-pale in the wash of moonlight, all crouched and curved together like a bow.

"It was coming!" she quavered. "I saw it in the mirror—over yonder, among those trees—"

Lanark glared across the little strip of water and the moonlit grass beyond. Ten paces away, between two trunks, something shone in the shadows—shone darkly, like tar; though the filtered moon-rays did not touch it. He saw nothing of the shape, save that it moved and lived— and watched.

He drew his revolver and fired, twice. There was a crash of twigs, as though something had flinched backward at the reports.

Lanark splashed through the water and, despite his limp, charged at the place where the presence lurked.

12. Jaeger

It had been some minutes before eleven o'clock when Jaeger reined in his old black horse at a distance of two miles from Fearful Rock.

Most of those now alive who knew Jaeger personally are apt to describe him as he was when they were young and he was old—a burly graybeard, a notable preacher and exhorter, particularly at funerals. He preferred the New Testament to the Old, though he was apt to misquote his texts from either; and he loved children, and once preached a telling sermon against the proposition of infant damnation. His tombstone, at Fort Smith, Arkansas, bears as epitaph a verse from the third chapter of the first book of Samuel: *Here am I, for thou didst call me.*

Jaeger when young is harder to study and to visualize. However, the diary of a long-dead farmer's wife of Pennsylvania records that the "Jaeger boy" was dull but serious at school, and that his appetite for mince pie amounted to a passion. In Topeka, Kansas, lives a retired railroad conductor whose father, on the pre-Rebellion frontier, once heard Jaeger defy Southern hoodlums to shoot him for voting Free-state in a territorial election. Ex-Major Kane Lanark mentioned Jaeger frequently and with admiration in the remarkable pen-and-ink memoir on which the present narrative in based.

How he approached Fearful Rock, and what he encountered there, he himself often described verbally to such of his friends as pretended that they believed him.

The moonlight showed him a stunted tree, with one gnarled root looping up out of the earth, and to that root he tethered his animal. Then, like Lanark, he threw off his coat, strapping it to the cantle of his saddle, and unfastened his "hickory" blue shirt at the throat. From a saddlebag he drew a trusty-looking revolver, its barrel sawed off. Turning its butt toward the moon, he spun the cylinder to make sure that it was loaded. Then he thrust it into his belt without benefit of holster, and started on foot toward the rock and its remains of a house.

Approaching, he sought by instinct the cover of trees and bush clumps, moving smoothly and noiselessly; Jaeger had been noted during his service in the Army of the Frontier for his ability to scout at night, an ability which he credited to the fact that he had been born in the darkest hours. He made almost as good progress as though he had been moving in broad daylight. At eleven o'clock sharp, as he guessed—like many men who never carry watches, he had become good at judging the time —he was within two hundred yards of the rock itself, and cover had run out. There he paused, chin-deep in a clump of early weeds.

Lanark and the girl as he surmised, must be well into the gulley by this time. He, Jaeger, smiled as he remembered with what alacrity Lanark had accepted the assignment of bodyguard to Enid Mandifer. Those two young people acted as if they were on the brink of falling in love, and no mistake. . . .

His eyes were making out details of the scene ahead. Was even the full moon so bright as all this? He could not see very clearly the ruined foundations, for they sat in a depression of the earth. Yet there seemed to be a clinging blue light at about that point, a feeble but undeniable blue. Mentally he compared it to deep, still water, then to the poorest of skimmed milk. Jaeger remembered the flames that once had burned there, blue as amethyst.

But the blue light was not solid, and it had no heat. Within it, dimmed as though by mist, stood and moved—figures. They were human, at least they were upright; and they stood in a row, like soldiers, all but two. That pair was dark-seeming, and one was grossly thick, the other thin as an exclamation point. The line moved, bent, formed a weaving circle which spread as its units opened their order. Jaeger had never seen such a maneuver in four years of army service.

Now the circle was moving, rolling around; the figures were tramping counterclockwise—"withershins" was the old-fashioned word for that kind of motion, as Jaeger remembered from his boyhood in Pennsylvania. The two darker figures, the ones that had stood separate, were nowhere to be seen; perhaps they were inclosed in the center of the turning circle, the moving shapes of which numbered six. There had been six of Quantrill's guerrillas that died in almost that spot.

The ground was bare except for spring grass, but Jaeger made shift to crawl forward on hands and knees, his eyes fixed on the group ahead, his beard bristling nervously upon his set chin. He crept ten yards, twenty yards, forty. Some high stalks of grass, killed but not leveled by winter, afforded him a bit of cover, and he paused again, taking care not to rustle the dry stems. He could see the maneuvering creatures more plainly.

They were men, all right, standing each upon two legs, waving each two arms. No, one of them had only an arm and a stump. Had not one of Quantrill's men—yes! It came to the back of Jaeger's mind that Lanark himself had cut away an enemy's pistol hand with a stroke of his saber. Again he reflected that there had been six dead guerrillas, and that six were the forms treading so strange a measure yonder. He began to crawl forward again. Sweat made a slow, cold trickle along his spine.

But the two that had stood separate from the six were not to be seen anywhere, inside the circle or out. And Jaeger began to fancy that his first far glimpse had shown him something strange about that pair of dark forms, something inhuman or sub-human.

Then a shot rang out, clear and sharp. It came from beyond the circle of creatures and the blue-misted ruins. A second shot followed it.

Jaeger almost rose into plain view in the moonlight, but fell flat a moment later. Indeed, he might well have been seen by those he spied upon, had they not all turned in the direction whence the shots had sounded. Jaeger heard voices, a murmur of them with nothing that sounded like articulate words. He made bold to rise on his hands for a closer look. The six figures were moving eastward, as though to investigate.

Jaeger lifted himself to hands and knees, then rose to a crouch. He ran forward, drawing his gun as he did so. The great uneven shaft that was Fearful Rock gave him a bar of shadow into which he plunged gratefully, and a moment later he was at the edge of the ruin-filled foundation hole, perhaps at the same point where Lanark had stood the night before.

From that pit rose the diluted blue radiance that seemed to involve this quarter. Staring thus closely, Jaeger found the light similar to that given off by rotten wood, or fungi, or certain brands of lucifer matches. It was like an echo of light, he pondered rather absently, and almost grinned at his own malapropism. But he was not here to make jokes with himself.

He listened, peered about, then began moving cautiously along the lip of the foundation hole. Another shot he heard, and a loud, defiant yell that sounded like Lanark; then an answering burst of laughter, throaty and muffled, that seemed to come from several mouths at once. Jaeger felt a new and fiercer chill. He, an earnest Protestant from birth, signed himself with the cross—signed himself with the right hand that clutched his revolver.

Yet there was no doubt as to which way lay his duty. He skirted the open foundation of the ruined house, moved eastward over the trampled earth where the six things had formed their open-order circle. Like Lanark, he saw the opened grave-trench. He paused and gazed down.

Two sack-like blotches of pallor lay there—Lanark had described them correctly: they were empty human skins. Jaeger paused. There was no sound from ahead; he peered and saw the ravine to eastward, filled with trees and gloom. He hesitated at plunging in, the place was so ideal an ambush. Even as he paused, his toes at the brink of the opened grave, he heard a smashing, rustling noise. Bodies were returning through the twigs and leafage of the ravine, returning swiftly.

Had they met Lanark and vanquished him? Had they spied or sensed Jaeger in their rear?

He was beside the grave, and since the first year of the war he had known what to do, with enemy approaching and a deep hole at hand. He dived in, head first like a chipmunk into its burrow, and landed on the bottom on all fours.

His first act was to shake his revolver, lest sand had stopped the muzzle.

A charm from the *Long Lost Friend* book whispered itself through his brain, a marksman's charm to bring accuracy with the gun. He repeated it, half audibly, without knowing what the words might mean:

"*Ut nemo in sense tentant, descendre nemo; at precendenti spectatur mantica tergo.*"

At that instant his eyes fell upon the nearest of the two pallid, empty skins, which lay full in the moonlight. He forgot everything else. For he knew that collapsed face, even without the sharp stiletto-like bone of the nose to jut forth in its center. He knew that narrowness through the jowls and temples, that height of brow, that hair white as thistledown.

Persil Mandifer's skull had been inside. It must have been there, and living, recently. Jaeger's left hand crept out, and drew quickly back as though it had touched a snake. The texture of the skin was soft, clammy, moist . . . *fresh!*

And the other pallidity like a great empty bladder—that could have fitted no other body than the gross one of Larue Mandifer.

Thus, Jaeger realized, had Lanark entered the grave on the night before, and found these same two skins. Looking up, Lanark had found a horrid enemy waiting to grapple him.

Jaeger, too, looked up.

A towering silhouette shut out half the starry sky overhead.

13. Lanark

The combination of pluck and common sense is something of a rarity, and men who possess that combination are apt to go far. Kane Lanark was such a man, and though he charged unhesitatingly across the little strip of water and at the unknown thing in the trees, he was not outrunning his discretion.

He had seen men die in his time, many of them in abject flight, with bullets overtaking them in the spine or the back of the head. It was nothing pleasant to watch, but it crystallized within his mind the realization that dread of death is no armor against danger, and that an enemy attacked is far less formidable than an enemy attacking. That brace of maxims comforted him and bore him up in more tight places than one.

And General Blunt of the Army of the Frontier, an officer who was all that his name implies and who was never given to overstatement, once so unbent as to say in official writing that Captain Kane Lanark was an ornament to any combat force.

And so his rush was nothing frantic. All that faltered was his lame leg. He meant to destroy the thing that had showed itself, but fully as definitely he meant not to be destroyed by it. As he ran, he flung his revolver across to his left hand and dragged free the saber that danced at his side.

But the creature he wanted to meet did not bide his coming. He heard another crash and rattle—it had backed into some shrubs or bushes farther in among the trees. He paused under the branches of the first belt of timber, well aware that he was probably a fair mark for a bullet. Yet he did not expect a gun in the hands of whatever lurked ahead; he was not sure at all that it even had hands.

Of a sudden he felt, rather than saw, motion upon his left flank. He pivoted upon the heel of his sound right foot and, lifting the saber, spat professionally between hilt and palm. He meant killing, did Lanark, but nothing presented itself. A chuckle drifted to him, a contemptuous burble of sound; he thought of what Enid had said about divining her stepfather's mockery. Again the cackle, dying away toward the left.

But up ahead came more noise of motion, and this was identifiable as feet—heavy, measured tramping of feet. New and stupid recruits walked like that, in their first drills. So did tired soldiers on the march. And the feet were coming his way.

Lanark's first reaction to this realization was of relief. Marching men, even enemies, would be welcome because he knew how to deal with them. Then he thought of Enid behind him, probably in retreat out of the gulley. He must give her time to get away. He moved westward, toward the approaching party, but with caution and silence.

The moonlight came patchily down through the lattice-like mass of branches and twigs, and again Lanark saw motion. This time it was directly ahead. He counted five, then six figures, quite human. The moonlight, when they moved in it, gave him glimpses of butternut shirts, white faces. One had a great waterfall of beard.

Lanark drew a deep breath. "Stand!" he shouted, and with his left hand leveled his pistol.

They stood, but only for a moment. Each figure's attitude shifted ever so slightly as Lanark moved a pace forward. The trees were sparse around him, and the moon shone stronger through their branches. He recognized the man with the great beard—he did not need to see that one arm was hewed away halfway between wrist and elbow. Another face was equally familiar, with its sharp mustaches and wide eyes; he had stared into it no longer ago than last night.

The six guerrillas stirred into motion again, approaching and closing in. Lanark had them before him in a semi-circle.

"Stand!" he said again, and when they did not he fired, full for the center of that black beard in the forefront. The body of the guerrilla started and staggered—no more. It had been hit, but it was not going to fall. Lanark knew a sudden damp closeness about him, as though he stood in a small room full of sweaty garments. The six figures were converging, like beasts seeking a common trough or manger.

He did not shoot again. The man he had shot was not bleeding. Six pairs of eyes fixed themselves upon him, with a steadiness that was more than unwinking. He wondered, inconsequentially, if those eyes had lids. . . . Now they were within reach.

He fell quickly on guard with his saber, whirling it to left and then to right, the old moulinets he had learned in the fencing-room at the Virginia Military Institute. Again the half-dozen approachers came to an abrupt stop, one or two flinching back from the twinkling tongue of steel. Lanark extended his arm, made a wider horizontal sweep with his point, and the space before him widened. The two forms at the horns of the semi-circle began to slip forward and outward, as though to pass him and take him in the rear.

"That won't do," Lanark said aloud, and hopped quickly forward, then lunged at the blackbeard. His point met flesh, or at least a soft substance. No bones impeded it. A moment later his basket-hilt thudded against the butternut shirt front, the figure reeled backward from the force of the blow. With a practised wrench, Lanark cleared his weapon, cutting fiercely at another who was moving upon him with an unnerving lightness. His edge came home, and he drew it vigorously toward himself —a bread-slicing maneuver that would surely lay flesh open to the bone, disable one assailant. But the creature only tottered and came in again, and Lanark saw that the face he had hacked almost in two was the one with bulge eyes and spike mustaches.

All he could do was side-step and then retreat—retreat eastward in the direction of Fearful Rock. The black-bearded thing was down, stumbled or swooning, and he sprang across it. As he did so the body writhed just beneath him, clutching with one hand upward. Hooked by an ankle, Lanark fell sprawling at full length, losing his revolver but not his sword. He twisted over at his left side, hacking murderously in the direction of his feet. As once before, he cut away a hand and wrist and was free. He surged to his feet, and found the blackbeard also up, thrusting its hairy, fishy-white face at him. With dark rage swelling his every muscle, Lanark carried his right arm back across his chest, his right hand with the hilt going over his left shoulder. Then he struck at the hairy head with all the power of arm and shoulder and, turning his body, thrust in its weight behind the blow. The head flew from the shoulders, as though it had been stuck there ever so lightly.

Then the others were pushing around and upon him. Lanark smelled blood, rot, dampness, filth. He heard, for the first time, soft snickering voices, that spoke no words but seemed to be sneering at him for the entertainment of one another. The work was too close to thrust; he hacked and hewed, and struck with the curved guard as with brass knuckles. And they fell back from him, all but one form that could not see.

It tottered heavily and gropingly toward him, hunching its headless shoulders and holding out its handless arms, as though it played with him a game of blind-man's-buff. And from that horrid truncated enemy Lanark fled, fled like a deer for all his lameness.

They followed, but they made slow, stupid work of it. Lanark's sword, which could not kill, had wounded them all. He was well ahead, coming to rising ground, toiling upward out of the gulley, into the open country shadowed by Fearful Rock.

He paused there, clear of the trees, wiped his clammy brow with the sleeve of his left arm. The moon was so bright overhead that it almost blinded him. He became aware of a kneading, clasping sensation at his right ankle, and looked down to see what caused it.

A hand clung there, a hand without arm or body. It was a pale hand that moved and crawled, as if trying to mount his boot-leg and get at his belly—his heart—his throat. The bright moon showed him the strained tendons of it, and the scant coarse hair upon its wide back.

Lanark opened his lips to scream like any woman, but no sound came. With his other foot he scraped the thing loose and away. Its fingers quitted their hold grudgingly, and under the sole of his boot they curled and writhed upward, like the legs of an overturned crab. They fastened upon his instep.

When, with the point of his saber, he forced the thing free again, still he saw that it lived and groped for a hold upon him. With his lip clenched bloodily between his teeth, he chopped and minced at the horrid little thing, and even then its severed fingers humped and inched upon the ground, like worms.

"It won't die," Lanark murmured hoarsely, aloud; often in the past he had thought that speaking thus, when one was alone, presaged insanity. "It won't die—not though I chop it into atoms until the evil is driven away."

Then he wondered, for the first time since he had left Enid, where Jaeger was. He turned in the direction of the rock and the ruined house, and walked wearily for perhaps twenty paces. He was swimming in sweat, and blood throbbed in his ears.

Then he found himself looking into the open grave where the guerrillas had lain, whence they had issued to fight once more. At the bottom he saw the two palenesses that were empty skins.

He saw something else—a dark form that was trying to scramble out. Once again he tightened his grip upon the hilt of his saber.

At the same instant he knew that still another creature was hurrying out of the gulley and at him from behind.

14. Enid

Lanark's guess was wrong; Enid Mandifer had not retreated westward up the gulley.

She had stared, all in a heart-stopping chill, as Lanark made for the thing that terrified her. As though of themselves, her hands reached down to the earth, found her dress, and pulled it over her head. She thrust her feet into her shoes. Then she moved, at only a fast walk, after Lanark.

There was really nothing else she could have done, and Lanark might have known that, had he been able to take thought in the moments that followed. Had she fled, she would have had no place to go save to the house where once her stepfather had lived; and it would be no refuge, but a place of whispering horror. Too, she would be alone, dreadfully alone. It took no meditation on her part to settle the fact that Lanark was her one hope of protection. As a matter of simple fact, he would have done well to remain with her, on the defensive; but then, he could not have foreseen what was waiting in the shadowed woods beyond.

She did carry something that might serve as a weapon—the hand-mirror. And in a pocket of her dress lay the Bible, of which she had once told Lanark. She had read much in it, driven by terror, and I daresay it was as much a talisman to her as was the *Long Lost Friend* to Jaeger. Her lips pattered a verse from it: "Deliver me from mine enemies, O my God . . . for lo, they lie in wait for my soul."

It was hard for her to decide what she had expected to find within the rim of trees beyond the clearing. Lanark was not in sight, but a commotion had risen some little distance ahead. Enid moved onward, because she must.

She heard Lanark's pistol shot, and then what sounded like several men struggling. She tried to peer and see, but there was only a swirl of violent motion, and through it the flash of steel—that would be Lanark's saber. She crouched behind a wide trunk.

"That is useless," said an accented voice she knew, close at her elbow.

She spun around, stared and sprang away. It was not her stepfather that stood there. The form was human to some degree—it had arms and legs, and a featureless head; but its nakedness was slimy wet and dark, and about it clung a smell of blood.

"That is useless," muttered once more the voice of Persil Mandifer. "You do not hide from the power that rules this place."

Behind the first dark slimness came a second shape, a gross immensity, equally black and foul and shiny. Larue?

"You have offered yourself," said Persil Mandifer, though Enid could see no lips move in the filthy-seeming shadow that should have been a face. "I think you will be accepted this time. Of course, it cannot profit me—what I am now, I shall be always. Perhaps you, too——"

Larue's voice chuckled, and Enid ran, toward where Lanark had been fighting. That would be more endurable than this mad dream forced upon her. Anything would be more endurable. Twigs and thorns plucked at her skirt like spiteful fingers, but she ripped away from them and ran. She came into another clearing, a small one. The moon, striking between the boughs, made here a pool of light and touched up something of metal.

It was Lanark's revolver. Enid bent and seized it. A few feet away rested something else, something rather like a strangely shaggy cabbage. As Enid touched the gun, she saw what that fringed rondure was. A head, but living, as though its owner had been buried to his bearded chin.

"What——" she began to ask aloud. It was surely living, its eyebrows arched and scowled and its gleaming eyes moved. Its tongue crawled out and licked grinning, hairy lips. She saw its smile, hard and brief as a knife flashed for a moment from its scabbard.

Enid Mandifer almost dropped the revolver. She had become sickeningly aware that the head possessed no body.

"There is the rest of him," spoke Persil Mandifer, again behind her shoulder. And she saw a heart-shaking terror, staggering and groping between the trees, a body without a head or hands.

She ran again, but slowly and painfully, as though this were in truth a nightmare. The headless hulk seemed to divine her effort at retreat, for it dragged itself clumsily across, as though to cut her off. It held out its handless stumps of arms.

"No use to shoot," came Persil Mandifer's mocking comment—he was following swiftly. "That poor creature cannot be killed again."

Other shapes were approaching from all sides, shapes dressed in filthy, ragged clothes. The face of one was divided by a dark cleft, as though Lanark's saber had split it, but no blood showed. Another seemed to have no lower jaw; the remaining top of his face jutted forward, like the short visage of a snake lifted to strike. These things had eyes, turned unblinkingly upon her; they could see and approach.

The headless torso blundered at her again, went past by inches. It recovered itself and turned. It knew, somehow, that she was there; it was trying to capture her. She shrank away, staring around for an avenue of escape.

"Be thankful," droned Persil Mandifer from somewhere. "These are no more than dead men, whipped into a mockery of life. They will prepare you a little for the wonders to come."

But Enid had commanded her shuddering muscles. She ran. One of the things caught her sleeve, but the cloth tore and she won free. She heard sounds that could hardly be called voices, from the mouths of such as had mouths And Persil Mandifer laughed quietly, and said something in a language Enid had never heard before. The thick voice of his son Larue answered him in the same tongue, then called out in English:

"Enid, you only run in the direction we want you to run!"

It was true, and there was nothing that she could do about it. The entities behind her were following, not very fast, like herdsmen leisurely driving a sheep in the way it should go. And she knew that the sides of the gulley, to north and south, could never be climbed. There was only the slope ahead to the eastward, up which Lanark must have gone. The thought of him strengthened her. If the two of them found the king-horror, the Nameless One, at the base of Fearful Rock, they could face it together.

She was aware that she had come out of the timber of the ravine.

All was moonlight here, painted by the soft pallor in grays and silvers and shadow-blacks. There was the rock lifted among the stars, there the stretch of clump-dotted plain—and here, almost before her, Lanark.

He stood poised above a hole in the ground, his saber lifted above his head as though to begin a downward sweep. Something burly was climbing up out of that hole. But, even as he tightened his sinews to strike, Lanark whirled around, and his eyes glared murderously at Enid.

15. Evil's End

"Don't!" Enid screamed. "Don't, it's only I——"

Lanark growled, and spun back to face what was now hoisting itself above ground level.

"And be careful of me, too" said the object. "It's Jaeger, Mr. Lanark."

The point of the saber lowered. The three of them were standing close together on the edge of the opened grave. Lanark looked down. He saw at the bottom the two areas of loose white.

"Are those the——"

"Yes," Jaeger replied without waiting for him to finish. "Two human skins. They are fresh; soft and damp." Enid was listening, but she was past shuddering. "One of them," continued Jaeger, "was taken from Persil Mandifer. I know his face."

He made a scuffing kick-motion with one boot. Clods flew into the grave, falling with a dull plop, as upon wet blankets. He kicked more earth down, swiftly and savagely.

"Help me," he said to the others. "Salt should be thrown on those skins —that's what the old legends say—but we have no salt. Dirt will have to do. Don't you see?" he almost shrieked. "Somewhere near here, two bodies are hiding, or moving about, without these skins to cover them."

Both Lanark and Enid knew they had seen those bodies. In a moment three pairs of feet were thrusting earth down into the grave.

"Don't!" It was a wail from the trees in the ravine, a wail in the voice of Persil Mandifer. "We must return to those skins before dawn!"

Two black silhouettes, wetly shiny in the moonlight, had come into the open. Behind them straggled six more, the guerrillas.

"Don't!" came the cry again, this time a command. "You cannot destroy us now. It is midnight, the hour of the Nameless One."

At the word "midnight" an idea fairly exploded itself in Lanark's brain. He thrust his sword into the hands of his old sergeant.

"Guard against them," he said in the old tone of command. "That book of yours may serve as shield, and Enid's Bible. I have something else to do."

He turned and ran around the edge of the grave, then toward the hole that was filled with the ruins of the old house; the hole that emitted a glow of weak blue light.

Into it he flung himself, wondering if this diluted gleam of the old unearthly blaze would burn him. It did not; his booted legs felt warmth like that of a hot stove, no more. From above he heard the voice of Jaeger, shouting, tensely and masterfully, a formula from the *Long Lost Friend*:

"Ye evil things, stand and look upon me for a moment, while I charm three drops of blood from you, which you have forfeited. The first from your teeth, the second from your lungs, the third from your heart's own main." Louder went his voice, and higher, as though he had to fight to keep down his hysteria: "God bid me vanquish you all!"

Lanark had reached the upward column of the broken chimney. All about his feet lay fragments, glowing blue. He shoved at them with his toe. There was an oblong of metal. He touched it—yes, that had been a door to an old brick oven. He lifted it. Underneath lay what he had hidden four years ago—a case of unknown construction.

But as he picked it up, he saw that it had a lid. What had Enid overheard from her stepfather, so long ago? ". . . that he would live and prosper until the secret writing should be taken forth and destroyed . . . it would never open, save at the place of the Nameless One, at midnight under a full moon."

With his thumbnail he pried at the lid, and it came open easily. The box seemed full of darkness, and when he thrust in his hands he felt something crumble, like paper burned to ashes. That was what it was— ashes. He turned the case over, and let the flakes fall out, like strange black snow.

From somewhere resounded a shriek, or chorus of shrieks. Then a woman weeping—that would be Enid—and a cry of "God be thanked!" unmistakably from Jaeger. The blue light died away all around Lanark, and his legs were cool. The old basement had fallen strangely dark. Then he was aware of great fatigue, the trembling of his hands, the ropy weakness of his lamed leg. And he could not climb out again, until Jaeger came and put down a hand.

At rosy dawn the three sat on the front stoop of Jaeger's cabin. Enid was pouring coffee from a serviceable old black pot.

"We shall never know all that happened and portended," said Jaeger, taking a mouthful of home-made bread, "but what we have seen will tell us all that we should know."

"This much is plain," added Lanark. "Persil Mandifer worshipped an evil spirit, and that evil spirit had life and power."

"Perhaps we would know everything, if the paper in the box had not burned in the fire," went on Jaeger. "That is probably as well—that it burned, I mean. Some secrets are just as well never told." He fell thoughtful, pulled his beard, and went on. "Even burned, the power of that document worked; but when the ashes fell from their case, all was over. The bodies of the guerrillas were dry bones on the instant, and as for the skinless things that moved and spoke as Mandifer and his son——"

He broke off, for Enid had turned deathly pale at memory of that part of the business.

"We shall go back when the sun is well up," said Lanark, "and put those things back to rest in their grave."

He sat for a moment, coffee-cup in hand, and gazed into the brightening sky.

To the two items he had spoken of as plainly indicated, he mentally added a third; the worship carried on by Persil Mandifer—was that name French, perhaps Main-de-Fer?—was tremendously old. He, Persil, must have received teachings in it from a former votary, his father perhaps, and must have conducted a complex and secret ritual for decades.

The attempted sacrifice rite for which Enid had been destined was something the world would never know, not as regards the climax. For a little band of Yankee horsemen, with himself at their head, had blundered into the situation, throwing it completely out of order and spelling for it the beginning of the end.

The end had come. Lanark was sure of that. How much of the power and motivity of the worship had been exerted by the Nameless One that now must continue nameless, how much of it was Persil Mandifer's doing, how much was accident of nature and horror-hallucination of witnesses, nobody could now decide. As Jaeger had suggested, it was probably as well that part of the mystery would remain. Things being as they were, one might pick up the threads of his normal human existence, and be happy and fearless.

But he could not forget what he had seen. The two Mandifers, able to live or to counterfeit life by creeping from their skins at night, had perished as inexplicably as they had been resurrected. The guerrillas, too, whose corpses had challenged him, must be finding a grateful rest now that the awful semblance of life had quitted their slack, butchered limbs. And the blue fire that had burst forth in the midst of the old battle, to linger ghostwise for years; the horned image that Jaeger had broken; the seeming powers of the *Long Lost Friend,* as an amulet and a storehouse of charms—these were items in the strange fabric. He would remember them forever, without rationalizing them.

He drank coffee, into which someone, probably Enid, had dropped sugar while he mused. Rationalization, he decided, was not enough, had never been enough. To judge a large and dark mystery by what vestigial portions touched one, was to err like the blind men in the old doggerel who, groping at an elephant here and there, called it in turn a snake, a spear, a tree, a fan, a wall. Better not to brood or ponder upon what had happened. Try to be thankful, and forget.

"I shall build my church under Fearful Rock," Jaeger was saying, "and it shall be called Fearful Rock no more, but Welcome Rock."

Lanark looked up. Enid had come and seated herself beside him. He studied her profile. Suddenly he could read her thoughts, as plainly as though they were written upon her cheek.

She was thinking that grass would grow anew in her front yard, and that she would marry Kane Lanark as soon as he asked her.

About MANLY WADE WELLMAN

Manly Wade Wellman's ancestry reaches back through the Confederate South to colonial Virginia, with the potent infusion of Gascon French and American Indian. And it is this fascination with country life and people that shows through most often in his work.

After working as a harvest hand, cowboy, roadhouse bouncer, and newspaperman, he began to write full time and settled permanently in North Carolina. Now he has some sixty-five books and several hundred stories and articles to his credit. As a historian, his work was nominated for a Pulitzer prize; but he has also written biographies, juveniles, mainstream fiction, mysteries, science fiction, fantasy and, of course, suspense. He was also one of the most popular writers for the legendary pulp magazine *Weird Tales*. He is the last of the old *Weird Tales* circle still actively writing.

Nominees—Special Award—Professional:

* *Ian and Betty Ballantine*   founders of Ballantine Books, pioneers in the fantasy genre, publishers of Tolkien, Burroughs, and Lovecraft

Donald A. Wollheim   helped establish the science fiction/fantasy reputation of Ace Books; began DAW Books, entirely devoted to fantastic literature

The Ballantines/*Special Professional Award*

Through the years fantasy has had no stauncher allies in mass circulation publishing than Ian and Betty Ballantine. During certain long stretches, Ballantine Books was just about the only place to go if you were an author with something particularly odd to sell, and the innovations and experiments they sheltered between soft covers are past counting.

When they began publishing science fiction on a regular basis, they were advised by Fletcher Pratt, and following his sensible guidance, they did not draw the hard line, one might almost call it a stone wall, that many editors and publishers did, and still do, between fantasy and its subdivision, science fiction. Under their flag, rocketships flew with dragons and trotting along beside the Martians were unicorns.

When I learnt that the Ballantines had deservedly won the First World Fantasy Convention Best Professional (to give it its full title) Award, I began to send them a series of nagging letters asking that they select two or three short stories, or selections from novels, or whatnot—the range of what they've printed is enormous—so that they might have a small anthology within this one.

I got a number of polite notes back from Ian Ballantine from their lair in Bearsville in upstate New York, explaining that Betty was "mulling" over my request. The matter slipped my mind, as did the whole anthology (I don't seem to have the properly *driven* attitude to put together an operation of this kind. I tend to wander off into other projects, or stare blankly at bare walls), and when I sent yet another nudging letter, I got one back, together with a very attractive book from their newest venture, Peacock Press, saying as how Betty was reluctant to choose the little group of favorites asked for. I was sorry about that as I'm sure her choice would have been excellent, and it would have been most interesting to see what it might have been, but I can most certainly understand her not wanting to go on record with such a limited culling from the riches they've brought out.

The letter did point out the tremendous importance of J. R. R. Tolkien in their publishing lives, mentioning that the success of those books permitted the Ballantines to print the first volume of Peake's Gormenghast trilogy, and that the said success also confirmed their belief—which was not and is not shared by as many editors as it should be—that there is a large and healthy market for fantasy out there in book buyer land.

So hurrah for the Ballantines, and for the lovely work they have done in this field, and may they flourish and thrive forever!

Nominees—Best Artist:

Lee Brown Coye horror illustrator for over thirty years; known for his gruesome *Weird Tales* and Arkham House drawings

Steven Fabian known for his delicately evil drawings and paintings, especially for *Galaxy* magazine

Tim Kirk fantasy painter who illustrated Tolkien's *Lord of the Rings* for his master's thesis

Gervasio Gallardo illustrator for many books in Ballantine's Adult Fantasy line

Jeff Jones primarily illustrates sword and sorcery

Frank Frazetta major illustrator for sword and sorcery; also known for his Conan covers

Lee Brown Coye/ *An Appreciation**

Among the other nice things it did, *Weird Tales* provided printing space and a marginal income for a number of interesting illustrators whose odd bents and eccentric styles made sales to straight markets such as *Colliers* and *The Saturday Evening Post* out of the question. True, a lot of ordinary pulp hacks worked the magazine through the years, and for a very long time the covers were the remarkably inappropriate work of Margaret Brundage showing pretty ladies being dismembered by something or other gently rendered in pastel, but there was Virgil Finlay, there was Matt Fox, there was Boris Dolgov and, suddenly and shockingly, there was Lee Brown Coye.

The first Coye illustration showed up in the March 1945 issue, and it was chock full of corpses, no less than eleven of them, and, friends, they were *corpses*. These were not the formal stylized cadavers of Fox, nor the sumptuous skeletons of Dolgov—these were honest to God dead bodies, and whoever had drawn them was obviously not fooling around.

The story that it illustrates was "Please Go Way and Let Me Sleep" by Helen Kasson, a pleasant little spoof involving the doings of a defunct family inhabiting a crypt, and it gave Coye the chance to show dead bodies in various states of decomposition. By God, he took it! Lovingly,

* Parts of this appreciation first appeared in *Whispers* magazine.

no other word for it, he showed you what happens when flesh dries up into a kind of bunched leather, or how it goes when mould takes over, or the various ways eye sockets tend to collapse—and the awful part of it was that you knew you were looking at the work of a man who knew what he was drawing about. Coye did not appear in the next issue, did the cover the one after that, did the cover and an interior drawing two issues after that, and so commenced his long and fruitful association with the magazine.

In 1944 Coye had begun his fortunate collaboration with August Derleth by illustrating Derleth's Farrar & Rinehart horror anthology, *Sleep No More*. This became the first of a trilogy, the others being titled *Who Knocks* and *The Night Side* which came out in 1946 and 1947, respectively. In 1967 he illustrated *Three Tales of Horror*, an Arkham House collection of Lovecraft stories, and in 1973 he did the drawings for Carcosa's Manly Wade Wellman volume *Worse Things Waiting*. This, his Arkham House covers, plus his magazine work (*Weird Tales, Fantastic,* and *Amazing*) constitutes the bulk of his work in the macabre field.

Coye's work has ranged widely in many directions from the fantasy area: he has done medical illustrations (one assumes they were properly gory), graphics of all kinds, paintings, water colors, murals, sculpture, including "white structure" abstractions in wood and metal, tried his hand very effectively at jewelry and silversmithing, and done a series of charming miniatures which includes a tiny little fisherman's shack together with full interior detail and wharf. He has exhibited at the Whitney and Metropolitan museums, and a large collection of his work is in the New York State University Library at Morrisville. He marks his seventieth birthday this year.

We have the honor of including a portfolio of his work in the center of this book.

NOMINEES—SPECIAL AWARD—NON-PROFESSIONAL:

Harry O. Morris, Jr. editor and publisher of *Nyctalops*, devoted to Lovecraftian horror

* *Stuart David Schiff* editor and publisher of *Whispers*, devoted to supernatural horror and fantasy

Roy A. Squires editor and publisher of special limited-edition high-quality printings of fantasy

STUART DAVID SCHIFF/*Non-Professional Award*

Stuart Schiff is an amateur in the classic sense, namely that he is a lover of this field and the work done in it. It's typical of him that when the Schiffs learnt they were to be blessed with an offspring, Stuart's first thought (possibly second—he may have congratulated his wife first, I am not sure) was to bring out a special edition of *Whispers* devoted to the theme of monstrous and ghastly babies. The child, one Geoffrey Ashton Schiff, is quite sweet-looking, and has intelligent eyes. I know this because Stuart proudly showed me a number of photos of the boy he carries in his wallet. He is, at least in some respects, reassuringly ordinary about being a father.

When Schiff was very slightly more than a baby himself, he got turned onto fantasy via "Aladdin," dreaming of djinn bringing him what he would; then, after a brief stay in the lands of classic mythology with the Gorgon and the Cyclops, he came across Poe, then the *Weird Tales* bunch, and was forever hooked. The sight of a Lee Brown Coye illustration of Arkham roused his avidity, and in an attempt to get the original drawing (which, ironically, he has yet to succeed in doing), he became immersed in the seductions of collecting. He pursued it with the earnestness, ingenuity, and determination which is so typical of him, and soon became a collector's collector.

For a while this occupied him completely, but as he perfected and completed his collection he found it becoming increasingly undemanding; what had been an all-out effort became reduced to tiny refinements, getting not just the first edition of such and such a book, say, but the one in the author's personal collection, not just any one, but the specific one which the author annotated and which was later bound in the author's skin. That sort of thing.

Stuart looked around for something which would give him a little more of a challenge and soon came up with *Whispers*. It began as a variation of the sort of thing August Derleth was up to in *The Arkham Collector* (he was astonished and shocked to learn the *Collector* was discontinued after Derleth's death): a compilation of short stories, essays, poems, and newsy items, all, one way or another, connected with fantasy, usually macabre. From the start the thing has been very much an extension of Stuart's particular personality.

The mood of the publication is exciting, it ranges all over the lot, its contributors vary from total tyros to the most professional pros, and it seems willing to try just about anything, written or drawn, which the editor feels is good or at least shows interesting promise. Those interested may contact *Whispers* at Box 1492–W Azalea Street, Browns Mills, N.J. One never knows what is lurking in the azaleas.

Herewith is a mini-anthology from Stuart Schiff's excellent and ever improving magazine. I hope it will encourage you to look for the full-scale collection he will be bringing out with this publisher, and, of course, to obtain *Whispers,* itself.

Fritz Leiber

THE BAIT

Fafhrd the Northerner was dreaming of a great mound of gold.

The Gray Mouser the Southerner, ever cleverer in his forever competitive fashion, was dreaming of a heap of diamonds. He hadn't tossed out all of the yellowish ones yet, but he guessed that already his glistening pile must be worth more than Fafhrd's glowing one.

How he knew in his dream what Fafhrd was dreaming was a mystery to all beings in Newhon, except perhaps Sheelba of the Eyeless Face and Ninguable of the Seven Eyes, respectively the Mouser's and Fafhrd's sorcerer-mentors. Maybe, a vast, black basement mind shared by the two was involved.

Simultaneously they awoke, Fafhrd a shade more slowly, and sat up in bed.

Standing midway between the feet of their cots was an object that fixed their attention. It weighed about eighty pounds, was about four feet eight inches tall, had long straight black hair pendant from head, had ivory-white skin, and was as exquisitely formed as a slim chesspiece of the King of Kings carved from a single moonstone. It looked thirteen, but the lips smiled a cool self-infatuated seventeen, while the gleaming deep eye-pools were first blue melt of the Ice Age. Naturally, she was naked.

"She's mine!" the Gray Mouser said, always quick from the scabbard.

"No, she's mine!" Fafhrd said almost simultaneously, but conceding by that initial "No" that the Mouser had been first, or at least he had expected the Mouser to be first.

"I belong to myself and to no one else, save two or three virile demidevils," the small naked girl said, though giving them each in turn a most nymphish lascivious look.

"I'll fight you for her," the Mouser proposed.

"And I you," Fafhrd confirmed, slowly drawing Graywand from its sheath beside his cot.

The Mouser likewise slipped scalpel from its rat-skin container.

The two heroes rose from their cots.

At this moment, two personages appeared a little behind the girl—from thin air, to all appearances. Both were at least nine feet tall. They had to bend, not to bump the ceiling. Cobwebs tickled their pointed ears. The one on the Mouser's side was black as wrought iron. He swiftly drew a sword that looked forged from the same material.

At the same time, the other newcomer—bone-white, this one—produced a silver-seeming sword, likely steel plated with tin.

The nine-footer opposing the Mouser aimed a skull-splitting blow at the top of his head. The Mouser parried in prime and his opponent's weapon shrieked off to the left. Whereupon, smartly swinging his rapier widdershins, the Mouser slashed off the black fiend's head, which struck the floor with a horrid clank.

The white afreet opposing Fafhrd trusted to a downward thrust. But the Northerner, catching his blade in a counterclockwise bind, thrust him through, the silvery sword missing Fafhrd's right temple by the thinness of a hair.

With a petulant stamp of her naked heel, the nymphet vanished into thin air, or perhaps Limbo.

The Mouser made to wipe off his blade on the cotclothes, but discovered there was no need. He shrugged. "What a misfortune for you, comrade," he said in a voice of mocking woe. "Now you will not be able to enjoy the delicious chit as she disports herself on your heap of gold."

Fafhrd moved to cleanse Graywand on *his* sheets, only to note that it too was altogether unbloodied. He frowned. "Too bad for you, best of friends," he sympathized. "Now you won't be able to possess her as she writhes with girlish abandon on your couch of diamonds, their glitter striking opalescent tones from her pale flesh."

"Mauger that effeminate artistic garbage, how did you know that I was dreaming diamonds?" the Mouser demanded.

"How did I?" Fafhrd asked himself wonderingly. At last he begged the question with, "The same way, I suppose, that you knew I was dreaming of gold."

The two excessively long corpses chose that moment to vanish, and the severed head with them.

Fafhrd said sagely, "Mouser, I begin to believe that supernatural forces were involved in this morning's haps."

"Or else hallucinations, oh great philosopher," the Mouser countered somewhat peevishly.

"Not so," Fafhrd corrected, "for see, they've left their weapons behind."

"True enough," the Mouser conceded, rapaciously eyeing the wrought-iron and tin-plated blades on the floor. "Those will fetch a fancy price on Curio Court."

The Great Gong of Lankhmar, sounding distantly through the walls, boomed out the twelve funereal strokes of noon, when burial parties plunge spade into earth.

"An after-omen," Fafhrd pronounced. "Now we know the source of the supernal force. The Shadowland, terminus of all funerals."

"Yes," the Mouser agreed. "Prince Death, that eager boy, has had another go at us."

Fafhrd splashed cool water onto his face from a great bowl set against the wall. "Ah well," he spoke through the splashes, "Twas a pretty bait at least. Truly, there's nothing like a nubile girl, enjoyed or merely glimpsed naked, to give one an appetite for breakfast."

"Indeed yes," the Mouser replied, as he tightly shut his eyes and briskly rubbed his face with a palm full of white brandy. "She was just the sort of immature dish to kindle your satyrish taste for maids newly budded."

In the silence that came as the splashing stopped, Fafhrd inquired innocently, "*Whose* satyrish taste?"

Manly Wade Wellman

THE VAMPIRE IN AMERICA

Our western hemisphere, accidentally discovered by clumsy European adventurers and settled more or less matter-of-factly by those who followed them, maintains its own climate of the supernatural. We have never needed to import ghosts—those were here anciently, recognized and respected by Indians. When Cotton Mather announced a whole fabric of organized witchcraft with some sort of focus in colonial New England, he noticed its sister cult among the aboriginal powwows. Other old-world curiosities—ogres, woodland sprites, shadowy elemental mischief-makers, even werewolves—are as native to America as to Europe and Asia, with both differences and similarities as with the American and European bison or Brazilian and African monkeys.

But the vampire, that outcast even among demons, the thing that dies and is buried under a curse and under a curse rises again to prey upon the living, is generally assigned to pagan origins in Slavic Europe. Count Dracula, who so long maintained his title of darkling nobility in foggy Transylvania, never lost his accented Continental charm, even when he came to horrify London. It was hard for him to get across the stormy channel, freighted in a coffin-load of his native earth. That was only two dozen miles. If there are vampires and flowing water stops them, how could they accomplish the two thousand miles of the Atlantic, to chill us while they intrigue us, here in America so far away from all that?

There is considerable evidence that they have done so. They have been reported as prowling and blood-drinking, up in bewitched New England, out in Illinois, among the shadows of the South. One must have a vigorous, deep-seated skepticism not to be nervous.

Decades of films, television thrillers and melodramatic fiction have made vampires a shudderingly fascinating familiarity. Dracula is as much a household name as Sherlock Holmes or Tarzan. But the folklorist Charles M. Skinner, writing about them in 1896, felt obliged to define the term: "A vampire is a dead man who walks about seeking those whose blood he can suck, for only by supplying new life to his cold limbs can he keep the privilege of moving about the earth." That was published a whole year before Bram Stoker's best-selling *Dracula,* and Skinner looked back half a century to when vampires reportedly plagued Connecticut.

The facts, if they are facts, are included in *The Vampire in Europe,* by Montague Summers, definitive scholar of the belief. Summers cites the Norwich, Conn., *Courier* of 1854, concerning the death and rumored subsequent activities of a citizen of Jewett City.

Horace Ray died during the winter of 1845, of a wasting disease, and was buried in the Jewett City graveyard. Three sons survived him, not all of them for long. The eldest succumbed to whatever strange blight had claimed the father. Then the second son pined, failed and died in 1852. The third son, in his melancholy turn, grew ghastly pale, thin and weak.

Friends and kinsmen held a stern council. It would be interesting, as today it is impossible, to learn what informed opinions they were able to procure; but someone convinced them that this series of tragedies meant that the dead rose to feed upon the living. They dug up the father and the two brothers and burned the bodies on a great pyre of logs. The ailing third brother, it is said, mended in health at once.

Apparently the tale was told—perhaps quoted from the *Courier*—across the Rhode Island state line a dozen miles away. It may well have impelled William Rose, of Placedale near Providence, to dig up his dead daughter in 1874, cut out her heart and burn it, "acting on the belief that she was exhausting the vitality of the remaining members of the family." This was chronicled in the Providence *Journal* of that year, and could have been quoted afar, for in 1875 a Chicago woman dead of "consumption" was similarly haled from her grave and burned by relatives who said she was drinking their blood.

The belief bobbed up in the old Dutch town of Schenectady. Skinner reports that the cellar floor of a house on Green Street showed a human silhouette in furry mould. Scrubbed away, it grew back again and again. People remembered that the house was built on an ancient burial ground; but "a darker meaning was that it was the outline of a vampire that vainly strove to leave its grave, and could not because a virtuous spell had been worked about the place."

This intriguing story returned eastward to Providence, home of Howard Phillips Lovecraft, six years old in 1896 and already beginning to read and treasure such things. He was to use Skinner's account for the plot of his own creepy tale, "The Shunned House," with a climax he successfully hoped would make the hair stand up on the reader's head.

It was, indeed, to Rhode Island that Skinner ascribed a special prevalence of the vampire belief. "In Northern Rhode Island," he wrote, "those who die of consumption are believed to be victims of vampires who work by charm, draining the blood by slow drafts (sic) as they lie in their graves. To slay this monster, he must be taken up and burned; at least, his heart must be; and he must be disinterred in the daytime when he was asleep and unaware." Which Skinner illustrated with another account of a grave-opening and heart burning at Exeter below Providence, in 1892.

These reports bespeak a complicated bracket of American folklore. The vampire, by name and fame, is ancient upon the European continent, and vampire stories date all the way back to classic Greece. It was argued that such creatures could not cross water and England, safe beyond the Channel, disregarded them for centuries. Henry More's mention of them in 1651 commanded only a small, educated audience, which does not seem to have become upset. More was told about vampires in the anonymous *Travels of Three English Gentlemen* in 1745. Some think it curious that the gothic novelists like Horace Walpole, Anne Radcliffe and Matthew Gregory Lewis did not bring vampires into their haunted castles. The vampire did not appear in popular English literature until 1813, when Lord Byron, always interested in creepy foreign folklore, wrote him into the ringing couplets of *The Gaiour* and explained him in an extended footnote.

John William Polidori, Byron's physician and uncle of the Pre-Raphaelite Rossetties, borrowed from Byron's material for his novelet *The Vampyre*. Published in 1819, it was more widely read and admired than its pedestrian style seems to deserve today. Thomas Peckett Prest was evidently influenced by it when he wrote *Varney the Vampyre, or The Feast of Blood*, 220 lurid chapters of it. Tedious though it was, it ranked among the most popular of Prest's many gory serials.

These matters help to demonstrate that Americans were long a separate culture and a nation before vampires were known and feared in the mother country a whole ocean away. Where, then, rose the ghastly assurance that unquiet graves must be disturbed to make them quiet again? Conjecture must serve our turn here, and we appeal to it with some interesting response.

Polidori's *The Vampyre* owed much of its popularity to the rumor that Byron himself had written it. Playwrights throughout Europe, including Alexander Dumas, dramatized it. Such plays had long runs, in many versions. At last the Irish actor-dramatist Dion Boucicault wrote it into three blood-freezing acts. He starred in the title role, at first in London in 1851, then in New York and other American cities. Boston, perhaps even Providence, saw him as the vampiric Lord Ruthven, with "phosphoric livid countenance."

Who, seeing the show, would not tell everyone about it when he got home, with all the play set forth about what a vampire is and how to go about destroying him to the last evil fiber?

Information like that may have influenced the Rays of Connecticut, the Roses and others in Rhode Island, those people in Chicago and Schenectady. Whatever the source of the belief, it did not die down in America, and in recent years it has come to notice in swampy Pasquotank County, North Carolina. There it was told, with considerable circumstantial detail, in the first person.

The teller was an old countryman named Benton, whose narrative got into the Raleigh *News and Observer* of June 1, 1950. Benton said that when he was a teen-ager, around the turn of the century, he got lost while wandering in the thick woods. The sun set and a billowy dark fog made it impossible for him to see where he was. Then a beautiful woman came toward him, dressed in a red robe. "Don't be afraid," she comforted him. "Come home with me, and maybe the fog will lift and the moon will come up and you can find your way home."

Pearl was her name, she said as she guided him through the darkness to a pleasant cabin among the tall trees. She gave him supper, which he ate with a grateful young appetite. Then, sitting on a red-cushioned stool before the blazing fire, he began to doze. He started awake, to find Pearl bending down to kiss him. He was embarrassed and somewhat frightened, but she crooned, "Just one more kiss and I'll stop." Again her lips fastened upon him, and he drifted off into deep slumber.

He awakened with the morning sun shining on his face and birds singing. He lay out in the woods, and he could not see the cabin nor the beautiful, red-robed, amorous Pearl. Trying to rise, he found himself too weak to stand, and he crept on all fours to a stream where he drank thirstily. The water revived him somewhat. He got to his feet and staggered away until he found familiar trees. At last he reached the door of his home, where his mother met him and said that he had been missing for three days.

Then she stared at his throat, and screamed. "You met the blood-witch!" she cried out. On the skin above his jugular vein were two puncture-like tooth marks.

In 1965, the newspaperman and folklorist F. Roy Johnson visited Pasquotank County to learn more about Benton's adventure. People knew it and told Johnson about it; but as for Benton, he was not in his old community, and nobody knew where he had gone, or whether he still lived. Another oldster, Joseph Berry, told Johnson that the blood-witch was a familiar and dismaying figure in local legend, and that his grandfather knew about the blood-witches far back in the nineteenth century.

This encounter seems far removed from the usual hoecake tales of the rural South. It sounds rather more like what John Keats tells us took place in *La Belle Dame Sans Merci*. Checked against the vampire lore of the Old World, the blood-witch seems plainly to be one of the traditional walking dead, luring and feeding upon its naive victims. If such a thing really happened to Benton, he lived long years to tell of it, but very probably he is dead now.

Or is he?

He was gone in 1965 from his Pasquotank County home. None of the old neighbors could say where. But if the blood-witch bit him, was he not infected with the vampire curse? Is there a grave somewhere else, with BENTON on the tombstone? And does it stay decently closed up, around midnight? Hadn't we better look for it, hadn't we better . . .

Ignore that suggestion. It's childish.

Yet, if you stroll a moonlit country lane, and meet a personable fellow in black, with an agreeable toothy smile, probably he's only acting in *Dracula* yonder at the summer theatre, and has stepped out between acts for a breath of fresh air.

Only be glad if you have a crucifix in your pocket, or anyway a clove of garlic.

Dave Drake

THE SHORTEST WAY

The dingy relay station squatted beside the road. It had a cast-off, abandoned look about it though light seeped through chinks in the stone where mortar had crumbled. Broken roofslates showed dark in the moonlight like missing teeth. To the rear bulked the stables where relays for the post riders stamped and nickered in their filthy stalls, and the odor of horse droppings thickened the muggy night.

The three riders slowed as they approached.

"Hold up," Vettius ordered, "we'll get a meal here and ask directions."

Harpago cantered a little further before halting. He was aristocratic enough to argue with a superior officer and young enough to think it worthwhile. "If we don't keep moving sir, we'll never get to Aurelia before daybreak."

"We'll never get there at all if we keep wandering in these damned Dalmatian hills," Vettius retorted as he dismounted. His side hurt. Perhaps he had gotten too old for this business. At sunup he had strapped his round shield tightly to his back to keep it from slamming during the long ride. All day it had rubbed against his cuirass, and by now it had left a sore the size of his hand.

The shield itself galled him less than what it represented. A sunburst whose rays divided ten hearts spaced around the rim had been nielloed onto the thin bronze facing: the arms of the Household Cavalry. Leading a troop of the emperor's bodyguard should have climaxed Vettius's career, but he had quickly discovered his job was that of special staff with little opportunity for fighting. He was sent to gather information for the emperor where the stakes were high and the secret police untrustworthy. There was danger in probing the ulcers of a dying empire, but Vettius found no excitement in it; only disgust.

Dama chuckled with relief to be out of his saddle again. He used his tunic to fan the sweat from his legs, looking inconsequential beside the two powerful soldiers. Though he was a civilian, a sword slapped against his thigh. In the backcountry, weapons were the mark of caution rather than belligerence. He nodded toward the still silent building, his blond hair gleaming as bright in the moonlight as the bronze helmets of his two companions. "If it wasn't for the light, I'd say the place was empty."

The door of the station creaked open, making answer needless. The man who stood on the threshold was as old and gnarled as the pines that straggled up the slopes of the valley. He faced them with wordless hostility. The last regular courier had passed, and he had been dozing off when this new party arrived. Like many petty officeholders, the stationmaster reveled in his authority—but did not care to be reminded of the duties that went with his position.

Vettius strode forward holding out a scroll of parchment. "Food for us," he directed, "and you can give our horses some grain while we eat."

"All right for you and the other," the stationmaster rasped. "The civilian finds his own meal."

"Government service," Harpago muttered. He spat.

Vettius began kneading one wrist with his other hand. The little merchant touched his friend's elbow, but Vettius shook him away. "I'll take care of it in my own way," he said. His temper had been worn thin on the grueling ride, and the stationmaster's sneering slovenliness gouged at his nerves.

"Old man," he continued in a restrained voice, "my authority is for food and accommodations for me and my staff. The civilian is with me as part of my staff. Do you dispute the emperor's authority?"

The stationmaster reared back his head to look the soldier in the eyes. "Even the emperor can't afford to feed every starving grafter that comes along," he began.

Vettius slapped him to the ground. "Want to call my friend a grafter again?" he grated.

The old man's eyes narrowed in hatred as he sullenly dabbed his bleeding lip, but he shook his head, cowering before the soldier. "I didn't mean it that way."

"Then take care of those horses—and be thankful I don't have you rub them down with your tongue." Vettius stamped angrily into the station, Harpago and Dama behind him.

"Food!" Vettius snapped. A dumpy peasant woman scurried to open a cupboard.

"I could have paid something, Lucius," the merchant suggested as they seated themselves at the trestle table. "After all, I came because I thought I could set up some business of my own here."

"And I brought you because I need your contacts," his friend replied. "The traders here won't tell me if they think the governor really is trying to raise money for a rebellion."

He paused, massaging the inside of his thighs where they ached from holding him into his stirrupless saddle since early dawn. "Besides," he added quietly, "it's been a long day—too long to listen to the gripes of some lazy bureaucrat."

Dama sighed as the serving woman set down barley bread and cheese.

"Not much of a meal anyway, is it?" he said. "I thought the empire fed its post couriers better than this, even way out here."

"And I thought that we were going to get directions here," Harpago complained. "If we don't get to Aurelia before the fair ends, we'll find all the merchants scattered; then how are we going to learn anything?"

"We'll find a way," Vettius assured him sourly. He took a gulp of the wine that the woman had poured him, then slammed the wooden cup back on the table. "Gods! That's bad."

"Local vintage," Dama agreed. "Maybe I should try to sell some decent wine here instead of silk."

The older soldier swigged some more wine and grimaced wryly. "Old man!" he shouted. After a moment the stationmaster came to the door. He limped slightly and his swollen lip was a blotch of color against his tight face.

The soldier ignored the anger in the old man's eyes. "How far is it to Aurelia?" he demanded.

"By which road?" the other growled.

Vettius touched the pommel of his spatha so that the long straight blade rattled against the bench. "By the shortest route," he said testily.

"You have to . . ." the stationmaster began, then paused. He seemed to consider the matter carefully before he started again. "The shortest route, you say. Well there's a road just past the station. If you turn north on it, it's only about twenty miles. But you'll have to look sharp, because nobody's been over that road for fifty years and the beginning is all grown over with trees."

The serving woman suddenly chattered something in her own language. The man snarled back at her and she fell silent.

"Could you catch any of that?" Vettius asked Dama under his breath.

The little Cappadocian shrugged. "She said something about bandits. He told her to be quiet. But I really don't know the language, you know."

"Bandits we can take care of," Harpago muttered, one finger tracing a dent in the helmet he had rested on the table.

"How else can we get to Aurelia?" Vettius questioned, half squinting as if to measure the stationmaster for a cross.

"You can keep going into Pasini, then turn back west on the Salvium road," the other replied without meeting the officer's eyes. "It's several times as long."

"Then we go by the shortest way?" Vettius said, looking at his companions questioningly.

Harpago rose and reslung his shield.

"Why not?" Dama agreed.

The stationmaster watched them mount and ride off. His gnarled face writhed in terrible glee.

"What did they do, tear the whole road up?" Harpago asked. Even with the stationmaster's warning they had almost ridden past the junction. The surfacing flags and concrete certainly had been taken up. Seeds had lodged in the road metal beneath. They had grown to sizable trees by now, so that the only sign of the narrow road was a relative absence of undergrowth.

"The locals must have torn up this branch because it wasn't used much and they were tired of the labor taxes to repair it," Vettius surmised. "They probably used the stone to fill the holes on one of the main roads."

"But if this leads directly to the district market town, it should have gotten quite a lot of use," Dama argued.

"At least it'll guide us to where we are going," Harpago put in, plunging into the trees.

The pines grew closely together and their branches frequently interlocked; riding through them was difficult. Vettius began to wonder if they should stop and turn back, but after a hundred yards or so the torn section gave way to regular road.

Dama paused, looking back in puzzlement as his fingers combed pine straw out of his hair. "You know," he said, "I think they planted those trees on the roadbed when they tore up the surface."

"Why should they do that?" Vettius snorted.

"Well, look around," his friend pointed out. "The road is cracked here too, but there aren't any trees growing in it. Besides, the trees don't grow as thickly anywhere else around here as they do on that patch of road. Somebody planted them to block it off completely."

The soldier snorted again, but he turned in the saddle. Dama had a point, he realized. In fact, the pines might even be growing in crude rows. "Funny," he admitted at last.

"Hey!" called Harpago, who had ridden far ahead. "Are you coming?"

Vettius raised an eyebrow. Dama laughed and slapped his horse's flank. "He's young; he'll learn."

"Sorry I sounded so pushy," the adjutant apologized as they trotted onward, "but I don't like wasting time on this stretch of road. It's too dark for me."

"Dark?" Vettius echoed in amazement. For the first time he took more than a cursory notice of the surroundings. The swampy gully to the left of the road had once been a drainage ditch. Long abandonment had left it choked with reeds, while occasional willows sprouted languidly from its edge. On the right, ragged forest climbed the slope of the valley.

Scrub pine struggled through densely interwoven underbrush to form a stark, desolate landscape.

But dark? The moonlight washed the broken pavement into a metal serpent twisting through the forest. The trees were too stunted to overshadow the road, and the paving stones gleamed against the contrast of frequent cracks and potholes. Even the scabbed boles of the pines showed silver scales where the moon touched them.

"I wouldn't call it dark," Vettius concluded aloud, "though you could hide a regiment in those thickets."

"No, he's right," Dama disagreed unexpectedly. "It does seem dark, and I can't figure out why."

"Don't tell me both of you are getting the night jitters," jeered Vettius.

"I just wonder why they blocked off this road," the merchant replied vaguely. "From the look of the job it must have taken most of the district. Wonder what that stationmaster let us in for?"

Miles clattered gloomily by under the horses' hooves. It was fell, waste land, a wretched paradigm for much of the empire in these latter days. This twisting valley could never have been much different, though. The humid bottoms had never been tilled; perhaps a few hunters had taken deer among its drooping pines. For the others who had come this way—lone travellers, donkey caravans, troops in glittering armor—the valley was only an incident of passage.

Now even the road was crumbling. Although only a short distance had been systematically destroyed, nature and time had taken a hand with the remainder. The flags had humped and split as water seepage froze in the winter, and one great section had fallen into the gully whose spring torrents had undercut it. They led their horses over the rubble while the pines drank their curses.

The usual nightbirds were hushed or absent.

Even Vettius began to feel uneasy. The moonlight weighed on his shoulders like a palpable force, crushing him down in his saddle. The moon was straight overhead now. Occasional streaks of light pierced the groping branches to paint the dark trunks with swordblades.

It *was* dark now. No white face would gleam from the forest edge to warn of the bandit arrow to follow in an instant. Was it fear of bandits that made him so tense? In twenty years of service he had ridden point in tighter places!

Letting his horse pick its own way over the broken road, Vettius scanned the empty forest. He took off his helmet and the tight leather cap that cushioned it. The air felt good, a prickly coolness that persisted even after he put the helmet back on, but there was no relief from the ominous tension. Grunting, he tried to hike his shield a little higher on his back.

Dama chuckled in vindication. "Nervous, Lucius?" he asked.

Vettius shrugged. "The woman at the station said there were bandits."

"On an abandoned piece of road like this?" Dama laughed bitterly. "I wish she were here now. I'd find out for sure what she did say. Do you suppose she knew any Greek besides 'food' and 'wine'?"

"No, she was too ugly for other refreshment," Vettius said. His forced laughter bellowed through the trees.

After a short silence, Harpago said, "Well, at least we should be almost to Aurelia by now."

"Look where the moon is, boy," Vettius scoffed. "We've only been riding for two hours or so."

"Oh, surely it's been longer than that," the younger man insisted, looking at the sky in amazement.

"Well, it hasn't," his commander stated flatly.

"Shall we rest the horses for a moment?" Dama suggested. "That pool seems to be spring fed, and I'm a little thirsty."

"All right with me," Vettius agreed. "I'd like to wash that foul wine out of my mouth too."

"Look," Harpago put in, "Aurelia must be just around the bend up there. Why don't we ride on a little further and see—"

"Ride yourself if you want to be a damned fool," snapped Vettius. He didn't like to be pushed, especially when he was right.

Harpago flushed. He saluted formally. When Vettius ignored him, he wheeled and rode off.

Vettius unstrapped his shield and looked around while the Cappadocian slurped water from his cupped hand. The adjutant was out of sight now, but the swift clinking of his horse's hooves reached them clearly.

"If that young jackass doesn't shape up fast, somebody's going to break his neck before he gets much older," Vettius grumbled. "Might even be me."

Dama dried his face on his sleeve and began filling the water bottles. "It's something in the air here," he explained. "We're all jumpy."

The soldier began scuffing at a stump fixed beside the roadway. Decayed wood flaked away under his hobnails and the wasted remnants of a bronze nail clinked on the pavement. "They crucified somebody here," he said.

"Um?"

"These posts along the road," Vettius explained. "There were a couple of others back a ways. They're what's left of crosses after the top has rotted away."

Around the bend the hoofbeats faltered and a horse neighed in terror. Vettius swore and slipped his left arm through the straps of his shield. Metal crashed on stone.

Someone screamed horribly.

The big soldier vaulted into his saddle. With one swift jerk Dama loosed the cloak tied to his pommel, snapped it quickly through the air to wrap protection around his left arm. He scrambled astride his horse.

"Wait!" Vettius said. "You aren't dressed for trouble. Ride back and get help."

"I don't think I will," the merchant remarked, drawing the short infantry sword that was belted over his tunic. "Ready?"

"Yeah," Vettius growled. His spatha shimmered in his hand.

They rounded the bend at a gallop. Wind caught at their garments. The Cappadocian's tunic bulked out into a squat troll shape while Vettius's short red officers' cape flew straight back from his shoulders. When a man looked up at their approach, the soldier let out the terrible banshee howl he had learned from his first command, a squadron of Irish mercenaries, as they slaughtered pirates on the Saxon Shore.

One of the men on the road howled back.

Harpargo's horse pitched wildly as two filthy, skin-clad men sawed at its reins. Startled by Vettius's howl, a dozen similar shapes in the middle of the road parted to disclose the adjutant himself. He lay on his back with his eyes wide open to the moon. One of his slayers was still lapping at the blood draining from Harpago's torn throat.

The bandits surged to meet them. A youngster with matted hair and a wool tunic too dirty to show its original color swung a club at Vettius. It boomed dully on his shield, and the bandit snarled in fury. Vettius struck back with practiced grace, felling the club wielder with an overarm chop, then stabbing another opponent over his own back as he recovered his blade. Dropping his reins, he smashed his shield down into the face of a third who was hacking at his thigh below his studded leather apron. Her rough cloak fell away from her torso as she pitched backwards.

Dama had ridden down one of the bandits. He was trading furious strokes with a second, a purple-garbed patriarch with a sword, when a third man crawled under his horse's belly and stabbed upward with a fire-hardened spear. The beast screamed in agony and threw the Cappadocian into the gully. He struggled upright barely in time to block the blow of a human thighbone used as a bludgeon, then thrust his assailant through the neck.

"Get Harpago's horse!" Vettius shouted as he cut through the melee to relieve his friend.

Dama caught at the beast's reins. A bandit, his mouth smeared with gore, clubbed him across the shoulders and he dropped them again. Stunned, he staggered into the horse—but before his opponent could raise his weapon for another blow, Vettius had slashed through his spine. Drops of blood sailed off the tip of the soldier's sword as each blow arced home.

Dama threw himself into the saddle. As he struggled to swing a leg astride, the purple-clad swordsman who had engaged him earlier slipped behind Vettius's horse and cut at the blond merchant's face. Vettius wheeled expertly and lopped off the bandit's right arm.

The handful of surviving bandits fell back in mewling horror. Then a baby bawled from the darkness as his mother tore him from her breast and dropped him to the ground. The woodline crackled with frantic movement. Savage forms rushed from the black pines—children scarcely able to walk and feral women. In the hush their bare feet scratched on the stone. Their men, braced by their numbers, surged forward purposefully.

All looked bestially alike.

Vettius took the reeling bandit chief by the hair and thrust his blade against his bony throat. The ghoulish horde moaned in baffled rage, but hesitated.

Then one of the women snarled deep in her throat and rushed at the riders alone. Dama, reeling in his saddle, slashed at her. She ducked under his sword and raked the merchant's leg with teeth and horny nails. Dama hacked awkwardly at her back. The woman cried shrilly each time the blade struck her, but only at the fourth blow did she sag to the pavement.

"Let's get out of here!" Dama cried, gesturing at the clot of savage forms. He could face their crude weapons, but the bloodlust in their eyes was terrifying.

Vettius was chopping at the bandit's neck with short strokes. At last the spine parted and the soldier howled again, flaunting his trophy as he kicked his horse into a gallop.

As they rounded the next bend, Dama glanced over his shoulder. Harpago's body was again covered by writhing men. Or things shaped like men.

A mile down the road they halted for a moment, looking to their wounds and gulping air. The merchant hung his head low to clear it. His face was still pale when he straightened.

Vettius had dropped his trophy into a saddlebag, so that he could grip the reins again with his left hand. He continued to rest the spatha on his saddlebow instead of sheathing it.

"We'd better be going," he said curtly.

The eastern sky was perceptibly brighter when their foam-spattered horses staggered into another stretch of dismantled roadway. The riders' skin crawled as they forced their way between the files of trees, but the passage was without incident. Beyond lay Aurelia, a huddle of mean houses surrounded by the tents of the merchants come for the fair.

Light bobbed as a watchman raised his lantern toward them. "Hey!" he called, "where did you come from?"

"South of here," Vettius replied bleakly.

"Gods," the watchman began, "nobody's come that way in—" The riders had come within the circle of lantern light and his startled eyes took in their torn clothes and bloody weapons. "Gods!" he blurted again, "Then the story *is* true."

"What story?" Dama croaked, his gaze fixed on the watchman. Absently, he wiped his sword on his ruined tunic.

"There was a family of bandits—cannibals, really—living on that stretch—"

"You knew that and did nothing?" Vettius roared, his face reddening with fury. "By the blood of the Bull, I'll have another head for this!"

"No!" the watchman squealed, cringing from the upraised sword. "I tell you it's been fifty years! For a long time they killed everybody they attacked, so it went on for years and years without anyone knowing what was happening. But when somebody got away, the governor brought in a squadron of cavalry and crucified them all up and down the road and left them hanging there to rot."

Vettius shook his head in frustration. "But they are still there!" he insisted.

The watchman gulped. "That's what my grandfather said. That's why they had to close that road fifty years ago. Because they were still there —even though all of them were dead."

"Lucius," the merchant said softly. He had opened his friend's saddlebag. A moment later the severed head thumped to the ground.

Rosy light reflected from the eyes that were suddenly vacant sockets. Skin blackened, sloughed, and disappeared. The skull remained, grinning at some secret jest the dead might understand.

Lee Brown Coye

FROM CHIPS AND SHAVINGS

"Chips and Shavings" was Lee Brown Coye's column for The Mid-York Weekly. *In it Lee could write about anything he pleased and the items it carried were often quite off-the-trail. The following is a reprint from the October 17th issue, 1963. It is a true story but reads like a horror-shocker in the best tradition of the genre. It shows Lee's talent at being able to educe the most macabre aspect of most anything he touches.*

Circumstances come about in the lives of men that try out emotional stability as surely and primitively as trying the lard out of a hog.

Most of us like to maintain the impression of toughness and immunity to the stark and nerve-wracking situations we are bound to encounter. But—by ourselves, alone in the house at night, the shell sloughs off and the toughest of us can awake from a nightmare with a scream and be scared beyond control.

Such an experience came to an old friend of mine and I have often wondered how much it contributed to his death. For the first few days after it happened, he was normally calm and discussed the horrid situation with me and other friends. He was able to get through the funeral arrangements without any outward show of emotionalism but—then it came about. His nights were plagued with sinister apparitions and his sleep was dogged with strange, realistic dreams of the horror he experienced.

This was the day of home-made radios, and he would spend late evenings with me, tinkering with the fascinating little box of wires and tubes. He would leave at a late hour, very tired and hoping for the sleep of exhaustion and release from his torture—but it was not to be and he was forever doomed.

His eyes became bright beads set in black sockets and his tall frame became emaciated and thin. Skin stretched over bones. Sometime later he died—from a gastric disturbance they said—but to me, in whom he confided his horror, it could have been something far more bedeviling than a physical complaint.

Floyd Griffin was a village character; highly respected yet strange and unpredictable in his actions. He was sort of a self-appointed overseer of the troubled. He could repair a clock, build a radio, fix a vacuum cleaner and do a thousand other chores so needed by people.

Among the townsfolk were two people, Andrew and Abigail Spencer, man and wife. They were dwarfs. Andy was almost five feet and Abby was several inches shorter. Miniature people beloved by all. Andy and Floyd were bosom friends and often seen together. It was a weird sight. People called them Mutt and Jeff with Floyd a skinny six feet and two inches in height.

Andy and Abby lived on a street near the outskirts of town, in a tiny house built especially to fit their stature. They were elderly, in their seventies they were, and one day Andy died of a heart attack. Abby wanted to run out her years in her little house and Floyd took care of it for her. He took care of all the necessary chores, mowed the lawn, shovelled the walk and kept the heating fires going.

One year they had a long cold winter with much snow and wind. On a bitter cold morning, Floyd went down to Abby's to take care of things. He found the house locked and empty. He knew she had gone to a church meeting the night before and thought she might have decided to stay with a friend because of the bad weather—yet it seemed unusual. He fixed the fires and carried out the ashes. He then shovelled the walk and left.

That afternoon the house was still empty and although he had inquired around the town, nobody had seen her since she had left the church the night before.

In the ensuing days there was much to-do. Relatives were contacted, the Syracuse police alerted, but it was to no avail.

Abby had disappeared.

The latter part of January turned out warm. They called it a January thaw. Snow melted and the drifts receded. At the corner of the Spencer house and along-side the walk to the side porch, the wind whipped and there was always a high drift.

One morning during the thaw, Floyd went down to check the fires and to see that everything was to rights. As he went up the walk to the porch, he saw something sticking up through the snow of the melting drift by the steps. He went over and took hold of it. He pulled on it. It was a tiny high-buttoned shoe with a pointed toe, and Abby was in it.

Dennis Etchison

THE SOFT WALL

The membrane was threatening to slip; he could feel it.
 "When the music's over," she said, "turn out the lights."
 The record finished (this time it was "The Masked Marauder" by Country Joe and the Fish, her choice, of course) and he did.
 "And if you take my pillow again tonight, I'll kill you. I really will."
 Mason sighed. So it was starting again. But then he should have known to expect it, the worst every night with Julie, and the best.
 He should have.
 "Why sure, princess. You can have the soft one. I don't care."
 She made a small sound, muffled, though some of the sharp edges still managed to get through, the ones that had been there continually since the illness. It was not until night, always by night that she came animated in the hard-to-speak-of ambivalences, beyond even what he might be equipped to discuss coherently with the well-meaning psychiatrist; not coherently enough, at least, to be of any further help to his wife, his own lovely girl, his dark night princess, his Julie.
 "Mmm. I want touchies now."
 "Okay, sweets. Just a sec." Blinking unnecessarily in the dark, he groped for the pack on the night table and drew a cigaret into his dry mouth. He flared the butane lighter in front of his face, and then filled his lungs.
 He blew out a long dream-cone of smoke. It seemed to flicker blue in the faint phosphorescence from the nightlight, the one that glowed perpetually now from the bathroom.
 "Mmm. Scratch my back?"
 He jerked the cigaret tip down sharply; it flashed, a star shooting in a wide arc by his face, and he almost made a wish.
 "Gerry?"
 "Okay, baby. Here I come."
 "No, listen: did Daredevil really kill the Masked Marauder, do you think?"
 "What?"
 "Daredevil. What I want to know, is, did you actually see the Marauder dead? I mean, could he come back again sometime? To menace DD anew?"
 "Well." Mason puffed mightily while he had the chance, inhaling right

down to the bottom of his bare feet. "Then. There. Now." He got up as steadily as could be expected and navigated to the bed, his toes sliding into an unavoidable pile of old Marvel comics and scattering them on the way. He still held his cigaret, the bright glow now appearing to lead the way for him, sort of like a tiny, dying torch. "You know, baby. You're the one who reads all the comics around here. You're the archivist. I haven't gotten past B.C. and the Wizard of Id."

He found his way around to her side of the round mattress, gripping the bedpost. It almost came off in his hand, and he fought down the memory of how easily it had come off for her just an hour ago, how swiftly she had wielded it when he had mentioned his first wife while trying to slip off to sleep. She had asked him about the other women he had known and, tired and unthinking, he had copped out with an appeasing remark or two about Jane. Julie never liked to hear that name. Never. And he should have known. He touched the still sensitive patch of scalp at the side of his head and realized for the hundredth time that he would never, not for any reason ever let himself mention Jane in this house.

It just wasn't fair to Julie.

He lowered himself to the edge of the bed, stabbing out the butt on the nightstand, and turned his eyes to where he knew her face would be.

The reflections from the nightlight did not reach this side of the room, but though the light from the quarter moon outside was almost nonexistent, in a few seconds he found her. The dark hair on the white pillow came up first, and then her softly diffused face, like a print developing in a darkroom tray.

He sighed, and put out his hand.

The cover—she was sleeping with only a sheet tonight—slid away, and faintly he saw the rest of his wife's withdrawn body, pale as the sheets and almost indistinguishable at first from them.

She had on her sheer linen shirt-dress, the one from India, and nothing else. Of course. She looked cool and inviting at this moment, not unlike some kind of angel who had decided, mercifully, to grace his tossed and sleepless bed for the night.

"You know what you are, baby? You're a very fetching, sexy little Peter Pan. Or is it Wendy? You know that, don't you?"

He let his fingers lay lightly along the gentle curve of her neck. Her skin was the temperature of the breeze one always hopes for in the middle of an Indian summer night. He allowed the flat of his hand to smooth over her shoulder, but only after his forefinger first touched the peach fuzz at her temple; and then he found the warm fullness of her arm and her side and the perfectly shaped convections that were her breasts. He stroked her; and he felt himself overcome with a sudden rush of enduring tenderness.

"And tell us," he breathed hoarsely, the old words catching surprisingly in his throat, "whose little girl are you?"

"Yours."

"That's right. That's right, princess. You haven't forgotten how it used to be, have you? Have you." He put his weary face between her breasts and shut his eyes, waiting for them to stop stinging. His fingers stirred and grasped her sides, his thumbs touching her nipples through the linen.

He heard her heart beating. Slowly.

"But . . . but what about it, Ger? I guess it wouldn't have mattered much if they had shown it. Like Dr. Doom. Remember how many times the Fantastic Four thought they'd seen him die?"

Mason started squeezing his eyes tighter. Until he saw dull lights flashing inside his eyelids.

"And then . . . well, you remember the way he came back to get revenge on them, one time by using old Daredevil. Re . . ."

"Baby," he said, his teeth grinding together involuntarily. "Baby. Do you have to—"

". . . member?"

He let out a long breath.

"Listen, babe. You know, don't you? You know I love you."

"W'll I should. You've only told me three million times today. My GOD, Gerry, can't you ever . . . ?"

"I only thought you might—I mean, you've been home a month already. Remember?"

She stiffened.

"Is that all you ever think about?" she hissed. "You don't care anything about what interests me. My God, I can't even have a conversation with you anymore, about anything." She squirmed and arched her back. "You're driving me insane!"

He stood. His fists were tight at his sides. *He could almost touch the membrane now, the one that had been slipping for longer than he could remember, but he held.* He saw her tense, angular little body, and he saw the shiny streaks appear on her quivering cheeks.

And he released a long, very long breath, and sat down again.

"Here. I shouldn't have upset you again. I guess I'm just tired. Here, let me. Let me."

Patiently his big, shaking hands coaxed her onto her stomach. He pushed up the thin cloth and began to draw his fingernails lightly over her back, the way she liked.

"Mmm. Mmmm. To the right. Up higher. Harder . . ."

As he did this, Mason swallowed hard and permitted his eyes to roam the bedroom. He saw without really seeing dark shadows of the familiar disarray of countless comic books which Julie had brought back from the hospital, and new clumps she had scattered literally all over the rug this week. They were all there, he knew: *Spiderman, Captain America, Iron Man, The Avengers, Daredevil, Conan, Fantastic Four, Thor, The Incredible Hulk.* All her new friends, they had kept her company in the hospital after the horror of the stillbirth and, according to Dr. Marber, she would be needing them, or some equivalent, a while longer. To provide for the transition, something to carry over from Camarillo, an assortment of friendly doormen back into her old life. A routine. She would need them. And she would be needing *him,* too. He was sure and he wouldn't let himself forget it. She would be needing him, soon. And any toll it might take on him would be worth it, to be sure, because of course he loved her. He knew that one thing: he had held to it for such a long time he was not about to let go now.

He loved his Julie.

"Mmm. That feels so good. I love you. But you know, Ger, sometimes I think I really hate you. You never do anything like this unless I ask you . . . *beg* you, practically. I do hate you. No I don't." She sighed. "Maybe I do. I don't care. Want to go to sleep now."

He heard the breath go out of her, heard the crickets outside the window massing in a thrushing chorus, heard even the street lamp at the curb buzzing itself on and on through the night. It seemed like hours since he had heard a single car drive by or the footsteps of any passing neighbor on the walks. He jammed his eyelids shut again, but couldn't even get the dull patterns of light to fire for him now. And still he continued to soothe his wife's cool, curving spine.

By and by he heard her foot begin to twitch beneath the sheet, unmistakable signal that she was finally asleep.

He slowed his fingers, trailing them off, and got to his feet.

He paused by the window. He thought of the night breezes, later, before dawn, when the air would be much cooler—too cool for her, he decided, and wound down the louvered windows and drew the curtain.

He probed his way to the bathroom, taking care not to mess up Julie's things; the moonlight from outside was cut off from him now, the nightlight ahead his only guide, and a poor one. Pushing back the door, he sidled in. As he did, he could not avoid noticing the splintered edge, reminder of Saturday, when she had locked herself in and threatened to take all the red pills. After pleading for an hour and a half, he had taken a crowbar to the lock. She was all right, though; sobbing in the empty bathtub, but all right. She had not swallowed a single one.

He ran cold water.

He dipped the washcloth and took a swipe at his face, his tired face, and then his chest under his shirt. He took off his shirt and tossed it over the shower curtain bar.

He took a long look at himself in the mirror, and it seemed in the pallid light that he was even more wan than usual. He saw nothing there that surprised him. There was nothing to figure out, nothing that didn't show.

It didn't matter anyway.

He left the bathroom.

At the door he hesitated. His wife was slumbering peacefully now. He saw her dimly illumined across the long room, her small hands outside the sheet, her lips parted and her tongue stilled at last. He wondered how she did it; he had never been able to fall asleep in that position, on his back. To do so, he found, required a certain mindlessness which he might have had as a small child, but had not known since, not for many years. He made out the time from a luminous dial on the nightstand: a quarter to two.

He reached behind him and turned off the nightlight, that surprising indulgence on which she had insisted. Well, it was only a few hours till sunrise. He thought, today I will walk into the Department Office and say to the secretary with the cheap jade eyes, Well hello, its back to my profession today; I'm off that 'extended leave of absence,' odious euphemism! My wife is better now, correction: my health is better, the doctor suggests I get down to business again. Yes, I'm sure. I'm fine. How are things in the Land of the Brownies? Don't bother, I'll tell him myself when I get to the lab. I'll tell that hack sub to go soak his head in hypo. I'll . . .

Maybe it will happen that way. Today. This week.

Maybe.

He hadn't bothered setting the clock radio: he never slept past dawn anyway: he couldn't any more. He knew he would be ready. As he had been ready last week. And the week before, and the week before. But he would make it to work this morning.

Unless Julie said she needed him, of course, unless she began begging again. Because he couldn't take that.

But this time, he felt now, he would make it out of here, out of this room, out of this room.

Maybe.

II

Slipping, about to tear.
He touched the wall.
Smooth and cool under his unsteady fingers, the firm texture of the plaster was welcome: steady and secure. He had made the mistake of staring right into the light, and now he discovered that he was quite blind. His eyes—they *felt* bloodshot, and he wondered in passing how bad they were by now; he hadn't noticed in the mirror—throbbed open and shut, open and shut and he cocked his head and squinted, but he could distinguish no single thing in the room ahead. There was the pulsating afterimage of light floating in some dimension in front of his eyes, but beyond that he could make out nothing, not yet. So it would take his eyes a few seconds to adjust. That was okay, too. *The deeper the shadows*—He had had to discover such holes in the fabric years ago, the first time they found him wandering the alleys in search of what? They locked him up, shot through with Thorazine. It was the night after the day Jane slipped away in childbirth. For his own good, they said. That was what they said. And by now he knew this room at least as well as that other, more terrible place. He thought so. He slid his hand around the peeling wood of the door frame, his feet dragging him full into the bedroom.
He reached for the wall.
A puzzle.
A second or two passed while he continued to extend his hand to where the wall should have been. He had a flash of himself standing there uneasily, hands moving helplessly like a blind man after a wrong turn. Then he found the wall and the image passed. Of course. He knew his apartment totally, the route from bed to bathroom and back particularly, of course. *Of course.* It was only another second until his right hand pushed into something solid. One of the pictures. He sensed it wavering after his touch for a protracted moment, only to slip loose suddenly of its mounting and fall crashing to the floor by his feet. With a sharp crack the corner of the frame struck what must have been the short space between the rug and the wall, and Mason started in spite of himself as the glass in the frame splintered in cold shards over his bare, vulnerable toes. He shuddered. Then, too tired to argue with it, he let his old instinct for order make the minor decision for him: to stoop and try to pick up the pieces.
He groped for the wall.
It must have been this: that his head went down too fast and something happened then with the blood. And he reeled. Too long, he

thought, too long without sleep. But he sighed, squared himself and thought instead of the cool sheets, the pillow soon over his head, the overdue dreams rolling through at last. He recalled vaguely just then a science fiction story he had read once, long ago: about a man who had the power to transport himself instantly over great distances by the power of thought alone. And he longed with a sudden and unexpected poignance to be able to do that now, to make it home safely before anything else could happen—Julie's waking up, say—that would keep him from it. Now. As irrationally as a child, and with the same intensity and single-mindedness, it seemed to him, as the obsessions of his boyhood, which he saw now as through the wrong end of a telescope; but he chuckled bitterly and bent again in a last effort, his final one for the night he was sure, to retrieve the fallen picture.

He lunged for the wall.

This time hit him hard. Too much blood surged down into his head and he felt his own weight toppling him over. His hand swung out like a shot, but too late.

He was falling.

"Gerry?"

He struggled to strike the floor or the wall with his hands but waited helpless to strike instead with his head, but his sense of equilibrium was capsized with the rest of him and he was unable to turn himself and for all he could tell in that microsecond of blackness, he could have been cartwheeling down a pit that had no end. Up and down and some other concepts that he didn't have time to consider were teetering madly.

A cat fell before his mind's eye, righting itself. He yanked at his muscles to do the same. But it was no use.

"Mmm."

Julie muttered across the spaces.

"For God's sake, Ger, let me sleep."

He located his voice. "Take it easy, honey. It's nothing. Go—"

Still he had not felt bottom, not yet. He wondered about the numbness.

". . . Never even answer me," he heard, and she rolled over in a rustle of bedclothes.

She hadn't heard his words—or wasn't listening.

And then, with an awful impact, he knew he had hit bottom.

Pain!

It sliced his hands, leaving them drained and shaking.

They found each other like blind fish as his head reeled on. They were warm-wet.

They were bloody.

The glass!

"Nothing, nothing," he tried again. This time his voice sounded too loud, as if trapped inside his skull. And again, no sound but his breathing and the blood pulsing in his ears.

"That is you, isn't it, Ger?" Julie sounded as though she had not heard him speak. "Sure it is," she answered herself in a muffled slur. "Would anyone else be wandering around my bedroom in the middle of the night? I should be so lucky."

"Take it easy. I'm turning in now," he managed.

Don't do me any favors, he expected. He waited several beats for her to say it.

She did not answer.

I must be on the floor, he thought. I must be. Down: glass. Up: the pictures on the wall, the other pictures. Gently, now. He didn't want to bring down the rest of the 11 × 14's he had mounted last year on the bedroom wall, Julie's mini-gallery. They came clearly to mind as he started reaching. Julie, caught and frozen for all time over dishes in the kitchen, the sunlight from the yard coruscating over her shoulders. Julie, laughing on the sands of Malibu: backlight again, flaring her hair into a halo of spun glass. Julie, mugging on the Henry Moore at the County Museum of Art. *Julie Julie Julie*. He raised his hands tenuously in a direction he thought to be up. He touched something.

"Hey."

He felt carefully. Wooden frames? Right angles? Glass?

"Hey, you."

No. Nothing like that.

"My God, answer me, will you? If you're not paying any attention to me tonight, at least do me the honor of answering."

She sounded wide awake now.

He wanted to talk to her and explain. But his fingers kept feeling around what they had found on the wall.

Nothing like that!

Nothing like pictures.

Nothing like them at all.

"I—I guess I got turned around somewhere, Julie. I guess I woke you."

Pause.

"Well, if you aren't going to answer me . . ."

Another pause.

While he felt some more.

There were two—somethings.

Round.

Slick.

Warm.

And—moist.

What the hell?

Sigh. "Well, darling, do you think the new Marvels are out yet? I mean, do you think this month's are on the stands yet?"

He inched up the wall with his other hand. The hand that was cut. A mistake. Pain again! And the wall, the damn wall must be smeared all over. But just let me get up off my knees and pointed in the right direction—

"I mean, do you think you could go to the drugstore for me tomorrow, and . . . ?"

And he felt two large, round, slick, warm, moist things there before him.

And he knew absolutely that there was nothing like that in his apartment. Anywhere. There never had been before. Anything. Like that. At all.

"And while you're at it . . ."

A chill went through him.

". . . do you think you could . . ."

A very cold chill.

". . . stop by Garry's . . . the doctor's . . . and pick up my prescription? I'm almost out."

He found he could walk again, and he moved his feet away from there as fast as he could.

As before, he had no sensation of movement.

"You know. You know how I am when I run out. Right?"

He moved ahead, soundlessly.

He kept moving.

He expected to run into the bed, or something.

He didn't.

"Maybe that's what's wrong with me. Maybe I need some new kind of pills. Something stronger."

Or something.

"Do you think?"

He nosed into another place along the kind of wall. A wall where he had never known one to be before.

"Huh?"

"Julie, keep talking, will you, honey? So I can hear where you are. I know it sounds crazy."

His moves were fast now. He covered several feet, then several yards of the wall. The wall that shouldn't have been there. The soft wall.

"Did you say something? Gerry?"

"Julie."
"I thought I heard your voice." Pause. "I guess not."
"Julie, *where are you?*"
"Good night, anyway. Creep."
"Julie!
"Julie!
"*Julie!*"

But there was no answer. All he knew was that he was feeling his way along an impossible wall. It went on and on, and it did not end.

His breathing roared in his ears.

He continued to follow it. He had no choice.

He came to a slope, and followed it down with his hand. It curved at something more than ninety degrees, and it too was warm and soft. Then he touched the further continuities of the wall that did not end, encountering bifurcations that ascended and changed directions and descended but progressed in unbroken lines and sweeps and junctures, all still remaining totally unidentifiable to him.

Time passed without meaning.

He toyed with the idea that he was losing his mind.

Mason kept moving, moving. Seconds became minutes or hours which he experienced as something much more and much less than he had known before. As he moved along the wall occasionally reshaped unexpectedly, extending further in pulsatile swells and planes which defied any known architecture, though he thought of pictures in a book he had owned once of round, organic buildings put up by a man named Goudi. Still he moved along, and after a while he was able to mark his progression only in units of space relative to his hand, time having receded for him until it was a ritual the rules of which he either chose or did not choose to forget.

The cool darkness fell upon his sweating back and he shivered.

At the same time the wall was becoming warmer. The surface became rough. It felt like very coarse and frayed burlap between his fingers. Two or perhaps three of his blunted fingers fell into a crevice. But he locked his elbow and pulled out. His pulse increased in a fierce battle to outlast the nightmare, and the hysterical energy continued to drive him forward beyond reason. He moved on.

At some length he came upon a different texture—the coolness of smooth cloth. He thought then that he had lost track of the warmth. For a reason not yet his to understand, he felt a terrible loss. He dragged his feet still faster, guiding himself with his one good hand.

Coolness.

Cooler.

Cold.

He stopped.

He strained. He twisted his body around almost 180 degrees but there was only empty air.

His arms plowed the darkness.

In desperation he took a step away from the wall and forced himself to turn around, and around again.

Only the cold darkness, almost palpable, met his swimming hands, and nothing else.

Nothingness.

He staggered. He braced his knees wide apart and fumbled his hands and knew panic. He was out of touch now. His body drew up in a jerking spasm, contracting toward an unseen center, slamming him back once more against the surface that felt like cloth, and shivered and couldn't stop shivering. He thought he let out a yell, but he could not be sure.

He was blinking madly, the air burning cold against his peeled, raw eyes. It did no good. An alien landscape tilted around him. His breathing churned a harsh and merciless white sound through and through his ears. He thought, this is unbearable; this is what is known as the breaking point. He thought, this is insanity!

Called to Julie. But she was no longer there/he was no longer here. Time swept over and through and caught in a hollow interior and blew on and away, carrying some part of him to a position for which there were no coordinates, would never be, and the wind blew through him and round about the landscape that made its own form and he was looking around and through it and the shapes, the cavernous whorls and the caged extrusions and the senseless, cancerous extensions, and he had never known it before, *it had not been known or seen before*, and he saw it without eyes and he felt it deeper than flesh, and the light was pulling away and then he was aware of the light fading and the shrinking measure of it, and he thought of Julie, and he thought, who will do for her the things she needs done if I am not there?

And he screamed. And he fought the air with violent motions. And he shook and he knew substance again and there were two and they were long and tubular and soft and he started to follow them, but almost as soon he knew that they might not end, and he remembered what it was to be confined, and he screamed and there was no sound. And there was no time. And there was no movement. And he was suspended in an eternity that was neither dark nor light.

And in his final paroxysm he flung himself into his suspension and tore at it with all he had, with his two hands. And the pain! And he remembered his flesh and he tore the remaining jagged blade of glass from the back of his hand and slashed and gouged and knifed at the separation with it until he was left with nothing but unresponsive pulp, past feeling. He was trying to free himself, trying to find his way, trying to get back.

III

Slipped.

And of course you must know the rest; but you already know; it's been written up more than once by now: the way they found him there, squatting silently in the middle of it all. Dr. Marber came to the house and finally broke the door in, and there was Mason, waiting. And there with him on the bed was Julie, of course; of course. He no longer followed the contours of her body with his hand, but he was still lost. He had cut her so badly the blood was everywhere, even on the ceiling of the tightly closed bedroom. It had been dark and when it was light, he refused it. He was there, withdrawn beyond hope. Perhaps, but not quite; and perhaps he should have been. He would not speak and he would not move unless they pressed their hands around him and used their strength for his own, and he would not move his head but saw only straight ahead, or did not see at all. He had lost and now he was staring and waiting. Waiting for it all to come to an end; waiting for the dawn.

Toward a Greater Appreciation of H. P. Lovecraft
The Analytical Approach
by
Professor Dirk W. Mosig

The analytical theory of Carl Gustav Jung, often used in literary analyses, provides an excellent framework for the interpretation of the works of H. P. Lovecraft. Almost without exception, HPL's stories lend themselves readily to interpretation in Jungian terms, though, as Professor Barton L. St. Armand suggests in his forthcoming study (*The Roots of Horror in the Fiction of H. P. Lovecraft*, Mirage Press Ltd., 1973), Lovecraft goes beyond Jung.

Since an understanding of some of the basic concepts of Jung's analytical theory is essential for the realization of the deep psychological meaning inherent in the Lovecraft opus, I shall sketch some aspects of the theory, and then show how they can be applied to HPL's writings.

For Jung, the human psyche is divided into *consciousness* and *unconsciousness*. The *ego* is the center of consciousness, and it relates to the outside world through the *persona*, a cloak or mask that presents the ego as it ought to be, or as it would like to appear, rather than as it really is. Much more important than the ego or consciousness, though, is the *Un-*

conscious. This includes the *personal unconscious*, comprising forgotten and repressed material, and the vast unfathomable ocean of the *Collective Unconscious*, which includes, in order of increasing depth, primitive instincts and emotions, irruptions from deeper layers, and, at the very unconceivable bottom, "that part of the Collective Unconscious that can never be made conscious." The Collective Unconscious is something that the individual has in common with the entire species, and consists of the accumulated actions, tendencies, experiences, instincts, etc. of all his ancestors, not only human, but also sub-human and pre-human or animal. It expresses itself in symptoms, complexes, images and symbols that we meet in fantasies, visions and dreams. Some of these are extremely powerful and universal, and are called primordial images or *archetypes*. The archetypes are reflections of instinctive reactions to certain situations and lead to modes of behavior that often appear irrational, inappropriate, or even insane, when seen from the rational viewpoint, but which are nevertheless psychologically necessary. The development of the ego and the persona are archetypal processes, even though they belong at least partially to the conscious sphere. . . . In addition to these, two other archetypes have become differentiated into separate psychic systems: the *Anima* or *Animus* (also known as the *Soul Image*), and the *Shadow*. The first one to develop is the Shadow, our "dark brother" which reigns in the miasmal black ocean of the unconscious, and consists of the conglomerate of inborn collective predispositions, consciously rejected, abhorred, and repressed by the ego because of the ethical, aesthetical, or rational reasons. The Shadow is the dark, shapeless Nemesis always threatening to block out the conscious principles of the ego. Archetypal manifestations of ego and shadow are common in literature: Gilgamesh-Enkidu, Abel-Cain, Faustus-Mephistopheles, . . . and in Lovecraftian fiction, Ward-Curwen, Blake-Haunter, Wilbur Whateley and his brother, the Outsider and his image, etc. The Shadow usually manifests itself in dreams and nightmares, though sometimes it irrupts into consciousness causing irrational and even insane behavior and thoughts. According to Jung, everyone carries a Shadow within himself, and the less it is embodied in conscious life (or the more alienated it is from the ego), the blacker and denser it becomes . . . a primitive, unadapted, savage, awkward lurker at the threshold of human sanity and rationality.

The Soul Image also individuates from archetypal material and consists of the complementary, contrasexual part of the psyche. All creatures are basically bisexual and man carries in his unconscious the archetypal image of woman (his Anima), while in the female's unconscious lurks the archetypal man (her Animus). The Anima or Animus also manifests itself in dreams and fantasies (Adam-Eve) and causes us to be unconsciously attracted to a person of the opposite sex that best embodies the characteristics of our unconscious contrasexual soul image. The dictum "opposites attract each other" has some foundation in Jung's theory, since the characteristics of the unconscious Anima or Animus are bound to be the opposite of the traits of the conscious ego. The soul image stands in direct relation to the persona. The latter consists of a person's habitual outward (intellectual) attitude, while the former reflects his habitual inner (sentimental) attitude. The persona mediates between the ego and the outside world, while the soul image mediates between the ego and the inner world. They stand in a compensatory relationship, which means the more rigidly the mask or persona cuts off the individual from his natural, instinctive life, the more powerful, archaic, and undifferentiated his soul image will become.

This theme of opposition in the form of compensatory relationships is fundamental to Jungian theory. The more the unconscious is repressed, the stronger it will become, until it irrupts compensating for its previous repression and reasserts itself in spite of the efforts of the conscious ego.

Jung recognizes four basic *functions* in the human psyche: thinking-feeling, and sensation-intuition (each pair composed of two opposites). One of these functions becomes the Superior Function, and reigns in consciousness, while its opposite turns into the Inferior Function, is repressed and operates in the unconscious. The other two functions become secondary or auxiliary, and can be used or known by the individual to a much lesser extent than the superior function. By the principle of opposition if, for example "thinking" is the superior conscious function, the unconscious will use mainly the "feeling" function; a conscious superior function of sensation is opposed by unconscious intuition etc. Jung also distinguished two main *attitudes*, or ways of reaching to outer and inner experience, in the human psyche: extroversion and introversion. Here the same principle applies, and a conscious attitude of introversion is opposed by an unconscious extroversion, and viceversa. This means that an individual who overtly appears to be, for instance, a thinking extrovert, is hiding a powerful feeling and introverted unconscious. . . . Small wonder that when the unconscious erupts into the conscious sphere it appears irrational and incomprehensible to the ego, not only because of a lack of differentiation, but because it is the exact opposite of the waking ego and the ephemeral island of consciousness.

A host of psychological problems result when the ego tries to completely deny, reject, and repress the unconscious. According to Jung, the ideal solution is a sort of fusion between consciousness and unconsciousness, resulting in the emergence of the *Self*. The Self is the archetypal image of the unification of conscious and the unconscious. The realization of the Self is the very goal of life, even though complete self-realization is impossible, since it implies the complete equalization of energy between psychic systems (total entropy) and no energy can flow without a gradient: this can occur only in death. Perhaps it is a somewhat twisted interpretation that the goal of all life is found only in death, but let us state it. The main symbolic representation of the Self is the mandala, or magic circle (the sun), and appears in literature as the "wandering hero" archetype (which stands for the sun's travel across the sky, that is, for the emergence of *Self*), and by other symbols.

The preceding brief summary of Jungian theory is by force most unsatisfactory and sketchy, and it is not intended to serve as a substitute for an adequate textbook of analytic psychology. The interested reader is referred to Jung's own writings and to the excellent paperback introduction to analytical theory by Jolande Jacobi, *The Psychology of Carl Gustav Jung*, Yale University Press, New Haven, 1962.

The following brief sketches are given as examples of how Lovecraft's writings can be interpreted in terms of Jungian theory and symbolism. They are not meant to be comprehensive or exhaustive (a long book would hardly suffice) but simply point the way for the reader interested in exploring the deep psychological meaning of the immortal works of H. P. Lovecraft.

I have taken the main tales in the order they appear in the three-volume Arkham House edition of the collected fiction of H. P. Lovecraft.

1. *Pickman's Model*

The subterranean labyrinth of tunnels represents the Unconscious where wander the archetypes or ghouls. Complexes with archetypes as nuclear elements, emerge into the conscious sphere through the old well in Pickman's basement study. The meaning of Pickman's paintings is purely psychological, depicting the archetypes and the Shadow which lurk behind steps, in the basement of the conscious mind. The Shadow is the dark changeling that exists, unsuspected, among images of rationality. Pickman himself is a Shadow figure, who returns to the unconscious and is never heard from again. The narrator, in whose psyche the whole eldritch conflict is taking place, is terrified when he realizes the reality of the primeval, bestial, savage images of the unconscious, which are "photographs from life," that is, mirror real and ever present forces in the Collective Unconscious.

2. *The Rats in the Walls*

In Delapore's dreams appear archetypal images (the swineherd, the fungous beasts) and manifestations of the Shadow (the rats). The descent down the stairs (personal unconscious) leads to the vast twilight grotto (the Collective unconscious) full of ruins and bones, which represent axial archetypal systems. Delapore's conscious ego is overcome by the Shadow as he reverts to archaic, primitive, sub-human and even pre-human levels. The atavistic fury of the long repressed unconscious has broken loose in the conscious sphere of Delapore's psyche, a slavering nightmare has emerged from the black putrid ocean to devastate the little island of deceptive security where the feeble ego lives the illusion of rationality. But Delapore is unable to accept the reality within himself, he denies the reality of the Shadow and projects the source of his inner conflict to the external world. He ends up in the insane asylum, still haunted by the rats in the wall of his own mind, from which there is no escape. In this powerful tale of madness and psychic disintegration, the cat stands for the anima, who is aware of the unconscious struggle but finally joins with the Shadow in that memorable final scene of ego-annihilation. Note that the servants and Norris do not hear the rats, but Niggerman does, which implies that the cat is part of Delapore's psyche. A male name for an anima figure would be consistent with Jung's principles of opposition and complementation (as represented in the t'ai chi t'u or yin and yang symbol). Incidentally, my interpretation here differs from the excellent discussion of this tale in Prof. St. Armand's paper. His interpretation is as valid as mine and no claim is made as to which is the "correct" analysis . . . my purpose here is merely to give examples of how reading HPL is enriched by an analytical reference or interpretation.

3. *The Outsider*

The subterranean castle is the Collective unconscious, while the black tower which protrudes through the "terrible trees" and ends in the vault, at the very edge of consciousness, is the personal unconscious. The underground library stands for the site of the archetypes containing the wisdom of all the primordial experiences of the species. The Outsider stands for the individuation of the ego, which deceives itself by its rigid persona and wants to join the gay party in the surface caste (which stands for the sphere of the consciousness). The illusion of rationality is shattered as he glimpses his Shadow, his own image in the Unconscious, a slavering nightmare of primordial savage and brutal instincts whose reality sears his consciousness in that fateful instant as he touches the mirror: he knows the Shadow, that monstrous appearance is himself—but unable to accept reality, uncapable of learning to live with the knowledge of his inner world, he escapes into insanity and psychosis, and in the "supreme horror of that second" forgets what has horrified him: the memory is repressed. He terminates in the insane asylum, where he "rides with the mocking and friendly ghouls . . . in the unknown valley of Hadoth . . . ," that is, with his fellow inmates in the sanatorium, with other unfortunate souls whose sanity was unable to survive the impact of the Shadow.

Here, of course, several alternative interpretations are possible. The Outsider can be viewed as the Shadow itself, erupting from the subterranean castle into the sphere of consciousness, with the conflict taking part in the mind of the writer (rather than in the mind of the Outsider). Non-analytical interpretations are also possible and meaningful. Within the framework of HPL's cosmic mechanistic materialism, the Outsider is man, emerging from the womb (the castle underground), filling himself of hopes and illusions, and finally coming to face the truth about man's insignificance in the Universe, devoid of purpose or aim . . . he sees himself as the abominable vermin polluting the grain of sand which is the earth, rather than as lord of creation, which is sufficient to send him back into madness, repression, and oblivion, an oblivion obtained by hanging desperately to those "sere memories" of childhood, that is, of man's innocence and blissful unawareness of reality before science opened new "terrifying vistas" from which he escapes into a new dark age. . . . The introductory paragraph of "The Call of Cthulhu" provides the key to the interpretation of "The Outsider" from a mechanistic frame of reference. Also an autobiographic interpretation is plausible (based Lovecraft's awareness of his "ugliness" and physical weaknesses, etc.) though it would be a much less powerful explanation than the preceding ones.

4. *The Colour Out of Space*

Here the meteorite stands for the Shadow, irrupting from the immense and unfathomable blackness of cosmic space (the Collective Unconscious). The farmland represents consciousness, which is masterfully depicted as gradually crumbling and disintegrating with the onslaught of madness and irrationality—the strange "living" radiation from the well (the personal unconscious) where the helpless ego (Nahum) has attempted to repress the Shadow. Nahum, the ego, is the center of the consciousness (farm and family) and is the last to perish (or disintegrate psychically) when the Shadow makes its final emergence from the well. When read in this context, Nahum's dying words become highly significant. . . . "The Colour Out of Space" is perhaps the most powerful symbolic representation in world literature of the gradual mental deterioration and disintegration taking place in the mind of a schizophrenic. Note that at the end of the tale the Colour returns to the black abysses of space—the Shadow returns to the unplumbed depths of the Collective Unconscious—but something remains: a permanent complex has encapsulated the conscious ego and there is no return from madness . . . the mind is now like the "blasted heath," where nothing ever grows.

"The Colour Out of Space" is undoubtedly among the best stories to come out of Lovecraft's incisive mind. One wonders whether consciously or unconsciously this tale was inspired by the dreadful fate of Lovecraft's father, who died in a sanatorium of general paresis when Howard was only eight years old, or whether it mirrors the gradual deterioration of his mother, who died a diagnosed psychotic years later.

6. *The Haunter of the Dark*

This is unreservedly one of the best and more richly symbolic tales in the Lovecraft opus. It is significant also that it is the last major tale that he wrote during his lifetime. For these reasons, we shall examine this work in slightly more detail.

The black, spectral Federill Hill represents the personal unconscious, perhaps even the upper layers of the Collective Unconscious. The phallic implications of the dark church steeple that dominates the hill's landscape is worthy of note (a sexual connotation that would delight the Freudian theorist). Blake explores the church in daytime while night (unconsciousness) is rapidly approaching. He unlocks the gate to the unconscious (opens the box with the archetypal trapezohedron) and becomes aware of the symbolic skeleton in the room (a traumatic event from the past which had been repressed into the personal unconscious) which later disappears again (a new repression to reduce anxiety). Looking through the "shining trapezohedron," Blake gets a glimpse of the unconscious. The Haunter is, of course, the Shadow, which starts emerging in Blake's dreams, particularly in that unforgettable nightmare where he awakens in the very phallic church tower of the unconscious and escapes in abject horror. The Haunter (Shadow), which exists only in darkness (in the unconscious, since light represents consciousness and reason), finally erupts from the church steeple (is ejaculated from the tower?) and speeds as a black Nemesis toward the ego (Blake). In the fateful instant when lightning strikes (the moment of truth, of understanding) Blake sees the Haunter, the Shadow, and recognizes it as the horror within himself . . . and perishes of fright and terror, unable to accept himself for what he really is, his consciousness seared by a knowledge sanity cannot endure. Note the final words of Blake, which become clear and meaningful now: "Light is still out . . . the thing is taking hold of my mind . . . trouble with memory. I see things I never knew before" (repressed material emerges from the Unconscious). "Dark" . . . "the lightning seems dark and darkness seems light" (reason and consciousness are fading while the Unconscious appears in a new light of dreadful understanding). This is followed by the frantic and pathetic (almost hysterical) attempt of the ego to re-assert itself, to erect again his persona as a feeble shield, a completely useless attempt because the threat is internal: "My name is Blake—Robert Harrison Blake of 620 East Knapp Street, Milwaukee, Wisconsin . . . I am on this planet" ("I, the ego, am real . . . the conscious world I am on is real"). Then comes the beginning of the final collapse: "Azathoth have mercy!" (Azathoth, the blind idiot god that blasphemes at the center of all chaos—and is mentioned in several Lovecraftian tales—is HPL's symbol for that part of the Collective Unconscious that can never be made conscious, the very origin of the Shadow, of irrationality, of all that is foul and evil—from the point of view of the ego—and reigns at the center of all chaos in the human psyche. . . . Note that Nyarlathotep, the Haunter—the Shadow, is often described as the messenger of Azathoth), . . . "horrible . . . light is dark and dark is light . . . far is near and near is far" (the Shadow was "far" from the ego, but is now "near" while reason, consciousness, and sanity are receding into the distance) . . . "Roderic Usher" (here, in a stroke of genius, Lovecraft compares the fate of Blake with that of Usher, recalling Poe's powerful picture of ego [Usher], anima [his sister], and Shadow [the house] which HPL unraveled in *Supernatural Horror in Literature* as three entities sharing a single soul [that is, existing in the same psyche] and meeting a common dissolution—sinking in the black swamp of the unconscious) . . . "am mad or going mad . . . the thing . . . I am it and it is I" (Blake realizes that he is the Shadow and the Shadow is himself) . . . "I want to get out" (he wants to escape from reality, to deny the reality of the slavering nightmare within himself) and then, the final breakdown, disintegration, and death in total and absolute horror. The triumph of the Shadow is complete and Blake is dead (or insane here if we interpret death to represent the annihilation of the ego). Lovecraft is communicating man's inability to achieve self-realization, to integrate consciousness and unconsciousness and escape insanity. Or perhaps we should read a deeper meaning in this, his last tale: the fusion of consciousness and the Unconscious has occurred, total entropy has taken place, and Blake discovers that the final purpose and goal of life is DEATH. Lovecraft, the mechanistic philosopher, has made his final statement on the futility of human existence.

7. *The Call of Cthulhu*

In this key story, Lovecraft states his psychological viewpoint, namely that man is basically unable to accept the reality of his own being, to accept the black horror that lurks in the slimy putrid ocean of the Unconscious, ready to flood the feeble island of the consciousness at any moment . . . This is a possible interpretation of that most famous introductory paragraph, "the most merciful thing in the world . . . is the inability of the human mind to correlate all its contents. We live on a placid island of ignorance" (consciousness) "in the midst of the black seas of infinity" (the Unconscious) "and it was not meant that we should journey far . . . someday the piecing together of dissociated knowledge will open up . . . terrifying vistas of reality, and of our frightful positions therein" (the relation of the ego to the vast miasmal ocean of the Collective Unconscious) "that we shall either go mad from the revelation or flee from the deadly light into the peace and safety of a dark new age." The alternatives are bleak: insanity or the return to a primitive dark age—man is unable to accept reality.

Naturally, other interpretations of the quoted passage are possible. For instance, the paragraph is quite meaningful when considered in the light of Lovecraft's mechanistic philosophy (the interpretation would be similar to that sketched earlier for "The Outsider" in this frame of reference).

In "The Call of Cthulhu", the ocean represents the Unconscious, from which emerges the city of R'lyeh and Great Cthulhu, who stands for the Shadow. It is significant to note the emergence of the Shadow (Cthulhu) in the dreams and fantasies throughout the conscious world, as would be predicted by Jungian theory. The Shadow erupts, leading to the desperate escape of the ego (the sailor), followed by his final collapse and insanity (the death of the sailor or ego). Or, if we assume that all is taking place in the psyche of the narrator, rather than the sailor, the emergence of the Cthulhu-Shadow is sufficient to shatter his own sanity, and the tale ends with the narrator anticipating his own disintegration or death. Notice that R'lyeh sinks again into the ocean of the Collective Unconscious, at the conclusion of the compensatory reaction symbolized by its emergence, but there remains the ever present threat of its reappearance in the future.

8. *The Dream-Quest of Unknown Kadath*

This is undoubtedly the richest Lovecraftian tale in terms of psychological symbolism. Even the title points toward the adequacy of an analytical interpretation. Randolph Carter descends the steps of the personal unconscious and penetrated the dream-world of the Collective Unconscious. Here it is explicitly stated that the entire action of this novel takes place in the protagonist's mind. An interpretation of the amazing wealth of symbols described in this unique work is completely beyond the scope of this paper. A whole book would need to be written to justly discuss and analyse this psychological epic, and a brief sketch would leave much to be desired. The reader is urged and urged to read and re-read DREAM QUEST, submerging himself into the realization of the deep meaning inherent in this surrealistic novel. Here we must be satisfied with briefly touching upon one aspect of the work, albeit perhaps the most important.

The climax of this novel, when the ego comes face to face with the deepest contents of the Unconscious, is extremely meaningful, because in Randolph Carter we have the only Lovecraftian hero capable of achieving at least a partial integration of the psyche, of obtaining some measure of self-realization. Carter represents the Wandering Hero archetype, the Self emerging after the mandala has been completed (even though imperfectly) and the psyche has attained some degree of wholeness by joining consciousness and the unconscious, ego and Shadow—but even here the union is not complete, as Carter finally escapes the confrontation with the unconscious psyche returning to the safety of waking and consciousness. This is to be expected, of course, as total equalization and entropy can occur only in death.

Randolph Carter, the wandering hero, is a waking introvert whose extroverted Unconscious is explored in this narrative. There is little doubt that Carter represents Lovecraft himself (as attested by several letters discussing the origin of this character) in his own search for self-realization. THE DREAM-QUEST OF UNKNOWN KADATH is probably the most detailed and memorable picture of the contents of the Unconscious in the annals of literature. Lovecraft describes literally hundreds of archetypes, complexes, etc., a wealth of symbols derived from his own dream-world—his own Unconscious.

Among the many Lovecraftian heroes and anti-heroes, Randolph Carter is the only one that shows hope in man's ability to develop the Self—a realistic attitude, as truly self-actualizing individuals are extremely rare. But Carter's victory is ephemeral and finally succumbs in THROUGH THE GATES OF THE SILVER KEY in a most ironic end.

The foregoing has been by necessity a sketchy and incomplete analysis. Many of the remaining tales should be included in a comprehensive analysis; as a matter of fact, I cannot think of a single piece of Lovecraftian fiction that would not lend itself readily to a Jungian interpretation. . . . "Beyond the Wall of Sleep," "Hypnos," and the remaining tales, as well as some of the collaborations (in particular "The Horror in the Museum," "The Mound," "The Curse of Yig," and "Medusa's Coil") show clear symbols of psychic conflict (ego vs.

Shadow, conscious vs. unconscious). In "The Curse of Yig," for example, we find the "snake of passions archetype" embodied in a Shadow figure, while a particularly powerful Anima symbol can be found in "Medusa's Coil," and the list is almost endless. . . . Incidentally, many of Lovecraft's unjustly neglected poems (such as "Nemesis," "The Outpost," "Psychopompos," the "Fungi from Yuggoth" sonnets, etc.) are also full of potent psychological symbols parallel to those found in the fiction. Another rich source of archetypal images, as mentioned above, is to be found in Lovecraft's dreams, and here the task has barely begun. Hopefully this paper will serve to encourage further criticism and research to help unravel the secrets of the vast unfathomable Lovecraftian mind, and that in so doing, we will arrive at a better understanding of ourselves.

A nice thing about Jungian analysis is that it is not necessary to assume that Lovecraft actually intended to consciously express such wealth of psychological meaning in his stories . . . an artist cannot help but express his personality and inner conflicts in his work, even though he may himself not be consciously aware of the implications of his creative output. The writer tends to express his psyche in his tales, even though few authors have done so as powerfully as HPL.

Nevertheless, taking into account several mentions of Freud and Jung in the *Selected Letters* volumes, as well as several passages discussing psychoanalytical theory, it becomes obvious that Lovecraft was well aware of Jung and his work, and that he had a keen understanding of psychoanalytic thought. It is then quite plausible that the gentleman from Providence intentionally chose symbols akin to Jung's to express his vision of the inner struggle of man.

As a final remark on the use of Jung's analytical theory for the purpose of literary criticism, I would like to remark that one does not need to be convinced of the validity of this approach in order to enjoy its application, or, in other words, you do not have to believe Jung's theory in order to enjoy reading Lovecraft's stories from an analytic frame of reference. Personally, as a mechanistic behaviorist, I do not attribute any significant degree of validity to Jung's hypothetical constructs, but I feel this viewpoint has enriched my appreciation of the immortal masterpieces of H. P. Lovecraft.

Addendum

Many have wondered about the riddle posed by the "incomprehensible" couplet of the mad Arab, Abdul Alhazred, mentioned in "The Nameless City," "The Call of Cthulhu," and other Lovecraftian tales:

"That is not dead which can eternal lie,
and with strange eons even death may die."

From an analytical point of view, the couplet becomes quite significative: the primitive, archaic instincts of man—the archetypal lore—are not dead, since they are able to "eternal lie" in the inherited Collective Unconscious, indefinitely transmitted genetically from ancestor to progeny and lying dormant in the depths of the human mind . . . and with strange eons, or in other words, when temporal circumstances require it, even "death" may die . . . the unconscious forces become "alive" and irrupt into the sphere of consciousness.

Also the famous couplet, "Ph'nglui mglw'nafh Cthulhu R'lyeh wgah'nagl fhtagn," ("In his House in R'lyeh dead Cthulhu waits dreaming") acquires a new psychological meaning, when we reflect that R'lyeh, stands for the Unconscious and Cthulhu for the Shadow. . . . The verse can now be translated as "In its House in the Unconscious, the apparently dead or dormant Shadow waits, while manifesting itself in dreams."

Joseph Payne Brennan

THE ABANDONED BOUDOIR

The abandoned boudoir
burns with ghosts
in nylon nightgowns,
silk negligees,
black satin garter-belts.

The lover-lecher
lugs his gin,
his mound of memories,
flesh gone flaccid,
brain cells blurred.

He lies on lustrous sheets
and curses clocks;
fallen white ladies,
attired in shreds,
repose in worm-infested beds.

H. Warner Munn

CRADLE SONG FOR A BABY WEREWOLF

Hush-a-bye, baby
  Cradle is rocking
Whip-poor-will calling
  Death-beetle knocking

Full moon is rising.
  Hear song of owl?
Father is hunting,
  We wait for his howl.

Soon he'll be coming,
  Bringing meat ripe and rich.

> Be glad he's a wizard
>> And your dam is a witch.
>
> Lie still, my darling,
>> Red dreams shall come true.
> High noon is for Man—
>> Midnight is for you!

Walter Shedlofsky

GUILLOTINE

> G hastly portent, each night the same dream of dread
> U nnerved and consumed his waking hours with fright:
> I mpelled by force, he climbed to a scaffold's height,
> L ed blindfold, he saw his head placed on the block:
> L oudly he screamed, as red blade came flashing down . . .
> O nly fancy, the doctor said, with a frown,
> T ravel, some pleasant cruise, will relieve the shock . . .
> I nsane screams caused the steward to break locked door:
> N eck prone on edge of bed lay he, while on the floor,
> E yes transfixed with horror, rolled the severed head.

David Riley

THE FARMHOUSE

As he left his carriage at the small, country station of Arrendale, to step down onto the platform, Melbury looked around for the nearest porter. Knowing that this was as far as the trains went in the direction that he was going he had intended catching a local bus the rest of the way, but when he asked they seemed of little use to him unless he was willing to wait until six o'clock in the evening, which he wasn't.

Consulting his map he asked if it wasn't possible to cut across the hills. "It nearly halved the distance," he added.

The porter, a red-faced man with a cheerful frown, said that he wouldn't advise it. "Bad 'ills to cross you see. They're nice enough now but come three they will be black with clouds, likely as not. Unpredictable. You wouldn't want to try crossing them. Bleak things to be on in a storm, I can tell you."

Melbury thought a moment, biting his lips till they were white. After eight years lecturing at a college, he was more used to giving than receiving advice. Somewhat tartly he said that he didn't see how the weather would change today. "It looks fine enough to me. Not a cloud in the sky."

No doubt noticing the well used rucksack by Melbury's feet and the look of one who felt himself to be an expert camper, the porter just said: "Maybe, maybe," and left it undecidingly at that.

Leaving the station, Melbury hitched his rucksack well up on his shoulders, put on a pair of polaroid sunglasses, and made his way through the village and out along a lane towards the hills. As he went he could not help picturing in his mind, as thoughts of everyday life were left further and further behind him, how like it was now this landscape must have been in the days of the Celts and Roman legions marching against rebellious Brigantes, of days before cars were invented and horses were the only means of travel besides one's legs.

Laughing to himself at the porter's advice he strolled across the first and smallest of the undulating hills, setting off from its windswept summit to where the sun, now and then, glittered on a meandering stream amidst a gathering of trees.

Feeling refreshed and invigorated by the walk so far after the warm drowsiness of the train, he half ran, half stumbled downhill, ending in a cautious clambering through the tangled undergrowth to thrust his hands gratefully into the cold water of the stream, splashing it across his face. Guelder rose and hazel grew luxuriantly about him with the buttressing trunks of several elms that had long since fallen at sharp angles against their still upright neighbours, brightly putrescent with honey agaric fungi and abundant patches of *Pleurotus sapidus,* alarmingly attractive with their lily-like caps set off against spreading rugs of moss. There weren't many trees and most further in were lying grotesquely yet pathetically on their sides with their shrunken roots poking the air. Some were completely overgrown with moss, speckled yellow where Jew's-ear fungus had grown.

"Are you lost?"

Surprised he turned round to see a girl—perhaps eighteen or nineteen—standing some five yards upstream. Like Melbury she was dressed for hiking, with a heavy floral blouse and blue jeans, a small white handkerchief which she'd just been wetting in the stream, as well as a small, slate grey rucksack held with one strap on her shoulders.

Taken aback—though pleased by the beauty of her hair, which lay attractively on her shoulders, and by the even contours of her face—he said that he wasn't. "Not really." Reconsidering the lameness of his reply he added that he was just admiring the view for the moment before continuing on his way. "I've more than a good idea of the geography of this place from my map." To underline the point he took it out of his anarak, making his way towards her safely if not elegantly across the ferns and slippery stones along the bank. Pointing at the map he said: "This is where we are now. I'm headed due east for Kendale. That's just across these hills here. It's not really far as the crow flies. Just a stiff walk."

"And worth it for the view," she said, looking around at the wind-brushed trees.

"Exactly how I feel. Can't stand the lanes. So many cars on them that you might as well be in the city at times. Which way are you going?"

"Tavestock. But I've got to go through Kendale to get there."

"Then we can go on together," he said. "It'll make a pleasant walk even pleasanter."

Having agreed they cooled themselves off at the stream before wading across it to make their way leisurely uphill. As they talked he learned that her name was Janet and that she came from Chethenham, using what free time she had before starting work in autumn to see as much of the better parts of English countryside as she could. Originally she'd been with a friend, but they had an argument and parted.

Very soon they were immersed amongst the hills. Yet, despite the many features about them, he found her company so utterly fascinating that it was not until they were rising from a valley several hours later on when they came upon a farmhouse that his attention wavered, though even then it was she as much as Melbury who aided this diversion by her repeated enthusiasm for looking closely at it.

Giving her a hand as they clambered over the debris surrounding it, he joked prosaically about the farm's weirdisms: the peculiar angle at which it sloped, the whole building being several degrees off the vertical, the ugly gash in its roof and the fungi that covered its walls like dilapidated veins. Over a colourless door at the front was an embossed stone with the legend 1743 upon it, although worn by age and caustic elements almost into nothing more than a weather-pitted plaque. Age showed from its every blurred contour as Melbury took out a torch from his rucksack and shone it through one of the grimy windows. "It's so old it must be deserted," he said finally. Inside were haphazard lengths of rotting wood entangled with flaking strips of plaster and even more ragged, veil-like drapes of webs, whilst the gash in the roof was mirrored by an even larger gash in the first story floor, the whole being dulled by damp and nightmarish shadows which resisted the torch beam with a dogged belligerence, loping about the quaking walls as he moved it about the room. In one corner were the remains of a table, whilst a gigantic hearth leered at them from one wall; a grotesquely shapen thing that was made of iron and served dually as a fire place and oven. A repugnant smell of decay surrounded the edifice like a vile miasma, whilst the ground near to it was slimy as though thick with mud.

"I wonder if this is the place all that fuss was about in the papers a few years ago," said Janet after a while, pushing open one of the fragmentary windows as she spoke.

"What fuss was that?"

"Don't you remember? About an artist—what was his name?—Preskett, I think—he painted surrealistic Biblical pictures: *The Four Horsemen of the Apocalypse, Wormwood, Babylon the Great, The Locusts* and things like these. He was supposed to have committed suicide in an old farmhouse around here."

"Supposed?"

"Yes, that was what all the stink was about. See that hole in the roof . . . ? Well that was really what made me think about it. According to the coroner, he killed himself by covering his clothes with petrol and setting himself alight, burning half the house down with him. But there was talk of other things besides suicide. Ritualistic murder for one. All very dark and mysterious. I'm surprised you don't remember it. One of the Sundays even did a serial about his life and works . . . all the juicier bits about his sojourns in mental homes, divorces, mysticism, drugs, midnight orgies on the hills, of course."

Melbury stood back looking the old building over. "I think I do remember something about it. Slightly mad, wasn't he? This was his retreat."

"But not his last. Somehow even this retreat held something that made him retreat into yet another: death."

Laughing, Melbury said that she made it all sound very mysterious.

"But I mean to," Janet said, laughing too. "Come on, let's have a look inside."

Seeing that he couldn't stop her, he led the way carefully towards the door. "I'll go first," he said. "It's not very safe and we don't want an accident in an isolated place like this."

The door gave way quite easily beneath his touch, swinging wide open on its crumbling hinges. The nauseous stench he'd noticed earlier now swept up into his face like the belch of something long dead and rotten. It dazed his senses and tore at his stomach, and almost made him collapse as he staggered through the pulpy debris that covered the floor inside: the decaying leaves and slime, puffed and discoloured by fungi and mould. Carefully he ran the torch beam across it reciting:

> "*I spied John Mouldy in his cellar,*
> *Deep down twenty steps of stone;*
> *In the dark he sat asmiling,*
>   *Smiling there alone.*"

"What's that?"

"A poem," he said, with a delicious facetiousness.

"I know it's a poem. Who wrote it? Not you?"

"No, not me. De la Mare. Come on, we'll go on a bit further."

An insipid glow seeped through a gash in the ceiling, making everything grey but the mysteriously black shadows. At one end of the room began a rotting staircase, whilst near to them stood several small but heavy cupboards, all of which seemed to have been modelled crudely from clay and chunks of dead flesh which had since been left here to fester into gangrenous mounds. Partly sickened, partly consumed by morbid curiosity, he looked around at the funnels and cones and hammocks of webs and the pus that dripped steadily from the moss-like remains of the ceiling. In one corner amidst a pile of plaster that had given way from the wall, he noticed a rectangle of red and black. He pushed his way through the rubble towards it.

As he leant over it he discovered that it was a metal box, much like the ones used for keeping petty cash in at offices.

"Wonder why that was missed when Preskett killed himself?" Janet said as she knelt beside him.

He shrugged. "*If* this was Preskett's home. But, besides, I'd say it was hidden in the wall by the look of it." Pushing more of the plaster from the wall, he put his hand into the gap behind. "Quite large," he said. "The rain and decay probably succeeded in doing what a search party couldn't."

Using a stone he snapped the padlock holding the box lid down and forced it open. Inside were several small books blackened by damp and stains from the in-running rust. Carefully—despite the bibliophile's pounding in his chest—he picked up the topmost book. Tucked inside the front cover was a sheet of paper. On it, written as though in some haste, was a quotation. Slowly he read it out loud:

> "Out—out are the lights—out all!
> And, over each quivering form,
> The curtain, a funeral pall,
> Comes down with the rush of a storm,
> And the angels, all pallid and wan,
> Uprising, unveiling, affirm
> That the play is the tragedy 'Man'
> And its hero the Conqueror Worm."

Janet shuddered. As she did so a light film of rain fell through the hole above their heads. Looking out through one of the deep set windows across the hills, Melbury saw the grey veil of a summer shower covering everything in a myopic blur.

Quickly they left the farm, deciding as they looked about the darkening hills to pitch one of their tents to give them shelter until the rain had died down. Deciding on his because it was larger, they erected it and retreated inside as sheet lightening flashed across the horizon. Lying back on the ground sheet Melbury said: "I wonder what all that writing was about?"

Janet pulled her face in false mockery. "The papers did say that Preskett was mad."

"If," he added, "the farm and the writing were his. One shouldn't jump to conclusions."

"And one shouldn't preach."

After talking for an hour they lapsed into silence. Rather than brightening the weather outside seemed instead to be getting even worse, darkening all the time. Already exhausted after the unusual exercise of his trek across the hills, Melbury began to doze amidst half thoughts of inns and warm beds, not meals and beer. It was with a feeling of profound and lasting shock that a short time later he jolted awake, a strange sense of solitude, of loneliness numbing him as though a deep iciness was permeating the air. Towns, railways, roads, and people seemed so far away, lost through vague vistas of eternity.

Sitting up, and striving to subdue these feelings, he looked across to where Janet had been lying, but she'd gone. Opening the tent flaps he leant out into the drizzle.

Melbury was surprised to see how long he'd been asleep.

"Janet," he called, stepping outside. He zipped up his anarak as the wind thrust itself against him. "*Janet.*" Looking across the hillside all he could see was grass and swaying trees, alive with motion as they threw their limbs into the air like maniacs in dismay. Still receiving no reply to his call, he wondered where she'd gone. Prone as he was to worrying, conjectures of the vaguest and, thus, most intrusive type stormed his mind with landsliding rapidity.

"Janet, where are you?"

The only cover in sight was the farmhouse. Besides this there was nothing that could hide her from view. But why should she be in there? Despite the tales about it there was nothing of interest in the thing. And even they were only guesses.

Pushing aside these doubts, he called her again. But still there was no reply.

Remembering the deceptive solidity of the farm's buttressed walls with their ever gaping cracks, and the burnt beams crisscrossed beneath the roof, the warped floor above, the rotting stairs, all with vivid images of incipient collapse, he felt a real sense of alarm. But, suppressing this with the knowledge that panic would only make things worse, he returned quickly to his tent for his torch. Without it a search would be practically hopeless.

As he flashed it on, he noticed a scrap of paper left where Janet had been lying earlier. Picking it up he read:

"In case you wake up before I am back (or, to get gloomy, in case I have an accident), I'm going off to the farm for those books we found. It's stopped raining now, but I don't want to risk them getting absolutely ruined if it starts up again.

                    Janet."

The paper fell forgotten from his grasp as he hurriedly rushed outside, the night air greeting him with an invigorating rush of cold water freshness. Without wasting a second, he ran towards the farmhouse. The books he'd left scattered in the debris fluttered wildly in the hollowing winds. A loose leaf from one blew against his leg. Picking it up he saw an etching of great, if diabolical quality. It was a squat, pig-like creature with great knobby joints, a formidable monstrosity admittedly, yet almost paradoxically showing in such vivid detail pain, agony and anguish on its twisted, entortured face that Melbury winced at regarding it.

What Hell must have been the inspiration of this artist? What forbidden delusions, dreams, nightmares had formed within him the inspiration for the ultimate blasphemy peeling, thrusting its nauseous self from the creature's floundering body: the snake-like creatures, the worms that gnawed at it like a cancer, springing from its paws, its legs, from its chest and ruptured stomach? Grünewald at his most insane could never have perpetrated such a blasphemy as this time worn etching. The realism was veritably obscene, a mockery of life itself. The very suggestion of what was depicted revolted Melbury, sickened him as confronting insanity would, as viewing the foulest of all foul deeds carried out by man. It was almost indescribable in its cacodaemonic entirety, only the etching itself could reveal what it so successfully did.

He threw away the paper. This was ridiculous. He'd never find Janet like this. "Janet. Where are you? *Where are you?*" He cupped his hands about his mouth and called again. As his cries echoed claustrophobically through the house, he saw something move in one of the corners amidst a stygian void of shadows.

"Janet?"

Awkwardly the girl stepped through the debris into the moonlight fanning through the roof. Her face was pale and still, her arms listless by her sides. It was like the calm tranquility just after a storm, or as one was about to erupt, the peaceful way she stood, statuesquely still in the moonlight.

Relieved, he ran towards her, the torch beam sending shadows fingering about her face, filling her eyes like the profoundest black gems, whilst making her blouse rumple in strangely sensuous ways with liquescent depths of blackness.

Before he reached her he stopped. Her body seemed to move, and yet did not move. Muscles shivered yet her limbs remained still.

Suddenly he began to scream. He couldn't stop. The whole world dissolved into an oblivion of tearing hysteria.

Something fell from her face. It was long and thin. Her mouth dropped and yet another slim, slithering object fell from her. Yet another from her hair, though it looked, even in the gloom, as though it came from her eye. One, two, then four as she collapsed upon the floor, hundreds more spreading out from her shrinking body into every conceivable direction, wriggling soundlessly into the shadows.

> *"Out—out are the lights—out all!*
> *And, over each quivering form,*
> *The curtain, a funeral pall,*
> *Comes down with the rush of a storm,*

> *And the angels all pallid and wan,*
> *Uprising, unveiling, affirm*
> *That the play is the tragedy 'Man',*
> *And its hero the Conqueror Worm."*

WITHDRAWN
No longer the property of the
Boston Public Library.
Sale of this material benefits the Library

Boston Public Library

Copley Square

General Library

PS509
.F3F5

2645709063

The Date Due Card in the pocket indicates the date on or before which this book should be returned to the Library.

Please do not remove cards from this pocket.